A CRY FROM BEYOND . . .

"ARE YOU READY, MS. LINDSTROM?" JACOBS asked. Unsealing one of the prosecution's clear plastic evidence bags, he pulled out a baby's bib printed with teddy bears. He displayed it to the jury, then placed the bib in Lindstrom's hands.

Dan grimaced. Why would Hector Muñoz want to put himself through the torture of a Violet's testimony? To look into those eyes and see the life you took staring back at you . . .

Lindstrom sat perfectly still for several minutes, the bib held between her palms. Then she let out a raw, throat-grating scream, and Dan saw several of the jurors blanch.

"Please tell us who you are," Jacobs instructed her.

"Rosa Muñoz." She said the name with a Spanish accent, and the soft soprano of her voice had lowered to a gravelly alto.

When Jacobs asked her to identify the man who murdered her infant son, she pointed to the defendant. "I started screaming. Called Hector the *asesino* he was. The last thing I remember was him grabbing my throat and yelling: *'Be quiet, bitch! They'll hear you!'*"

She pressed the bib to her face and shut her eyes, shuddering. "The baby follows me everywhere. I'm the only one he knows there, and he never leaves me. Do you know what that's like, Hector? *Just the two of us, crying in the dark. . . .*"

Through Violet Eyes

Stephen Woodworth

A DELL BOOK

THROUGH VIOLET EYES
A Dell Book / September 2004

Published by Bantam Dell
a division of Random House, Inc.
New York, New York

ISBN 0-553-80337-9

Manufactured in the United States of America
Published simultaneously in Canada

OPM   10   9   8   7   6   5   4   3   2   1

This book is for
CELIA LOUISE HAMILTON WOODWORTH
and
HARRY HOLLIS WOODWORTH,
who gave me love, encouragement, and support
above and beyond the call of parenthood.
I love you, Mom and Dad.

Acknowledgments

Many saints have laid hands upon this book to ensure its success, and the author would like to thank all of them for the benefit of their blessings: Anne Lesley Groell, my estimable editor at Bantam Dell; Jimmy Vines, superagent extraordinaire, and his intrepid assistant Dana Grayson; my foreign rights agent Danny Baror; Greg Bear, Octavia Butler, Gordon van Gelder, Nancy Kress, and Gwyneth Jones, my instructors at the 1999 Clarion West Writers Workshop, as well as Dave Myers, Leslie Howle, and the whole Clarion West backstage crew; my fellow CW '99 alums Sarah Brandel, Christine Castigliano, Duncan Clark, Sandy Clark, Monte Cook, Dan Dick, Andrea Hairston, Jay Joslin, Leah Kaufman, Margo Lanagan, Ama Patterson, Elizabeth Roberts, Joe Sutliff Sanders, Tom Sweeney, Sheree Renee Thomas, and Trent Walters; my family and friends; and, most of all, my dearest Colleague, Collaborator, Soul Mate, Spouse, and Partner-in-All-Things, Kelly Dunn. I love you, sweetheart!

"If I were in heaven, Nelly, I should be extremely miserable."

"Because you are not fit to go there," I answered. "All sinners would be miserable in heaven."

"But it is not for that. I dreamt once that I was there."

"I tell you I won't harken to your dreams, Miss Catherine! I'll go to bed," I interrupted again.

She laughed, and held me down, for I made a motion to leave my chair.

"This is nothing," cried she. "I was only going to say that heaven did not seem to be my home, and I broke my heart with weeping to come back to earth; and the angels were so angry that they flung me out into the middle of the heath on the top of Wuthering Heights, where I woke sobbing for joy. . . ."

—Emily Brontë

He who does not fill his world with phantoms remains alone.

—Antonio Porchia

Through Violet Eyes

1

The Faceless Man

CROUCHING BEHIND THE WOODEN TOOLSHED along the back fence, the man watched the little strawberry-blond girl at play in the yard. Perspiration blotched the featureless weave of the black veil that obscured his face, and sweat oozed under the latex of his gloves as he flexed his fingers.

It hadn't rained in Los Angeles for almost six months, and the haze of accumulated smog cast an amber pall over the pink bungalow house and its tiny backyard. The late September heat wave had dried the grass to brittle yellow needles, and patches of bare dirt mottled the lawn like mange. An inflatable wading pool decorated with *Winnie-the-Pooh* characters sagged in the center of the yard, and the girl squatted in its shallow water, wearing a one-piece bathing suit with Tigger on the front. Her wispy hair hung in horse-tail tangles about her freckled face as she made her naked Barbie doll swim in big circles around her.

The man's breath quickened, the air hot and stifling underneath his mask of crepe. The child's mother was at work, and the babysitter had gone into the house more than twenty minutes ago. It was the first time in three days that the man had seen the girl left unattended. Nevertheless, he hesitated.

Then he saw her begin to twitch.

She dropped the doll in the water and clapped her hands over her ears. "Somebody's knocking! Somebody's knocking!"

The man tensed and mouthed words under his breath. He imagined that he could hear the soundless whispers now sifting into the girl's skull.

They had found her.

The girl stumbled out of the pool, still clutching her temples, jerking her head as if in the throes of a seizure. *"Somebody's knocking! Somebody's knocking!"*

The man shot a wary glance toward the back door of the house and lunged toward her.

Seeing him, the girl yelped and broke into a zigzagging run toward the house. He blocked her, but she dodged his grasping hands and doubled back on him, scrambling toward the backyard gate. When he cut her off, she scampered to the chain-link fence that bordered the neighbors' yard, locked her fingers on its wire mesh, and shook it, screaming.

As he took hold of her shoulders, though, a sudden exhaustion seemed to overwhelm her, and she drooped against the fence. Her face pinched with concentration, she whispered the letters of the alphabet like a rosary. *"A-B-C-D-E-F-G…H-I-J-K-L-M-N-O-P…Q-R-S-T-U-V…"*

Her voice trailed off. The contours of her face subtly changed, her expression darkening.

Strength surged back into her small frame, and she whipped around, snarling, and clawed the fabric of his mask, trying to pull it from his face. Anticipating that she would do this, the man caught hold of her arms and forced them down.

"Who *are* you?" The girl's voice resonated with adult authority. "Why are you doing this to us?" She glared at him with gleaming violet eyes.

The smooth, shallow hollows of his masked face betrayed no emotion, but the man trembled visibly. Holding the struggling child at arm's length, he clasped her head with his rubber-skinned hands in an almost tender caress.

And then, with a single brisk twist, he snapped her neck.

2

Summoning a Witness

TRAFFIC CLOTTED THE HOLLYWOOD FREEWAY THAT morning, and Dan missed the start of the Muñoz murder trial. By the time he arrived at the Criminal Justice Center, the prosecution was already preparing to summon the victim to testify.

Since he was running late, he decided to park in one of the privately owned downtown lots rather than search for the law-enforcement garage. The Bureau could eat the fourteen-dollar charge. He regretted the choice before he'd walked even half a block, though, for he could feel sweat dampen the dress shirt beneath his blazer.

Despite the oppressive heat, spectators and television news crews clustered around the courthouse entrance, the crowd held at bay by a cordon of uniformed guards from the Sheriff's Office. A Violet was due to take the stand today, an event so rare that it made headlines. Usually, the mere threat of a Violet's testimony served to force a plea bargain, yet Hector Muñoz had insisted upon his not-guilty plea and demanded his day in court.

Dan nudged his way through the crowd to the roped-off area surrounding the entrance and flashed his ID at the beige-shirted officer standing there, who waved him toward the door.

Relieved to be in the building's cool foyer, Dan showed the Bureau badge again at the lobby's security checkpoint. "Okay, Agent...Atwater." The white-shirted guard, a beefy Hispanic man, read the ID and handed it back. "If you like, I can keep your gun for you until you pass through the detector...."

Dan gave him a tight-lipped smile. "No need. I'm not carrying." He emptied his pockets into a wooden box and strolled through the door-shaped booth without setting off the alarm.

The guard grinned. "In that case, have a wonderful day!"

Dan touched two fingers to his forehead in a Boy Scout salute and collected his loose change and car keys.

A placard beside the elevators warned him that "All Persons Will Be Searched On 9th Floor," and he discovered that even his Bureau badge couldn't save him from further delay. Dan didn't mind, however. Violets creeped him out, and he would be spending enough time with this particular Violet in the days to come. No need to rush it.

Superior Court 9-101 exhaled a cold, air-conditioned draft as Dan eased open one of its double doors and stepped inside. The room was nearly filled to capacity, but Dan located a seat at the back of the gallery while the judge finished her mandatory admonition to the jury.

"The statement of the victim should be considered as carefully, and with as much skepticism, as that of any other witness when you decide upon your verdict." The matronly black justice peered at the jurors over the tops of her spectacles, her furrowed face stern. "You must weigh the testimony of the deceased against the other evidence presented by both the prosecution and the defense in order to determine the truth for yourselves. Do you understand your responsibilities as I have described them to you?"

The jurors murmured their assent, although several of them seemed apprehensive. Compulsively drumming his fingers on the defense table, Hector Muñoz shifted in his chair and leaned over to whisper something to his attorney. She merely shook her head, a drawn look on her face.

"Very well." The judge nodded to the assistant D.A., a tall, studious man with flawlessly combed black hair. "Mr. Jacobs, you may call your next witness."

"Thank you, Your Honor." Jacobs rose from his chair. "Bailiff, would you show in Ms. Lindstrom?"

A stocky man in uniform opened a door to the left of the judge's bench and ushered a gaunt, pale young woman with a shaved head into the room. Dan craned his neck for a better view of the Violet he'd be living with for the next few weeks.

She wore a long-sleeved shirt and slacks that both seemed a size too large for her, making her appear frail in the antiseptic illumination of the courtroom's fluorescent lighting. Nevertheless, she spoke with a quiet, understated strength as the bailiff swore her in.

A high-backed reclining chair had been placed on the witness stand for her testimony. Heavy nylon straps dangled from the chair's back and legs. "Please state your name for the record," Jacobs instructed the woman once she'd seated herself.

"Natalie Lindstrom."

"And you are a licensed member of the North American Afterlife Communications Corps?"

"That's correct."

"And do you intend to serve the court today with complete honesty and to the best of your abilities?"

"I do."

Jacobs turned to a portly, bespectacled man who stood to the right of the witness stand. "Mr. Burton, would you prepare the conduit for testimony?"

Pulling a penlight from the inside pocket of his suit coat, Burton shone the light in both of Lindstrom's eyes to make sure she wasn't wearing colored contact lenses. Although there were now more sophisticated ways of verifying the authenticity of a "conduit," this method had become traditional, for, as their nickname implied, all Violets were born with violet irises.

Burton wheeled a pushcart bearing a SoulScan unit up to the witness stand and connected Lindstrom to the device by attaching a series of electrodes to her bare head with surgical tape. Like most Violets, she'd had the twenty contact points tattooed on her scalp as a constellation of tiny bluish spots.

Jacobs explained to the jury how this sophisticated electroencephalograph could detect the electromagnetic presence of the victim's soul as it suffused the conduit's brain. "You'll be able to see for yourselves the precise moment of inhabitation," he said, indicating a large, greenish monitor mounted on the wall above Lindstrom's chair. Dan noted that Jacobs failed to mention the function of the large red button on the SoulScan console. Known as the "Panic Button," it would send a powerful electric shock through the wires to the Violet's head and forcibly eject a soul that became violent or refused to leave the conduit's body. Through rigorous mental discipline, trained Violets could usually evict an unruly soul at any time, but the Panic Button was there as a safeguard, for the dead were always unpredictable.

Burton stepped away from the witness stand, leaving Lindstrom with a forest of wires sprouting from her brow. These wires twisted into a ropelike bundle that snaked down to a port on the SoulScan unit. Burton flicked on the machine, and a series of green lines appeared on the monitor. The rhythmic little zigzags of the top three lines represented the alpha waves of Lindstrom's conscious thought. The bottom three lines lay flat, awaiting the inhabiting entity.

"Are you ready, Ms. Lindstrom?" Jacobs asked.

"Yes." She leaned back in her chair and closed her eyes, while Burton fastened the nylon straps around her legs and torso and bound her wrists together with a ratcheted plastic band.

It's for her own safety, Dan reminded himself, but the thought failed to reassure him. Painful as the restraints were, Lindstrom would soon suffer worse.

Jacobs unsealed one of the prosecution's clear plastic evidence bags and pulled out a baby's bib printed with teddy bears. He displayed it to the jury, then placed the bib in Lindstrom's hands.

Dan grimaced and shook his head. This D.A. pulled no punches. He could have selected almost any item touched or worn by the victim to serve as the touchstone. A hairbrush, a house key, a driver's license—all of these items would retain a faint quantum link to the dead woman and would draw her electromagnetic essence to the conduit like a lighting rod. Instead, Jacobs had chosen to use her child's clothing for the emotional impact it would have on the jurors. Why Muñoz would want to put himself through the torture of a Violet's testimony, Dan couldn't comprehend. To look into those eyes and see the life you took staring back at you…

Lindstrom shaped silent words with her lips, and the alpha waves that scrolled across the top of the SoulScan monitor became more measured and even. Soon, she would withdraw into her own subconscious and cede control of her body.

Jacobs glanced over his shoulder at the crowd in the gallery. "Please remain quiet," he admonished them. He needn't have bothered. The silence made it seem as though everyone in the room had stopped breathing.

Lindstrom sat perfectly still for several minutes, the bib pressed between her palms. The tension in the courtroom eased as people became bored with their unresolved suspense. Feet shuffled. Chairs creaked. Someone coughed. Only Muñoz sat frozen in place, eyes fixed on the woman on the witness stand.

Dan's sweat dried to clamminess in the air-conditioned room, leaching the heat from his skin. He was shivering by the time the first squiggles appeared on the bottom half of the SoulScan monitor. The hair stiffened on his scalp, and he imagined that the entire room was charged with the static of dead souls.

Lindstrom's body became rigid, her back arched, her belly straining against the straps that held her to the chair.

Her bony hands constricted on the bib, and she bucked and twisted with epileptic fury.

This is a bad one, Dan thought. If the touchstone summoned more than one soul, the conduit needed to fight to stave off the other entities so the desired individual could inhabit her. Untrained Violets had been known to bite their own tongues off during such a fit.

Her head thrashing from side to side, Lindstrom let out a raw, throat-grating scream, and Dan saw several of the jurors blanch. No doubt most of them had only seen Violets in movies or on TV cop shows. The real thing was an entirely different experience. Dan had probably seen them fifty times or more during his career, and each time seemed worse than the last. Particularly during the past two years.

Lindstrom's eyes snapped open, and she gaped around the courtroom like a rabbit in a wolves' den. Without changing in any physiological way, the muscles in her face had reconfigured themselves to suggest a new countenance, knitting the brows, thrusting out the chin, inflating the cheeks. She whimpered and tried to wriggle free of the chair's restraints. Then her gaze locked on Hector Muñoz, and she fell silent, staring at him.

Muñoz clutched at his temples with trembling hands, unable to look away. *"Rosa…"*

Jacobs stepped forward to address the woman in the witness stand. "Do you remember me?" he asked her.

She glanced at him and nodded. No doubt the prosecution had previously summoned the victim in order to question her.

"Please tell us who you are," Jacobs instructed her.

"Rosa Muñoz." She said the name with a Spanish accent,

and the soft soprano of her voice had lowered to a gravelly alto.

"Let the record show that the witness has identified herself as the victim." Jacobs attempted to reestablish eye contact with her. "Do you know where you are?"

Her eyes remained fixed on Hector Muñoz as she shook
her head.

"Do you recognize anyone else in this room?"

The woman in Natalie Lindstrom's body didn't respond, for she was looking down at the bib she held in her
hands. "Oh, God—Pedrito!"

"Pedrito…he was your son, wasn't he?" Jacobs
prompted. "Tell us about Pedrito."

"*He* killed him. My *cerdo* of a husband." She thrust her
bound hands forward to point at Muñoz. "He killed my
baby!"

Muñoz slumped over the defense table as though he'd
been shot. His lawyer patted him on the shoulder, but offered no words of encouragement.

Jacobs turned toward the jury. "Let the record show that
the witness has identified the defend—"

"You and your goddamned *speed*!" Trembling, the
woman in the witness stand glared at Muñoz with Lindstrom's fathomless violet eyes, her face wrinkled with contempt. "Always the goddamned speed. And Pedrito crying,
getting on your nerves. 'Shut up! Shut up!'" She mimed a
shaking motion with her hands. "Well, you got him to shut
up, didn't you, Hector?"

Muñoz didn't look up.

"And then what happened?" Jacobs asked.

"And then I started screaming. Called Hector the

asesino he was. The last thing I remember was him grabbing my throat and yelling at me: *'Be quiet, bitch! They'll hear you!'*" She pressed the bib to her face and shut her eyes, shuddering. "He follows me everywhere. I'm the only one he knows there, and he never leaves me. Do you know what that's like, Hector? *Just the two of us, crying in the dark.*"

Hector Muñoz raised his head, his face streaked with tears. "Oh, God, Rosa, *lo siento, lo siento!*" Before his attorney could stop him, he clambered over the defense table and bolted toward the witness stand, hands reaching out in supplication to his dead wife. Two guards lunged forward and grabbed him before he got there. *"Perdóneme! Perdóneme!"* Muñoz sobbed as they wrestled him to the floor.

He knew all along he couldn't win, Dan realized. He'd wanted a trial simply because it was his only chance to beg forgiveness of the wife he'd strangled.

The woman in the witness stand strained forward in her chair, and Dan could hear the nylon straps stretch to the point of breaking. *"Never,"* she rasped. Her voice rose to a shriek, and the air vibrated with the force of her hatred. "You hear me, Hector? *NEVER!*"

On the SoulScan monitor, the smooth, measured waves of Lindstrom's dormant consciousness turned spiky and frenetic. Her facial features contorted.

With a worried look, Burton reached for the Panic Button.

The corners of the Violet's mouth stretched wide to expose gritted teeth, as though she wore a mask that had been pulled too tight. Then her quivering flesh settled into a melancholy composure, and Lindstrom straightened her posture in the chair, breathing deeply.

Burton withdrew his outstretched hand. Jacobs nodded to him, and the assistant began removing the straps and wires from Lindstrom's body.

The guards handcuffed and chained Hector Muñoz, who moaned inconsolably as they led him out of the room. His attorney, a seasoned public defender appointed by the state, had apparently anticipated such an outcome from the beginning, for she calmly asked for an adjournment to allow her time to revise her client's defense in light of recent developments. Although the prosecution objected to the delay, the judge granted her request. The bailiff helped an exhausted Lindstrom shuffle out the side door.

As the people around him filed out the courtroom's double doors, Dan discovered that his eyes had become dry and sticky from staring so long. His tongue seemed wrapped in gauze, and he popped an Altoid into his mouth to try to work up some saliva. Rosa Muñoz's final word still reverberated in his head.

NEVER ...

He dawdled in the courtroom for more than five minutes before he felt ready to meet Natalie Lindstrom.

As long as she doesn't touch me ...

Straightening his tie, Dan made his way to the courtroom's side door and showed his ID to the guard standing there. He passed through the door into a private waiting room, where he found Lindstrom stretched out on a sofa, one arm folded over her eyes. Her wrists were red from where the plastic bands had rubbed the skin. The knotted tension in her cheeks and brow still bore an afterimage of Rosa Muñoz's expression, like a photographic double-exposure.

"Ms. Lindstrom?"

Startled, she sat up and regarded him with suspicion.

"Sorry to bother you." He almost gave her his hand to shake, but put it in his pocket instead. "Special Agent Dan Atwater, FBI. Investigative Support Unit. That was … quite a performance out there."

She slumped back on the couch. "If you say so."

He knelt until he was almost eye level with her. "I know you must be tired, but we really need your help with one of our current cases. When you hear the details, I think you'll agree—"

"I know the details." Her eyes shifted to meet his. "*They* told me."

3

Dead Violets

THE HAIR PRICKLED AT THE NAPE OF DAN'S NECK. "'They'?"

She half-closed her eyes. "You know who I mean."

He chewed on his lower lip. "How many of 'them' have you talked to?"

"Four. Why? How many are missing?"

"As of yesterday, seven." Dan stood and paced the room, giving himself the excuse to avoid her violet stare. "If we don't act soon, you could be chatting with a bunch more."

"Mmm. And if I refuse to help?"

He pretended to examine the shine on his Florsheims. "Then I'll have to take you into protective custody. You're a prime target, after all."

She sighed. "I didn't think I had a choice, but I always like to make sure." She swung her feet off the couch and sat up. "Mind if I change?"

"Depends who you change into." Dan smiled, but Lindstrom gave him an icy look. He cleared his throat. "Yeah, do whatever you need to do."

She unzipped an overnight bag that lay beside what looked like a hatbox on a nearby table. Pulling out a folded outfit, she glanced over her shoulder at Dan. "Uh...could you leave for a minute?"

"Afraid not. The Bureau wants you under watch twenty-four/seven."

"You mean they're afraid I might skip out on them."

He shrugged. "Hey, the killer could be hiding right outside that door."

"Or even standing here in front of me."

Dan chuckled. "Touché. Although, as 'they' probably told you, the killer never lets his victims see his face."

"True enough. But if I get killed, I'm going to report you to the Bureau myself. You mind turning around?"

"Uh...sure." He faced the wall and folded his arms. "I've read a lot about you," he said with the forced pleasantry of someone speaking to a mental patient.

"I bet."

Behind him, cloth whispered against skin. He dredged up more words to keep himself from visualizing her in nothing but lingerie. "Nice work on the Aqueduct Killer case."

"My work is never 'nice.' How about yours?"

Dan was glad she couldn't see his grimace. "It has its ups and downs."

"You can turn around now."

He put on the most amiable face he could manage and turned around. Lindstrom now wore a sleeveless white blouse and a pair of blue jeans that highlighted her slight but shapely figure. She pulled her black Doc Marten boots back on and tied them, then picked up the discarded long-sleeved shirt and slacks and threw them in her bag. Pawing through her purse, she pulled out a portable makeup mirror and a contact lens carrying case.

"How long you been working for the Feds?" she asked as she placed a colored lens in each eye.

"Five years. Before that, I was a detective here in L.A."

"You must be a glutton for punishment." Pulling a roll of double-sided tape out of the overnight bag, she tore off strips of the sticky plastic and applied them in an arc across her scalp and down to her temples. She then opened the hatbox and took out a long, straight, copper-colored wig, which she carefully arranged on her head. "So, where do we go from here?"

"The LAPD admin building—we've set up a meeting there for your convenience. We can take my car to avoid the press."

"Nah. Let's walk." Examining her reflection in the mirror, Lindstrom pressed the wig into place and combed out its tangles with her fingers. "They won't recognize me."

With some rouge and red lipstick from her purse, she added color to her pallid face. The change in her appearance was startling. The long hair hid the skeletal starkness of her tattooed scalp and softened the planes of her cheeks and chin, while the contacts lightened her eyes from dark purple to crystal blue. Not a trace of Rosa Muñoz remained.

"Anyone ever tell you you look good as a redhead?" he asked with a tentative grin. It wasn't simply a lame icebreaker line, either. He meant it. If she weren't a Violet…

Lindstrom's face may have changed, but her expression didn't; it remained resentful, resigned, and a trifle sad. "Here. Make yourself useful." She held out the overnight case and wig box. "Let's go out the back."

Dan remained quietly courteous, but took great care to

make sure his fingers didn't brush against hers when she handed him the luggage. He knew that Violets could use people as touchstones, and unlike Hector Muñoz, Dan had no desire to speak to ghosts from his past.

It's only for a few days—a week or two at most, he reminded himself. *As long as she doesn't touch me....*

They left the courthouse through the restricted-access portion of the building, the pathways reserved exclusively for judges, police officers, and prisoners. If they'd used the elevator, they would have been on the ground in less than five minutes, but Lindstrom insisted they take the stairs.

Dan raised an eyebrow. "Claustrophobic?"

"It's good exercise" was all she said as they entered the emergency stairwell at the ninth floor.

"Easy for you to say. You're not the one carrying the suitcase."

Reporters and shutterbugs still loitered outside the courthouse, no doubt hoping to snap pictures of the Violet in all her bald-headed, purple-eyed strangeness. But no one spared a glance at Lindstrom when she and Dan emerged from the building and strolled down Temple to Los Angeles Street.

A security checkpoint at the corner allowed only authorized vehicles to enter, but the street was open to foot traffic, and they proceeded halfway down the block toward a cement glacier propped up by cylindrical concrete columns—the monolithic entrance of Parker Center, the LAPD's administration building. After walking through the blast-furnace heat outside, Dan savored the refreshing chill as they passed beneath the glacier and into the air-conditioned police headquarters.

He led Lindstrom up to the second floor and rapped on the door of a small conference room. A dour-faced man with mocha-colored skin and tightly wound black hair let them in. The knot of his tie hung loose below the unbuttoned collar of a white dress shirt that had been pressed with military precision. "About time! I was beginning to wonder if we'd have to add you two to the victims list."

"Allow me to introduce my boss, Earl Clark," Dan said to Lindstrom as Clark stepped aside for them to enter. "He's the Special Agent in Command for this case. Earl—Natalie Lindstrom."

SAC Clark extended a hand, which she shook without enthusiasm. Dan winced. In that brief moment of contact, he wondered, did she get a glimmer of the dead people in Clark's past? Did it bother Earl to think that she might?

Setting Lindstrom's overnight bag and wig box by the door, Dan gestured toward a dark-haired woman in a beige pantsuit who sat at a long table that was covered with open file folders, photographs, and miscellaneous items of evidence. "And this is Yolena Garcia, detective from the LAPD's East Los Angeles Division."

Garcia stood and offered her hand to Lindstrom. "Pleased to meet you." Much like Lindstrom, Garcia never seemed to smile, and she conducted herself with the overzealous professionalism of one who has had to fight to be respected by her peers.

"Detective Garcia's in charge of the local investigation," Dan explained. "Natalie—can I call you Natalie?—Natalie says she's been in contact with some of the victims."

Clark and Garcia exchanged a glance.

"That's interesting." Clark picked a three-by-four-inch snapshot off the table and handed it to Lindstrom. "Heard anything from her?"

For the first time since the trial, Lindstrom's stony expression faltered: eyes glistening, mouth trembling. Peering over her shoulder, Dan saw that the photo depicted a little girl with strawberry-blond hair and violet eyes. Her broad, goofy grin was missing two upper teeth on the left side, and she held a butterscotch tabby cat that was almost as big as she was. Dan recognized the snapshot from the briefing Garcia had given him that morning.

Lindstrom passed the photo back to Clark. "No, she hasn't knocked. Is she ...?"

"We were hoping you could tell us. She disappeared yesterday. We haven't found a body yet, if that means anything. Of course, we haven't found any of the others, either." Clark tossed the photo beside the open file folders. "He moves the bodies after they're dead, so even the victims can't tell us where they are."

"Who was she?" Lindstrom's use of the past tense made Dan wince.

"Laurie Gannon," Garcia replied. "The babysitter who was supposed to be watching her was asleep in the house when she heard Laurie shouting in the backyard. By the time she got outside, Laurie was gone. The babysitter saw someone in dark clothing climb over the backyard fence and run away. From the size and posture of the figure, she's pretty sure it was a man." The detective frowned. "He had a bulging plastic garbage bag slung over his shoulder."

"You come up with anything at the crime scene?" Dan asked.

"No prints or fibers—the guy worked clean. About all we got was this." The detective held up the plaster cast of a shoe sole. "Reeboks, size ten and a half. Brand new, by the look of it. Found the tracks on some of the dusty patches in the back lawn."

"Great. That narrows the field to a few million suspects. What about the killer's car?"

Garcia set aside the shoe imprint and shook her head. "We figure he parked here, in the alley that runs behind the back fence of the Gannon residence." She tapped her finger on a schematic diagram of the crime scene and its environs. "We've canvassed the neighborhood, but no one remembers seeing a car drive in or out of that alley—most of the people in that area are away at work during the day. About the only good news is that we didn't find any traces of the girl's blood, for whatever that's worth."

"Why wasn't she at the School?"

Lindstrom's question took Dan and the others by surprise. "Funny you should ask," Clark said. "Her mother pulled her out of the School last week, before we even considered the children possible targets for the killer. Ms. Gannon's now convinced that *we* took her daughter."

"Did you?" Lindstrom had restored her frigid calm, and Dan fancied that he could see her violet irises radiating through the blue shells of her contacts.

Clark glared at her. "We had nothing to do with this."

"No doubt the Corps has all the other kids in custody now."

"For their own safety," the SAC responded in an arch tone.

Dan moved to break the tension between the two of them. "Why don't you tell us which of these have contacted you?"

He indicated the open file folders, and Garcia pushed them forward for Lindstrom's inspection. A photo of each missing Violet had been paper-clipped inside each folder, along with a background sheet containing personal data, family information, and a North American Afterlife Communications Corps registration number. The flat, institutional Polaroids all resembled criminal mugshots, each one featuring a man or woman with a bald head and violet eyes.

Without bothering to look at the typewritten name on the data sheet beside it, Lindstrom pointed to the photo of a wizened black man with hollow cheeks. "Jem's knocked." Her finger moved to a picture of a plump, middle-aged woman with a mole at the corner of her mouth. "And Gig." Then a skinny, squirrelly man with thick, bulbous glasses and a lopsided smile. "Russell." Next, a copper-skinned Puerto Rican woman. "Sylvia."

Lindstrom stopped abruptly, her fingertips lingering on the unshaven face of a young man with thick black eyebrows. "Evan…"

"Heard from him, too?" Dan asked.

"No. And I should have." She looked up at him with indignant suspicion. "How do you know he's dead?"

"Russell Travers summoned him. We have the deposition on video, if you want to see it."

Laying her palms flat on the table, she braced herself to

remain upright, and Dan pulled a chair out for her. She sank onto it.

"I'm sorry you had to find out this way," he said. "You were friends?"

"You could say that." She stared at Evan's photo. "They were all my friends. All but...what was her name? Laurie?"

"Yes. It was your familiarity with the other victims that made us select you for this investigation, Ms. Lindstrom," Clark said. "That, and your...expertise in dealing with violent crime." He pushed another folder forward. "Was she a friend of yours, too?"

"Not exactly." The frown lines at the sides of Lindstrom's mouth deepened as she examined the photo of a fair-skinned young woman with a broad, heart-shaped face. The woman's head was turned away slightly and her eyes downcast, as though the government photographer had caught her by surprise. "I knew Sondra, but she hasn't come to me, either. Last I heard, she and Evan were together."

Dan detected the acid aftertaste of jealousy in her tone. Had Lindstrom and Evan Markham been an item once? Dan had worked with Evan on the Philly Ripper case last year, and found the Violet to be a sullen, standoffish sort.

They'd make a perfect couple, Dan thought. He was strangely disappointed in Lindstrom, though, for choosing such a misanthrope as a boyfriend.

"When did Whitman and the others start 'knocking,' as you put it?" Clark asked her.

"End of August. Jem was the first. He was trying to warn as many of us as he could." She gave Clark a cold look. "He knew the Corps wouldn't."

The SAC's mouth twisted, but he didn't contradict her.

Dan glanced from one to the other in alarm. He'd heard nasty things about the NAACC, but nothing like this. "The Corps didn't alert their membership?"

"Of course not," Lindstrom said. "They didn't want us to panic and run. Isn't that right, Mr. Clark?"

The SAC answered without meeting Dan's questioning gaze. "Corps Security wanted the opportunity to contain the problem before it got out of hand."

"But it *did* get out of hand, didn't it?" Lindstrom pressed. "When Jem warned her, Sylvia tried to hide, but the Corps dragged her back...."

Turning his back on her, Clark raised his voice and pointed to a U.S. map that had been thumbtacked to a bulletin board on the wall. "Whitman disappeared in D.C. on August twenty-eighth, Gig Marshall two days later in Baltimore. Conduits have a history of taking unscheduled vacations, so we figured they'd turn up eventually."

"When Corps Security tracked them down," Lindstrom added.

The SAC calmed himself before continuing. "Sondra Avebury and Evan Markham were working for us at Quantico, and both reported that Whitman and Marshall had come to them and told them they'd been killed by a man wearing a black mask. Within a week, Avebury vanished, followed by Markham a day later. That's when we knew our killer had a thing for Violets.

"The N-double-A-C-C turned the case over to us, and we called in Russell Travers to summon all the previous victims for their testimony. Because of the geographic clustering of the initial victims, we thought the UNSUB might be a Maryland or Virginia local," Clark explained, using the acronym that designated the "unknown subject" of the investigation. "The Corps took steps to protect the members in the immediate area. Then the killer got Travers in New York on September tenth and Sylvia Perez in Miami on the twelfth. Both were taken in their sleep, so they couldn't tell us anything new about the UNSUB. Now he's come to the West Coast for Laurie Gannon, and we have no idea who's next." He paused for effect, leaning toward Lindstrom. "Maybe you."

Dan noted the pulse in her neck. "You've done an admirable job of keeping it out of the papers."

Clark snorted. "So far, yes. But it's only a matter of time before someone connects the disappearances—or a body turns up. That's why we need to catch this nutcase now."

"All right, then. What do you want from me?"

"Well, as you can see, we can't even find a corpse to examine." The SAC indicated the avalanche of data spread over the table. "In the past, murderers who've worn masks or disguised their appearance have always left us something to work with—trace forensic evidence, a motive buried in the victims' memories, even the body language the killer displayed while committing the crime. In this case, the killer hasn't left so much as a hair at the crime scene, and none of the victims has a clue who he is or why he kills."

"What makes you think I'll be able to find out any more about him than the other Violets?"

"We need to talk to the girl," Dan suggested. "Laurie. She doesn't seem to fit the pattern of the other victims. She was only a kid, not a full Corps member. Maybe she can tell us something about why the killer chooses the Violets he does."

Lindstrom sighed. "I'll need a touchstone."

Garcia selected an evidence bag from the scattered items on the table and held it up. A naked Barbie doll with disheveled nylon hair smiled through the plastic. "Would this work?"

In spite of her artfully layered makeup, dark shadows of weariness reappeared around Lindstrom's eyes. "Yep. That'd do it."

She made no move to take the doll.

"We've had a room specially prepared for you." Clark jerked his head in the direction of the exit. "Detective, would you ... ?"

"Sure." With the bagged Barbie in hand, Garcia crossed the room and pulled open the door. "Ms. Lindstrom?"

The Violet collected her luggage and stalked out with Garcia beside her. Dan was about to join them when Clark laid a hand on his shoulder.

"Wait." He looked like a father whose son has failed a final exam. "Where's your gun?"

Dan shoved his hands in his pockets. "I have it. It's in the trunk of my car."

"Wrong answer, Agent Atwater." Clark's expression softened. "Look, I know what you're going through, but you can't let it get in the way. Remember: You're not only her partner—you're her last line of defense."

Dan shook his head. "And I thought this was gonna be a desk job," he mourned with a thin chuckle, and left the room.

4

Laurie

DAN GOT TO THE INTERROGATION ROOM JUST AS
Garcia finished strapping Lindstrom into her chair. When
the detective started to untangle the electrode wires of a
nearby SoulScan unit, however, the Violet balked.

"That won't be necessary," she snapped.

Garcia looked to Dan for guidance. "You sure about
that?" Dan asked Lindstrom.

She brushed a hand through the strands of her wig. "I
just did my hair."

"We won't have access to the Panic Button."

"I can handle it. And I really don't enjoy electric shocks."

"Your call." He waved Garcia off, and the detective
wound the electrode wires back into a neat bundle. From a
nearby corner of the room, she took a camcorder on a tri-
pod and moved it in front of Lindstrom, but Dan told her
to put it back.

Garcia didn't budge. "Regulations require that all conduit depositions be videotaped."

Dan waited for Lindstrom to object as well; when she
didn't, he edged closer to Garcia and lowered his voice. "Detective, we're about to yank a little girl out of the blackness
of death and ask her for intimate details about how she

was murdered. She'll be frightened enough without having a camera lens shoved in her face. Don't you agree?"

The detective's officious demeanor faltered, and she withdrew the camera.

Lindstrom gave Dan a slight nod.

He placed two folding chairs in front of the Violet while Garcia handed her the evidence bag containing Laurie Gannon's Barbie. Lindstrom ran her fingertips over the doll's face, but seemed reluctant to remove it from the bag.

"Want me to take it out for you?" Garcia offered.

"No. I can do it." Uttering a rapid, repetitive whisper, Lindstrom tore open the plastic.

With spastic suddenness, her hand tightened around the doll's waist, her forearm becoming a bas-relief of taut tendons and veins. A kaleidoscope of shadows shifted across her face as the musculature of her cheeks and brow rippled and reshaped.

Dan thought of the little girl with the strawberry hair and missing baby teeth and felt a queasy sense of dread bubble up from his gut. He braced himself against the back of a chair and realized he hadn't taken a breath for almost a minute.

Garcia gave him a sympathetic look. "First time?"

"Yes and no." Dan licked his dry lips. "Every time seems like the first. I'll be back in a sec."

He stepped out of the room and tugged the knot of his tie away from his Adam's apple. The soundproofed door closed behind him, cutting off the plaintive wail of a child that bawled with Lindstrom's voice. Dan sighed and ambled down the corridor to an alcove on the right where vending machines dispensed bottled soft drinks and packaged snacks. The blood returned to his face in a blush. He was acting like a total rookie.

He rubbed his eyes with the heels of his hands, then fished a dollar out of his wallet and fed it into one of the machines. It spat out a Kit Kat bar along with his change. He grabbed the coins and candy and returned to the interrogation room, pausing outside the door in order to put on his game face.

"It's okay, it's okay," Garcia repeated in a motherly tone as Dan entered. "We're not going to hurt you...."

Lindstrom hunched in her chair, the long locks of the wig hanging down over her face as though she were trying to hide behind the curtains of copper hair. She chewed on the thumb of her left hand while clutching the Barbie to her chest with her right.

Maintaining eye contact with her, Garcia introduced the two of them. "Laurie, I'm Yolena, and this is my friend Dan. We were hoping you could help us."

Lindstrom looked up at Dan with large, liquid eyes. It reminded him of the shy way his niece met strangers for the first time. *What a thing for a kid to go through,* he thought, but smiled reassuringly as he seated himself on the chair beside Garcia's. "Hey, Laurie. It's nice to finally meet you. Here, I brought you something...." He held up the Kit Kat. "You like chocolate?"

She nodded.

Dan unwrapped the bar and broke off one of the chocolate-coated cookie sticks for her. "Want some?"

She looked at the candy he offered, but made no move to take it. Her eyes scoured the room. "Is Mommy here?"

Dan swallowed to relieve the tightness in his throat.

"No, honey. But she wanted us to tell you that she loves you and thinks about you all the time."

"Oh." Disappointment. Since her mother was not waiting to give her a hug, she took the thumb from her mouth and pointed to the chocolate stick. "I can have it?"

"Sure."

She took the stick from him, stuck it in her mouth, and started to lick the coating off the soggy wafers. Saliva dripped down onto her fingers, and her lipsticked mouth became smeared with melted chocolate. The doll she still held close to her heart.

"Laurie?" Garcia leaned forward. "Can you tell us the last thing you remember? The last thing you saw... before..."

"Before I died?" She stared at the detective with the hard, grim gaze of a Violet, reminding Dan that this little girl had been denied the comforting ignorance of mortality enjoyed by most children. She had known death every day of her brief life.

"Yes, Laurie," Dan said. "Can you tell us how you died?"

She shook her head.

"Why not? Were you asleep?"

"Sort of." She bit off some of the bare wafer and chewed it. "Someone was inside me."

"Someone was inside you? Someone dead?" Garcia took a ballpoint pen and a small notepad from her jacket pocket. "Who was that?"

"Jem. He used to be one of my teachers." She finished the chocolate stick and licked her fingers. "He was the one who told me about the man with no face."

She pointed sheepishly to the rest of the candy bar in

Dan's hand. He broke off another stick for her. "Did you see the man with no face?"

She nodded and pulled her elbows close to her sides as if cowering in a cold draft. "He came, just like Jem said he would."

"What do you mean when you say he didn't have a face?"

"It was just, like, a black lump. No eyes or nose or mouth or nothing."

"A mask," Garcia commented. "Same MO as the others."

"When did you first see the Faceless Man?"

"When he jumped out at me. I got scared and tried to run away."

"Then what happened?"

"Jem came in. He wanted to help, but he was too late."

"That's all you remember?"

"That. And being dead." Her gaze lost its focus, and the chocolate stick wilted in her hand, forgotten.

Dan touched her forearm. "Laurie? Laurie? Why did your mom take you out of the School?"

"Because that's where Jem said he'd be." Her voice was distant, small, and sad. "The man with no face."

"Jem told you about him while you were still at the School? Did you ever see the man while you were there?"

She considered the question, and her mouth opened. Then she shook her head.

Garcia scribbled something in her notebook. "Can you tell us anything else about the Faceless Man? Do you know why he'd want to hurt you?"

"Uh-uh."

"How about Jem?" Dan asked. "Did *he* know why the man was coming to get you?"

"He thinks the man hates us."

"Us?"

"The special ones. The dead-talkers. That's why Jem was trying to warn us. He said he'd visit me as much as he could to make sure I was okay."

"Did anyone besides Jem visit you at the School?"

"Not me. But some others came to my friends there."

"And they said the same thing? About the Faceless Man?"

She nodded.

"What did the teachers at the School do when you told them what Jem said?"

"They said he was just trying to scare us and that everything would be okay."

That's the Corps for you, Dan thought. *They obviously wanted time to "contain the problem" before the parents started yanking their kids out of the School.* "Is that when you asked your mommy to take you home?"

"Uh-huh."

"I see." Dan silently pitied Ms. Gannon. By saving her daughter from the government, she exposed her to the killer. "Thank you for helping us, Laurie." He looked at Garcia. "You have anything else?"

The detective scanned her notes. "Not at the moment."

"Mister?"

Dan glanced back to find Lindstrom peering at him intently. "Yes, Laurie?"

"Please don't let him hurt my friends."

It took Dan a moment to find his voice. "We won't," he said at last, and hoped he could keep the vow.

With the questioning complete, an awkward silence descended on the interrogation room. Dan tried not to stare at the grown woman in front of him as she hugged her doll and ate her chocolate stick. Was Lindstrom aware that they were done? Dan knew that experienced Violets could monitor the thoughts of the souls that inhabited them. How long did she need to reassert control? Perhaps, if the spirit left willingly...

He leaned forward to make eye contact with her again. "Laurie? We need to talk to Natalie now...."

She pouted defiantly. "I don't want to go back."

Pinpricks of panic danced across Dan's scalp, but he kept his voice level and calm as he chided her. "Laurie, you can't stay."

"I miss Mommy. I miss my friends. I miss my kitty. I miss them all so much!" She started to cry, drool spilling over her lower lip with each hiccuping sob.

Garcia glanced toward the unused SoulScan unit and gave Dan a questioning look, but Dan signaled for her to wait. He got out of his chair and knelt in front of Lindstrom. "What's your cat's name, Laurie?"

She sniffled and gulped the spit in her mouth. "Tigger."

"Tell you what: I'll get Tigger a big can of tuna and tell him it came from you."

Her shuddering breaths began to quiet. "What about Mommy?"

"I'll tell her that you love her and miss her a lot."

She chewed on her thumb and pressed Barbie's face to her cheek. "Can I have the rest of my candy before I go?"

"Sure, honey."

He gave her the rest of the Kit Kat bar, and she made sorrowful little mewling sounds while she finished it. As she licked the chocolate residue from her fingers, shadows settled in the hollows of her eyes, aging her expression into one of adult exhaustion. Lindstrom wiped the saline trail of a tear from her face, and ended up smearing her cheek with brown stickiness. Her grief tainted with embarrassment, she looked at her chocolate-slicked hand in helpless annoyance. "Can somebody get me a napkin?"

"Here." Dan took a folded handkerchief from his back pocket and shook it out for her. "We'll let you clean up in the bathroom before the debriefing."

He signaled Garcia, who undid Lindstrom's restraints. She handed the Barbie to Dan, and Garcia led her down the hall to the women's lavatory.

Lindstrom had recovered her composure by the time they returned to the interrogation room. Dan noticed, though, that she seated herself in what had been *his* chair, leaving him the chair with the dangling nylon straps. He chose to remain standing instead.

Garcia poised her pen over a blank page of her notepad. "What can you give us?"

"Not much," Lindstrom responded. "Perp definitely seems to be a man. Slender, but well built, weight between one-seventy and one-ninety. Height is a little more difficult to guess; Laurie's perspective is a lot lower than mine, and he was hunched over when she saw him. Could have been anywhere from five ten to six three. Wore a black veil, dark clothes, latex gloves."

"Did he say anything?"

"No, not to Laurie. Her sensory memories ended as soon as Jem took over, though."

"At least Whitman spared her the physical pain. What about the School?" Garcia flipped back a few pages. "When I asked Laurie if she'd seen the Faceless Man there, she seemed unsure of herself."

"There *was* something—the memory of a man sitting on his haunches in front of a large metal tank."

"Did you recognize the location?" Dan asked.

"No." Lindstrom shut her eyes, as though to recapture the image. "The man wore some kind of uniform, like a jumpsuit, and he had a toolbox with him. He wasn't wearing a mask, though."

"He wasn't? What did he look like?"

"Give me that sketchbook and I'll show you." She indicated the table by the door, where a drawing pad and pencils had been provided for use by police sketch artists.

Dan brought her the drawing materials and watched in fascination as she deftly rendered a picture of the stranger Laurie had seen at the School: a Caucasian man with curly blond hair, full cheeks and lips, and a bushy mustache and eyebrows. *Blue eyes,* Lindstrom scrawled at the top of the black-and-white drawing.

"This is the best I can do." She tore the finished sketch off the pad and gave it to Garcia. "Laurie didn't get too good a look at his face; as soon as he saw her standing behind him, he stood up and hurried away."

Garcia frowned at the portrait. "So why would she think this guy was the Faceless Man?"

"Obviously, she didn't," Dan said. "That's why she didn't mention him."

"She saw a resemblance, though."

Garcia glanced at Lindstrom. "What do you mean?"

"It was something about the body language." Her hands groped the air as she strained to define the impression. "In both cases, Laurie sensed some...*hesitation* in the man. More than that: reluctance—dread, even."

"Doesn't sound like your typical psycho." The detective angled the drawing toward Dan. "Should I circulate this?"

"Hold off for now—a kid's hunch by itself isn't enough to link this guy to the killer." He turned to Lindstrom. "How would you feel about a visit to your old alma mater?"

"Can I get a root canal instead?"

"Great! We'll leave first thing in the morning."

"Where are we staying *tonight*?"

"My hotel room." He raised his hands to calm her. "It has two beds."

"Joy. Can I at least stop by my apartment and get a few things?"

"Of course."

"Good." Lindstrom picked up her purse and thrust her overnight case and wig box at Dan. "Dinner's on you."

"Fair enough." He accepted the luggage without complaint, then took a business card from his wallet and handed it to Garcia. "Thanks for your help, Detective. Call my cell phone if you get any news."

"Sure." She tucked the card in her jacket pocket along with her notepad. "Where you going now?"

"To give Ms. Gannon some bad news."

5

The Missing Tigger

UNDER MOST CIRCUMSTANCES, DAN WOULD HAVE eaten lunch behind the wheel while driving to the Gannon residence, but, out of courtesy, he treated Lindstrom to a twenty-minute snack break in the open square behind the courthouse. While he wolfed a ham sandwich, she settled for a banana, an apple, and a bottle of water.

When they got to the Ford Taurus he'd borrowed from the Bureau's L.A. office, Lindstrom inspected the vehicle like a finicky car buyer. "Does this thing have antilock brakes?"

Dan flipped through the keys on his key ring. "You bet."

"Passenger-side air bags?"

"I think so...."

"Side-impact air bags?"

He glared at her across the roof. "I don't know. Why the *Consumer Reports* survey?"

She folded her arms. "I like to be careful, is all."

"Well, I guarantee it's safer than walking in this town." He popped open the car's automatic locks. "Get in."

"What's your driving record like?"

"I haven't killed anyone, if that's what you mean." *At least, not in a car,* a voice in his mind added.

"Have you ever talked to the victim of a head-on collision?"

"No, but I'm sure it's fascinating. *Get in.*"

She finally opened her door and slid into the passenger side.

Dan swung in behind the wheel and lifted Lindstrom's bag over onto the backseat. The moment he slammed the door, though, he remembered Clark's orders. "Aw, hell."

Lindstrom snapped her safety belt in place. "What is it?"

"Give me a sec...."

Dan got out and opened the trunk. Folding back the canvas tarp inside, he revealed a leather shoulder holster and a rectangular lockbox with five numbered buttons on top. After surveying the parking lot to make sure that no one was watching, he punched in the combination and opened the box.

Nestled inside on a bed of foam rubber was a Smith & Wesson Model 10 six-shot .38 revolver. In the contoured notch beside it rested a case of bullets.

Although he'd dutifully brought the gun with him, Dan had never fired it. In fact, he hadn't even removed it from the case since the Bureau issued it to him eighteen months ago. But he knew well enough what the pistol would feel like—knew exactly the heft it would have in his hand, the tension required to pull its trigger, the jolt its recoil would send shivering up his arm. He'd carried a gun just like it, once.

A night-darkened alley. Above a door, a dim lightbulb caged in thick wire. Silhouetted in the light's feeble glow, a man stands rattling the knob of the door. The three of them— he, Ross, and Phillips—train their guns on the figure's back, and Phillips shouts at the man to freeze. The man turns around, there's something in his hand, and someone fires first....

He'd been thinking with his spinal cord. Like when the doctor taps your knee with a hammer—it was all reflex.

The dark face looks up at him, eyes wide and white and uncomprehending. It is not the face Dan expected to see. "For God's sake, call an ambulance!" Dan screams at Ross and Phillips, who stand behind him, dumbfounded. In desperation, Dan presses his wadded FBI windbreaker against the man's chest wounds and feels warm liquid pooling beneath the plastic....

Dan slapped the lockbox shut. He hadn't even cleaned or oiled the damned gun. For all he knew, it'd blow his hand off the first time he fired it.

He had started to close the trunk when he caught sight of Lindstrom's profile through the Ford's back window. She gazed idly out the side window.

You're her last line of defense.

Dan let the trunk lid spring open again. His eyes fixed on the lockbox, he shrugged off his jacket and put on the leather holster.

A few minutes later, he got back in the car, pulling his blazer snug around his shoulders. Beneath the coat, the holstered .38 chafed against his left side.

Lindstrom gave him a quizzical look. "Do what you needed to?"

"I hope so." Dan blotted the sweat from his forehead with his chocolate-stained handkerchief and started the car.

As they drove south down the 101 and merged onto the

Santa Ana Freeway, Dan became acutely aware of Lindstrom's aloof presence in the confined space of the Taurus. To distract himself, he fiddled with the air conditioner, cranking it up because it seemed too warm and turning it down a few minutes later when it got too cold.

"You aren't married," Lindstrom said, as though remarking on the weather. It was a statement, not a question.

Dan drummed his ringless fingers on the steering wheel and gave a dry chuckle. "Brilliant deduction, Holmes." He cast a sidelong glance at her. "Neither are you."

"Mmm." She stared straight ahead. "Were you?"

Dan nosed the car over a lane. "You don't waste time with small talk, do you?"

She brushed off the sarcasm with a wave of her hand. "Fine. Never mind."

For a while, the only sound in the car was the breath of the A.C.

"Yes," he said at last.

Lindstrom cocked her head. "What?"

"The answer to your question. Can you find me that Thomas Guide on the floor there? It's under your seat."

She pulled the thick map book from underneath her feet, while he exited the 5 at Ditman Avenue. Pulling into the parking lot of a small Mexican grocery store along Olympic Boulevard, Dan took the guide from her and looked up the surrounding residential district.

Lindstrom eyed him as he squinted to read the street names. "You mind if I ask what happened?"

"Yes." He set the open book on the seat beside him and took the key from the ignition. "Come in with me. I need to get something."

"Can't I just wait here?"

"Sorry, ma'am. I have to keep you with me at all times."

She rolled her eyes. "Whatever. Just don't call me ma'am."

With Lindstrom in tow, Dan strode into the market and worked his way over to the canned meats aisle. There he grabbed four cans of tuna from the shelf.

"Don't tell me that's our dinner," Lindstrom muttered.

"No. Just keeping a promise." He indicated the grocery-laden shelves around them. "Need anything?"

"A new identity." She trudged toward the cash register at the front counter.

With the plastic shopping bag of canned tuna on the seat between them, they drove on into the surrounding neighborhood, Dan slowing the car at each intersection in order to read the street signs.

"I forget. Do we go right or left on Crescent?"

"For the two-hundred block? Right." Lindstrom rotated the map book 180 degrees and peered at it more closely. "No, left."

Dan turned onto a quiet street lined with brightly col-ored bungalow houses. Chain-link fences surrounded the rain-starved lawns, and wrought-iron bars bracketed most of the windows. The sun hung low and bloated in the west, and the orange hues and soot-black shadows it cast gave the impression that the entire area had been scorched by fire.

Scanning the street numbers, Dan parked the car across from a weather-faded house whose pink stucco resembled goose-pimpled skin. "Two forty-seven. This is it."

Lindstrom left her seat belt fastened as she leaned forward to look at the house through the driver's-side window. "What do you expect me to do here, anyway?"

"I don't know. We'll find out when you do it." He grabbed the bag of tuna and got out of the car. She scowled and punched the seat belt's release button.

Hangnails of peeling paint curled up at the edges of the front door to number 247. As they reached the front step, Dan dug out his Bureau badge and pushed the doorbell, watching for the moment when the home's occupant eclipsed the pinpoint of light in the peephole.

"Ms. Gannon? Special Agent Atwater of the FBI." He flipped open his ID and presented it to the peephole. "May we talk to you for a moment?"

A dead bolt and chain rattled, and the door jerked open about two inches. A gaunt woman with stringy black hair peered out at them across the bar of a security latch. "Do you have Laurie?"

"No, ma'am. But my associate, Ms. Lindstrom, and I have spoken with her. May we come in?"

"Yeah, right. Come back when you have her."

She moved to slam the door, but Dan stopped her with his voice. "Laurie's dead, Ms. Gannon. I'm sorry."

The woman leaned forward again. "Why should I believe you? For all I know, you're the bastards who took her."

Dan stepped aside. "Ms. Lindstrom, would you show her your credentials?"

Lindstrom studied both his expression and Gannon's, and bowed her head. Holding her eyelid open with one hand, she removed the contact from her right eye and, with the lens balanced on the tip of her index finger, looked up at Gannon with mismatched irises. "It's true."

Laurie's mother stared at Lindstrom's unblinking violet eye and trembled. "No…no, you're lying. You're *lying!* YOU'RE LYING!" She collapsed against the doorjamb and slid to the floor, shrieking.

Stranded on the doorstep, Dan stood in helpless awkwardness as Amelia Gannon wept. Even the slightest twitch of his neck or hands made him feel like a spear-carrier upstaging the tragic heroine, and he didn't know whether it was a greater sin to watch her anguish or to avert his gaze. Lindstrom evidently felt the same paralysis, for she was too self-conscious to replace the lens that sat on her fingertip.

"I'm sorry. We thought you should know." Dan wasn't sure that Gannon even heard him. "We can come back another time—"

"No! Wait." Still on her knees, she rubbed her eyes clear and pushed the door shut. Metal scraped against metal as she disengaged the security latch.

When the door swung open again, Gannon was gone. Dan entered the house in time to see her hurrying down a short hallway. "Give me a minute," she called out.

Lindstrom put her contact back in and stepped into the gloomy living room as Dan shut the front door. The orange light that slanted through the crack in the drawn drapes served only to accentuate the dinginess of the room's matted shag carpet and threadbare thrift-store furniture. A chaotic mosaic of cigarette butts littered the bottom of an ashtray on the scuffed coffee table, and the bottled air in the house tasted of nicotine. Lindstrom coughed, and Dan panted for breath in the carbon monoxide miasma.

The sound of running tap water shuddered through the home's old pipes for a few minutes before Amelia

Gannon reemerged, her face slack with shell shock, her hair pulled back in a haphazard ponytail. Her oversized lavender T-shirt accentuated the livid skinniness of her arms, and the hole in her right jeans leg resembled ragged flesh torn from the bony kneecap it exposed. "Can I get you something?" she asked, her voice toneless. She was clearly flying on autopilot. "I could make some coffee...."

"No, no, that's all right. May we?" Dan indicated the defeated-looking sofa.

"Oh...sure."

Dan and Lindstrom seated themselves on the couch, while Gannon perched on the edge of an adjacent easy chair and drew a fresh cigarette from a pack of generics on the coffee table. "Sorry about the way I treated you at the door. Since you're from the government, I thought you might be working for the Corps."

She lit up, exhaled smoke. "You said you spoke to Laurie. Was she...okay?"

Lindstrom cleared her throat. "She didn't suffer."

"She misses you a lot," Dan added before the Violet could elaborate.

"Yeah." Gannon took another drag, the worry lines at the corners of her mouth and along her brow growing deeper. "Could I talk to her?"

Lindstrom shifted uncomfortably. "I don't think that would be a good idea right now."

Gannon sniffed and nodded. "You're probably right. I just wanted...to tell her I'm sorry." She pressed a fist to her mouth, swallowing a sob. "If I hadn't had to work, I'd never have left her with that stupid sitter."

"Do you know who might have wanted to hurt your daughter?" Dan asked.

The tip of Gannon's cigarette flared orange as she inhaled more smoke. "Just those bastards at the N-double-A-C-C. They told me if I made one wrong move, Child Protective Services could take her from me."

"I see their tactics haven't changed," Lindstrom said, a cynical edge in her voice. "But the Corps would never kill her. She's too valuable to them."

"I thought I was doing the best thing for her," Gannon continued, as if to herself. "The fits she kept having—I couldn't handle it. They seemed so nice at the School...."

Dan sought to refocus her attention. "What about Laurie's father?"

"Jeff?" She scrunched her face in disbelief and let out a bitter chuckle. "Hasn't sent so much as a birthday card since she was born. Soon as he saw what she was, he was outta here."

She spat out another plume of smoke, and Lindstrom coughed again.

"I'm sorry. I'll put it out." Gannon stubbed out the half-burnt butt on the edge of the ashtray. "I quit when I got pregnant, y'know? Cold turkey. Six years, and I didn't even take a drag 'til yesterday. Doesn't really matter now, does it?" She contemplated her extinguished cigarette for a moment, then slid it back into her pack for later consumption.

Lindstrom cleared her throat again. "Laurie had trouble at the School...."

"She seemed to like it in the beginning," Gannon replied. "It was the first chance she had to make friends who were...like she was. Then, about a month ago, she got really scared of the place. Every time I talked to her on the phone—every time they *let* me talk to her—she begged to come home."

She ground her teeth. "*They* told me it was just a phase, that she'd settle down once she'd been there a full year. 'Screw that!' I said. 'Give me back my kid!' As it was, I had to schedule a month in advance just to spend a weekend with her."

Her face crumpled. "She'd only been home a few days."

"Did Laurie ever mention a man she was afraid of—a man without a face?" Dan asked quickly, before she could break into tears again.

"Yeah." Gannon bit her thumbnail, and Dan noticed that all her nails were ragged, their black polish flecked off in places. "I thought it was just one of those kid things, y'know? Like the bogeyman. If I'd known..."

"What about a man with curly blond hair and a bushy mustache?" Lindstrom said. "Someone she saw at the School. Did she ever talk about him?"

Gannon frowned and shook her head. "Do you think he's the one?"

"We don't have anything definite yet, but we're following every lead we've got. We'll let you know as soon as we find out anything." Dan glanced around the living room. "Um, Laurie said you have a cat?"

Gannon appeared perplexed. "Tigger? What about him?"

Dan lifted the shopping bag into his lap. "I don't quite know how to ask this but...do you have a can opener?"

When he explained what he wanted to do, Gannon smiled, her eyes misty, and carried the plastic bag into the kitchen. An electric can opener hummed. She returned with a small bowl of drained tuna and a sheet of newspaper and led Dan and Lindstrom down the narrow hallway to a small bedroom. "He's probably in here. He's used to sleeping with Laurie."

She flicked on the light switch, and the room glowed pink, the color of the pastel ponies on the wallpaper. A vacant Barbie Dream House languished atop the nightstand, and assorted stuffed animals huddled about the foot of the bed like faithful pets.

Curled up on top of the bed was a butterscotch cat. The animal lifted his head warily as Dan spread the newspaper on the floor and set the bowl of tuna on top of it. "Here you go, Tigger. With Laurie's regards."

The cat leapt off the bed and padded onto the paper. He picked at the tuna with mincing little bites while Dan stroked his velvety back.

"It's gone...."

Dan looked up at Gannon, who stared at the bed in puzzlement. "What?"

"Laurie's stuffed Tigger." She pointed. "I left it on her pillow for when—for when she came back."

Dan stood and surveyed the bed. The pillow was bare.

Reaching into his right jacket pocket, he pulled out a pair of surgical gloves. "When did you put it there?"

"Just last night."

Dan put on the gloves, the latex snapping as he tugged them tight, and he gingerly lifted one fold of the lace-fringed comforter to peer under the bed. "Could the cat have dragged it somewhere?"

"I guess so, but I haven't seen it."

He let the bedspread fall back into place. "Would you mind taking a look around for it?"

"Uh ... sure." She hurried out of the room.

Watching from outside the door, Lindstrom moved to take Gannon's place. "What is it?"

Dan motioned for her to stay back. With as few steps as possible, he made a wide circle around the end of the bed, hugging the wall until he came near the room's sole window. Bracing himself against the adjacent wall, he leaned in to examine the window sash. Shiny abrasions glinted on the sliding metal frame around the window's latch. A streak of black rubber marred the white paint along the sill.

"He must have wanted a trophy," Dan mused, pushing himself upright.

Gannon returned, her puzzlement turned to apprehension. "I don't see it anywhere."

"I don't think you will. Have you vacuumed this room today?"

"No."

"Good. Don't. We might be able to get some shoe impressions or fiber samples here. Did you let anyone else in the house after the police left yesterday?"

She shook her head emphatically.

"I see. Look, I'm going to have to call another evidence team in here." He took his cell phone from his belt and punched in Detective Garcia's number. "Would you like me to arrange for you to spend the night somewhere else?"

Gannon's mouth hung open. "I don't know." She covered her face with her hands.

Lindstrom put an arm around her shoulders and gently

steered her toward the master bedroom. "Why don't you lie down for a while? We can handle this."

Dan conferred with Garcia, and twenty minutes later a pair of LAPD patrol officers came to secure the crime scene until the evidence team could arrive. Gannon hid away in the master bedroom; at her request, Lindstrom brought her the lighter and cigarettes from the coffee table.

Lindstrom remained silent and pensive as Dan briefed the cops. "So you think he took the stuffed tiger as a souvenir?" she asked when they left the house and returned to his car.

"Looks that way."

"But why not take it the day of the crime? Or take some other toy? Why risk coming back?"

Dan glanced out the window at the sad façade of 247 Crescent Street. "It's hard to say. Sometimes a killer gets a sadistic thrill from revisiting the scene of his crime. Grabbing one of the victim's personal items would help him relive the murder."

"If you say so."

Smiling with strained gaiety, Dan started the car and drove off. "Well, Ms. Lindstrom, I think we've earned our dinner. Where do you want to eat? Remember, we're on the Bureau's tab, so money is no object."

"Surprise me."

"How does Italian sound?"

"Wonderful. Can we stop and get my stuff first?"

"You bet."

She studied him a moment, as though noticing a facial feature she'd missed before. "That was a very kind thing you did."

The compliment caught Dan off guard. "I beg your pardon?"

"With the cat. And before that, with the chocolate bar."

Dan shrugged. "I don't know. It doesn't really amount to much."

"More than you think. By the way, you can call me Natalie."

Sid Preston nudged aside the window's musty lace curtain to focus his Nikon on the Suit and the Redhead.

He zoomed in on the faces of the blue-blazered man and red-haired woman as they left the Gannon place and got in their white Ford Taurus. Click-*whirr,* click-*whirr,* click-*whirr* went the camera. Preston had already scribbled terse descriptions of the couple on the legal pad in his lap, and now, as they pulled away from the curb, he trained the Nikon's lens on the license plate number, which he added to his notes.

When the car had disappeared from view, Preston slouched back in his chair and doodled on the notepad, chewing his gum with the deliberation of a bull masticating its cud. The license number he'd written began with the letter E circumscribed by an octagon, and he sketched arrows pointing to the polygon and added the caption "govt." below it.

Well, well, well: His investment had finally paid off. True, the house he occupied would never make the cover of *Good Housekeeping*—the carpet reeked of dog farts from the renters' ancient cocker spaniel, and dead flies dotted the front windowsill. But the charming white-trash couple who lived there were more than happy to let him use the place during the day for a modest fifty-dollar-per-diem fee, no questions asked, and the house had a lovely view of Amelia Gannon's front door across the street.

Preston idly traced over key words on the notepad with his pen. The Suit was easy enough to peg—obviously a Fed of some sort. *But who's your pretty companion, Mr. G-man?* Perhaps his informants in the LAPD could run this plate number and tell him something about Ms. Gannon's guests.

Stretching the gum with his tongue, Preston blew a pink bubble until it popped.

6

A Night on
the Town

"HOW CAN YOU LIVE IN L.A. WITHOUT A CAR?" DAN marveled as they drove through the security gate of the Toluca Lake apartment complex.

"When they need me, they send someone to pick me up. Other than that, I don't go out much." Natalie pointed to a pair of lighted windows on the ground floor of one of the Lego-like modular buildings in the complex. "That's mine. You can park in the garage over here. I'll click you in."

Dan couldn't help but shade his eyes when they moved from the evening darkness outside to the glare of Natalie's living room: He counted at least eight glowing lamps and light fixtures in the small den.

She's afraid of the dark, he realized. Was it because it reminded her of that other darkness—the darkness that never ended?

"Now I know why we have a power crisis," he quipped to disguise his own discomfort at the thought.

"They're all fluorescents," Natalie shot back over her shoulder. "Besides, it cheers up the place." She snatched a couple of ragged paperbacks out of one of the shelving units that flanked the sofa. "This won't take long. I'm used to packing in a hurry."

She bustled on through the door to the bedroom and out of sight, leaving Dan to browse the contents of her bookshelves. A couple of volumes were now missing from a set of Jane Austen novels, which shared space with such classic romances as E. M. Forster's *A Room with a View* and Charlotte Brontë's *Jane Eyre*. Other shelves boasted an extensive DVD collection—mostly screwball comedies and MGM musicals of the thirties and forties. Framed posters from *Gigi* and *Singin' in the Rain* adorned the far wall, and a huge photo of Ginger Rogers and Fred Astaire in evening attire hung above the modest entertainment center opposite the couch.

If only the world were all champagne and romance, Dan mused sadly.

A vase of shriveling lilies sat on the coffee table in front of the sofa, and around it lay several large pastel drawings of the flowers, done in a style reminiscent of Georgia O'Keeffe. Dan cocked his head right and left to view each of the scattered pictures right side up until he saw the open sketchbook that rested against a rack of pastel chalks.

With a furtive glance at the bedroom door, he picked up the drawing tablet and flipped through its pages. In addition to other still lifes, he found a series of pastel, pencil, and charcoal sketches—character studies, mostly, some of famous people, others of strangers seen on the street. Although all the drawings looked good to Dan, at least half of them had been crossed out with angry black X's.

"I like your artwork," he called toward the bedroom. "You have a great eye."

"Oh." The pitch of her voice flattened with embarrassment. "Well, I can draw something besides ax murderers."

"Why don't they have you working with van Gogh or Rembrandt or somebody?"

"Because the Corps needs murders solved more than it needs Old Masters painted." A scorpion-sting of bitterness in her tone. "There're only a half-dozen positions in their Visual Arts division, and I didn't make the cut. After I graduated, they put me in Archaeology for a few months, then shunted me into the West Coast Crime section, and here I am."

"Sorry to hear that. You have a lot to offer." He turned back another leaf of the sketchbook, to one of the first drawings in it.

Evan Markham stared up at him from the page, eyes mournful, full lips in a poet's pout. Natalie must've drawn it from memory, and she evidently remembered Evan very well, for it was a perfect likeness.

What a waste, Dan thought, without analyzing whether he referred to her unused artistic ability or her unfortunate taste in men.

A shuffling sound from the open doorway startled him. He hastily returned the sketchbook to its original page and set it back on the coffee table, then ambled into the bedroom. "Need any help?"

"No. Almost done."

Natalie stood before a theatrical makeup table whose mirror was surrounded by glowing bare lightbulbs. Six identical mannequin heads sprouted from the tabletop, three on either side of the mirror. All but one were bald; as a wry joke, tattooed node points dotted their smooth white scalps, and violet irises had been painted into their blank eyes. Natalie plucked the blond wig off the last head and placed the hairpiece inside one of the six wig boxes that filled an open suitcase on the bed. Then she turned back toward the makeup table.

"Forget something?" Dan asked.

Her gaze fixed on a necklace hanging from one of the mirror's light sockets, and for a moment, the banked snow of her expression threatened to crumble into an avalanche. She lifted the chain to peer at the pendant that dangled from it. Its silver ring encircled a pair of snakes that twined to form a horizontal figure eight.

Dan had seen one just like it before, of course. Russell Travers had used it as the touchstone to summon Evan Markham.

Natalie's lips whitened, and she let the necklace swing like a slowing clock pendulum. "No. I've got everything."

She's a tough one, Dan thought, now ashamed of his snide reaction to her portrait of the dead man.

Natalie zipped up the bag containing her wigs and gave it to Dan, along with another suitcase and her overnight bag.

"Now," she said, "as I recall, you promised me dinner...."

Verdi's was packed that night, and they had to wait almost an hour before a hostess led them to a booth at the back of the restaurant. As they slid into their seats, Lindstrom dubiously surveyed the trompe l'oeil mural of a Venetian canal and the plastic grapes and fairy lights that dangled from a trellis on the ceiling above them.

"Nice place. Who does their decor, Disneyland?"

Dan started to remove his blazer, then remembered the holster under his arm. "Hey, lighten up. Most people love this stuff."

He nodded toward a large party in the center of the room. A group of waiters and waitresses in black vests and bow ties had gathered around the table to sing an operatic rendition of "Happy Anniversary" to a blushing, laughing older couple and their assembled children and grandchildren. The sight seemed to sadden Lindstrom—that is to say, *Natalie,* Dan corrected himself.

"Yeah. I see what you mean." She sighed and rubbed her face. "Don't mind me. I'm just tired and cranky."

She barely looked up at the waiter who came to their table—a struggling actor, Dan guessed by the guy's *GQ* handsomeness and perfectly moussed hair. Dan ordered Verdi's celebrated eggplant parmigiana and a half-carafe of cabernet sauvignon, while Natalie merely asked for pasta shells with marinara sauce and ice water to drink.

"Aren't you technically on duty?" she asked as the waiter brought his wine.

"Call it R and R." Dan poured himself a glass. "Want some? You look like you could use it."

"No, thanks. Every drink of alcohol kills brain cells, you know."

"I don't mind, as long as they're the *right* brain cells." She didn't even smile. "That's a joke, by the way."

"Is it?" Her artificially blue eyes bored into him.

Dan swirled the wine in his glass. "Boy, am I looking forward to *this* drink."

He downed the first gulp so fast that it barely registered

as a tingle on his tongue. What *was* it with her health and safety obsessions, anyway? The elevator, the car's air bags, the vegetarian diet…

Because she knows that endless darkness is waiting for her, a voice inside him replied. *It scares the hell out of her, and she's determined to delay the inevitable as long as humanly possible. And it's waiting for you, too, isn't it, Dan?*

Yes, it was, and if he knew it as intimately as she did, he'd probably cower under his bedcovers and never set foot outside his apartment. *She's a tough one, all right,* he thought as he guzzled the rest of his wine and poured himself another glass.

A burst of cheers and applause drew Natalie's attention back to the family at the anniversary table. "You have kids?"

"Nope. That was one mistake I didn't make." Dan was grateful for the conversation, no matter how unpleasant.

"Any other family?"

"You seem awfully interested in my personal history.…"

"Just trying to get up to par. I don't have a file on *you*."

Dan gave a tight-lipped smile. "All right. My parents are retired, live up in northern California near my brother's family. My niece turns six in October. I was hoping to be there for her birthday, but…" He shrugged and took another sip of wine.

"And your ex-wife?"

The waiter intervened. "Spinach salad with raspberry vinaigrette for the lady and Caesar for the gentleman." He set the plates on the table. "And here's some warm bread and olive oil. Anything else I can get you folks?"

Dan chuckled. "Saved by the appetizers! No, we're fine for now."

As the waiter hustled away, Dan tore off a hunk of bread and dipped it in the shallow bowl of olive oil, pretending that he'd forgotten Natalie's last question. "How about you? See your folks much?"

She picked at her salad with a fork. "I visit Mom every now and then, but…you know."

Dan paused in chewing his bread, realizing what a faux pas he'd made. He now remembered reading that Nora Lindstrom had spent the last twenty years in a private mental hospital in Ventura. "Yes…I'm sorry. It must be hard for you."

The sympathy washed off her like waves on a rock. "My dad and stepmom live in New Hampshire," she added in an offhand manner. "I go there for Christmas sometimes, but we haven't been close. Not since Dad sent me to the School."

Laughter erupted from the anniversary party. The family patriarch, a portly man with a bald crown and wire-rimmed glasses, had just unwrapped a pair of baggy boxer shorts printed with red hearts and cherubs. The grandkids whistled as he waved the shorts in front of him with a silly grin.

The noise seemed to heighten Natalie's anxiety. She fidgeted in her seat as if she'd left the oven on at home.

"Something wrong?" Dan inquired.

"There's a place I need to go tonight," she said. "Do you have anything to wear that doesn't scream 'Fed'?"

* * *

There were only 183 known Violets still alive in all of North America, but to look at the shops along Hollywood and Vine, you'd think that every one of them lived in L.A. Nearly anyone with enough money to buy a pair of purple contact lenses could set himself up as a professional speaker for the dead. The government attempted to crack down on the fraud by making it illegal for conduits to operate without being licensed by the NAACC, but thousands of self-proclaimed "spiritual intermediaries" still plied their trade among the grief-stricken and gullible across the country. Several of these charlatans had opened businesses among the tarot readers and tattoo parlors in West Hollywood, and it was to one such establishment that Natalie led Dan that night.

Hooking his thumbs in the pockets of the sweatshirt he now wore, Dan scanned the dark storefront and wondered if the proprietor was even there. He'd wanted to call ahead, but Natalie informed him that her eccentric friend didn't own a phone.

Unlike its neon-glaring neighbors, the shop's front window bore only the words *Spiritual Counseling* and a painted pair of purple eyes. Those eyes were as blatant an advertisement as the triad of golden balls above a pawnshop. Sheets of aluminum foil masked the interior of the glass, making the window a cloudy mirror of the street.

"Charming place," Dan remarked. "Are you a customer or an employee?"

Natalie silenced him with a reproving look. They opened the foil-lined front door and stepped into a small entryway illuminated by two hissing Coleman lanterns hanging from hooks on the walls. Sheets of aluminum covered every square inch of the ceiling and walls, down to the rubber mats that blanketed the floor. *Must play hell with the guy's TV reception*, Dan thought.

Approaching a door on their left, he and Natalie peered through a rectangular window crisscrossed with a mesh of chicken wire. In the room beyond, two people sat at a round table. Candelabra stood in each corner of the chamber, illuminating the occupants with the wavering flames of white tapers. Although Dan could see only the back of the first figure, he judged her to be a woman from her slight build and collar-length curled hair.

Her attention was focused on the man seated across from her, who looked to be in his early sixties, with wavy silver hair and jowly cheeks. He wore a white oxford shirt, unbuttoned at the collar, that highlighted the mottled redness of his skin. His facial fat rippled as he overplayed the agonies of a Violet's inhabitation, emoting like an actor in a silent movie. An oil lamp on the table heightened the dramatic effect by casting portentous shadows on his face.

"Your friend's quite the performer," Dan said. "Does he do bar mitzvahs?"

Natalie scowled and held an index finger to her lips.

In the adjoining room, the man moaned one final, unheard pronouncement, then slumped sideways in his chair, panting with exertion. The woman leapt from her seat and crouched before him, clasping one of his limp hands in hers. He gave her an exhausted smile and patted her head paternally.

Dan and Natalie drew back from the window as the "spiritual counselor" and his client moved to leave the room. A bell jingled as the door swung inward, and the counselor's words became audible.

"...at least you know he's happy now." With his arm around her shoulders, he steered his client through the entryway toward the shop's exit. His beatific smile flattened a bit when he saw Dan.

The woman appeared to be in her mid-forties, with a pointy nose and a mouth shriveled from worry. She pushed her rimless, round glasses up to her forehead and dabbed at her eyes with a wadded tissue. "Thank you so much, Yuri." She took a sealed business envelope from the pocketbook in her hands and passed it to the man. "I just wish I could get Harold to come here. He hasn't been the same... since it happened."

"Yuri" nodded. "Some people aren't prepared to encounter the Other Side. Give him time—I'm sure he'll come around." He folded the envelope in half and slid it into his shirt pocket. "Now, don't hesitate to come back if you need me."

She sniffed and returned his smile. Squeezing his hand once more, she left the shop.

"Yuri" turned to Natalie. "Boo! It's good to see you."

"Arthur." Her voice exuded more warmth than Dan had heard before, and she wrapped her arms around the man's beefy frame.

So it's "Arthur" now, is it? Dan examined the counselor's face more closely. The eyes were a shade of purple a bit too dark—more blue-violet than violet—indicating the presence of contact lenses, just as Dan would have expected. But there was something naggingly familiar about the tiny pockmarks that dotted the man's cheeks, scars left by some horrendous case of acne.

The charlatan reflected Dan's suspicion. "Who's your friend?" he asked Natalie.

She pulled away from him. "My *acquaintance* is Dan Atwater, FBI agent."

Uncertainty flashed across their host's face. "What's going on, Boo?"

"Not what you think. May we come in?"

Arthur, a.k.a. "Yuri," considered the two of them a moment, then opened the door to his consultation room. A small brass bell above the door jingled on the end of a coiled spring to herald their entrance into the inner chamber.

Here, tie-dyed cloth banners bearing signs of the zodiac draped the walls. Dan noted, however, that aluminum foil glinted along the room's baseboards, where the hems of the banners failed to reach the rubber matting of the floor. The place smelled of incense and aftershave—both cheap.

Four chairs were arranged around the circular table, but their host did not offer them a seat. Instead, he proceeded to one of the candelabra and began to extinguish its flames. "I was just about to close." He blew out the first candle. "What can I do for you, Boo?"

"Jem's dead."

The man paused, hunched over the candleholder. "He was ready." He snuffed out another taper.

"Gig, Sylvia, and Russell, too. Even Sondra and Evan, I'm told."

The man looked at her.

"They were killed. Murdered."

He turned to Dan, as though demanding an explanation.

"I'm afraid so, sir." Again, Dan tried to match the older man's features with a face in his mental file of mug shots. *Arthur…Arthur…Arthur…*

Shaken, the old charlatan lowered himself onto the nearest chair and let his head droop. "I can't help you."

"We're here to warn you." Natalie knelt beside him and touched his hand. "The killer's in L.A. He took another Violet—a little girl—yesterday. One of us may be next. I figured the others wouldn't be able to tell you, so that's why I came."

Dan peered more closely at the man's brow and saw a bluish tattooed point lurking amidst the silver roots of his hairline. The clues clicked into place like the wheels of a slot machine.

"The contacts are a nice touch," Dan blurted. "They add an authentic phoniness to your whole fake-psychic shtick."

The man glared up at him with his too-purple eyes. "It's called hiding in plain sight, Agent Atwater. You might say it's my way of ensuring my retirement."

"You'll have to excuse Dan," Natalie interposed. "Like most Feds, he was born tactless."

Dan tried to placate the former conduit. "I'm a great admirer of yours, Mr. McCord. Your work on the Bundy and Hillside Strangler cases—you saved a lot of lives."

"And taught the best Violets of the past thirty years." The proud way Natalie lifted her chin told Dan that she was one of McCord's alumni.

"That's right! You taught at the School, didn't you? Before your disappearance.…"

"My *retirement*. The only way a Violet *can* retire and retain a shred of health or sanity. And I'd like to keep it that way."

"It's a free country. No one can force you to do anything you don't want to do."

McCord laughed bitterly. "Obviously, you've never been considered a scarce resource, Mr. Atwater. As we say in the business, 'Necessity is the mother of oppression.' Society needs our services, and there are only a handful of us born in each generation. That gives our benevolent government quite a motive for ensuring our continued employment, wouldn't you say?"

"Maybe so. But you left the Corps for *this*?" Dan swept his hand around the room, with its guttering candles and Gypsy decor.

Natalie moved between them. "Dan, that's enough."

"No, Boo." McCord nudged her aside. "Want to know why I really left the Corps?" There was an almost manic gleam in his eyes. "Because I'm *sick* of listening to the dead. I don't want to hear them again until I'm one of them."

He rose from his chair and walked over to the nearest wall. "Do you know what a Faraday cage is, Mr. Atwater?"

Dan vaguely remembered the term from his high school physics class. "Something to do with electricity, right?" He pointed to the wall. "The foil...?"

McCord nodded and pulled aside a fold of the banner beside him, revealing the aluminum sheet beneath. "These rooms are entirely encased in several layers of metal and insulation—even the floors. The metal conducts any incoming electromagnetic energy around the outside of the shop before it has a chance to get in. I tell my clients that it keeps radio waves from disturbing the spirits." He chuckled. "It actually keeps the spirits from disturbing *me*."

"You mean souls can't get in here? Is that why you don't believe in electric lights?"

"Or telephones, or refrigerators, or TVs." He let the banner fall back into place. "Anything that might conduct the souls' energy into my home." He indicated a doorway in the back corner of the room that was covered by a beaded curtain. "At last, I don't have to feel them pounding on the gates of my head day and night, like a horde of attacking Huns. Otherwise, I'd have ended up like poor Nora."

"You don't need to bring her into this," Natalie said softly.

McCord bowed his head. "Sorry, Boo. Your mother deserves better."

"Then all that was...?" Dan jerked a thumb in the direction McCord's client had gone.

"Humbug. Yes."

"Doesn't that bother you?"

"Not really." He pointed to where the weeping woman once sat. "You think Barbara there really wants to hear that her son got high and crashed his motorcycle because she's an overprotective harpy and her husband's a domineering tyrant? I doubt it."

"You know that for a fact?"

"I can guess it from what she's told me. You get good at that sort of thing in the fortune-teller's game. I tell them what they want to hear; they like it better than the truth anyway."

"So you've had no contact with the dead in...how long?"

"Oh, must be six years, at least."

"And you had no idea that Jeremy Whitman and the others had been murdered?"

McCord shook his head.

Natalie moved closer to him. "Arthur, can you think of anyone who'd want to kill us?"

He snorted. "Too many. Most of them ought to be behind bars, though. You check recent paroles and escapes?" he asked Dan.

"One of our first thoughts, too. We haven't turned up anything yet, but we're still looking."

"Maybe it isn't someone we caught," Natalie suggested. "Maybe it's someone who doesn't *want* to be caught. All of the Violets killed so far went to the School. Maybe we know something the killer doesn't want us to tell."

"Well, that place has done its share of dirty tricks, God knows," McCord muttered. "Conning and cajoling people into selling their kids into slavery....I'm surprised the parents haven't torn it apart, brick by brick. What does your suspect look like?"

"No one can tell us," Dan admitted. "Whenever he kills, he wears a mask and says nothing."

"Although he may have wavy blond hair and a bushy mustache," Natalie added. "And blue eyes. The last victim saw him at the School. Somewhere around six feet, a hundred eighty pounds. Late twenties, early thirties."

"Sound like anyone you know?"

Again, McCord shook his head. "No. But then, I haven't been near the School in seven years, and haven't worked a case in almost ten. This guy may not even know I exist."

"If he's obsessed with Violets, he'll know about you."
Natalie touched his forearm. "Watch your back, Arthur."

He smiled and enfolded her in a bear hug. "You, too, little Boo-berry." He looked at Dan. "Guard her well. She's my
star pupil."

"I'll do that, sir. But I can't leave you alone like this. I'll
arrange for some police protection."

Gently breaking his embrace with Natalie, McCord
gave a sardonic chuckle. "Mr. Atwater, if there's anything I
fear more than death, it's police 'protection.' "

Dan shrugged. "If that's the way you want it—"

"Yes. It is."

Dan inhaled sharply and nodded. "All right."

"Thank you." McCord held out his hand.

Dan gawked at the plump fingers as though they were
covered with smallpox. The longer he hesitated, the more
Natalie's stare seared his face with shame.

Hope that Faraday cage really works, he thought, and
gave McCord's hand a soft-gripped shake. His arm flinched,
as if a stove burner he'd touched turned out to be cold instead of hot.

Nothing happened.

"It was an honor to meet you." He hid his relief as Mc-
Cord nodded and let go of him.

Natalie embraced her old teacher once more, and her
gaze lingered on him as she and Dan headed for the door.

McCord smiled and waved good-bye. "Don't be a
stranger, Boo."

Dan studied Natalie's expression out of the corner of
his eye as they passed through the metal-lined entryway

and out onto Vine Street. He jerked his head toward the shop they'd just left. "So, is that how it is for you?"

She paused beside him. "How what is?"

"You know—about the souls." Dan hunched his shoulders inside his sweatshirt, which now felt too thin to turn the cool evening breeze. "About them talking to you all the time."

"Yeah. Pretty much." She didn't even blink at the question.

"What do they want?"

She regarded him with mild surprise. "They want back in, of course. Wouldn't you?"

The muscles in his gut tightened like a drumhead. "*Which* ones want back in?"

"All of them." Natalie waved her hand through the viscous night air, which suddenly seemed laden with phantoms. She proceeded up the street toward their car, glancing back when he fell behind. "You coming?"

Dan drew a deep breath and jogged to catch up with her.

7

The Happy Couple

DAN DROVE THEM TO THE EMBASSY SUITES NEAR LAX, where he'd phoned in a reservation for "Kent and Josie Mitchell."

Natalie rolled her eyes when he told her about their cover story in the hotel carport. "Perfect. You sure you got us separate beds, *darling*?"

"Of course, *dear*. I know how you hate it when I hog the covers. Here." Dan took a small, velvet-covered box from his duffel bag. "Put these on."

She opened the box and pretended to admire the engagement ring and wedding band inside. "Oh, Kent! How romantic. I don't know what to say—it's all so sudden."

"Enough! This is for *your* benefit, remember." He slid a matching gold band on his own finger. The familiar constriction around his knuckle made him wince; he hadn't felt it for more than a year. "Let's go register."

"I'll wait here." She put on the rings and modeled them for herself with feigned insouciance. Dan just watched her until she met his gaze. "I *will*," she assured him.

Now he rolled his eyes. "Come on, Natalie. It won't be as painful as you think."

"Says you." She unfastened her seat belt. "And the name's Josie."

Dan chuckled, shaking his head, and followed her into the hotel lobby. They approached the front desk, and he was about to ask the clerk for their room key when she touched him.

Not merely a brief brush of the elbow, either. She slung her arm around his shoulders and snuggled up to him, nuzzling his cheek.

He staggered back a step, hands flailing to keep her away. *"Don't!"*

"Relax, *honey*." She grabbed him around the waist and pulled herself close, crinkling her nose with cheerleader perkiness. "We're on vacation, after all."

His heart stuttering, Dan watched her face for signs of inhabitation. There were none. She was simply playing "Josie" to tweak him. But how long would it be before the man he'd shot that night in the alley started "knocking"?

The front desk clerk witnessed their domestic squabble with an expression of polite blandness. If the hotelier thought the exchange odd, he didn't let it show.

Dan steadied himself, and tried to ignore Natalie as she ruffled his hair. "Reservation for Mitchell."

"Certainly, sir." The clerk tapped a few keys on his computer terminal, then handed Dan a card key and a printed Visa slip for him to sign. "Here you go, Mr. Mitchell."

"That's *Dr.* Mitchell," Natalie told the clerk in a sunny voice, rubbing Dan's left biceps. "My Kenny's the keynote speaker at the gynecologists' convention. We met at his office, believe it or not. But that's probably more than you wanted to know." She put her fingers to her lips and giggled, leaning heavily on Dan. "God, I am *so* drunk!"

The clerk failed to suppress a grin. "Room eight-oh-five. Elevators are to your right."

Dan felt his face flush as he signed the receipt and gave it back. "Can we get a wake-up call for five A.M.?"

"You got it."

"Thanks. Come on, *honey*." He swiveled Natalie toward the lobby entrance.

"You folks have a good night, now!" the clerk called to them as they lurched away, arms around one another.

Natalie waved back at him. "Bye!"

As soon as they were out in the carport, she let go of Dan, and her face returned to its usual solemnity. "You're right. That wasn't nearly as painful as I thought."

Dan slammed the car door when she tried to open it. "Spare me the attitude! Your life is in danger, and I'm trying to protect it. For someone who's so afraid of dying, you oughtta appreciate that."

Natalie's eyes widened, and she shook with dumb-founded fury. For a moment, he thought she might stalk off into the night without him.

Uh-oh, Atwater. Now you've done it. Not for the first time, he wished his mouth had an Erase button.

Then her head drooped. "I know."

He lowered his voice. "What you did in there could've blown our cover. Don't let it happen again."

She nodded without looking at him. He suddenly missed "Josie."

"Hey, it's all right." He grinned. "I always wanted to be a gynecologist."

The corners of her lips twitched upward, and she let out a small snicker.

After parking the car, Dan unloaded Natalie's cases as well as his own bags and lugged them inside like an overworked bellboy. He paused by the elevator and gave Natalie a pleading look.

"Eight floors up. Could we...?"

She considered the metal doors. Her mouth crinkled.

"I'd rather not," she said diffidently.

The frozen mask of her face betrayed her fear by its very blankness. She was scared out of her wits by the thought of stepping into that steel box, but too proud to show it. Had she summoned the victim of an elevator crash before? Dan wondered. Did she hear the whip-crack of the snapping cable, feel the instant of sickening weightlessness as the carriage plunged, the spaghetti spatter of pulverized flesh as it hit bottom? Is that what she imagined every time she stepped up to a pair of sliding safety doors? If so, who could blame her for wanting to take the stairs?

"On second thought, forget it." Dan hitched the straps of the suitcases higher up on his shoulders and gave her a cheery smile. "As you said, it's good exercise."

Natalie looked surprised and even a little embarrassed.

"Look...I can take these." She unburdened him of her luggage, and together they set off in search of the emergency stairs.

When they finally reached their room, Dan doublelocked the door and dropped his bags on the nearest bed. "Not much chance of anyone coming through the window at this height," he said, still trying to catch his breath. "I'll sleep here to guard the entrance."

"Whatever. Dibs on the bathroom." She headed there with her overnight bag in hand.

"Wait." He checked the bathroom to make sure it was empty. "Sorry. Standard procedure."

She pushed past him, shaking her head, and shut the door.

Dan took off his sweatshirt and pulled the .38 from under the waistband of his pants, where the butt of the gun had been grating against his navel. He shoved the revolver under his pillow, then stripped off his remaining clothes and changed into a white T-shirt and a pair of gray flannel boxer shorts.

The bathroom door opened a crack, and Natalie called to him through the gap. "Are you decent?"

"I'm better than decent, I'm fantastic!" He chuckled at her groan of disgust. "Relax. I've clothed my manhood."

When she emerged, Dan realized how accustomed he'd become to her red hair and blue eyes. She now looked like an invading alien. The tattooed spots seemed to perforate her shaved scalp like microphone jacks, and the event horizons of her purple irises swallowed the light that entered them. She had changed into an oversized T-shirt and loose-fitting gym shorts, and Dan caught himself peeking at the sleek shapeliness of her bare calves and lower thighs, their skin smooth and cream-pale.

"Can I *help* you?" She set her overnight case at the foot of her bed and regarded him with suspicion. She'd obviously seen him staring.

Dan blinked and cleared his throat. "Umm…you're done with the bathroom? I'll just be a minute." He grabbed his duffel bag and hastened through the door.

By the time he'd brushed his teeth, Natalie had already crawled under the covers of her bed. She lay board-stiff on the mattress with the sheet pulled up to her chest and her bare arms stretched out at her sides, like a cadaver awaiting a morgue attendant. Only the restless motion of one nervous foot caused her blanket to flutter.

Dan clambered into his own bed and reached over to turn off the lamp between them. Her voice stopped him.

"Don't."

He looked over at her, his fingers still on the switch. "What is it?"

Her face tightened. "Please. Leave it on."

Dan thought of the desperate banishment of darkness in her apartment.

"Whatever you say." He let go of the lamp and lay back on his pillow.

"Sleep is a very... *vulnerable* time for me," Natalie said, as though he'd demanded an explanation. "If I have to wake myself up in the middle of the night, I like to see my surroundings. It helps me ground myself again. Is that okay?"

"Sure, sure—no problem." He settled down under his sheets, shut his eyes, and tried to ignore the orangey glare that filtered through his eyelids.

"Thanks, Dan," she said before he dozed off.

He'd been asleep for some time—precisely how long he couldn't say—when his animal senses jarred him awake. Opening his eyes, he lay still and waited for his conscious mind to understand what his instinct told him.

Someone in the room was whispering. The half-formed words rose and receded in his ears like autumn wind.

Dan took hold of the .38 under his pillow. He made his best guess at where the sound was coming from and sprang forward in bed, aiming the gun in that direction.

There was no stranger in the room. Instead, the hiss of shaped air issued from Natalie's moving lips. She tossed from side to side, her eyelids straining to open, her hands gripping the sheets as if to keep her body from floating away.

Dan lowered the gun.

Natalie's breath caught in her throat, and she gagged. Then a strange calm stamped itself on her face, and she spoke aloud.

"There's a long list of lambs, child. You better watch for the wolf wearing the wool coat." The voice was Natalie's, but pitched much lower—a raspy growl from deep within her chest. "He knows us, child. He *knows* us."

Her back arched, and she resumed her manic, inarticulate whispering.

The gun in his hand forgotten, Dan watched her toss to and fro and debated whether to wake her. Would she still be Natalie if he did?

At length, he decided that whatever was happening to her was something only she could handle. Stashing the .38 back under his pillow, he scrunched under the blankets and pulled the sheets over his head.

It took him a long time to get back to sleep.

8

An Elevator
without Cables

DAN DRIFTED BACK INTO CONSCIOUSNESS EVEN
before the morning wake-up call, roused by a rhythmic
gasping on the other side of the room. Wondering if
Natalie was still in the grip of her ghosts, he glanced over at
the bed next to his, but it was empty.

He shoved aside the covers and sat up. Natalie was sitting on the floor between the foot of her bed and the
dresser. She had stretched her legs out until they were
nearly doing the splits, and, with her hands locked behind
her head, she swiveled her torso left and right, leaning forward each time as if to touch her toes with her elbows. Instead of her baggy T-shirt and shorts, she wore a skintight
two-piece workout outfit, and he could see the sweat that
glistened on the bare skin at the small of her back.

Dan, who hadn't even dated since Susan left him,
watched the movement of the muscles in Natalie's hips
and back and felt himself getting an unwelcome erection.

Great, he thought wryly. *If we ever have sex, all our dead
relatives can join us in bed.*

Natalie must have seen that he was awake, for she

folded her legs and turned toward him. Dan yanked the blanket back over his bulging boxers.

"Sorry. Hope I didn't wake you." She panted between words.

"No. No problem—I've been wishing I could get to a gym myself." He noted the dark puffiness beneath her eyes. "Did you…sleep well?"

"Yeah…sure." If she reacted to the question, she didn't show it. "Okay if I hit the shower?"

"Be my guest."

Dan reclined in bed and tried not to stare at her lithe body as she snatched some clothes from her suitcase and went into the bathroom. When she'd shut the door, he lifted the blanket on his lap and peered beneath it. "You can relax," he told his penis. "She's gone now."

While waiting for his turn to shower, Dan did a few sets of push-ups and selected a suit to wear for the trip to New Hampshire. He bathed, shaved, and dressed in the bathroom, and when he returned, Natalie was standing in front of the dresser mirror, buzzing the stubble off her bare scalp with a Lady Remington.

"We're going to the School." She flicked off the razor and ran a hand over the crown of her head.

"Yep."

"And we're going to fly."

"Yeah." Dan put on the shoulder holster and nestled the .38 back inside it. "Is that a problem?"

"A plane is just an elevator without cables." After sticking double-sided tape to her cranium, she opened one of the boxes in her second suitcase, took out her blond wig, and pressed it into place on her head. Its wheat-colored locks were shorter and wavier than the red wig's, making her face appear broader than before, and the hair was parted on the right rather than in the middle, allowing a lazy wisp to fall across her brow. She put in her blue contacts and applied a pink metallic lipstick. "All right. Let's get it over with."

"Let's." Dan zipped up his duffel bag and cast a sidelong glance at her. "By the way…anyone ever tell you you look good as a blonde?"

A hotel shuttle dropped them off at LAX about twenty minutes later. As usual, checking in and getting through airport security became even more of a hassle than usual because of the paperwork Dan had to fill out to take his .38 on the plane. He'd been tempted to leave the damned gun in the trunk of his car, but if Clark ever found out…

Natalie grew more sullen and silent as they made their way toward the gate, her eyes hidden behind a pair of sunglasses with tortoiseshell frames. Dan bought them both some breakfast—a cheese Danish and coffee for him, a plain bagel and orange juice for her—and he picked up an abandoned *Wall Street Journal* from the seat next to him and scanned the headlines while they waited for their flight to board.

When he set aside the paper, he saw that Natalie still stared at the bagel and cup of juice she held as if they were a pair of dead fish.

"You okay?"

She didn't seem to hear him. Concerned, he stretched his hand toward her, but shied back.

For Christ's sake, get over it! he thought, and forced himself to touch her bare forearm. "Natalie?"

Her skin quivered with suppressed tension, and she started so violently that her juice sloshed on both of them.

"Jeez! Sorry." He took a napkin and blotted the damp spots on their clothing. "My God, you're shaking like a leaf."

She retained her stony expression. "I told you—I don't like to fly."

"Why not? I thought flying was the safest way to travel."

Movement flickered behind the black lenses of her sunglasses. "Maybe so. But I've worked with the FAA on a couple of crash investigations. They summon the pilots, you know, to find out what happened—"

"Whoa! Don't even go there. I get the picture."

"You asked." She offered him the juice and bagel. "Want these?"

"No, thanks." His remaining appetite had vanished.

Natalie stalked over to a nearby trashcan and threw away her breakfast. "You sure you're up to this?" Dan asked as she sat down again.

She shrugged. "Flying's the fastest way to get there and back. And the longer it takes us, the greater the chance that more of my friends will die."

Dan pursed his lips and nodded.

Their flight boarded about ten minutes later. As they joined the queue of passengers entering the gangway, a man in a dark windbreaker and a New York Yankees baseball cap trained the telephoto lens of his Nikon upon them.

As the couple came into focus, Sid Preston saw the

blonde lean over to whisper something in Atwater's ear. The G-man looked anxious for a moment. Then, with a shaky smile, he offered her his hand, which she clutched tightly as they entered the plane.

Click-*whirr*, click-*whirr*, click.

Preston lowered his camera and grinned. It appeared that Agent Atwater was quite the ladies' man.

His sources at the LAPD had managed to get him Atwater's flight information, but the ticket reservations were under cover names—they couldn't tell him who the agent's lovely traveling companion was. Sid would have to find that out for himself.

When the couple disappeared from view, he dug a piece of Bazooka bubble gum out of his pants pocket and unwrapped it. He put the pink block of gum in his mouth and jawed it into a sticky wad as he read the comic strip in the wrapper. He chuckled at his good fortune; it was one he didn't have yet.

Taking out his billfold, Preston tucked the little slip of waxed paper in among the other Bazooka Joe strips that cluttered the wallet, along with assorted business cards and fast-food coupons. Then he grabbed his backpack from the seat beside him, pulled his boarding pass from his back pocket, and ambled over to follow the other passengers onto Atwater's plane.

9

The Alumna Returns

THE WALLS OF GRAY GRANITE BRICK AND GATES OF twisted wrought iron had not changed since Natalie had last seen them seven years ago. They hadn't changed in the hundred years before that, either. Dirty and dull with age, the gilded letters that arced over the main entrance read IRIS SEMPLE CONDUIT ACADEMY. To the students sentenced to spend their childhood there, however, it was simply known as "the School."

Natalie had pictured these gates in her mind so many times that seeing them come into view of the rental car's windshield felt like déjà vu. She kept staring at the School's name as Dan parked the car in the gravel driveway and switched off the engine.

"You ready for this?" he asked.

She glanced at him, grateful for the distraction. "Can't be any worse than the plane ride."

He gave her a weary smile, and they got out of the car. The School's long shadow touched Natalie with a cavern's chill.

Dan removed the padlock and chain on the twin gates and punched a code into an alphanumeric keypad mounted on a post to the left. For the dozenth time since leaving the airport in Manchester, Natalie surreptitiously studied his face. Although she'd taken him for just another government drone at first, she had to admit that she now appreciated Agent Atwater and his little acts of kindness. When they hit a patch of turbulence over the Midwest, he let her hold his hand for nearly an hour as every buck and dip of the 737 sent spasms of terror through her.

She also suspected that, despite his desperate cheerfulness, Dan knew as much about living with the dead as she did. It was written there in the premature lines etched on his boyish face and the scattered strands of gray that highlighted his wavy brown hair. She felt it in his touch as well: Someone knocked every time he made contact with her skin. A dead relative, perhaps? It didn't matter. Natalie brushed the soul away with her protective mantra, and took comfort from the warm pressure of Dan's hand.

The twin gates yawned open with an electric hum. Beyond stood the imposing Victorian facade of the School itself, its entrance flanked by Ionic columns of chiseled granite.

A paved path led them across a well-groomed lawn to the semicircular steps of the front entrance. Ascending the steps, Natalie felt like she was five years old again, the age she'd been when she first came to the School. The feeling gave her the jarring impression that everything was too small, from the columns to the doors to the cathedral windows along the ground floor, as though she'd swallowed too much of Alice's "Eat Me" cake.

Dan selected another labeled key on his key ring and unlocked the heavy oaken double doors. "Just how big is this place?"

"Not that big. There were never more than twenty of us here at any given time." Natalie shivered in her pullover sweater; after the oppressive heat of L.A., she wasn't prepared for the nip of New Hampshire autumn.

She entered the vacant Common Room, the soles of her Doc Martens squeaking on the lacquered hardwood floor. Ordinarily, the students would come here in their free time, the younger ones to play on the floor with their toys, the older ones to read or study. "So where did they take the kids?"

"No idea. The N-double-A-C-C's only telling people on a need-to-know basis."

"Mmm. Naturally."

With the sun already low in the sky, scant light came through the windows that faced the courtyard. A blue gloom shrouded everything—the massive Persian rug, the crushed-velvet easy chairs, the wooden mantelpiece with its scuffed scrollwork—making the room seem faded and worn and grimy compared to Natalie's memory of the place. The thought made her sad...the sort of pity a child might feel for a strict, even cruel, parent who now wasted away in a cancer ward.

"Could I wander around for a while?" she said in a distant voice. "Alone?"

Dan assessed her with a look. "All right. I'll only be a few steps behind you. If you find anything, call me."

"Yeah."

She drifted away down the hallway to her right, toward the classrooms where she first learned what she was. They must've shut off the heating system when they closed the School, for the air was even colder in here than outside.

With the strange, disembodied sensation of being the third-person observer in a dream, she entered the first of the empty rooms and imagined that she could see a five-year-old Natalie, her arms wrapped around her folded legs and her chin propped on her knees, cowering among her five violet-eyed classmates. They all sat on the floor on foam-rubber mats and looked at Arthur McCord, who presided over them, Buddha-like, with his legs in a lotus position. In her memory, Arthur was younger and thinner, his shaved scalp waxy under the classroom's fluorescent lights.

"Death is like a big black room," he told the children in front of him, the oldest of whom was nine. "You're feeling your way around in the dark, and you're not sure where to go. The things you touched while you were alive, the places you went, the people you knew—all of these are like closed doors leading out of that room. When a Violet touches one of these things, she throws open one of those doors, and your soul runs toward the light...."

Natalie felt her scalp prickle the way it did that day. She still had hair then—long, straight sandy-blond locks held back at the temples with pale blue barrettes. Years later, she learned the scientific explanations for everything Arthur said that first day at the School: about the quantum composition of the soul and about Bell's theorem, and how subatomic particles that come into contact with a soul's energy retain a connection to that soul after it leaves its body. But even today, whenever Natalie thought about death, she pictured that big black room filled with blind souls groping for an exit.

Arthur took a lace-bordered handkerchief from his shirt pocket and fluttered it in front of his pupils, as if he were about to perform a magic trick. The corner of the cloth was embroidered with the initials RM.

"This was my mother's," he said, "and right now, I can feel her pushing at my mind, trying to get out of that black room. In my head, I see flashes of her memories, I think little pieces of the thoughts she's thinking. But I use my own thoughts to keep her out of my head."

He asked Kevin, the nine-year-old, to come sit beside him. A shy black boy with a slight overbite, Kevin crept forward and resettled himself next to Arthur.

"Hold out your hands."

The boy's purple eyes shone with suspicion, but he did as he was told.

"Close your eyes."

Again, Kevin obeyed, his mouth shrinking with anxiety.

Arthur dangled the handkerchief over the boy's upturned palms. "Now, Kevin, I want you to say your ABC's. Keep saying them over and over again, no matter what happens. Don't think about anything else, and don't stop until I tell you to."

Kevin's eyelids quivered with concentration, or maybe fear. "A-B-C-D-E-F-G-H-I-J-K-L-M-N-O-P…"

Arthur waited for him to hurry through several breathless repetitions of the alphabet. Then he lowered the handkerchief into the boy's hands.

The letter K caught in Kevin's throat. His fingers clamped onto the handkerchief, and his head jerked upright.

"Come on, Kevin, where's that alphabet?" Arthur urged. "What comes after K?"

The boy's jaw strained against the paralysis of his lips. "Mmm…mmm…"

"Yes! That's it! Say it, Kevin!"

"Mmm…mmm…EMMM!"

"Yes! And what's after that?"

"Nnn…nnn…ENNN!"

"Good! Keep going."

"…O…puh-PEEEE! K-k-KYEW!"

With each letter, his stammer subsided, and soon he was chiming out the alphabet as rapidly as he had before. A big grin spread across his face.

Arthur retrieved the handkerchief from Kevin's hands. "And that, class, is how you can keep dead people from running your life."

Natalie and the other children looked at each other with awe and excitement. All of them had lost minutes, hours, even days, of their young lives to the souls that invaded them. Now, this teacher promised them salvation, a way to reclaim their own consciousness.…

But Arthur lied, Natalie thought as she surveyed the barren floor and the dusty rubber mats stacked in the far corner of the room. Not every soul could be turned away as easily as that of Arthur's mother. And, in one way or another, a Violet's life would always be ruled by the dead.

She left the room and continued on down the hall, glancing through the window of each door she passed. The building was essentially a large square, with this side devoted to the younger students, and every classroom resurrected another memory: intense training sessions in the morning, followed by lessons in math, reading, science, and history in the afternoon. Within the first two years, she progressed beyond the alphabet mantra to more sophisticated mental disciplines that allowed her to remain a conscious observer as she shared her body with another soul.

The techniques were ancient, passed down from Violet to Violet through the ages.

At the far corner of the building where the corridor turned to the left, Natalie came to the infirmary. She pushed open one of the swinging double doors, but didn't go inside. From where she stood, she could see the examining table surrounded by shelves stocked with first-aid supplies. Here, the School's doctor and nurses bandaged scraped knees, gave vaccine shots, and even set the occasional broken limb.

As Natalie leaned through the doorway, the twin barber's chairs on the opposite side of the room came into view. A rack beside the first chair held an assortment of combs, scissors, and electric hair trimmers. Beside the second chair sat a small cart supporting a SoulScan unit and an array of gleaming stainless steel tattoo needles.

There were five of them scheduled for that day: three girls and two boys. All of them would soon be moving to the other side of the School, where the advanced students lived. But first, they had to visit the infirmary. Milling about outside, they teased each other to relieve the tension.

"No more split ends," Sylvia said, smiling weakly.

"Yeah." Natalie tried to smile back. "Save a lot of money on conditioner, too."

She fidgeted with a strand of her flaxen hair, which now spilled down past her shoulders. She was the youngest of the five—only twelve, while they were thirteen. It didn't seem fair.

The infirmary doors swept open with a loud thump, and Sondra pushed her way out into the corridor.

"Well, guys, what d'ya think?" Sondra sashayed and posed

for them, a cocky tilt to her shaven head. "Am I gorgeous or what?"

The boys, Evan and Forrest, whistled and clapped. "Sexy mama!" Evan whooped.

Sondra locked her hands behind her head and ground her hips. A brash brunette an hour ago, she exuded the natural confidence of an early bloomer, her budding breasts bulging impressively beneath her tight tank top.

Natalie, who wore shapeless, oversized T-shirts to hide the fact that she had nothing to hide, stood back and sulked. Sondra acted as if the whole ordeal were some big party; in fact, she'd volunteered to go first. Natalie squinted at the tiny spots of blood on Sondra's scalp, now drying to scabs. Was it possible that she really didn't care?

"Natalie?" A nurse propped open one of the doors. "We're ready for you."

Natalie sucked on the strand of hair she'd been twirling and shuffled forward.

Evan grinned at her, eyes bright beneath his heavy black brows. "You can do it, Boo."

She giggled as he led the others in a chant of support. "BOO! BOO! BOO!"

The cheer urged her on into the infirmary, where it was cut off by the swinging door.

The nurse, a pleasant hazel-eyed woman named Terry, directed her toward the first barber's chair. "Have a seat."

Natalie dropped herself into the chair and tried to relax with some measured breathing techniques she'd learned in her yoga class. But she couldn't help watching Rob, the other nurse, sweep the last clippings of Sondra's brown locks into a dustpan. The School had promised all of them a wig made from their own hair.

Rob set aside the broom and dustpan, tugged his white shirt taut over his paunch, and tucked a nylon cloth under her chin. "So, how do you want it?"

Very funny, Natalie thought. How many times have you used that one this century?

"An inch off the back," she deadpanned.

He laughed, and plucked his scissors from the rack. It didn't take long: He tied most of her locks in careless braids and cut them off, then laid the thick ropes of hair on the counter beside him. A flick and a buzz, and Natalie's head reverberated with the hum of the clippers as they removed the tufts that remained. While Rob cleaned off the stubble with shaving cream and a razor, Natalie looked toward the other barber's chair, where Dr. Krell was preparing a fresh, sterilized tattoo needle.

Like the rest of the medical staff, Dr. Krell was not a Violet. Rather, she was an ordinary middle-aged woman with green eyes, sharp cheekbones, and a prominent chin. To demonstrate solidarity with her patients, however, she kept her own head shaved, and the gesture, along with her amiable bedside manner, made her a favorite with the schoolchildren.

"Hey, Boo! How's that shoulder been treating you?" she asked as Natalie moved into the second barber's chair.

"Oh…fine." In reflex, Natalie rubbed her right shoulder, which she'd dislocated during a soccer match when she was nine.

"Well, compared to that, this'll be a cinch. Let's get you hooked up." The doctor first cleaned Natalie's scalp with rubbing alcohol, then picked a bracelet made of hair off the cart *beside her. Its woven brown strands looked dry and brittle. "No need to worry. Ginny's a gentle soul. When you're ready…"*

Natalie muttered one of the advanced mantras that Arthur had taught them that year. After a moment, she held out her hand.

Images flickered in Natalie's mind the moment the coarse bracelet brushed her palm. A farmhouse surrounded by cornfields. Shucking peas on the front porch while rocking a cradle with her foot. A boy in gray knickerbockers chasing chickens in the yard.

My children, my children! Ginny implored, weaving in and out of the fissures of Natalie's brain. *Where are they? What has become of them?* It occurred to Natalie that these children were probably great-grandparents now—if they were even still alive.

"Good." Dr. Krell placed the cold metal circle of an electrode against the skin of Natalie's scalp and observed the resulting readout on the SoulScan monitor. "Now, let's see if we can locate your receptor nodes.…"

She edged the electrode left and right, up and down, as though using a stethoscope to seek a heartbeat. When at last satisfied with the wave patterns she saw on the monitor, she lifted the electrode and marked the chosen spot with a surgical grease pencil.

She repeated this process until she'd pinpointed each of Natalie's twenty SoulScan nodes, and took back the hair bracelet. Ginny's personality dissipated, leaving Natalie with a residual dizziness.

Dr. Krell gave her an encouraging smile. "That was the hard part. Now sit very still."

The doctor steadied Natalie's head with one hand and

*started the tattoo needle with the other. A high-pitched whine
made Natalie's ears tingle, and the first jolt of pain stabbed
into her skull....*

The door slapped shut on the twin barber's chairs.
Natalie recoiled from the infirmary, massaging her temples
to fend off an incipient headache and muttering Psalm 23,
one of her strongest defensive mantras, under her breath.
For the first time since she'd seen the snapshots in Dan's
FBI case files, the realization closed in on her: Evan was
dead. His presence permeated this place, and he might
come to her at any moment. Natalie wasn't sure she could
stand that.

And then there was Sondra. She was dead, too, and, in
death, had Evan all to herself, once and for all. Would she
come back from the grave just to gloat?

With growing uneasiness, Natalie continued down the
hallway, past the dining hall and gymnasium, the administrative offices and the library, and on around into the side
of the School dedicated to the older students. Here, like
novices in a monastery, shaven-headed teenagers learned
from their bald masters the roles society expected them to
play. It was unlikely that Laurie Gannon had been here
when she saw the man in the jumpsuit, and Natalie didn't
see any door or room that seemed to match the scene in
Laurie's memory.

Dan paced the hall several yards behind her, hands in
his pockets. Despite his evident impatience, Natalie
stepped out a side door into the courtyard. The air in the
building was too cold and musty, she told herself. A walk
outside would clear her head.

But that wasn't really the reason she wanted to go.

Cement paths crisscrossed the courtyard at right angles, dividing it into four quarters. Maple trees stood in each grassy quarter, their bowers of three-pronged leaves forming a canopy of shade over the walkways. A small fountain rested in the center of the courtyard, its pond now still, its stone fauns no longer spouting water from the pan-pipes they played. Natalie rubbed her arms, shuddering from a chill far deeper than the briskness outside.

The temperature must have been in the single digits that day, but that was why they had come outside—to be alone. The fountain, drained of water for the season, had filled with snow, and the skeletal maples bled sweet sap into wooden buckets that hung from taps hammered into their trunks. The younger children would later take this syrup and make maple sugar candy of it, molding it into honey-colored stars and hearts. It was here that Evan brought her to say good-bye.

"I'm not coming back after Christmas." He pulled his stocking cap down until it almost covered his eyebrows in a vain attempt to keep his head warm. *"They're short on Violets at Quantico, and they want to start my training early."*

Although her nose was numb and needles of cold pricked through the weave of her own cap, Natalie smiled and stroked his cheek with her hand, her glove snagging on the stubble he'd grown on his cheek. "Don't worry. I turn eighteen next October—I can be there in less than a year—"

"No." He gently took her hand from his face and pressed it between his palms. *"Don't come, Boo, even if they assign you. That place eats people."*

"It's all right. I can handle it."

"No, you can't. No one can." Always gloomy, he looked even more morose than usual. *"Like your mom—"*

Natalie yanked her hand from his grasp. "I am NOT my mother! I wish everyone would just shut up about her already!"

"Hey, take it easy."

He moved to embrace her, but she swatted his arms away. Hot breath steamed from her nose and mouth in white billows. "And if it's so dangerous, why are YOU going?"

Evan sighed and folded his arms. "Because they've threatened to foreclose on my parents' house if I don't. And my dad could lose his job."

She folded her arms, mimicking him. "Lucky for you they've assigned Sondra there."

He groaned and threw up his arms. "Aw, Christ! For the last time, there's nothing going on between Sondra and me."

"Really? And why aren't you telling HER to stay away from Quantico?"

"Ha! You know Sondra. You think it would do any good?"

"Of course not. It's her big chance."

He put his hands around her head, forcing her to look directly into his mournful eyes. "Boo, I swear, I'm only trying to protect you. Pray for the Art Division. You're good—they've got to take you. But don't let them stick you in law enforcement. Run away, if you have to."

"Yeah? And what about this?" Taking off a glove, Natalie slid her right hand under the layers of clothing at her neck and pulled out the chain that hung there. Still warm from her chest, the pendant cooled quickly when exposed to the air: two snakes entwined to form the symbol for infinity.

"I thought this meant 'forever.' Do you even HAVE yours anymore, Evan?"

He put his hand to his chest and nodded.

She stared at him in silence, her jaw set, unwilling to forgive him for abandoning her. The caring and regret in his eyes melted her resolve, however, and she hugged him as closely as their down jackets would allow. "Please don't say I'll never see you again," she whispered in his ear.

He didn't reply. She held him there by the frozen fountain for several more minutes, while the cold made the moisture in her eyes cut like glass. . . .

"Natalie."

The courtyard snapped back into focus. The leaves on the trees were just beginning to turn red, and the water in the fountain was stagnant and tainted with algae, the color of a rotting lime.

Natalie turned to the voice that had pulled her back to the present and found Dan standing in the doorway behind her. "Don't want to disturb you, but we don't have much time. Did you find the spot where Laurie saw the suspect?"

She shook her head, unable to speak for a moment. The tableau of that winter afternoon still enveloped her. Was Evan here? Why didn't he knock?

The awful possibility occurred to her that maybe he didn't *want* to knock—that maybe he and Sondra were happy in their nonlife together, their souls intertwined like the snakes on the pendant. . . .

She repelled the idea by forcing herself to listen to what Dan was saying.

"Could Laurie have seen him upstairs somewhere?" he suggested.

"I doubt it. There's nothing but dorm rooms up there." She rejoined him in the hallway, the specter of Evan still clouding her thoughts. "That's what I don't understand. It was a part of the School I'd never seen before."

Dan rubbed his chin as he looked up and down the hall. "You said the guy was wearing a uniform, like he was some kind of handyman. Where's the maintenance department?"

"I don't know—in the basement, I suppose. But Laurie couldn't have gone down there. The staff keeps those doors locked for safety."

"Yeah. But this guy wasn't a real member of the staff."

He stalked down the corridor, and Natalie kept pace with him.

"Laurie would've been over here with the younger students, right?" he asked as they passed through the Common Room and returned to the east wing. Dan marched past the classrooms until he came to a windowless door stenciled with the words *Employees Only* in black paint. He tried the knob, but it was locked, so he fished the key ring out of his pocket. After scrutinizing the blue ballpoint scrawls on several of the labeled keys, he picked one and inserted it in the lock. The knob rotated as he turned the key, and the door opened into a darkened stairwell.

Dan located the light switch on the wall to their right, and a pair of fluorescent bars overhead showered the concrete steps with gray illumination. The smell of damp cement gave Natalie gooseflesh as they descended the stairs.

"This is it," she whispered.

When the stairwell emptied out into a concrete-floored corridor, Natalie took the lead. The orange doors, the beige walls, the fluorescent lights—she'd seen these before. Quickening her stride, she advanced to the third door on the left and reached for the handle.

"Wait." Dan pulled on a pair of latex gloves as he came up beside her. He opened the door with one gloved hand and flipped the light switch inside. A single bare bulb on the ceiling shone on the green metal of a large furnace. A square duct rose from the top of the furnace and split into smaller ducts, which ran up through the roof of the room. A horizontal pipe connected the furnace to an enormous tank of heating oil.

"Where did you see our mystery man?" Dan asked.

"Over here." She crossed the room and sat on her haunches beside the huge black cylinder of the oil tank, which lay on its side in a steel framework that held it about a foot off the floor. "He was squatting here, clasping his hands in front of him like this." She folded her hands and bowed her head.

Dan knelt beside her and pulled a penlight from the inside pocket of his jacket. "What were you doing here, Mr. Mystery?"

He darted the penlight's beam over the grimy surface of the tank, but found nothing unusual about it. Lying on his side on the floor, he directed the light on the underside of the tank. "Oh, boy."

Natalie crouched on her hands and knees until she could see where the oval of light fell. A small package was duct-taped to the bottom of the oil tank. Two galvanized pipes protruded from the package, and insulated wires looped from the end of each pipe to a black switch affixed to the bottom of the bundle. A liquid-crystal display above the switch blinked the digits "90:00."

Natalie looked at Dan. "Is that…?"

"A bomb," he confirmed.

10

New Problems

DAN WAS ON HIS CELL PHONE FOR ALMOST TWENTY minutes, leaving Natalie with little to do but shiver and stare at the derelict edifice of the School. Although Dan didn't think the bomb had been activated, neither of them wanted to risk staying in the building, so they stood out front in the dimming light of sunset.

Finally, he hung the phone back on his belt and came over to brief her on the situation. "Removal squad's on its way. The package is strictly a homemade job, by the looks of it, but whoever made it knew what they were doing. Blasting that oil tank would've brought the whole place down. Needless to say, Clark's fit to spit. This blows the whole case wide open, if you'll pardon the pun."

"Even the President couldn't pardon *that* pun." Natalie scanned the School's forbidding face, trying to read its expression. "Do they have any ideas?"

"That's the problem. Now we have *too many* ideas. It could've been a revenge plot, a mob hit, a terrorist act. We could be dealing with a lone psychotic or with a team of professional assassins. Assuming, of course, that this bomb incident is even related to the murders."

"It is. I'm sure of it." She thought of Laurie's memories—

of the hesitation she sensed in the Faceless Man just before he killed her. "Why didn't he start the timer?"

Dan raised an eyebrow. "That's the real question, isn't it? That, and why he'd travel three thousand miles to murder a girl he could've killed right here." He frowned at the School. "Anyway, some local cops are coming to secure the area until the squad arrives. Clark wants us back in L.A. pronto for a powwow, so I booked an eight P.M. flight."

Natalie sighed. "Swell."

Dan pulled his suit coat tighter around him. "I don't know about you, but I'm freezing out here. Let's get back to the car."

They started down the cement walkway toward the main gate, but Dan abruptly fell a few steps behind. "What the hell…?"

Natalie turned and saw him lift his right foot.

A gooey strand of pink bubble gum stretched from the pavement to the sole of his shoe.

11

The Black Room

IT WAS THE LAST SÉANCE OF THE NIGHT, AND Arthur McCord couldn't wait for it to end.

The customer was an older woman named Beatrice Rose, whom he had not seen before. In her sixties, she teetered on that cusp between middle and old age, after the flesh begins to sag but before the soul's fire burns to embers. Although her shoulders were already hunched with weariness and incipient osteoporosis, she perched attentively on the edge of her chair, her eyes bright, her silver hair curled with a girlish perm.

She'd walked in off the street yesterday to schedule an appointment, and Arthur had had little time to prepare. Ordinarily, he would have paid that college kid Bonner to do the research for him—check county records, obit sections in local newspapers, even the credit history of the subject and her deceased husband—anything that might give him some convincing facts to sprinkle into the session. As it was, he had to do the summoning cold, making educated guesses and prompting Mrs. Rose to give him the information he needed. "Plucking the feathers off her," as they called it in the fake Violet trade.

"I know why you've come, Bea." He smiled and caressed her cheek. "I know what you want to ask me."

"Oh, Davey!" She stroked and kissed his hand. "But how...?"

"I've been with you all along. I know how hard it's been for you—how hard you've had to work since I left." Actually, this was nonsense. Shut in their black room, the dead could see the living only through the window of a Violet. But Arthur knew Mrs. Rose was in financial straits from the way she haggled over the price of his consultation. The calluses that he felt on her palms must have come from long hours of pushing a mop or vacuum cleaner, and the fact that she'd come to him at ten o'clock at night told him that she was probably working overtime.

"Yes. It's been hard." Her tears seeped between his fingers. "I've missed you so much."

"But something's about to change, isn't it?"

She turned her face from him in sudden shame, sniffling. Arthur easily guessed her dilemma.

"There's someone new, isn't there? Another man."

She said nothing, but her head drooped lower, and she fidgeted with the wedding band and engagement ring on her left hand.

"Bea, do you remember what I told you on our honeymoon?"

"In Hawaii?" Mrs. Rose's brow furrowed. "When?"

"You remember. On the beach."

"That...that you loved me?"

"That I would *always* love you," Arthur amended. "Forever. No matter what. You're my 'Honey Bea,' after all." The pet name was a gamble. If he'd guessed wrong, she'd probably dismiss it as irrelevant; if he was right, she'd be convinced he was her husband.

The gamble paid off. She pressed her hands to her face, trembling. "Davey! Oh, sweet Lord, I'm sorry...."

"Don't be. I want you to be happy, even if that means marrying someone else." Arthur wondered if the real David Rose would be as understanding. He hoped so.

She jumped from her chair and collapsed on top of him, sobbing. "It's not 'cause I stopped loving you! I never stopped loving you!"

"I know." Patting her back as he cradled her, Arthur decided that this was a good time to end the session. "I have to go now, Honey Bea. But I'll always be close by, watching over you, enfolding you in my love."

Arthur kissed her forehead, then allowed his body to go limp in the chair, hyperventilating as though he'd just run a marathon. His eyes shut, he heard Beatrice Rose weeping, felt her shuddering against him.

When Mrs. Rose had cried herself out and blown her nose, Arthur walked her to the door. She thanked him effusively and pressed him to take an extra ten dollars as a token of her gratitude. He politely declined and bid her good night.

What a life, he thought bitterly as he locked the shop's front door and shut off the Coleman lanterns in the entryway. *Spinning lies like a mentalist in a Vegas lounge act.*

Of course, he wouldn't have had to resort to such flimflam if he simply summoned the dead as he claimed to do. But Arthur treasured his hard-won solitude of soul, and refused to surrender it even for a moment.

He shuffled back into the séance room and started

blowing out the candles. Maybe he should have left the country after his "disappearance"—although he'd heard that some foreign nations were even more ruthless with their Violets than the NAACC. If you refused to cooperate in the U.S., the Corps could blacklist you, repossess your car, audit your family; in Paraguay, the government would mail you your spouse's fingers one at a time until you came back to work.

Arthur also couldn't convince himself to leave the only family he'd ever known: Jem and Gig, Evan and Boo, Lucy... even Simon. They were the only people he trusted enough to reveal the true identity of "Yuri," the only genuine Violet in West Hollywood.

Now half that family was dead.

The circle of illumination in the room shrank to the size of the central table, where the oil lamp still cast a wavering ring of amber light. Arthur picked the lamp up by its handle and carried it through the bead-draped rear door of the room and into what had once been the shop's back office. He'd turned it into his living quarters by installing a small shower in the bathroom—all plastic pipes, like the rest of his plumbing—and by moving in a cot, a dresser, several shelves of books (mostly Eastern philosophy), and a propane camp stove. He got by without a fridge by subsisting mostly on canned goods, fresh fruit, root vegetables, and prepared foods he had delivered to him regularly. Like the rest of the shop, the walls here glinted with the dull reflection of rumpled aluminum foil.

The only electrical device in the room was a flashlight that lay on the floor beside the bed, and out of habit, Arthur switched on the light to make sure the batteries still worked. With the ambient light from the street blocked out by the foil-covered windows, the store became black as a cave when the lamps weren't lit, and he hated trying to feel his way to the bathroom in the middle of the night.

Beside the flashlight lay an unregistered .45 revolver that he'd bought off one of the crack dealers on the Boulevard.

Arthur set the oil lamp on the dresser and changed into his pajamas. After brushing his teeth at the bathroom sink, he removed the too-purple contacts and stored them in saline solution for the following day. Then he settled himself on the cot, lifted the fluted chimney off the lamp, and extinguished the flame.

Just as the broad wick of woven string smoldered into blackness, a sound whispered in from the séance room—a soft, metallic *ting*, whose resonance abruptly stopped.

Wrapped in palpable darkness, Arthur sat perfectly still, trying to convince himself that air pressure alone had pushed the séance room door against the bell that hung above it. But that didn't explain the sudden silence, as if fingers had seized the bell to muffle its vibration.

Moving by touch and memory, Arthur picked up the revolver and flashlight. Pulling back the hammer of the gun, he switched on the light, half expecting to find the killer standing there in front of him. A quick sweep of the flashlight beam reassured him that he was alone in the room.

Arthur then pointed both the light and the gun at the strings of purple beads that curtained the doorway. Imagined sounds made his ears twitch, but he heard nothing.

How long he froze there, listening, hardly daring to

blink, he didn't know. More than an hour it seemed. It occurred to him that he could maintain this Mexican stand-
off all night: He had the advantage, after all, for the
intruder—if there was one—couldn't enter the room without getting shot. The following day, some of Arthur's clients
would come, and Arthur could get them to call the police
by firing his .45, assuming the intruder hadn't fled by then.

The muscles in his arms started to cramp, and he be-
rated himself for his cowardice. The man who'd murdered
Jem and the others might be hiding in that room. If Arthur
let him sneak out the way he'd crept in, his next victim
might be Lucy or Boo.

For the first time in six years, Arthur McCord wished he
owned a telephone.

He lowered the flashlight beam to the floor beneath the
bead curtain. No feet stood there.

Flexing his finger on the trigger of the cocked pistol,
Arthur stood and padded toward the door. He pressed himself back against the wall to the right and nudged aside a
few strings of beads with the barrel of his gun so he could
shine light into the séance room. Starting with the nearest
wall, he zigzagged the flashlight's beam around the room's
perimeter. Constellations and zodiacal symbols floated in
and out of the circle of illumination, which became larger
and dimmer as it reached the far wall of the chamber. He
leaned into the doorframe just enough to be able to direct
the beam at every corner of the room.

He found no one.

He trained the light on the door diagonally across from
him. It was ajar, its top edge resting against the forward rim
of the bell. Was the intruder still behind that door, hiding

in the entryway? How did he get past the locked front door?

With equal concern, Arthur eyed the cloth-draped table in the center of the room. Plenty of room to crouch under there. But how to check under the table or behind the door without exposing himself to ambush from the other location?

Arthur advanced toward the table as if it were a sleeping lion. Keeping the door within the circle of his flashlight beam, he knocked over the table with a quick kick of his right foot. The table landed on its round edge and rolled to a stop, the tablecloth deflating around its wooden legs.

The floor underneath was bare.

Arthur licked at the sweat on his upper lip. The flashlight beam hovered on the door—a spotlight waiting for an actor. Had the crack at the door's edge widened since he first looked at it? Or had he left it ajar himself when he closed the shop?

He sidled around to the hinge side of the door and glanced through the wire mesh of the window. Nothing. He couldn't be sure, though, unless...

Holding the flashlight with his thumb, he hooked the fingers of his left hand under the door handle. He tightened his grip on the gun in his right hand and yanked the door open.

From behind him came the susurration of rippling cloth.

The banners, Arthur realized before he could turn around. *He was behind one of the banners.*

Razor-thin piano wire bit into the flesh of his throat and collapsed his windpipe.

Arthur jerked backward, his mouth gaping but unable to draw air. His trigger finger twitched in reflex, firing a shot at the wall. Although he managed to hold on to the gun, the flashlight slipped from under his thumb and bounced on the floor, creating a useless puddle of luminescence at his feet.

Arthur's brain screamed for oxygen as blood flow stalled in his constricted carotid arteries. Like a panicked bull, he thrust his body forward, lifting his attacker off the floor and onto his massive back.

The killer clung to the garrote while Arthur whipsawed him from side to side. Stumbling backward, Arthur slammed him against the nearest wall and pinned him there. The killer groaned in pain.

Checkerboard patterns shimmered over Arthur's vision, yet he ignored the viselike pressure in his head and pointed the gun at the man trapped behind him.

The garrote fell away, and a hand seized Arthur's right wrist, its skin the clingy, gelatinous texture of rubber. The killer forced the gun's barrel up toward the ceiling as Arthur squeezed off another round. There was a light *snick* sound behind him, and a knife plunged into Arthur's neck.

The pistol slid from his numb fingers. His wattles oozed hot wetness, and when he tried to breathe, his trachea gurgled like a backed-up drain. Conscious thoughts flashed off in his mind like bursting lightbulbs, leaving only one still glowing: *Boo* . . .

Weaving drunkenly, Arthur marshaled the anaerobic strength left in his muscles and drove his right elbow into the killer's solar plexus. When the man doubled over, Arthur grabbed him around the waist in a wrestler's bear hug and used the momentum of his 318-pound bulk to push the off-balance attacker to the floor.

As he collapsed on top of the killer, Arthur slipped into unconsciousness momentarily, but fought to open his eyes when he felt the man squirming to get out from under him. The murderer's veiled head had fallen within the oval of illumination from the flashlight, the crepe pulsing with his labored breath.

With fingers he could barely feel, Arthur gripped the web of fabric at the man's temples and started to push the mask off his face. *Give me one look. One look for Boo...*

The killer sensed the threat and thrashed his head to shake off Arthur's hands. The base of the mask slipped out from under the collar of the man's black shirt, revealing the white of his neck. Arthur dripped blood and red saliva on the exposed skin. The mask slid up a bit, but caught on the killer's chin. Arthur continued to tug at it. *Just a little more...*

Then the knifepoint flashed toward the jelly of his eyes.

The final shards of his consciousness shattered with the white-hot pain of his punctured corneas. He felt blood seep into vitreous fluid in the cups of his eye sockets, but the sensation was like the last foot of film on a projector reel; the tail end of the experience slap-slap-slapped at his memory, forever unresolved.

Death arrived not as a sleep, but as an awakening. Gradually, Arthur became aware of the absence of pain—the absence, indeed, of any sensation at all. Reaching to touch something, he discovered that he was no longer bound by the confines of flesh.

Arthur expanded like vapor into a strange new void, a

blackness that was not black for it lacked all conception of color. The sense of freedom gave him a giddy euphoria, and he wondered if he could stretch himself all the way to the stars.

Something stopped him. The barrier did not touch him in any physical way, but it exerted a magnetic repulsion on his mind, fencing in his disembodied thoughts. He pressed his essence against the force, searching for a chink in the walls surrounding him, but encountered the same resistance on all sides.

The Faraday cage, he remembered, and panic crackled through his soul.

Growing frantic, he swirled and pushed and pounded his immaterial essence against the sides of the cage, but it was no use. Created to keep other souls out, it now boxed his in.

Trapped and alone, Arthur McCord groped in vain for an exit from a black room of his own construction.

12

An Open Door

THEY DIDN'T ARRIVE AT MCCORD'S SHOP UNTIL after noon. By that time, Dan was starving and Natalie looked like hell.

They'd taken a night flight back from New Hampshire and hadn't reached their hotel until almost one A.M. Dan managed to catch a few winks on the plane, but he knew that Natalie had quivered with fear, wide-awake, for the entire trip. SAC Clark, of course, insisted that they meet him at LAPD headquarters at seven sharp, and they spent the entire morning reviewing the case.

Dan's complimentary continental breakfast had sustained him only until ten o'clock or so, and a hunger headache now pulsed in his temples. "You sure you don't want to come back later?" he asked Natalie, who lay draped on the passenger seat like a wrung-out rag. "You could use some food and sleep, in that order."

"No. I have to let Arthur know what's going on." She grabbed the door handle and pulled herself upright. "It'll only take a minute."

"Your call." He got out and jogged around the car to join her at the shop's entrance. They found the front door unlocked, yet the entryway was still dark when they stepped inside.

"Mr. McCord's late lighting the lanterns today." Dan switched on his penlight as the front door cut off the sunshine from the street. "Could he be out somewhere?"

"Arthur doesn't *go* out." Natalie's weary voice was suddenly charged with dread. "Something's wrong."

She pushed open the door to the séance room, the bell jangling with incongruous cheeriness in the pitch dark. Even before he lowered the penlight's beam to the floor, Dan felt the stickiness under his shoes, smelled the odor that stank like rank sweat and rust. Natalie staggered back and braced herself against the door as the dim circle of light drifted over the shape in front of them.

Dan's empty stomach shriveled. "Good God…"

The blood had spread over most of the rubber matting at the room's center. Arthur McCord lay in the middle of the congealed pool, his bare feet pointed toward the door. The front of his pajama shirt had been ripped open and red graffiti etched into the livid skin of his chest:

An open door
Come on in

Below the writing, McCord's mountainous belly had been slit from breastbone to navel and his hands placed on either side of the wound, as though he were holding the flaps apart to permit entry to his bowels. The killer had carefully unraveled the corpse's small intestine and pulled it out through the wound to form a talismanic circle around the body. McCord's throat bore ligature and stab wounds, and his violet eyes had been gouged from their sockets.

"Natalie…" Dan moved to guide her out of the room, but froze when the beam of his penlight fell on her face. Her eyes were nearly all white, the corneas rolled up under her fluttering lids, and she leaned back against the door as if standing on the window ledge of a skyscraper.

Her head jerked twice, and the irises rotated back into view. "Boo…thank God you're here."

Dan tensed at hearing the low, sonorous register of her voice. When she bolted for the exit, he blocked her way.

"Mr. McCord, I presume."

Natalie threw herself against him, snarling. *"LET ME OUT!"*

"Not yet." He moved into the doorway, and she growled in frustration: McCord was clearly unused to having such a lightweight body. Dan grabbed Natalie's wrist. "Who was it?"

"I don't know!"

"What did you *see*?"

McCord stopped struggling. "I didn't *see* anything. He stabbed my eyes out."

"Why would someone want to kill you?"

"I said I don't know!"

"Who else knew you were hiding here besides Natalie?"

For the first time, McCord paused to consider the question. "Lucy Kamei…and Simon."

"Is that it? Are you sure?"

"Yes, I'm sure! Everyone else is *dead*."

McCord thrashed again, twisting the features of Natalie's face. Dan became aware of how tightly his hand was clamped on Natalie's arm, how much he must be hurting her. He let go and stepped aside.

McCord drove Natalie forward, past Dan and through the front door. Dan followed them out to the sidewalk and saw McCord tilt her face toward the welcoming sun and raise her arms like a bird spreading its wings.

Natalie balanced there for an instant, then crumpled. Dan caught her before she dropped, and eased her down onto the pavement beneath the shop's violet-eyed sign.

As she rested her cheek against the wall, Dan punched Clark's number into his cell phone. No chance of lunch now, but that was okay—he'd lost his appetite anyway.

Congested at the best of times, the traffic along Vine Street slowed to the pace of a funeral procession as uniformed LAPD officers tried in vain to shoo the rubberneckers away from McCord's shop. An evidence-gathering team had gone inside to photograph the scene and collect clues while Clark grilled Dan out front.

"You want to tell me why we didn't know about this guy?" the SAC asked, sounding a lot like the vice principal at Dan's old high school.

"I looked up the records on McCord's disappearance in case there might be a connection with the murders," Dan lied. "With Natalie's help, I was able to get some new leads on his present whereabouts, but I didn't want to divert the investigation until I had something definite. Unfortunately, the killer got to him first."

The story didn't impress Clark. "I look forward to reading your *official* report, Agent Atwater," he murmured, and turned to the crime scene technician who'd just emerged from the shop. "What'd you get?"

"We'll have to wait for the coroner's report, but the skin's lividity and the insignificant decomposition of the body suggest that death occurred within the last day—possibly as little as fifteen hours ago." The technician, a chunky woman named Estelle Blair, lowered her clipboard and raised her reading glasses onto her forehead. "Looks like the killer tried to strangle McCord, then stabbed him in the neck to finish him off. Size of the puncture wound indicates a hunting knife or similar blade."

"Any weapons?"

"Just a forty-five revolver, which apparently belonged to the victim. Two shots fired. We found one bullet in the wall, but we're still looking for the other one; the foil everywhere makes it tough to spot the holes. Don't know if any of that blood in there is the killer's, but we're sending plenty of it to the lab for analysis."

"Anything else?"

"Some bloody shoe prints that look like they match the impressions taken from the Gannon backyard. Also, the lock on the front door shows signs of tampering. Whoever broke in knew how to pick it."

Clark nodded and shifted his attention back to Dan. "Lindstrom ready to talk?"

Dan glanced over at Natalie, who still slumped like a vagrant on the sidewalk, her head resting on her knees. "Give her 'til tomorrow."

"How about seven tonight?"

"*Tomorrow*, Earl."

Clark looked at Natalie, and his mouth twitched. "Okay. Tomorrow *morning*." He and Blair stepped aside to confer.

Dan squatted beside Natalie and tapped on the bare skin of her arm, like a father rousing his child from a bad dream. She lifted her head and half opened eyes that were too tired to cry.

"You ready to go?"

She acquiesced with an almost imperceptible nod, and let him help her to her feet.

13

Vulnerable Time

NATALIE DIDN'T SPEAK DURING THE WHOLE TRIP back to the Embassy Suites, even when Dan stopped at a Carl's Jr. drive-through to buy their dinner. Although she didn't place an order, he got her a Charbroiled Chicken Salad-To-Go, figuring that was the closest thing to health food on the menu. At the hotel, she still insisted on trudging up the eight flights of stairs to their room, but slumped into bed without even taking off her shoes.

Sitting cross-legged on his own bed, Dan watched her comatose form with concern as he ate his Famous Star cheeseburger. Fear, grief, exhaustion—she'd been through the wringer and had every right to pass out for a few hours. But was something else going on? Should he take her to a hospital?

"You know, that stuff'll kill you," she murmured in a sleepy voice.

Dan smiled and munched a french fry. "Better than starving. You want some of this salad I got you?"

She yawned. "No. But thanks for thinking of me."

"I'll put it in the minibar. Maybe you can have it for breakfast." He set aside his burger. "How you doing?"

"Right now? Not so good." Her expression became

pinched, as if with sudden pain. "Dan, tell me something about your life. Something nice—something you like."

The request startled him. "Well…there's lots of things…."

But nothing came to mind at first. Certainly the last two years didn't offer much to brag about: the trial, the transfer to Quantico, the divorce from Susan…and the rest of it. He rewound his memory until it came to the last good thing he could recall.

"Last spring I was going through a bad time, what with my divorce and all." He cleared his throat and wished that his tongue didn't taste like onions. "I'd moved into an apartment in Virginia by that time, and didn't really know anyone there except the people I met at work. My brother Sam knew I was going to be on my own for Easter, so he invited me out to his place on the edge of Clear Lake in northern California to spend the weekend with his family.

"When I got there, I found that he'd invited my parents, too. I guess he wanted to surprise me." Dan chuckled. "Since Mom and Dad took the guest bedroom, I got put on the living room couch. But that was okay—it reminded me of the times I used to sleep over at my grandparents' house.

"Anyway, I was late getting there—I could only get a Saturday afternoon flight, and Sam's house is about a two-hour drive from the Sacramento airport—but my little niece Tina had stayed up to wait for me and *insisted* that we decorate Easter eggs that night." He laughed and wiped his eye with the back of his hand. "So there we were—me and Tina, Mom and Dad, Sam and his wife Liz—all dyeing hard-boiled eggs at eleven o'clock at night the day before Easter. I think my fingers were purple for a week after that.

"They let me sleep in the following morning when they went to church. Liz told me later that Tina could hardly keep from giggling as she tiptoed past me while I snored there on the sofa. I was up by the time they got back, and we all went out for a big Easter breakfast at the little coffee shop there in town. After that, I got to follow my niece with the Easter basket as she picked up all the plastic eggs Sam hid for her in the yard.

"In the afternoon, Dad and I sat out on my brother's dock and fished. Didn't talk much, and didn't get a single bite, but I didn't mind. Then we ate Easter dinner, and no one asked me about the divorce or how the new job was going." Dan swallowed and found that his mouth had become dry and sticky. "And that was when I knew that, no matter what I did, no matter how bad I screwed up...these people would always take me back."

He stared into the vacant air, his half-eaten burger lying forgotten on the flattened paper bags in front of him.

"Must be nice." The springs of Natalie's bed creaked as she shifted position. "Easter. Do you believe in that?"

"Hmm? What do you mean?"

"You know: Rebirth. Renewal. Whatever."

Dan felt the recoil of the .38 in his hand, saw the wadded windbreaker on the man's bleeding chest and the bewildered face staring up at him. "God, I hope so." He glanced over to see her lying on her side, her eyes shut. "What do you think?"

She didn't answer for a long time, and Dan thought she'd fallen asleep.

"I've heard stories," she said at last. "About people you

can't call back. Souls that Violets can't summon, that go on to someplace beyond our reach."

"Do you believe those stories?" Dan examined the palms of his hands, as if trying to read his own future. "I mean, there must be *happy* souls somewhere, right?"

"I don't know." The question seemed to trouble her. "I never get to talk to the happy ones."

Dan wasn't sure what to say to that, so he quietly wrapped up his burger and fries and threw them in the trash. Just before he went into the bathroom to brush his teeth, she called to him again.

"Thank you. For sharing your Easter."

He paused at the door to smile back at her. "Thank you for reminding me of it."

When he returned, she was snoring softly. He left the light on for her, nevertheless.

Sometime later, Dan twitched to the tempo of a nightmare.

In the dream, he stood in the alley. The caged lightbulb above the door gleamed with an unnatural incandescence, its whiteness blindingly bright, yet cold. Phillips and Ross were nowhere to be seen; the street was vacant except for a figure with its back to Dan, its head bowed.

Lowering his gaze, Dan saw that the figure stood in a reflective puddle of blood. The stranger wore a dirty jacket and jeans like those of the man they'd killed, yet when it lifted its head, the light illuminated the white skin of its bald scalp.

Although every instinct screamed at Dan to run away, the inevitability of nightmare compelled him to approach the figure. The echoes of the alley converted his footfalls into whispered accusations.

The figure turned—it was Natalie. Her features bore the stamp of another face, and her eyes glinted with icy resentment. Dan stopped as she lifted her arm to point a gun at him. It was his own .38.

"You stole my life," she said in a low voice he had never heard before. He knew who had spoken, though, even before she emptied the gun into his chest....

Dan jerked awake, limbs flailing as if the bed were falling out from under him. Sinking back on the pillow, he pressed his hands to his face, waiting for the hummingbird beat of his heart to slow.

"Couldn't sleep?"

The words seemed to have risen out of his dream. Dan sprang up and shot a glance at the bed next to him.

It was still well before dawn, and the shaded light from the lamp submerged the room in a stale yellow pall. Natalie sat on the edge of her bed, wearing only her oversized T-shirt. She must have undressed after Dan went to sleep, for she had also removed her wig and contacts, and now regarded him with a hungry intensity in her eyes.

"You seem tense." Her bare legs held apart, she ran her fingertips up and down the skin of her inner thighs. "Maybe I can help." With a loose-limbed nonchalance, she rose and padded over to him.

The memory of his dream still flickering in his mind, Dan flinched as she stroked his cheek. *Night is a very vulnerable time for me,* she'd told him.

"You're not Natalie. Who are you?"

The left corner of her mouth pulled back in a lopsided

smile. "Natalie's asleep. Let her rest." She brushed a strand of hair out of his eyes.

"Whoever you are, you need to leave. Now." Not sure what else to do, Dan bluffed. "I have a stun gun in my suitcase. I'll use it if I have to."

"Now, now! No one wants to hurt Natalie. Least of all me." There was an affected lilt to her voice, a tone of jaded amusement. "I'm an old friend of her mother's."

Before Dan could get up or move to the other side of the bed, she hitched her right leg over his waist and straddled him. Trying to ignore the warmth of her hips, he strained to remember names from the files of the missing Violets. "Gig Marshall?"

Again, the off-kilter grin. "Shh, shh." She touched a finger to his lips to chide him, then, rising in his lap, she pulled the bedsheet off his body. As she settled back into position, the down of her pubic hair brushed against his skin.

His penis stiffened without his consent, and a wave of both excitement and revulsion shuddered through him. "Sylvia Perez?"

Ignoring the question, she spread her hands on his chest and massaged his pectoral muscles, leaning close enough for him to feel her breath on his cheek.

Dan grabbed her wrists, holding her at bay while he compared her expression with those in the file photos of the victims. It didn't seem to match, unless...

His mouth dropped open. He had seen that half-grin before. *"Russell Travers."*

She snickered like a schoolboy who'd been caught mimicking his teacher. "It's all right. I'm a girl now."

Squirming back against the headboard, Dan struggled

to superimpose the bulbous spectacles and sagging cheeks of the fifty-three-year-old man over Natalie's porcelain visage. He now recalled reading that Travers was gay.

"She won't mind," Travers promised him in Natalie's voice. "She likes you. You know that, don't you? I've seen it in her mind."

Dan's breath became so rapid that it made him light-headed. He released his grip on Natalie's wrists.

She slipped her arms around his chest and pulled him against her breasts. She wasn't wearing a bra, and he could see her hardened nipples outlined by the fabric of her T-shirt. The lopsided grin faded. *"Please,"* Travers begged. "There's no one to touch where I am. Please touch me."

She kissed him on the mouth, but Dan kept his lips pursed and pushed her back. "Come *on*, Natalie. Wake up!"

"Please." Wriggling against him, she wormed her hands up under his T-shirt, her palms searing his skin. "I've been so cold and lonely…."

Dan gently tilted her chin up to look into her eyes. "I'm sorry."

Then he slapped her cheek. An open-handed smack, just enough to sting. She blinked in shock and shook her head like a dog bitten by fleas. Her facial muscles spasmed and shifted, and the desire in her eyes dimmed to disorientation. She recoiled from him, wiping her hands on her shirt as if to cleanse them, and glanced from his body to hers in a panic. "Oh, my God. What happened?"

Dan held a hand out to her. "Natalie—"

She scuttled, crablike, off the foot of the bed, and hid her face in her hands. *"What have you done?"*

Dan couldn't tell to whom she shrieked the question. "It's okay! Nothing happened."

Twisting away from him, she ran into the bathroom and slammed the door.

Dan sighed and sagged back against the headboard. *Another brilliant Atwater maneuver.*

He waited for several minutes before crossing the room to tap on the bathroom door. "Natalie? Do you want to talk?"

No answer.

Dan stood by the door for another minute, but went back to bed without knocking again. Staring at the ceiling, he watched the urine-yellow cast of the room give way to the bluish predawn sunlight filtering through the hotel's tinted windows. Eventually, the phone beside him jangled with his morning wake-up call.

It was unnecessary.

14

Slide Show

"TELL US WHAT WE'RE SEEING HERE," CLARK COM-manded from the other side of the conference table, his glasses reflecting the projected image of Arthur McCord's eviscerated body.

Dan blinked his sleep-deprived eyes and directed his laser pointer at the screen behind him. "Well, the killer obviously staged the body to humiliate and dominate the victim. With its feet toward the door, the corpse was arranged for maximum emotional impact on whoever entered the room. By placing McCord's hands inside this abdominal incision, the killer demonstrates his mastery over his victim. The circle..." He cleared his throat. "...the circle formed by the small intestine suggests that the perpetrator perceives the killing as a sort of ritual sacrifice, possibly to gain mystical power of some kind."

He pressed the remote control in his left hand, and took the opportunity to glance at Natalie as the slide changed. She'd chosen to wear a collar-length wig of straight black hair and a pair of contacts that made her eyes a rich chocolate brown. She'd hardly looked at him all morning and even now sat with her eyes shut. Perhaps she'd fallen asleep, or perhaps she simply couldn't bear the horrors of the slide presentation.

The latest photo was a close-up of the words carved into Arthur McCord's chest. The coroner had placed a ruler in the picture to show the exact size of the letters. "With the grotesque humor of the pun on 'open door,' the killer further debases his victim. He also suggests that, by performing this ritual sacrifice, he is establishing some connection with the world of the afterlife—a connection once possessed by the deceased conduit."

Clark leaned back in his chair and arched his fingers. "And what would be your profile of the UNSUB?"

"From what Natalie saw of the victim's memories, McCord apparently tried to remove the killer's mask. Although he didn't succeed, he saw enough of the UNSUB's throat to make us believe the killer is a Caucasian male in his late twenties or early thirties with a clean-shaven chin. Is that right?"

She lifted her head just long enough to nod.

"The fact that he could subdue McCord, a much larger and heavier man, suggests that the killer is in good physical condition. The ME found no sign of sexual abuse on the body, and the UNSUB has shown no preference as far as race, age, or gender in his choice of victims. Therefore, sexual gratification does not seem to be the principal motive for the crime.

"Rather, the UNSUB seems to be an individual who is intimately acquainted with Violets and harbors intense rage against them, possibly arising from some irrational envy of their ability to communicate with the dead. By killing them, he intends to prove himself superior to them.

He may also believe that he is collecting the power of his victims. That would explain why he carved out the eyes." Dan pressed the remote again, and a close-up of McCord's face flashed onto the screen, its empty sockets red and gaping, tear-trails of blood and vitreous fluid streaking the cheeks.

The frown lines on Clark's face grew a bit deeper. "Why now?" He thrust a hand toward the desecrated face onscreen. "Why this? Before, the guy wouldn't even let us find a body. Now he's decorating them to impress us. Why?"

Dan set the pointer and remote on the table. "Serial killers tend to escalate the violence of their crimes. Their rage feeds on itself, and with every murder, they grow bolder, more eager to intensify their violent fantasies. It's possible this guy needed to 'practice' on a few victims before he got up the nerve to flaunt his handiwork.

"The good news is, the cockier the killer gets, the more he lets us know about him. The incisions he used to form the letters on McCord's chest seem to have been made left to right, suggesting that the UNSUB is right-handed."

Clark rolled his eyes. "That narrows it down to a little more than half the white male population. You turn up anything, Yolena?"

Seated opposite Natalie, Detective Garcia shook her head. "Not much. The bloody footprints taken from the floor of the shop match the ones from the Gannons' backyard."

"Which means we're only dealing with one guy."

"Not necessarily. Those footprints don't match the impressions we found in the carpet in Laurie Gannon's bedroom, so either the perp changed shoes or there's someone else at work here."

"Swell. What about the bullets from McCord's gun?"

"We finally found both slugs, but no traces of blood on either of 'em." Estelle Blair, the crime scene technician, consulted her clipboard. "All the samples we took from the floor are McCord's blood type, although we've sent them off for DNA analysis, just in case. Unfortunately, it looks like McCord missed."

"Um-hmm. And how does all this fit in with the bomb plot at the School?"

Dan switched on the conference room's overhead fluorescents. The light whited-out the projector screen except for the dark pits of McCord's eyes. "Another act of rage against Violets. The killer wants to make a statement, and all the victims have ties to the School. I think it's highly probable that he either worked there or knew one of the students who went there. Maybe a friend or family member."

"Cheery thought. For what it's worth, we've already obtained School employee files for the past twenty years." Clark shoved a stack of manila folders down the table toward him. "A few misdemeanors and juvenile offenses, but no criminal records. They're pretty picky about who they let work there. What about these friends of McCord you mentioned?"

"McCord said that only a handful of people knew where he was hiding from the Corps. The only ones left alive are Lucinda Kamei, his younger brother Simon ... and Natalie."

She didn't react. Her eyes were open now, but they

seemed to be staring inward, oblivious to the proceedings in the conference room.

"Mmm. You think these people might know something?" Clark asked.

"They might know who else could have found Arthur McCord. And they might be our killer's next targets."

"Where are they?"

"Kamei's in 'Frisco, Simon McCord's in Seattle. Both under police protection. I thought, if they compared notes with Natalie, we might turn up something."

"All right, go with it. But keep your cell phone handy in case we need you."

Clark, Garcia, and Blair all rose to leave, but Natalie still slouched in her chair.

"I suppose this means I have to *fly* again?" she muttered.

Dan smiled, relieved to hear her complaining. Another strained silence ensued when they were alone, however. Dan collected Clark's stack of manila files under his arm, and Natalie accompanied him to the conference room exit without saying a word.

He stopped her at the door. "Listen, about what happened—"

"It wasn't your fault." She avoided his gaze. "I wasn't ready for Russell. I'm sorry. It won't happen again."

"Don't worry about that. I just wanted you to know that I didn't—you know, that nothing—"

"I know." This time, she looked him in the eye and touched his arm. "I only wish you hadn't seen me that way."

In his head, Dan heard Russell Travers tease him with Natalie's voice: *She likes you, you know....*

He hugged the files to his side. "I don't know about you,

but I'm starving. Can I treat you to lunch? No fast food, I promise."

The melancholy clouding her face lifted a bit. "Actually, I am kind of hungry, now that you mention it."

"Great." He opened the door for her. "By the way . . . anyone ever tell you you look good as a brunette?"

The corners of her mouth turned upward. "Not lately, no."

Dan feigned shock. "Wait! Is that an actual *smile* on your face? You can't be Natalie. Who are you?"

She laughed. "Watch it, Dan, or you'll wish it *wasn't* me."

15

Distant Transmissions

THE MAN IN THE PRIMER-GRAY CAMARO WAITED
until well past three A.M., an hour after the last of the gang-
bangers had left, before getting out of his car.

While biding his time, he reclined the driver's seat so
that his profile was out of view and angled his rearview
mirror to reflect the entrance of the abandoned shop
across the street, which fluttered with strips of torn yellow
POLICE LINE DO NOT CROSS ribbon. Wearing a pair of Pana-
sonic headphones, he stuck the long black nose of a directional microphone in the corner of his rolled-down
window and turned it right and left, eavesdropping on the
nightlife of Vine Street.

Clement Everett Maddox was a careful man, and the
problem of getting into Arthur McCord's former residence
posed a particular challenge for him. After the murder, the
police had chained the door shut and sealed the place as a
crime scene. Clem could have gotten past these obstacles
on his own, but he was concerned that the police might put
the shop under surveillance, at least for the first week or so.
Better to let someone else do the dirty work and draw out
any cops who might be watching, he decided.

The night after the cops collected their evidence and

left, Clem had gone to buy a few rocks of crack from one of the pushers on Hollywood Boulevard, a beefy bulldog named Pedro. Clem didn't use drugs—he flushed the rocks down the john when he got back to his fleabag motel—but the deal gave him an excuse to chat up the dealer. "Hey, you hear what happened to that dead-talker down on Vine? Wild, huh?"

"Yeah." Murder was hardly newsworthy in Pedro's business. He ignored Clem and scanned the street for his next customer.

"Killer must've been looking for his money."

"Uh-huh." Pedro still didn't look at him. "And how would you know?"

"Used to deliver the guy's groceries." This was a lie, but it piqued Pedro's interest. "Crazy bastard. Never left his shop, so he paid me to bring all his stuff to him. Always cash. And I know for a fact he never went to a bank. If I had any balls, I'd go for his stash myself."

The dealer turned to him, eyes unreadable behind midnight black shades. "What makes you think it's still there?"

"Because the cops couldn't find a motive for the killing. Said so on the police band of my CB. If the place'd been robbed, they'd've reported it as both a one-eighty-seven *and* a four-sixty—homicide and burglary." This was another lie, but Pedro didn't know that. "Won't matter, though. In a couple days, the cops'll rip the place apart and give whatever they find to the state."

"Yeah. That's a pisser, all right." Pedro walked away without a backward glance.

Clem couldn't tell whether Pedro bought the BS, so he formulated plans to break into the shop himself if the dealer wimped out on him. Nevertheless, Maddox stationed himself across the street from McCord's place the following night, just in case. He counted on the fact that crack dealers tended to be addicts themselves and would find it hard to pass up any opportunity to score cash for their next fix.

Clem was about to give up hope when, around two in the morning, Pedro finally showed. He and two of his buddies sauntered up the street and stopped in front of McCord's shop, where they met a couple of their comrades who happened to be walking the other way. Clem admired their acting. They high-fived each other with the enthusiasm of friends meeting purely by chance.

Pedro and his two tallest, broadest-shouldered pals lit cigarettes and started talking with one another, casually blocking the view of the shop door. Wearing baggy coats too heavy for the warm night, their two smaller friends disappeared behind them. Through his headphones, Clem heard a muffled crunch as they punched out the glass at the base of the door.

The B&E boys must've had some trouble getting past McCord's layers of chicken wire and insulation in the shop, because the guys out front chained an entire pack of smokes while waiting for them to finish their strip-mine search of the shop's interior. Finally, the two smaller men emerged from behind their beefy friends, their faces betraying no emotion. Clem aimed the directional mike at them.

"You get it?" Pedro asked one of them, his voice distorted and tinny in Clem's headphones.

"Not here, man. Tell you later." If he was angry about

not finding any money, he didn't let it show. *Who knows?* Clem mused. *Maybe ol' Arthur really did have a few bucks lying around.*

Pedro and his pals stamped out their cigarette butts, gave each other another round of high-fives, and parted company as calmly as they'd arrived, leaving a huge hole of darkness in the bottom half of the shop's front door.

Clem remained in his car, watching. No cops came. He checked the street with his mike as best he could but didn't catch any conversations that sounded like police. A Winchell's Donut shop clerk stepped out onto the sidewalk for a cigarette. A customer holding a cruller and coffee joined him, and they discussed the Lakers' upcoming season. Not plainclothes, Maddox decided.

He nudged the headphones' right speaker off his ear, turned up the volume on his CB radio, and scanned the police band. No 460s for this area. If anyone had noticed the break-in, they hadn't bothered to report it. Not surprising—this was West Hollywood, after all.

When he sensed that it was safe to proceed, Clem set aside his mike and got out of the Camaro. Although he could easily have jaywalked across the street at that hour, he strolled down to the nearest intersection and used the crosswalk. With his shaggy hair, unshaven face, and dirty, oversized Army jacket, he could easily pass for a homeless veteran. If a cop caught him in the shop, he'd claim he was simply seeking a place to flop for the night.

Pedro's friends had knocked most of the glass out of the lower part of the shop's door, then cut through the chicken wire and insulation and peeled it forward to protect themselves from the jagged edges of the hole as they crawled through it. Seeing no immediate threat on the street, Clem wriggled through the opening into the shop's coal-pit darkness.

Once inside, he took a palm-sized flashlight from one of his coat pockets and used it to scan the foil-lined walls of the entryway. He got to his feet, grinning. McCord's Faraday cage fascinated Clem, and he toyed with the idea of making one just like it.

Pushing his way through the door into the séance room, Maddox flinched a little as the bell jingled on its coiled spring, then smiled at his own jumpiness. Nothing to worry about now, of course.

He swept the flashlight beam around the room. Pedro's boys had done a job on it. The cloth banners had been ripped from the walls and the underlying insulation slashed.

His excitement growing, Clem held the flashlight in his teeth while he scooped a cheap Sony AM/FM radio out of another coat pocket and put on the headphones. Switching on the radio, he thumbed the tuner slowly across the dial. McCord's cage worked well: Clem heard nothing but static, as though he were standing under a metal bridge.

He wasn't searching for music, however. When he got to one end of the dial, he reversed direction, working his way back through the radio spectrum, sifting for a whisper of intelligence among the formless fuzz of white noise. And again, walking around the room and swinging the radio from side to side like a dowsing rod or Geiger counter. Nothing.

It appeared that the genie had escaped its bottle. What a pity.

Still, Clem would not leave empty-handed. While he ordinarily sought some personal item from the deceased, he knew that, in this case, he could obtain something far more effective.

Removing the headphones, Maddox knelt on the floor and pointed the flashlight at the patch of dried blood that coated the rubber matting at the room's center. The police had taken copious samples as evidence, but there was plenty more to be had.

Blood was perfect for Clem's purposes. Blood was *resonant*.

He set aside his Walkman, reached in yet another pocket of his coat, and withdrew a Swiss army knife, a three-by-five index card, and a glassine envelope. Holding the flashlight in his mouth, he used one of the knife's blades to loosen flakes of blood off the mat. He scraped a small pile of the rusty dust onto the card and poured it into the envelope, which he carefully sealed and put back in his pocket.

Struck with sudden inspiration, Clem picked up his Walkman and pried off its back cover with the knife's flathead screwdriver. Collecting some more brandy-brown dust on the three-by-five card, he salted the powder into the radio's exposed circuitry and snapped the cover back into place.

"Soon, Amy," he whispered. "Not much longer now...."

Clem shoved the radio and his other belongings in his pockets, keeping only the flashlight in hand to find his way back to the hole in the front door. He wanted to test the radio's reception as soon as he'd wriggled out of McCord's cage and into the open air of Vine Street, but he forced himself to wait until he returned to the shelter of the Camaro.

Reclining in the driver's seat with the Sony's head-phones on, he again scanned the dial. This time, bursts of music and snatches of deejay jabber swelled in his ears with each station he passed. He didn't stop at any of these sta-tions, however, but paused instead at the dead spaces of in-terference between them, listening to the fog of static.

He'd nearly reached the far end of the radio's spectrum when a barely audible murmur penetrated the hiss of white noise, like a transmission broadcast from a distant star.

Clem took his thumb from the Walkman's tuner with a smile of satisfaction, as if listening to the strains of a fa-vorite melody.

16

DWG

THE STREETS OF SAN FRANCISCO'S PACIFIC HEIGHTS district resembled overstocked bakery shelves, with Victorian houses packed roof-to-roof along the sidewalks like so many gingerbread confections. Lucinda Kamei's house shared the eclectic architecture of its neighbors. Ornamented with a round tower at its left front corner and frosted with burgundy paint and lacy, wedding-cake white trim, it managed to look both ostentatious and charming at the same time.

The curbs along the street were already crammed with cars, so Dan and Natalie had to park their rented Buick several blocks away. Although better rested today, Natalie still seemed shell-shocked, her eyes downcast as they walked back to the house. As far as he knew, she hadn't permitted herself to cry over Arthur's death. Or Evan's either, for that matter.

They were just kids back then....She's gotta be over him by now, Dan thought, wondering why her former love life was suddenly so important to him.

From the corner of his eye, he tried to read the stony blankness of her expression. "You okay?"

She exhaled and squared her shoulders. "I just realized...it's been almost six years since I saw Lucy last. When she taught at the School, she was like my big sister. I don't know—I can't believe it's been that long."

"Yeah. Time flies even when you're not having fun."

A man with close-cropped black hair sat in a deck chair on the porch of the house, and as they approached he stood and descended the front steps to meet them.

"Hey, there!" He smiled broadly. "What can I do for you folks?"

Dan noted the loose-fitting Hawaiian shirt the man wore over his white T-shirt. He was willing to bet there was a holstered automatic there. "We wanted to speak to Ms. Kamei for a few minutes."

"She's a bit busy today. Mind if I ask who you are?"

"Dan Atwater, FBI." He handed the man his ID. "And this is Natalie Lindstrom of the N-double-A-C-C."

The man examined the badge and passed it back. "Oh, yeah—we heard you were coming." He extended a hand, which Dan and Natalie shook in turn. "John Ruehl of the Corps Security Division. Let me see what Ms. Kamei's up to."

He tilted his head to one side, directing his voice toward the collar of his Hawaiian shirt, and held a hand to his right ear. "Hey, Steph, I got Atwater and Lindstrom here. Okay if they come in?" He chuckled at some unheard response. "Yeah, I'll warn 'em. Later, babe!"

He beckoned Dan and Natalie to follow him up the porch steps. "Ms. Kamei's at work right now, and there's no telling when she'll finish. Interrupt her at your own risk." With a wry smirk, he opened the front door for them.

The house welcomed them inside with the lemon-oil scent of polished wood. Persian and Chinese rugs of various sizes formed padded pathways over the parquet floor, while ornate Victorian cabinets and marble-topped tables of cherry and walnut displayed exquisite carvings of jade and ivory. A crystal chandelier glittered above the carpeted staircase, the teardrops of glass refracting tiny rainbows onto the walls.

Dan whistled appreciatively as Ruehl shut the door behind them. "Your friend Lucy sure knows how to decorate."

"One of the perks of working for the Art Division. She gets royalties on every piece of music she transcribes."

Dan detected a note of envy in Natalie's voice. He nudged her with his elbow and smiled. "Can't buy you happiness, right?"

"Maybe not, but it makes misery a lot more comfortable."

They started to move forward, gaping at the museum-quality antiques around them, but a stocky woman wearing jeans and a black suit coat hurried toward them with her hand raised. "Stop!"

Dan and Natalie exchanged a perplexed glance.

The woman pointed at their feet. "Take off your shoes."

A bit nonplussed, Dan slipped off his Florsheims and picked them up, noticing as he did so that the woman was also in her stocking feet. She indicated a rubber mat to the right of the front door, where a pair of woman's Reeboks already sat. "Over there."

When he and Natalie had placed their footwear in the designated spot, the woman relaxed. "Sorry about that. You wouldn't believe how old some of these damn rugs are." She shook hands with them. "Stephanie Corbett, Corps Security. Ms. Kamei's in the front parlor."

She led them to a pair of sliding lacquered doors on their left. In the room beyond, someone played a piano, repeating the same turbulent, minor-key theme over and over with subtle changes in its tempo and phrasing.

"If she asks, this was *your* idea," Corbett whispered, rapping on the door.

The melody ended with a thunderous, dissonant chord that resounded with the player's fury. *"Mein Gott!"*

The guttural voice continued to curse in German for more than a minute before falling silent. Corbett leaned toward the door. "Ms. Kamei?"

She lifted her fist to knock again, but the door jerked open a few inches to reveal the silhouetted figure of a woman. Light outlined the pale surface of her bald scalp.

"Didn't I tell you not to bother me?" the woman snapped in perfect English as she tore the Soul Leash off her head. Resembling a miniature pair of headphones, the electronic Leash served the same precautionary function as the Panic Button on a SoulScan. "It's bad enough you invade my home. Now I can't even work in peace!"

"Sorry, ma'am, but the folks from the FBI are here."

Corbett stepped back, allowing Kamei to see her guests. "Boo?"

"Hey, Lucy." Natalie raised a hand in greeting. "Been a long time."

"God, I'm sorry! Come in, come in." Kamei slid the double doors open for them. Dan thanked Corbett with a look as she took her post outside the room.

He and Natalie entered a rectangular chamber paneled with golden oak. Lace curtains softened the sunlight coming through the curved windows where the base of the round tower formed one corner of the room. The temperature here was noticeably cooler than in the rest of the house, and a humidifier sat on a table in one corner, exhaling cold steam. The reason for the climate control was obvious: The parlor housed at least a half-dozen antique musical instruments. The crowded room contained an early pianoforte with a boxy, triangular case and an even older harpsichord inlaid with mother-of-pearl and ivory and trimmed with gold leaf. A glass case displayed a viola and two violins that Dan surmised were either Strads or something equally priceless. In electric contrast to the room's other items, a charred Stratocaster guitar with a broken neck dominated the wall nearest the door, flanked by neon-colored prints of a Keith Haring dancing man and Andy Warhol's silk-screen portrait of Marilyn Monroe.

The two Violets embraced like long-lost twins. "Arthur told me," Kamei said as Natalie opened her mouth to speak.

Akin to her house, Lucinda Kamei was an intriguing amalgam of apparent contradictions. From reading her file, Dan knew that she was forty-six years old, but he could not have guessed her age from her hairless head and smooth, soy-milk skin. Her Japanese features made her violet eyes all the more striking since one would have expected them to be brown. Though surrounded by turn-of-the-century elegance, she wore a sleeveless Led Zeppelin concert T-shirt and a pair of black sweatpants.

"Forgive us for disturbing you, Ms. Kamei," Dan said. "Unfortunately, our questions can't wait."

"I understand. And you'll have to pardon Ludwig for his

temper." She pronounced the name *Loodvig*. "He can get pretty grumpy sometimes."

Her casual remark left him starstruck for a moment. He pointed to the pianoforte, upon which sat an old-fashioned calligraphic pen, an inkwell, and the scattered pages of an incomplete musical score. "You mean...?"

"Yeah. He likes to continue his work now that he can actually hear the music again. That piano was his—I use it as a touchstone when we collaborate. You must be Agent Atwater." She smiled at his surprise. "Arthur said you'd probably come to visit."

"Oh...yeah." *Someday,* he thought, *I'll get used to dead people talking about me behind my back.* "What did Mr. McCord tell you about his death?"

"About what you'd expect."

"He said that you, Natalie, and his brother were the only people alive who knew where to find him."

Kamei frowned. "And? Surely you don't think *we*—"

"I think what Dan's saying is that the killer could only have found out about Arthur from one of us," Natalie interjected. "Can you think of anyone who might have spied on you when you wrote or visited him?"

Kamei considered the question, but sighed and shook her head. "Maybe the Corps or the School, but they wouldn't kill Arthur. They'd want him alive."

"If they *had* tracked him down, could someone at the Corps or School have found out about it?" Dan asked. "An employee, say?"

"Maybe."

He took some papers out of the inside pocket of his suit coat and unfolded them. They were photocopies of some of the photos of School employees that Clark had given him. "Do you recognize any of these people?"

She scanned the sheets he handed her. "I remember some of them, sure, but it's been a long time. I haven't been to the School since I taught a music class two years ago."

"Do you recall anyone there acting strangely? Anyone who might've had something against Mr. McCord or Violets in general?"

"No. The Corps always screened out the weirdos with psych tests and background checks."

"And did you ever tell anyone else where Mr. McCord was?"

"Never."

Natalie bit her lower lip in hesitation. "What about Simon?"

Kamei shot an indignant glare at her. "Arthur was his *brother*. He didn't have anything to do with this."

Dan waited for one of them to elaborate, but both women seemed reluctant to discuss the subject. "Did Simon McCord have something against Arthur?"

Kamei drew a sharp breath. "Arthur and Simon had very different attitudes about their careers...."

Natalie snorted. "You can say that again. Simon's a religious nut."

Kamei grimaced but didn't contradict her. "Simon believes conduits have been given a gift from God and that we have a holy duty to use our ability for human enlightenment. He was royally pissed at Arthur for leaving the Corps."

Dan looked at Natalie. "You think Simon would rat out Arthur to the Corps?"

"No. If anything, Simon was jealous of all the attention Arthur got. He sees himself as some kind of über-Violet, and always felt like he was living in his brother's shadow. He wouldn't want Arthur back in the Corps." She gave Kamei a guarded look. "But…he might want to make an *example* of Arthur as a warning to other Violets who want to run away."

Dan sighed. "That would fit the profile, all right. But what about the other victims?"

"Well, Laurie Gannon's mother pulled her out of the School. And I know that Evan and Sondra hated their work at Quantico. The job there is infamous for driving conduits crazy. As for Jem, Gig, and the others, I don't know—job dissatisfaction is high among us."

"And the bomb plot at the School? Why kill all those kids?"

Natalie shrugged. "Simon used to teach there, before the Corps let him set up his own conduit training program at his commune in New Mexico. Since then, he's been pushing the Corps to give him control over education of *all* Violets. Blowing up the School would eliminate the competition."

Kamei shook her head. "Simon's weird, but I can't believe he'd do anything like this."

"Maybe so, but we'd better have a talk with Mr. McCord regardless. You realize, Ms. Kamei, that until we have the killer in custody, you're in terrible danger. Are you sure you'll be safe here?"

She smiled with a touch of disdain. "Don't worry about me. I'm under house arrest 'til this thing is over. If I even sneeze, Steph and John'll come running."

"If you say so. But if you want to move to a safer location, call me." Dan gave her his business card. "Thanks for your help."

She nodded, her face suddenly aged with concern. "If there's anything else I can do..."

"We'll be in touch."

Natalie gave Kamei a good-bye hug. "Lucy."

"Boo." She rubbed her hand up and down Natalie's back. "You don't need to wait for someone's death as an excuse to come visit, you know."

"I know."

They separated, both glassy-eyed but habitually unwilling to weep.

As he and Natalie moved to leave, Dan let his gaze linger on the charred Stratocaster mounted on the wall. "Do you work with Jimi as well?" he asked Kamei.

She gave him another bitter smile. "No, Jimi's not in the Corps canon—not a DWG."

"A what?"

Natalie chuckled. "Dead White Guy."

Kamei walked to the guitar and ran her fingertips over the blackened patch where Hendrix had squirted lighter fluid on the Strat and set it ablaze. "I bought this for myself at a Christie's auction. Had to outbid Paul Allen and the Hard Rock Café. I've tried using it to call Jimi—on my own, without the Corps' knowledge. He never comes, though." She lowered her hand. "It gives me hope."

Dan glanced at Natalie, who answered his silent question with her eyes: Yes, this was one of the stories she'd heard.

"Thank you," he said to Kamei in a hoarse voice. As they

left Kamei's house and began the long walk back to their car, Dan clenched his hands into fists so Natalie wouldn't see them shaking.

"You up for a flight to Seattle?" he asked, trying to brighten the mood.

"Does it matter?" she said.

"No. But at least we can grab some dinner first. I remember this great little seafood restaurant—"

In turning his head toward her, Dan caught sight of the cars parked on the opposite side of the street. A Toyota Camry about halfway down the block had its driver's-side window rolled down. As they walked forward, the glare on the windshield diminished, giving Dan a glimpse inside the car.

The man in the driver's seat lowered his camera and blew a big pink bubble until it popped.

Dan flashed back to the School and the gooey-fresh bubble gum stuck to his shoe.

Natalie became wary as he slowed his steps. "What is it?"

"I don't know." He avoided staring at the car so as not to spook the driver. "But why don't you go and keep Agent Ruehl company for a minute?"

He gave her an encouraging nudge back toward the house. She frowned but did as he suggested.

Keeping the Camry in his peripheral vision, Dan jay-walked across the street, glancing at his watch to give the impression that he was a busy man with appointments to keep. When he reached the opposite sidewalk, he kept walking with the same purposeful stride—brisk, but not hurried.

The car remained where it was.

Dan quickened his steps down the street. He was less than twenty feet away when the Camry's engine started.

Breaking into a run, Dan pulled out his Bureau badge and held it open in front of him. "FBI! Get out of the car *NOW!*"

The car backed up a foot, then peeled out from the curb. Dan tried to block the way before it could accelerate, but the driver swerved around him. The man behind the wheel was a nondescript white male wearing a baseball cap.

Instinctively, Dan drew his .38, but froze before pulling the trigger. He cursed and ran after the Camry as it squealed up the street, its tires smoking rubber. He kept it in view long enough to read the license plate number, which he recited to himself while watching the car disappear.

Holstering his gun, he wrote the number in his pocket memo book and returned to Kamei's house to get Natalie. His face must've told her how angry he was.

"What happened?" she asked.

"I think I just let our prime suspect get away."

17

In Between

NATALIE WATCHED HIM FROM THE BUICK'S PASSEN-ger seat. "Well?"

Dan folded up the cell phone and hung it back on his belt. "The Camry was a rental from a local Hertz agency. The cops are going to have the agent look up the renter's ID and see if they can track him down for questioning."

"You really think it was *him*?"

Dan drummed his fingers on the steering wheel. "I hope not...."

Natalie touched his shoulder. "You couldn't shoot a man for chewing gum."

"Maybe not. But I *could* have blown a hole in his tire if I wasn't so trigger-shy."

"Better safe than sorry, right? You can't take back a bullet, you know."

"Oh, yeah. I know."

Neither of them was overflowing with joy at the moment. Dan, of course, had added yet another blunder to his record-breaking streak, while Natalie had been sliding steadily into an even deeper funk than usual. Perhaps her grief for Arthur had finally caught up with her.

Or maybe it's for Evan, the little sly voice in his head added. *Let's not forget about dear, departed Evan.*

On second thought, Dan amended, *let's MAKE ourselves forget about Evan.*

"So what do we do now?" Natalie asked. Her tone implied that all the possible alternatives would be equally dreary.

Dan knew of only one sure way to snap her out of it: He would have to make her really, *really* mad at him.

He pasted a cheery smile on his face and rubbed his hands together. "I have some bad news and some good news. The bad news is Clark sees no reason why we shouldn't go on up to Seattle to chat with Simon McCord. The good news is our flight isn't 'til nine tonight, which means we have about ten hours to kill. Let's have some fun, shall we?"

She looked askance at him. "You think it's a good idea to go out on the town when there's a murderer running around?"

"A moving target is harder to hit."

Natalie pinched the bridge of her nose. "Dan, I appreciate your trying to cheer me up, but I'm really not in the mood."

"I know." With barely a flinch, he took hold of her hand. "I just hate to see you live your life in a box."

She yanked her hand away. "What's *that* supposed to mean?"

"It means I've been living in a box for the past two years, and it hasn't been worth it."

"What's *your* life got to do with *mine?*"

He turned his face toward the window. "I only wanted to say that you shouldn't be afraid—"

"What, I'm some kind of loser because I take the stairs instead of the elevator and don't eat junk food? And you're a fine one to talk about being afraid! You don't have someone out there who wants to cut open your stomach and rip out your eyes."

"You're right," Dan replied softly. "And hiding away might help you live longer. But what's the point of living longer if you're stuck in a room your whole life?"

His words seemed to short-circuit her anger, and she drooped in her seat with a defeated look. "Yeah. A big black room."

"What?"

"Never mind." She sulked like an eight-year-old in detention. "Where did you want to go, anyway?"

Dan started the car. "The last place the killer would ever think of looking for you."

He answered her scowl with an enigmatic smile. She remained sullen, so he switched on the radio to fill the silence during the hour-long trip to Santa Clara.

"You've *got* to be kidding," she groaned as they finally arrived at Paramount's Great America amusement park.

Dan drove into the massive parking lot. "You have to admit, your chances of being disemboweled here are pretty slim."

"Yeah, I'll die of a heart attack instead. Honestly, do you really think risking my life on a bunch of rickety roller coasters is my idea of a good time?"

"Relax. You don't have to go on any rides. We can just walk around and laugh at all the people waiting in line."

He paid the fee to the attendant in the booth at the entrance and parked the car as close to the main gate as possible. "Shall we?" he asked, removing his tie and unbuttoning the collar of his shirt.

Natalie sighed, but got out with him.

They purchased their admission tickets, and Dan treated Natalie to dinner at the Pasta Connection, the furthest thing from fast food Great America had to offer. After their meal, they strolled around the park's midway, taking in the kaleidoscopic landscape of colored lights and the sonic clash of rock-and-roll and circus music as they moved from one attraction to another.

Natalie gravitated toward the park's diverse array of roller coasters, which bore such forbidding names as The Demon, Greased Lightnin', and Invertigo. The tortuous tracks of wood and metal and the Doppler-shifting shrieks of the riders held a perverse allure for her. She studied the people on the rides as though they were an alien species, the fascination on her face a mixture of disbelief and childlike admiration as she saw them wave their arms over their heads to enhance their sensation of helplessness. "Why? Why would you ever take the chance?"

Dan watched Invertigo turn its passengers upsidedown with a 360-degree loop. "Sometimes coming close to death makes you feel more alive."

"I suppose." Natalie didn't seem convinced, yet she kept her gaze fixed on the riders as they screamed up and down the coaster's dips and around its curves, mesmerized by their casual indifference to danger.

With dusk descending, they returned to the main gate

and the enormous, two-tiered Columbia Carousel. Dan nudged Natalie. "How 'bout it?"

She gaped, openmouthed, at the rotating cavalcade of fiberglass horses and circus animals, and shook her head. "Oh, no! You said I didn't have to go on any rides."

"I know, I know, but this is just a merry-go-round. They have safety belts, and I'll be right there beside you. Nothing's gonna happen. Why, I bet you haven't been on one of these since you were a kid."

Her mouth became very small, and she gazed at the carousel as though it were a poster in a travel agency window. "I've *never* been on one."

He gently took her hand. "Trust me."

She peered into his eyes for a moment, then permitted him to lead her into the crowd of children, parents, and amorous couples waiting in line. Natalie's hand tightened on his as the carousel slowed to a stop and the previous riders dismounted.

The ride attendant out front unfastened the chain that held back the waiting crowd and waved them forward. They stepped onto the carousel platform, and Dan guided Natalie to a white charger with a flowing mane and tail, its mouth frozen in a permanent whinny. "Put your left foot in the metal loop there and swing your other leg over—"

"I *know* how to do it. I'm terrified, not stupid." She brushed off his attempt to give her a boost and grabbed the pommel to pull herself into the saddle. Buckling the canvas safety belt across her lap, she seized the metal pole in front of her in a white-knuckled grip. "If I die, I'm going to have Lucy bring me back just to bitch at you."

A female ride attendant came around the carousel and

directed Dan to the white tiger next to Natalie's stallion. "You'll have to take a seat, sir—we're about to start."

Dan patted Natalie's knee and got on the tiger. "Hang on. You'll be fine."

The carousel lurched into motion, and their mounts bobbed up and down.

"Yee-haw!" Dan whooped, grinning encouragement at Natalie.

She kept her face turned outward, toward the accelerating swirl of people and lights surrounding the merry-go-round. But the arch of her back and the pressure of her knees against the sides of the horse told Dan that every muscle in her body was as taut as a violin string, and she clung to her horse's pole as if it were the topmost mast of a sinking ship.

Guilt wore down his grin. *I shouldn't have pushed her so hard,* he thought as the merry-go-round drifted to a halt. He swung off his tiger and went to Natalie, who remained paralyzed on her fiberglass steed. "Thanks for being a good sport. Hop off, and we'll go get some ice cream."

She looked down at him, eyes shining. "Can we go again?"

Dan never managed to talk her into trying any of the roller coasters that night, but they did ride the carousel five more times before they had to leave. On their way out of the park, Dan bought some soft-serve, which they consumed while tramping back to their car.

Natalie giggled at him as he slid into the driver's seat, munching the last remnant of his cone. "You've got chocolate all over your face."

She moistened the corner of a crumpled napkin and swabbed his cheek clean. Dan laughed, but the playfulness of her touch made him pause. He snuck a sidelong glance at her face as she examined his mouth.

"That ought to do it," she concluded, and caught him staring at her.

Both their smiles faded. *Uh-oh*, Dan thought. *Busted*.

Natalie withdrew her hands with a guilty air. "I had fun tonight." She fidgeted with the dirty napkin in her lap. "I can't even remember when I had so much fun."

They took turns avoiding each other's gaze.

"I'm glad." Dan smiled and slipped the key into the ignition. "I only hope it makes up for tonight's plane flight—"

"Wait." She grabbed his hand. "Someone's knocking."

His pulse fluttered as Natalie pressed her palms to her forehead and mumbled to herself. "What can I do? Should we go somewhere?"

"No, it's okay. I know who—" Her body undulated as if wrenched by natal contractions, her head banging against the window, and Dan was afraid she'd smash right through the safety glass.

The convulsions soon passed, however, and she calmly righted herself in the seat and cocked her head toward Dan, her eyes half-lidded like pistachios peeking out of their shells.

"Natalie?" He frowned when she didn't respond. "Who am I talking to?"

"The name's Jeremy, son. But friends call me Jem." She spoke with a cultured southern lilt, her voice husky, and held her hands in an arthritic curl.

Someday I will get used to this, Dan vowed. "It's an honor to meet you, Mr. Whitman," he said aloud. "Dan Atwater, FBI. To what do I owe this unexpected pleasure?"

Whitman gave him a lazy smile that reminded Dan of lemonade and long afternoons. "Just doing what I can to watch the flock while the wolf's on the prowl."

The phrase jarred Dan's memory. "You came to Natalie before, in the hotel room. You said something about a wolf in sheep's clothing."

Whitman's grin went flat. "The man you're looking for *knows* us, inside and out. He might even be one of us."

"Like Simon McCord?"

Whitman mulled over the idea, sucking at Natalie's upper lip like there was a shred of beef caught between her teeth. "You know, I've been trying to talk to little Simon, but he turns me away every time I get close. Boy's good at his defensive mantras."

"What do *you* think about him?"

"Not sure. Simon's an odd bird, no mistake. Very full of himself. Keeps in prime shape, too, but could he snap that little girl's neck like a chicken's? Don't know. He has some students who could do it, though."

Dan raised an eyebrow. "Laurie Gannon said you were there when she died...."

Whitman nodded, the weary fatalism of the old etched onto Natalie's fresh features. "Tried to help, but got there too late. Takes longer to find a Violet when you haven't been summoned, and I've been bouncing around like a pinball trying to warn everybody. I was there at the end, though—at least I spared her that much."

"Weren't you the one who told her about the Faceless Man?"

"Yep. Her and some of the other kids. Think I scared little Laurie enough that she begged her mom to take her out of the School. Much good that did."

The tension in Dan's muscles eased, and he almost forgot that this elderly black man was inhabiting a young woman's body. "Laurie saw a man at the School—young-looking, blond hair and mustache—who planted a bomb there. Natalie says that both he and the man who killed Laurie seemed to hesitate. Did you notice that?"

Whitman snorted. "Didn't think twice when he strangled *me*. But Laurie? Yeah…he had second thoughts about her."

They ruminated in silence for a bit, like two pigeon-feeders on a park bench, Dan afraid to speak the question that endlessly circled the Möbius strip in his mind. Finally, he asked it anyway.

"What's it like?"

Whitman studied him with Natalie's narrowed eyes, which now seemed unspeakably ancient. "You really want to know?"

Dan's answer caught in his throat. He bowed his head under the intensity of Whitman's stare.

"You remain whatever you were on this side," Whitman said quietly. "Your thoughts, your feelings, your memories—they become your world over there. And you can let your soul intersect with another's, each of you sharing everything you are."

"And is that…it?" Dan flushed, suddenly feeling stupid and shallow. "I heard there might be something…*beyond* that."

"Oh, there *is*." Whitman grinned. "See, most folks are so

caught up in things on this side, they can't let go, even when they pass on. They get stuck *in between*, afraid to go on, always wanting to go back. That's why you've got to make peace with your life while you can, so you can wave it good-bye when the time comes."

"Then some people *do* go on?"

"Sure. I'd go on myself if I wasn't watching after little Boo here." He glanced down at Natalie's pale arms and jutting breasts and laughed. "Wouldn't my mama pitch a fit to see me as a white girl!"

Dan couldn't help but laugh as well, despite—or, perhaps, because of—the macabre absurdity of the situation. "Why does everyone call her 'Boo,' anyway?"

"Oh! Well…" Jem chuckled as if remembering the punch line to a favorite joke. "When little Natalie first came to the School, she was such a skittish pup, scared of her own shadow. Arthur used to joke that he only had to say 'Boo!' and she'd jump right through the ceiling. He made that his pet name for her, and the rest of us picked it up." His expression sobered. "You keep a close eye on Boo, son. She's not ready to wave good-bye yet."

"I know." Dan forced himself to look directly into those bottomless eyes. "I will, Mr. Whitman."

"Told you, son—the name's Jem." He winked. "Guess I'd better excuse myself before I wear out my welcome. Dan, it's been a pleasure." He leaned back and closed Natalie's eyes.

"Jem?"

Whitman roused himself and looked at Dan.

"I hope we talk again soon."

"No offense, son," the old man grimly replied, "but I hope we *don't*."

He reclined in the passenger seat and seemed to nod off for a long-awaited nap. Natalie's body went slack, and a moment later she shivered to consciousness.

Dan held her hand while she reoriented herself. "Welcome back."

"You met Jem." She massaged her temples. "Did he give you any new ideas?"

"Sort of." He started the car and smiled. "You ready for another plane ride, Boo?"

"Don't call me that," she snapped.

His smile fell. *Nice work, Dan. Why not simply wave a picture of Evan right in her face?*

"Sorry. Didn't mean to offend."

"You didn't." She peered out the window at the receding glow of the amusement park as they pulled away. "I'm just sick of being scared."

18
Simon

A GLOOMY GRAY DRIZZLE HAD DESCENDED ON Seattle by the time they arrived at Simon McCord's apartment house the following morning.

A utilitarian square tower in the city's Capitol Hill district, the six-story building was quite a comedown for a man of McCord's self-importance. According to Natalie, he owned a twenty-acre ranch in northern New Mexico, where he trained the handpicked Violets she referred to as his "disciples." However, he and a couple of his students had traveled to Seattle to assist the local police in investigating the murders of several male prostitutes, and the city had rented out the entire top floor of this tower as a safe house for McCord's group.

Entering the foyer of the building, Dan and Natalie confronted the dented gray door of an old elevator.

Dan dabbed dew from his face. "Well?"

Natalie contemplated the decrepit door for a moment.

"I'll save my risk-taking for merry-go-rounds," she said, and strode past it.

Smiling, Dan followed her to the emergency stairs.

When they reached the sixth-floor hallway, a portly man with a thinning pompadour folded the newspaper he'd been reading and rose from his chair to intercept them. The .45 he wore on his hip told them what he was even before he introduced himself.

"You just missed him," he said when they asked to see Simon McCord. A Corps Security agent named Bender, he spoke with a Brooklyn accent, hooking his thumbs under the waistband of his one-hundred-percent polyester slacks. "He and them students of his went out to some graveyard."

Natalie grew wary. "Graveyard?"

"Yeah. To practice raising the dead or whatever. You know them freaks."

Dan saw Natalie stiffen, but she didn't let on that she was also one of "them freaks."

"Mr. McCord *does* know his life is in danger, doesn't he?" he asked Bender.

"Hey, that's exactly what we told him! But he's got a bug up his ass about this training he does."

Natalie chuckled. "That's Simon, all right."

"Can you tell us which graveyard they went to?" Dan said.

"Aw, crap! What was it?" Bender rubbed his forehead to summon the answer. "I forget the name, but it's where Bruce Lee's buried."

"Thanks. I'm sure we can find it."

Natalie glowered at him, but didn't say anything until they were back in the stairwell. "You want to meet Simon in a *cemetery*? Why don't you just have me walk through a minefield?"

"It's either that, or stay here with Bender and wait for him. Besides, what's the big deal?"

She sighed as they rounded the fourth-floor landing and continued down the stairs. "You'll see...."

Lake View Cemetery resided just north of Seattle's Volunteer Park, and served as the final resting place for Doc Maynard, Henry Yesler, and many of the city's other founding fathers. There, the forbidding mausoleums and iconic headstones of the past shared ground with the flat, in-soil grave markers of the present.

Dan and Natalie walked along the asphalt road that wound through the memorial park, the air around them heavy with dew and redolent of wet grass. The grayness of the day had dimmed the vibrant green of the rolling lawns and towering trees, making the landscape look flat and monochromatic, like an underexposed Polaroid.

Dan scanned the necropolis for Simon McCord. "Where is he likely to be?"

Natalie indicated an eclectic group of obelisks and bed-like sarcophagi off to their right. "Among the older graves; they're less likely to have metal-lined coffins. A Violet can use a buried body as a touchstone as long as there's no metal in the way. The soul jumps between the corpse and the conduit like a spark."

Dan stopped at the fringe of the grass. "Is that why...?"

"I'll be all right." She drew a lungful of breath and straightened her posture, rapt in yogic concentration. Mouthing words to herself, she set out across the turf, taking pains to walk far around any graves in her path.

Perhaps it was only the power of suggestion, but Dan became equally reluctant to tread on the deceased. When he inadvertently crossed the foot of one grave, he flinched back like a child afraid of stepping on a crack in the pavement.

Skirting a stand of pines, they came upon a broad expanse of grass lined with precise rows of headstones. Spectrally bright in the dreary afternoon, three white figures passed between the monuments, resembling cartoon ghosts in bedsheets. As he got closer, Dan saw that the sheets were actually monastic robes. One of the robed figures stalked ahead of the others, leading them at a rapid pace across a string of graves.

"That's him," Natalie said, and resumed her soundless mumbling.

McCord and his two apprentices all had shaved heads and held their hands pressed together in front of them. Their expressions twitched with facial tics, and their voices rose and fell in a weird chorus of seemingly random exclamations, like radios tuning in to different stations.

Those were souls, Dan realized. McCord and his disciples were donning and doffing dead personae as easily as a bunch of old hats.

A woman in a dark pantsuit moved to stop Dan and Natalie from reaching McCord's group. "Sorry, folks, this part of the cemetery is temporarily closed. Are you here to visit a loved one? We should be out of your way in a few—"

A sharp cry came from behind her. One of McCord's students stumbled and fell on his hands and knees behind a chiseled granite slab. McCord waited for his fallen protégé with the impatience of a supercilious schoolmaster.

A baby-faced young man with pink pale skin and blond eyebrows so fair as to be almost invisible, the student staggered to his feet, calling out in a high, thin voice. "Margery? Margery?" He clutched his head in apoplectic fear, eyes bulging. "Oh, my God, where am I? *MARGERY!*" He ran off through the garden of sprouting tombstones, tripping repeatedly on the hem of his robe.

Natalie's repetition accelerated, and the words became audible: " *'The Lord is my shepherd, I shall not want….'* "

McCord turned to his other pupil, an androgynous African-American with a shrewd, angular face. "Go after him," he commanded, his voice dripping with contempt.

The apprentice bowed and set off after the wayward disciple.

Distracted by this little drama, the woman in the pantsuit turned back to Dan and Natalie. "It looks like we might be done sooner than I thought. If you'd like to wait here—"

"Actually, we wanted a few words with Mr. McCord." Dan presented his Bureau badge.

"Oh! Agent Atwater—we heard you were coming." She glanced dubiously at Natalie, who still recited the Twenty-third Psalm like an autistic eulogist. "I'll see if he's available."

She went over and exchanged words with McCord. He smiled at Dan and Natalie and beckoned to them, evidently enjoying the opportunity to grant an imperial audience.

Simon McCord had no use for colored contact lenses; he let his violet eyes blaze in all their unsettling splendor. Although Simon was whipcord-lean and younger than his dead brother Arthur, Dan immediately noted the family resemblance of the wide nose and broad, flattish face. With free-hanging lobes, Simon's large ears stuck out from his bald head like mutant butterfly wings.

"Mr. Atwater, good to meet you." He clasped his hands in front of him in an affectation of piety. "And you—Lindstrom, isn't it?"

Natalie's lips worked furiously, but her words had slipped into silence again.

"I almost didn't recognize you with that unflattering wig. Too busy with that protective mantra to greet your old instructor?" Without even blinking, McCord stepped onto the grave in front of him, positioning himself directly over the heart of the buried corpse beneath him. "Perhaps you need a refresher course...."

Natalie snapped her mouth shut, and her face hardened into a mask of cold resentment. "That won't be necessary, Professor."

She stepped onto the grave nearest to her and put her hands on her hips with mocking nonchalance.

McCord laughed. "Perhaps you haven't forgotten *everything* I taught you. I presume you're here about my brother's death."

"His murder, you mean," Dan corrected. "Since you're one of the only people alive who knew where Arthur was hiding, we wondered if you might know who killed him."

"I have no idea. I didn't make it my business to keep track of Arthur and his acquaintances."

" 'Am I my brother's keeper?' " Natalie quoted darkly.

McCord glowered at her. "It's no secret that Arthur and I were never...close. But he was still my brother, and I would never betray my own flesh and blood."

"You don't seem too broken up about the killing."

He resumed his smile of paternal beneficence. "Because I know that death is merely a prelude to the True Life."

Natalie quivered with outrage, but Dan cut her off before she could express it. "Can you tell us where you were Friday night?" he asked McCord.

"Of course. I've been here in Seattle for the past two weeks, suffering police protection in that dismal apartment building."

"And what about your students?"

McCord's smile slipped. "What about them?"

Dan nodded in the direction of the departed disciples. "They seem very devoted to you. Very obedient."

"Need I remind you that I teach conduits to *catch* killers, not to become them?"

"How many students do you have?"

"Nine, at the moment."

"Where are the others?"

"Back at my ranch in New Mexico, as far as I know."

"Any of them Caucasian men?"

"A few. Tell me, is this leading anywhere?"

"Maybe. We still don't know whether these Violet murders were committed by one person or several working together."

McCord brushed aside the implied accusation with a wave of his hand. "Now, why would I want to slaughter the Lord's Chosen Ones?"

"Perhaps you didn't think they were fit to serve Him." Natalie suggested, eyes glinting like poison-tipped arrows. "Maybe they weren't *your* 'Chosen Ones.'"

McCord's nostrils flared. "It is not my place to question the Lord's wisdom in selecting His servants."

"But you did condemn your brother's decision to leave the Corps, didn't you?" Dan said.

McCord put a finger to his lips as he chose his words, the way a father might prepare to explain to a toddler where babies come from. "Did you know, Mr. Atwater, that most modern scholars believe that the Witch of Endor was actually a conduit? Or that Tiresias may have only seemed blind to the people who saw his violet eyes?"

"That's all very interesting. What's your point?"

"The *point* is that, from the beginning of recorded history, conduits have been revered as humanity's connection to the World Beyond. In every culture and in every epoch, we have been spiritual leaders and prophets: priests of Anubis in ancient Egypt, Dalai Lamas in Tibet, *houngans* in Haiti, shamans in Siberia."

McCord seated himself on the headstone beside him, a monarch on the throne of the dead. "Now, of course, science calls us a genetic anomaly, and society treats us like a commodity—mere tools to be exploited. We're welcome only when we're needed; otherwise, we can't even show ourselves in public." He cast a disparaging glance at Natalie, with her wig and contacts. "But that doesn't change the fact that we are blessed by God."

"So was your brother."

"Yes." McCord leaned forward. "And he rejected God's gift. *Mocked* it, even, by becoming a carnival fortune-teller! That's like Jesus going to work in a winery. It was a *sin*."

"Did you punish him for that sin?" Natalie sneered.

He grinned with righteous satisfaction. "I didn't have to, my dear. He punished himself."

Dan leveled his gaze at the imperious Violet. "And how

about you, Mr. McCord? You ever resent having to roll over and fetch for the N-double-A-C-C?"

McCord's eyes darkened, but they flicked toward the woman in the dark pantsuit, who stood just within earshot, her face impassive.

"I have always been a loyal Corps member," he said with the tact of a diplomat negotiating with an enemy nation.

The missing disciples returned then, the fair-skinned one leaning on his comrade for support.

"Ah! You found him, Serena," McCord said to the shrewd-faced apprentice, who was apparently a woman. "What do you have to say for yourself, Master Wilkes?"

Still unsteady on his feet, the male student couldn't seem to catch his breath. "I'm—I'm sorry, Professor. It—it was a—careless mistake. It—won't happen again."

"We'll see about that." McCord rose from the tombstone. "It appears we have a good deal more work to do, so if you'll excuse me ..." He gave Dan and Natalie a dismissive nod and moved to lead his students back through the rows of memorials.

"Thanks," Dan called out after him. "By the way, Jem said to say hi."

McCord paused, but did not turn around.

"He's been wanting to talk to you, but you haven't let him in. Why is that, Mr. McCord?"

This time, he did face Dan. "Lots of people try to talk to me, Mr. Atwater. I *choose* the ones I allow to speak."

"I see. And you realize that, if you're *not* behind these killings, you might be the next victim?"

McCord chuckled. "The Lord protects His own." He

tipped his head to Natalie. "Ms. Lindstrom—always a pleasure."

"So long, *Simon.*" She turned her back on him and stalked off without even waiting to appreciate the look of affront on his face.

Dan gave McCord a shrug and followed her as she marched right across the graves without so much as a twitch of her marble face. Only when they rounded the stand of pines and returned to the asphalt drive, far out of Simon McCord's sight, did she crumple to her knees, shivering like a diver racked by the bends.

His face flushed, McCord waited for Lindstrom and the FBI agent to vanish from view before addressing his students. He glanced with disdain at Wilkes, who now sat panting on the grass, then looked to Serena.

"Follow her."

She bowed her head and, with a sly smile, began to unbutton her cassock.

19

News Item

DAN'S CELL PHONE STARTED RINGING BEFORE THEY got back to the cemetery parking lot. It was Clark, and he wasted no time with small talk.

"It's hitting the fan. Get Lindstrom back here *now*."

"What happened?" Dan asked.

"We found out who rented that car in 'Frisco."

Dan looked at Natalie, who was still peaked after walking across the graves. "Yeah. I'll call you when we get in."

"Don't call. Just come. We'll be here."

"Yeah...okay."

He hung up and immediately dialed the airline.

Natalie rubbed her arms as if to ward off a chill. "Let me guess. We're going to fly again."

Dan put the phone to his ear. "Hey, I thought you'd be used to this by now."

"I am. I'd just like to spend more than two nights in the same city for a change."

"You may have your chance," Dan replied, but didn't explain.

* * *

By the time they arrived at LAPD headquarters that evening, the minicam crews were already swarming around the concrete barriers at the top of Los Angeles Street. Network news vans beamed live updates to the world through satellite dishes.

"Jeez! Did someone shoot the Pope?" Dan exclaimed as he and Natalie approached the security checkpoint.

When he pulled up to the guardhouse to show his ID, a swarm of photographers mobbed the car. Both he and Natalie blinked and shaded their eyes as a dozen camera flashes flooded the Ford's interior with light. The rolled-up windows reduced the collision of voices outside to a muted roar, like a riot heard from inside an aquarium, and uniformed police officers pushed back the paparazzi long enough for Dan to give the guard at the checkpoint his badge. He let them pass into the relative serenity of the blocked-off street, where they parked in the administration building's secure lot.

Inside Parker Center, many of the administrative offices were already closed for the day. Dan and Natalie proceeded upstairs to the conference room, where Clark awaited them, as promised. Seated at the table with him was a gray-haired man with severe, wire-framed glasses whom Dan had not met before. Behind them stood a guy with the build of a linebacker and a tall, wiry woman, both wearing suits and military-style crew cuts. The strangers didn't offer to introduce themselves.

"Dan. Ms. Lindstrom." Clark exuded all the eagerness of a man anticipating an IRS audit. "Have a seat."

Dan and Natalie pulled up a couple of chairs on the opposite side of the table. Sensing this was no time for chitchat, Dan decided to open with the obvious question. Natalie beat him to it.

"Who was he?"

Clark took a deep breath. "The car was rented to one Sidney R. Preston, a reporter for the *New York Post*."

Dan's stomach went sour. "You traced him through the Hertz records?"

"Didn't have to." He unfolded the tabloid paper that lay on the table and slapped it down in front of them.

WHO IS PLUCKING THE VIOLETS? the front page blared.

Although the headline had been printed in type at least an inch high, the publishers still found room for a nice big picture of Dan and Natalie coming out of Laurie Gannon's house, along with a file photo of a bald Natalie on the witness stand in court. *Could the unidentified woman seen here with FBI Special Agent Daniel Atwater (left) be conduit Natalie Lindstrom, whose dramatic testimony was the highlight of the Muñoz murder trial?* the caption speculated.

"Look inside," Clark said. "It gets better."

Acutely aware of the three officious strangers staring at him from across the table, Dan opened the paper to the featured article. The two-page spread contained shots of the bomb squad entering the School, crime scene workers loading Arthur McCord's bagged body into a police van for transportation to the county coroner's office, and Dan and Natalie conferring with Agent Ruehl outside Lucinda Kamei's house. Although photos of Violets were hard to come by, the paper had managed to scrounge up a decade-old picture of Russell Travers, who'd testified at a high-profile New York murder trial back in the early nineties, and a head shot of Kamei taken from one of her recent Mozart CDs.

The byline above the text was *Sid Preston*.

Natalie pulled the paper closer. "Oh, my God..."

She turned the page and discovered blown-up photos of herself in all her colored wigs, accompanied by a caption that invited readers to compare the similarities of facial features with the photo of her bareheaded courtroom appearance. She also found an entire sidebar devoted to Dan.

G-Man No Stranger to Death, the subhead proclaimed, above a picture of Dan, Ross, and Phillips behind the defense table at their own murder trial. "Absolved by the jury, Agent Atwater still possesses an itchy trigger finger, and came close to firing upon this reporter," Preston wrote, no doubt relishing his revenge.

"At least he's thorough," Dan murmured, his voice hoarse.

Natalie looked up from the paper, eyes wide with disbelief. "The man was innocent?"

Dan couldn't bring himself to answer her. His gaze dropped to his hands, which now felt heavy as wood.

"Dan, this is Delbert Sinclair, Director of Security for the N-double-A-C-C." Clark indicated the gray-haired man. "They want to take Ms. Lindstrom under their protection."

Anger jolted Dan out of his self-pity. "Now wait a minute! What gives you the right—"

"Given your background, Agent Atwater, I wonder what gives you the right to be here at all," Sinclair said without raising his voice. "If a common muckraker was able to get this close to Ms. Lindstrom, it's obvious that her security's been compromised."

Dan strived to remain civil. "I assure you, her life's never been in danger. I've been with her twenty-four/seven since I was assigned to her." He glanced at Natalie for confirmation, but she'd retreated from the conversation, the shades drawn on the light in her eyes.

"We're not questioning your commitment. But we've lost some of our best people already, and we can't afford to have a Corps member running all over the country while there's a killer at large. Especially when the man charged with protecting her is a loose cannon."

Clark intervened in Dan's defense. "For the record, Agent Atwater was cleared of any wrongdoing."

"*For the record*, Mr. Clark, our members have enough on their minds without having to worry about being killed by friendly fire."

"Director Sinclair, I understand your concern about this article," Dan conceded, "but Ms. Lindstrom's assistance is crucial to this investigation."

"And she will continue to assist the investigation once the Corps takes control of it."

Stunned, Dan looked at Clark.

"They have friends in high places," the SAC said.

Sinclair pushed himself up from his chair. "Well, if that's settled, Agents Brace and Lipinski here can escort Ms. Lindstrom to the Corps safe house."

"Maybe you should ask Ms. Lindstrom what *she* wants," Dan snapped.

Everyone's attention turned to Natalie. Sinclair spread his hands in the air, as if to ask, *Well?*

Dan silently pleaded to her: *Give me a chance to explain.*

Natalie cleared her throat. "Maybe it's for the best," she said quietly, her eyes glistening.

Dan deflated in his chair, the tension in his muscles draining from him along with his hope. It was the relief of total defeat.

"Excellent." Sinclair moved around the table to Natalie's side, accompanied by the two Corps Security goons. "Agent Atwater, if you wouldn't mind lending Agent Brace your car keys, he can fetch Ms. Lindstrom's bags."

Dan dug the keys out of his pocket and dropped them in the outstretched hand of the linebacker guy. "It's the white Taurus."

Brace nodded, and Dan began to wonder whether he and his partner were capable of speech.

Natalie got up from the table. "Thanks, Dan. For everything."

He couldn't lift his head to respond.

She lingered a moment longer, then left with Sinclair and the others. Clark followed them out, pausing to clap his hand on Dan's shoulder in silent commiseration.

Abandoned, Dan held his face in his hands and waited for Brace to bring back his keys.

Sid Preston's article attracted the notice of many readers that day. But Clem Maddox was undoubtedly its most avid fan.

He sat cross-legged on the dingy bed in his room at the E-Z-Sleep Inn, a rent-by-the-hour motel that hadn't redecorated since the sixties and didn't particularly care whether its guests registered with their real names. Around him lay several copies of that day's *New York Post*, open to sequential pages of the Violet story, and Maddox set to work on them with his rusty scissors, clipping out each and every panel and column of the feature.

When Clem heard about the article during a newsbreak on his car radio that morning, he immediately went to every newsstand in the area in search of the *Post*. This being the West Coast, New York papers were hard to find, but he eventually tracked down a stack of them in a Borders bookstore and bought every copy they had.

Maddox trimmed the fringe of paper from the fourth picture of Natalie Lindstrom. God, she was pretty. He especially liked her with that short black hair—kind of like Amy's used to be. Lindstrom: He was sure he'd already devoted a couple of pages to her, what with that Muñoz trial and all.

He set aside the clipping and picked up a huge binder from the floor beside the bed. Setting it in front of him, he flipped past several sheets of stiff cardboard covered with plastic. Normally used for displaying snapshots, they were crowded with magazine and newspaper articles, many of them yellow with age. Some had been cropped from *National Geographic*, some snipped from the *Weekly World News*, but the subject matter was always the same: the exploits of famous Violets.

A few of the pages also featured obituaries.

Maddox found his Natalie Lindstrom pages and inserted a blank cardboard sheet among them. Peeling back the protective plastic, he pasted the pictures of Lindstrom on the cardboard's pregummed surface, arranging them in a circle around the one of her with black hair, his favorite.

After smoothing the plastic back in place over his hand-iwork, Clem set aside the binder and picked up his rusty shears again. He shuffled through the papers around him until he found a sheet already tattered from previous clippings. The picture of Lucinda Kamei's Victorian house remained intact, though, and he began to cut around its edges, smiling. He was a huge Lucinda Kamei fan, and already owned most of her CDs.

He'd always wondered where she lived....

20

A Quiet Night

JOHN RUEHL, SECURITY AGENT FOR THE NORTH American Afterlife Communications Corps, flexed the already broken spine of his Tom Clancy paperback and refocused his eyes on the page he'd been reading. Rereading the paragraph where he'd left off, he found himself unable to keep his eyes open to the end of it. It didn't help that the room's only light source was an antique electric chandelier whose bare bulbs shone as dimly as the candle flames they imitated.

Shaking himself awake, Ruehl tossed the book on the table beside him and gulped the last swig of cold coffee from his plastic travel mug. They'd arbitrarily stuck him on graveyard shift at the Kamei place after he'd been working mornings for a week, and he'd had a hell of a time adjusting his sleep schedule. Good thing these eighteenth-century chairs were so damned uncomfortable or he might've dozed off an hour ago.

He got up and paced the sitting room's parquet floor to get his blood flowing again, and wished he could go down to the kitchen for more coffee. The grandfather clock in the corner told him it was nearly half past two in the morning. Still more than three hours to go. Maybe he'd call Hawks, the agent on duty downstairs, and have him order a Domino's pizza and some Cokes.

Ruehl had wedged the sitting room door open so he could keep watch on the entrance to the master bedroom. Kamei evidently slept like a baby in there, for she hadn't made a sound since she went to bed.

"Must be nice," he grumbled. Taking care to tread lightly on the creaky floorboards, he walked down the hallway to the second-floor landing to stretch his legs.

On the other side of the bedroom door, Lucinda Kamei lay in the plush opulence of her canopied four-poster bed. Despite the luxury, she did not sleep well. Her breaths came quick and shallow, and she knotted herself in the satin sheets, rolling with night terrors. Her mouth yawned open, but the scream lodged in her throat like a bone fragment. She fought to disgorge it, her abdominal muscles heaving.

Then a leaden calm smoothed the rumpled fabric of her flesh. With cool deliberation, she opened her eyes and swung her feet out of bed and onto the floor.

The sheets slid off her bare body as she sat up on the edge of the mattress. She smiled at the blue nudity of her breasts in the dark and lightly touched the concavity of skin between them. Her smile soon faded, however, replaced by a frown of cold efficiency.

With feline stealth, she crept from the bed to the door that led into the hallway. She eased the door inward a millimeter at a time until she'd opened a crack barely wide enough for one eye to peer through. The gap permitted her to see cross-sections of Ruehl as he walked up and down the hall.

She nudged the door shut and allowed her eyes to re-adjust to the darkness. Orange light from a sodium-vapor street lamp outside sifted through the lace curtains of the curved windows in the corner. There, in the center of the cylindrical tower, a set of metal steps corkscrewed around a post, spiraling up to a trapdoor in the ceiling.

Without bothering to clothe herself, Kamei crossed the room and climbed the stairs, pausing at the top to raise the trapdoor until the brackets of its hinges held it upright. Stepping up onto the floor above her, she lowered the door back into place.

She now stood in the topmost room of the tower, a per-fectly round chamber paneled with polished California redwood. Dimly visible above her, a pyramid of wooden beams supported the conical roof. In the center of the room sat a chair, a sheet music stand, a twelve-string acoustic guitar on its own stand, a flute case, and a four-track recording system that Kamei used to tape demos of the songs she wrote in her spare time. Every 90 degrees around the circle, a window looked out. The two windows nearest the street lamp provided the room's scant illumina-tion, while the others offered a view of the clear night sky.

One of the sky-side windows was inked over by a black silhouette.

Like a bride eager to elope, Kamei hastened to the win-dow, unfastened the latch, and pushed up the sash. The dark figure who had been squatting on the gabled roof out-side ducked through the opening with simian agility. Once inside, he drew himself up to his full height before Kamei, his head and body a featureless oblong of ebony.

She smiled and took his latex-wrapped hands in hers, pulling him down with her as she lay, naked, upon the hardwood floor.

Back in the sitting room, Agent Ruehl plopped himself back into the uncomfortable eighteenth-century chair and re-opened his book.

At half past three, Hawks came upstairs with their pepperoni-and-black-olive pizza and a couple of bottled so-das, which they consumed while complaining about the Corps' health plan in hushed half-whispers. Stephanie Corbett relieved the bleary-eyed Ruehl at six, taking his post in the sitting room.

When Lucinda Kamei didn't emerge by ten o'clock that morning, Corbett considered rapping on the bedroom door, but thought better of it: Given how much Ms. Kamei detested interruptions, Corbett would hate to wake her from a pleasant dream. Besides, John reported that the night had been quiet and dull.

Corbett returned to the sitting room and her copy of *Time* magazine. She read it cover to cover.

Noon came. Kamei still hadn't appeared.

Approaching the bedroom door, Corbett hesitated only a moment before knocking. "Ms. Kamei? Everything all right?"

No reply.

She knocked again, louder this time. "Ms. Kamei? You okay?"

The silence thickened.

"I don't want to scare you, Ms. Kamei, but I'm coming in." Corbett drew the .45 from her shoulder holster and opened the door.

A gray dimness persisted in the bedroom, the noontime sunlight dampened by the drawn curtains. The canopied bed sat unmade and vacant.

Corbett eyed the door to the adjoining bathroom. She was moving toward it when she heard the dripping.

Pit...pit...pit...

Dark droplets fell into an opaque puddle on the floor beside the spiral staircase. Corbett's gaze followed the chain of drips upward, and she saw the spreading scarlet stain on the ceiling.

21

Consequences

SOME MEN TURN TO ALCOHOL OR HEROIN FOR THE negation of self. Dan Atwater used cable TV.

Lying on a bed in his Embassy Suites hotel room, he let the opiate of an HBO stand-up comedy special numb his aching neurons. He didn't laugh, and wasn't even listening to what the comics were saying, really; all that mattered was the shifting, soothing patterns of color on the picture tube.

In the days following the shooting two years earlier, when he was suspended without pay and due to stand trial for murder, when he spent every moment of conscious thought replaying the memories of the blood oozing into the windbreaker and the man's uncomprehending face asking *whywhywhy*, Dan had congratulated himself on not seeking refuge in a bottle the way Ross did or resorting to the sort of self-righteous denial that Phillips cowered behind. He found that watching enough mindless entertainment put his brain to sleep, kept it from torturing itself. TV would help him get through this, he thought at the time. It would save his health, save his marriage, save his sanity.

He'd been watching Cartoon Network for thirty-eight consecutive hours when Susan told him she was leaving him.

The comedy special ended and an Al Pacino movie came on. *Donnie Brasco.* He'd already seen it. He wanted to change the channel, but that would mean reaching over to the nightstand, where the remote had been bolted to the wood.

Getting away from the press had been a trick. They'd surrounded LAPD headquarters, all set to tail him wherever he went. Since they'd spotted him and Natalie on the way in, they knew what he was wearing and what his car looked like, so he requested a new car from Clark and borrowed some street clothes and a fake mustache and glasses from the LAPD's undercover division. He ended up looking like his high-school chemistry teacher. *Now you know how Natalie feels,* he thought as he scrutinized the disguise in a restroom mirror before leaving the police station.

The whole getup now lay in a heap on the hotel room's other bed. Dan had stripped to his boxers the moment he got to the room, and he'd barely moved in—what was it now?—ten hours at least. In that time, he'd almost forgotten about the *Post* article and the paparazzi and Delbert Sinclair and all the rest of it.

But he couldn't forget about Natalie.

The afterimage of her many faces seemed to hover in front of the television screen: red-haired Natalie and her deadpan sarcasm, blond Natalie and her wistful frown, brunette Natalie and her reluctant smile. Through dry, sticky eyes that ached for sleep yet refused to close, he saw her sharing dinner with him at Verdi's, doing yoga in their hotel room, and triumphantly riding her stallion on the carousel. Especially her on the horse, grinning into the wind.

He also saw the look of horror she gave him after reading how he'd killed an innocent man. It rose before his eyes, unbidden, again and again.

Dan still hadn't eaten or slept when his cell phone rang at two that afternoon. It took twelve beeps to convince him that the caller wasn't going to hang up.

"Pack your bags," Clark commanded, his voice fading in and out, when Dan finally picked up the phone. "You're back on the case."

Dan sniffed in disbelief. "That was quick. Sinclair die or something?"

"No, Lucinda Kamei did."

Dan sat up. "When?"

"Last night, and right under the noses of Corps Security."

"How?"

"Same as McCord. Looks like you nailed the killer's profile. How soon can you leave?"

The phone held between his cheek and shoulder, Dan bounded out of bed, grabbed some clothes, and headed for the bathroom. "On my way out the door...."

He almost left the hotel without putting on his fake mustache and glasses, but changed his mind at the last minute. It turned out to be a wise move, for a sea of reporters had surrounded Lucinda Kamei's house by the time he arrived at seven that evening.

Brandishing his Bureau badge, Dan shooed newspeople out of his way until he reached the police barricade. Once there, however, his disguise backfired, for the cop on duty didn't believe he was really Dan Atwater.

"Go get Earl Clark," he told the officer, rather than trying to explain his appearance.

The cop called one of his comrades over to watch his post while he went into the house in search of Clark. When he returned with the SAC at his side, the throng of correspondents pelted Clark with questions.

"Agent Clark! How did the Violet Killer murder Ms. Kamei?"

"Do you have any suspects yet?"

"Is it true you tried to cover up the first eight murders?"

"Where's Natalie Lindstrom? Is she next on the killer's list?"

Refusing to make eye contact, Clark merely raised his right palm, silently telling them all to "talk to the hand" as he ushered Dan up the front steps and into the house. "Much more of this crap and I'm gonna get me one of those mustaches," he muttered when they were safely inside.

"Nah, I think you'd look better with a goatee." Dan took off the fake eyeglasses and rubbed the bridge of his nose. The coffee he'd drunk on the flight was already wearing off.

Clark frowned at him as they climbed the main staircase, sidestepping a white-coated crime scene technician who was on his way down. "You get *any* sleep?"

"Oh, at least ten, twenty minutes on the plane."

They reached the second-floor landing, and Clark indicated an open door to the left. "There."

In the sitting room, they found Agent Ruehl sulking in a chair with Agent Corbett standing beside him, her arms folded, both of them wearing the pallid dread of school-children waiting outside a principal's office.

"Ms. Corbett. Mr. Ruehl. You look about as bad as I feel."

Ruehl squinted at Dan's face. "Agent Atwater? What's with the...?" He pointed to his own upper lip.

"Don't ask."

"Kindly tell Mr. Atwater what you saw and heard last night," Clark said.

Ruehl exhaled in exasperation. "*Nothing*, that's what I've been telling you! Ms. Kamei went into that room at half-past eleven. The shower in the bathroom ran for about fifteen minutes after that, and then... *nothing*."

"You're sure?" Dan pressed. "It was late. You might've dozed off—"

"No! Absolutely not."

"We can understand why you might be reluctant to tell us if you did fall asleep, but I promise you that—"

"*No!* For the thousandth time, no! Much as I might've *wanted* to, I did *not* go to sleep!"

Corbett cleared her throat. "I've worked with John lots of times before. He would never let something like that happen."

Dan nodded as though her testimony had resolved his doubts.

Clark redirected his aim at Corbett. "And why didn't you check on Ms. Kamei until after noon?"

She grimaced, obviously regretting her decision to speak. "Well, sir, as Mr. Atwater can tell you, Ms. Kamei doesn't like to be disturbed." Her mouth twitched. "Didn't, I mean."

"How did you find the body?" Dan asked.

"Well, when Ms. Kamei didn't respond to my voice, I entered the bedroom, and..." She faltered. "Well, you'll see. I tried to preserve the scene as much as possible, but I had to climb the stairs, you know, just in case she was still alive." The longer Dan and Clark stared at her, the more Corbett drooped. "It was a long shot, I admit, but I had to be sure."

"We understand, Agent Corbett. We're just trying to figure out how this happened. If you'll excuse us..." Dan nudged Clark, and they proceeded from the sitting room to the adjacent door in the hallway. Clark nodded at the police officer standing guard there, and she let them into the bedroom.

"Do you believe them?" Dan asked when he and Clark were alone.

"Actually, I do. Let me show you why."

Clark led him around the canopied bed and pointed to the bloodstains on the floor and ceiling. "These led Corbett to check the room above us. As far as we can tell, the killer never even came down here. Kamei apparently woke from a deep sleep, got out of bed butt-naked, and climbed these stairs under her own power. We found partial prints of her bare feet on the steps."

"Maybe he *was* down here," Dan suggested. "Maybe he forced her at gunpoint."

"Sure, if he did it without making a sound, without any signs of a struggle, without leaving so much as a scuff mark on a waxed hardwood floor in a house where no one's allowed to wear shoes."

"Hmm...I see what you mean."

"Wait—I haven't even come to the best part yet."

He motioned for Dan to follow him up the spiral

stairway. "Crime scene unit's already come and gone. Body's at the morgue. We'll go there next."

"Oh, joy."

"We're waiting for the autopsy to make it official, but an initial examination showed no bruises, abrasions, scratches, or ligature marks." They stepped up onto the floor of the tower room, and Clark waved a hand toward the enormous patch of congealing redness near the trap-door. "She let him cut her guts out without even slapping his wrist."

Dan's nose wrinkled at the rusty-urine stench. "Maybe she was already unconscious by then. Drugged or chloro-formed."

"That still wouldn't explain why she let him in the house." Clark directed his attention to the nearby window, where whitish scratches marred the polish on the redwood sill. "He entered through here. Some of the wooden shin-gles on the roof outside show fresh cracks; the houses are so close together here, we figure he probably came over from the roof of the place next door to avoid being seen.

"He didn't force the window, though. Kamei opened it for him. We found her prints on the latch and the sash." Clark shook his head. "Why would she help the man who'd come to kill her?"

"Maybe it wasn't her." Feeling short of breath, Dan re-membered the way Natalie crouched on the edge of her hotel bed, peering at him with Russell Travers's lust.

Night is a very vulnerable time for me....

Clark gave him a quizzical look.

"We need to talk to Lucinda Kamei" was all Dan said.

"Should we tell Lindstrom about this?" Clark nodded toward the patch of blood.

The sweat on Dan's upper lip had loosened his mustache, and he pressed it back in place. "I have a feeling she already knows."

22

Safe House

SITTING CROSS-LEGGED IN A WIDE EASY CHAIR, Natalie shut her battered copy of *Sense and Sensibility* and shoved it down between the seat cushion and armrest. She'd already read it twice in the past week, but the only other book she'd brought with her was *Northanger Abbey*, which she'd read four times. Nevertheless, Jane Austen still seemed preferable to the Jackie Collins potboiler Agent Lipinski offered to loan her. The Corps "safe house" turned out to be a dingy little two-bedroom mobile home in the desert wastes outside Victorville, and with nothing else to do, Natalie had read until her head throbbed from sensory deprivation.

She sighed and looked over at Lipinski, who sat with board-straight military posture in a high-backed chair on the opposite side of the bedroom. Wearing a khaki U.S. Army T-shirt and a hip holster with a .45 automatic, she incongruously passed the time by knitting a scarf, her hands scissoring the long blue needles together with robotic speed and precision.

"I'm thinking about going to bed," Natalie announced.

"Be my guest." The staccato clicking of Lipinski's needles didn't even slow.

Natalie waited for her to get the hint, but the agent didn't budge, nor did she bother to speak again. Lipinski apparently viewed conversation as an unnecessary distraction. They'd been together almost twenty-four hours, and the woman had yet to mention her first name. Natalie thought of Dan's breezy smile and bad jokes, and felt a loneliness more desolate than she'd ever known in the cell of her little apartment.

"You can *go* now," she told Lipinski, more sharply than she'd intended.

"Nope. Not tonight."

Natalie tensed with suspicion. "You stayed outside last night…."

"Orders changed."

"Why?"

This time, Lipinski missed a purl. "Tighter security. That's all."

"Mmm." Gazing out the window at the lightless desert surrounding them, Natalie tried to fill the emptiness with a vision of the glittering carousel and its charging horses. She groaned and unfolded her legs to restore their circulation, for her toes had begun to tingle.

The prickling sensation did not go away, however, but spread instead to her other extremities—her fingers, her earlobes, the tip of her nose. The throbbing of her head intensified as well, causing her vision to shimmer with migraine starbursts. Her mind rolled through unfamiliar images like a television with no vertical hold.

Someone was knocking.

Out of habit, Natalie shut her eyes and recited her protective mantra in her mind. *The Lord is my shepherd; I shall not want. He maketh me to lie down in green pastures: he leadeth me beside the still waters. He restoreth my soul. . . .*

The anaesthetized feeling in her limbs subsided, and her mind cleared. But the haze of an alien persona still lingered behind her eyes, and it now repeated Natalie's words, although slightly out of phase, like an echo in her skull. As it synchronized itself with her thoughts, Natalie felt the numbing tingle in her fingertips return.

She gasped. *It knew her mantra,* and now it was trying to worm its way around her mental barricades.

"You okay?" Lipinski asked from a million miles away.

Ignoring her, Natalie shifted from her protective mantra to her "spectator" mantra, which let her monitor the consciousness of the invading soul while permitting her to resume control over her body if necessary.

Row, row, row your boat, gently down the stream!

Merrily, merrily, merrily, merrily! Life is but a dream. . . .

Images again poured into her mind, but clearer this time: delicate sienna-tinted hands fingering yellowed ivory keys, a circular room paneled with redwood, a charred and broken Stratocaster guitar.

Boo, let me in. . . .

Natalie opened her eyes, her parted lips quivering. "Lucy."

"What?" Lipinski had dropped her knitting and now stood over Natalie, regarding her with the sort of professional concern a mechanic might show a car engine that started to rattle. "Can I help?"

Before the Security agent could stop her, Natalie bolted from the bedroom into the adjoining bathroom and locked herself inside.

Life is but a dream....

Numbness stuffed her limbs like cotton, and her muscles quivered with conflicting nerve impulses as she relinquished command of her flesh to Lucy. Her knees buckling, she fell against the shower door and slumped into a rag-doll heap on the linoleum, the shower stall shuddering with the impact.

Row, row, row your boat...

The doggerel verse kept Natalie's personality circling in a holding pattern within the recesses of her own subconscious, permitting Lucy's soul to seep like a damp draft into her brain. Lying with her cheek flattened on the cool floor, Natalie could still see a sideways view of the base of the toilet, but she felt detached from the scene, as though watching it through a closed-circuit security camera.

...gently down the stream!

Sense-memories unspooled in the mind she now shared with Lucy: the mint tang of toothpaste in Lucy's mouth as she left the bathroom, the orange glow of the streetlight outside the curtained windows as she climbed into the canopied bed, the slide of satin sheets against sweat-moistened skin as she grappled with the soul that infiltrated her dreams.

Natalie heard her own voice speak to her. "They got me at night, while I was asleep. I tried to block them out, but couldn't."

How, Lucy? Natalie asked. *How did they get in?*

"They knew me. They knew my mantra and subverted it."

Who was it? Who could do that?

"I don't know—they shut me out. I couldn't monitor

their thoughts. They had their *own* mantra that I couldn't penetrate. I never even saw...the end."

You said they. *Was it more than one?*

"Yes...I think so. One dead and one living. But I never saw the living one. The one that killed me."

With the weariness of Atlas, Lucy pushed Natalie's body up from the floor and stood on legs of gelatin, bracing herself against the bathroom sink. "Watch out, Boo," she warned the reflection in the medicine cabinet mirror. "Don't let your guard down, even for a second."

Her soul dissipated like a dry-ice fog, and Natalie sank to her knees before the basin. She gradually became aware of the insistent knocking on the door and Lipinski's harsh voice calling her name.

"What happened in there?" the agent demanded as Natalie strode back into the bedroom.

"I need a ride to L.A." She scooped her clothes, hangers and all, out of the closet. "And a plane ticket to San Francisco."

"What the—? Are you *nuts*?"

Natalie hefted her first suitcase onto the bed and unzipped it. "Would you rather I hitchhike?"

Lipinski slapped the bag's lid shut. "You can't leave this house."

"What are you going to do? Shoot me?" Natalie threw the lid open again.

"You realize you're risking your life by leaving Corps Security, don't you?"

She resumed packing her clothes. "For some reason, Agent Lipinski, Corps Security doesn't make me feel as safe as it used to."

23

Master of the Doors

LUCINDA KAMEI DID NOT SEEM DISTRESSED ABOUT lying on a stainless steel autopsy table in the San Francisco County Morgue. In fact, Dan fancied that he could see a faint smile on her livid face, although that may have been a rictus caused by rigor mortis in her cheek muscles.

She didn't have much to smile about. Her rich almond skin tone had been leached to whiteness, except where the blood had pooled inside her to form bruise-purple discoloration along her back and the undersides of her arms and legs. The coroner had slit open her chest from each shoulder to the lower tip of the sternum and sawn open the rib cage in order to remove the heart and lungs. The UNSUB had saved him the trouble of making the lower part of the traditional Y incision, for, as with Arthur McCord, the killer had slashed through the abdomen from the breastbone to the navel and parted the flesh to pull out the entrails. The small intestines that had formed a mystic circle around Kamei's corpse now coiled like a knotted worm in the metal pan of the autopsy scale.

Deputy Coroner Delaney, a tall man with a beaklike nose and blasé manner, was in the process of inventorying and weighing all the internal organs. "I want to be sure he didn't take anything *else* with him," he explained, his words muffled by the surgical mask he wore.

Without really wanting to, Dan gazed into the empty red sockets where Kamei's eyes should have been. He and Clark also wore masks as they examined the body. Dan shuffled through some police photos the SAC gave him to see how the body had been positioned at the crime scene. "Any signs of sexual assault?"

"We didn't find any semen, if that's what you mean," Delaney replied.

Dan held up one of the photos. "But she was nude when they found her...."

"That doesn't necessarily mean anything," Clark interjected. "Kamei was known to sleep in the buff."

The coroner shook his head. "You never know what gets these guys off. This, for example." With latex-gloved fingers, he pulled down a flap of skin tissue that had been folded back over Kamei's clavicle. It flopped down inside the vacant chest cavity like a flag of surrender, revealing puckering red scratches that formed a crude number 9. "For all we know, that's our man's idea of a good time."

"Maybe." Dan tried to make the 9 fit with the "open door" message on McCord's chest. Kamei, McCord, Gannon, Travers, Markham, Avebury, Marshall, Perez, Whitman...the most obvious answer was the number of victims. But nine was a mystical number as well: three times three, the Trinity squared. Could the numeral have additional significance for the killer? "Any signs she'd been drugged?"

Delaney scratched his head through the turquoise-green hairnet of his surgical scrubs. "Not that we've found, though we're still waiting for the toxicology report. But as far as I can tell, she should've been stone-cold sober."

The swish of a swinging door drew their attention from the cadaver, and they turned to see a nattily dressed Chinese-American man enter the morgue. He held up a sheet of paper. "Agent Clark, I think you'd better see this."

"Ah! Stuart." Clark pulled down his surgical mask and walked over to him. "Dan, this is Stuart Yee, San Francisco PD. He's heading up the Kamei investigation. Stuart—Dan Atwater, FBI."

"Agent Atwater." Yee tapped his upper lip. "You better fix that."

Embarrassed, Dan touched his false mustache, half of which had peeled off when he'd pulled down his own mask.

"The hell with it." Chuckling, he yanked off the rest of the fake facial hair.

"What have you got?" Clark asked.

Yee handed him the photocopy he held. "Killer mailed this to the *Chronicle*. They called us as soon as they read it."

"Good thing he didn't send it to the *New York Post*—we wouldn't have seen it 'til tomorrow's front page." Clark skimmed the letter's contents. "Where's the original?"

"With forensics."

"They find anything?"

"No prints on the paper, the envelope, or the stamp. The stamp was self-adhesive, so no saliva. Paper and envelope were common brands available in most office supply stores. Typescript seems to be a standard Word 2000 twelve-point Courier font, most likely printed with an HP inkjet. Not much help, all the way around."

Clark passed the paper to Dan. "Sounds like our guy."

The boldface, single-spaced lines were perfectly centered in the middle of the page:

> **Dear Ed:**
> **Nine doors open,**
> **so many still to go.**
> **I'm saving the eyes in a jar....**
> **All the better to see you with!!!**
> **Gotta run now, more work to do.**
> **You'll hear from me soon.**
> **Forever yours,**
> **MASTER OF THE DOORS**

"Not exactly Shakespeare." Dan gave the page back to Yee. "How do we know it's not just some wacko who wants to claim credit?"

"Because the envelope was postmarked yesterday," the detective replied.

"If nothing else, it backs up your profile," Clark said. "And tells us what that nine on Kamei's chest means."

"Why doesn't that make me feel better?" In his mind, Dan saw Lucy touch Hendrix's guitar, her eyes shining.

Her eyes...

He turned back toward the dissection table, peering at Kamei's placid white face. "You find any vitreous jelly in her eyes?" he asked Delaney.

The coroner didn't even bother to look up from the body. "Nope. He plucked those suckers out clean and whole. Minimal lacerations to the eyelids suggest he used his fingers instead of a knife."

Clark saw Dan's frown. "What is it?"

Dan indicated the letter in Yee's hand. "If he really is collecting their eyes, Arthur McCord's pair wouldn't have made very good specimens. Either he botched that job, or he's getting better at his work. Or..." He hesitated.

"Or he had help this time," the SAC finished. "Is that what you're suggesting?"

"Maybe. Someone who couldn't get past McCord's soul cage, but who *could* let the killer into Kamei's upstairs studio. Someone who could keep Kamei absolutely silent and still while he did the job right."

Clark and Yee exchanged a dark look.

Before they could respond, Dan's cell phone chirped. He excused himself and withdrew a few footsteps to take the call. "Atwater here."

"Dan! Are you in San Francisco? I'm on my way."

He lowered his voice. "*Natalie?* I thought you were holed up God-knows-where."

"I was. Look, my plane gets in at eleven-thirty. United Airlines Flight one-oh-oh-eight. Can you pick me up?"

Dan took out his pen and notebook and jotted down the flight information. "Sure, but why are you coming here?"

"I talked to Lucy."

"I see." He glanced back at the dissection table. Delaney had peeled the flesh from Kamei's forehead down over her face. Wielding a cranial saw, the coroner began to carve out an oblong section of her skull for removal of the brain. The whine of the saw's rotating blade dropped in pitch as it ground through the bone. "What did she have to say?"

"Someone's helping the killer. Someone dead."

Dan's face tightened. "That's what I was afraid of. See you at midnight."

"I can't wait."

The longing in her voice left him speechless for a second. "Yeah," he said at last. "Me neither."

But only a dial tone replied.

24

Gone

AFTER WHAT LUCY HAD TOLD HER, NATALIE KNEW
she absolutely, positively could not let herself go to sleep.
To make sure she didn't doze off, she resorted to two things
she never thought she'd do. She drank a grande cup of
Starbucks coffee, which would probably give her colon cancer in twenty years, and she took a window seat on the
flight to San Francisco. When the caffeine buzz began to
wane, she forced herself to look down at the pinpoint lights
of San Jose below her. Reminding herself that she was riding in a little metal box twenty thousand feet in the air gave
her a jolt of pure, vertiginous terror that snapped her
awake again.

She slapped the shade shut and pressed herself back in
her seat, hyperventilating. The passenger across the aisle
from her, a thin black man with a neatly trimmed beard,
smiled and cupped a hand to his mouth for a stage whisper.
"Don't worry! We'll make it."

She laughed at her own skittishness. Really, she ought
to be proud of herself. It was the first time she'd ever flown
alone.

Not that Lipinski hadn't threatened to come with her.
Indeed, she forced Natalie to phone Delbert Sinclair, who

hinted darkly at the punishments that awaited her family if she left Security protection.

"I understand that your father's business just won a substantial government contract," he murmured. "It would be a shame to see that contract canceled. And then there's the matter of your mother's long-term care insurance—"

Natalie hung up before she could change her mind. Her only regret was that she didn't have Dan's hand to hold during the twin traumas of takeoff and landing.

When her plane at last arrived at its gate, Natalie exited the gangway and scanned the area for Dan's face. At midnight, the San Francisco International Airport terminal was a desolate place. The few people who still languished on the padded benches looked as forgotten as the soft-drink cups and outdated newspapers that littered the seats beside them. Natalie felt a prickle of panic when she didn't see Dan among them.

Her flight had been only half full, and the passengers poured out and dispersed like bubbles from an uncapped soda bottle. As the stream of travelers thinned, Natalie saw a man with horn-rimmed glasses and a slim brown mustache standing nearby, the knot of his tie hanging loose and his shirt collar unbuttoned. He held up a hand-lettered sign that read JOSIE MITCHELL.

She couldn't help but giggle as she sauntered over to him. "Dr. Mitchell, I presume?"

"Ah, Josie! I can't tell you how much I've missed you, honeybunch." Dan shoved the sign under his arm and grinned. "By the way…has anyone told you how good you look with brown hair?"

"Why, no." She fluffed the feathery locks of her latest

wig. "But thanks for noticing, Kent, darling. Incidentally, I like the mustache, but the glasses have *got* to go." She put her arms around him in a tentative hug. "I missed you."

His hands squeezed her back. "Missed you, too."

They let go of each other with a guilty air. "You have any other luggage?" Dan asked, indicating the overnight bag on her shoulder.

"Yeah. One suitcase I had to check."

"You have a good trip?"

"The plane didn't crash, if that's what you mean. I don't think I'll ever get used to—"

Natalie didn't finish the complaint. Heading for the escalator down to baggage claim, they'd entered a corridor lined with fast-food counters, gift shops, and newsstands, most of which had already closed for the night. A frenetic mumble from the right caught her attention, but it took her a moment to comprehend what the voice said.

"—*two times two is four, two times three is six, two times four is eight*—"

It was like a ghost had brushed her shoulder. She turned and saw an unshaven homeless man standing near the men's restroom. Greasy black curls snaked out from underneath his stocking cap, and dirt darkened the grooves of his brow. He hunched inside his nappy blue overcoat and clamped his hands over his ears to shut out some imaginary clamor. Apparently sensing that he was being watched, he limped into the lavatory and disappeared.

Dan followed the line of her stare to the men's-room door. "What is it?"

"Did you hear what that man was saying?"

"The bum? Sounded like gibberish to me."

"Yeah. I guess you're right." Natalie watched the rest-room entrance, but the man did not emerge. She took hold of Dan's arm. "Can we get some coffee before we go?"

He stared at her like she'd asked to go skydiving. "Sure... whatever you say."

It turned out that he needed the caffeine even more than she did. He came close to nodding off behind the wheel while driving them back to his motel.

She rubbed his forearm. "How long has it been since you slept?"

"Oh... forty-two hours or so. Nothing I didn't do in college."

She sighed and gazed out at the white dashes of the freeway lanes zipping through the circle of their headlights. "I'm sorry. I'd offer to take the wheel, but I never learned to drive."

"That's okay. Just jab me in the ribs if I start to zone out."

She studied his face in the light reflected from the road: the determined set of his stubble-covered jaw, the creases of anxiety at the corners of his mouth, the eyes clinging to the world of the visible, afraid to close.

It might have been the face of a Violet.

When they got to the less-than-lavish accommodations of San Francisco's Walkright Inn, Dan automatically took her suitcases and trudged toward the emergency stairs. "Sorry," he said over his shoulder. "If I'd known you were coming, I would've reserved something on the ground floor."

"It's okay." Natalie hooked her hand around his elbow. "Let's take the elevator."

He blinked his bleary eyes. "You don't have to—it's only two flights...."

She shrugged and smiled. "Hey, what're the odds a seven point six is gonna hit in the next three minutes?"

He saw that she was serious and let out a laugh. "Well, you don't have to twist my arm. Lead on!"

Natalie managed to keep a cool front during the brief ride up to the third floor, although she held her breath the whole way and folded her hands to keep them from shaking.

"Home sweet home!" Dan exclaimed as they entered his room. He set her bags on the dresser and took off his jacket. "I was thinking about rinsing off in the shower before bed. You want to go first?"

"No, help yourself." Drawing a deep breath, she sat on one of the twin beds. "Dan...would you tell me about it?"

He took off his tie and started to unbutton his shirt. "About what?"

"You know."

Dan lowered himself onto the edge of the other bed, his back to her.

"I want to hear your side of the story," Natalie said when he couldn't or wouldn't respond.

"Yeah. I guess I owe you that." He smoothed back his hair, but didn't turn to face her.

It didn't take him long. The drug bust, the fleeing suspect, the silhouette in the alley, the wrong man dying on the pavement—he'd obviously told this tale many times before. When he finished, his voice was hoarse, and he looked down at his hands as if he didn't recognize them.

"Who was he?" Natalie asked quietly.

"Alan Pelletier." Pronouncing the name seemed to cause Dan physical pain. "Night janitor at the Laundromat there. Had a wife and two kids."

Moving from her bed to his, Natalie pressed her palm on his back. "You're a good man. You didn't mean to do what you did."

He sniffed and rubbed his nose. "It doesn't help to know that."

"Would it help if you talked to Pelletier himself?"

Dan shrank from her touch. "*No*. No way—that's just insane—"

She held on to his arm. "You told me you've been living in a box for two years. Maybe this is the way out."

Dan pushed his hands into the hollows of his eyes. "What could I possibly say?"

"Tell him what you feel. How sorry you are. Ask his forgiveness. All those things you wish you'd done that night."

She took his hand. It quivered in her grasp. As he looked up at her, she saw that trapped tears had fused together the lashes at the corners of his eyes. His fingers tightened on hers.

"Do it."

Natalie nodded and closed her eyes.

Row, row, row your boat…

She hadn't even finished the first round of the spectator mantra before the soul began pricking at her fingers. It hummed along the lines of Dan's palm and sparked off the hairs on the back of his hand. Alan Pelletier had obviously been waiting for this moment.

...life is but a dream....

Sense-memories of Pelletier's past fluttered through her mind: She clapped callused black hands as a small boy in a bright red helmet and jersey carried a football into the end zone; she nuzzled the cheek of a smiling, chocolate-skinned woman, inhaling the lavender scent of her perfume; she laughed as a baby girl in diapers scampered across the floor in pursuit of a little wind-up dinosaur.

Then the force of Pelletier's personality hit her like the leading edge of a cyclone.

Natalie fought to keep her face from revealing the torrents of his grief and rage. Grief for the world Pelletier had known, still so fresh and beautiful yet already dead to him, like a cut rose withering in a vase. And rage—all-consuming, murderous rage—at the men who'd robbed him of his future.

Would he even give Dan a chance to atone? Or would he simply strangle him with her hands?

Jaw muscles aching from gritting her teeth, Natalie thought of Arthur and his fake séances, of the mother weeping with gratitude for words of consolation her dead son had never spoken. *I tell them what they want to hear*, Arthur said. *They like it better than the truth anyway*.

Keeping her face an immobile mask of meditation, Natalie switched from her spectator mantra to the Twenty-third Psalm.

The Lord is my shepherd....

Pelletier's soul shrieked in silent fury. In vain, he clawed to hold on as she swept him from the eaves of her mind, cursing her for depriving him of life a second time.

Natalie swallowed the shudder that squirmed in her mouth. Thank God she wasn't hooked up to a SoulScan unit.

"He's not there," she said.

Dan lifted his head, gulped the pooled spit in his mouth. "What?"

"I can't summon him. He's gone."

"Gone?"

"Gone." Natalie gently rocked him as he wept on her shoulder. In her mind, she saw Lucy touch the burned Stratocaster. *It gives me hope,* Lucy had said.

Dan trembled in her arms the way he'd trembled that day—with hope.

Had she done the right thing? Would Alan Pelletier have shown Dan mercy if she'd given him the chance? Natalie wasn't sure. But one wasted life was enough. Maybe now Dan could live his.

Gently encouraging him to climb onto the bed, Natalie let Dan cry himself out, until he finally slipped into a placid doze. She spent the rest of the night beside him, watching the infantile repose of his face and occasionally brushing her fingertips over the tufts of his disheveled hair.

25

Touchstone

ROTATING THE GLASS CUTTER AROUND A CENTRAL axis like the lead of a compass, Clement Maddox etched a fine white circle on the bedroom window. The suction cup still adhered to the circle's center, and Clem wiggled the cup's handle to snap the disk free of the surrounding glass. When he'd removed the disk, he shoved the glass cutter/suction cup unit in his belt pouch, next to the security-code scanner he'd used to get past the front gate, and zipped the pouch shut.

Hunkered down behind the shrubs along the bedroom wall, Maddox scanned the surrounding apartments for witnesses. It was now past three A.M., and all the windows were dark. Since it was a weeknight, most people ought to have been resting up for work the next day, although you couldn't count on that in L.A.

Seeing no immediate threats, Maddox wormed his hand through the hole in the window and unfastened the inside latch. With practiced agility, he opened the window, vaulted over the sill, and eased the window closed behind him in less than twenty seconds.

Now cloaked in the bedroom's darkness, Clem took a penlight from a loop on his belt and began searching for a suitable touchstone. He waved the tiny circle of light toward the open closet, but quickly moved on: Half the hangers were already bare, and clothing was bulky to carry. Besides, Clem preferred a more personal item for his purposes—something with greater resonance.

He'd failed to obtain a suitable item from Lucinda Kamei's house after the murder. Too many cops around. Fortunately, he already owned a CD she'd autographed for him at a Virgin Megastore a couple years back. Hardly ideal, but she *had* touched it, and it would have to do.

From now on, though, he would plan ahead, and take what he needed in advance. That's why he'd driven all night to come to Los Angeles. Already his hands shook from the effects of too many Red Bulls and Nō-Dōz tablets, and he would be driving even farther before he slept again.

The penlight's beam danced over the bare mannequin heads on the makeup table, its firefly brightness reflected in the mirror's gloom. Silver glinted in the passing glare, and Maddox trained the beam on the hanging necklace. He smiled.

"Soon, Amy. *Very* soon."

He took the snake pendant in his palm and rubbed it for luck.

26

Old Friends

DAN AWOKE WITH A STALE SNOT TASTE ON HIS breath and a snail-trail film coating his mouth. He scraped his tongue with his teeth and groaned as he rolled over onto his back, his memory of the previous night still hazy from sleep.

When a hand brushed his forehead, he opened his eyes and saw Natalie gazing down at him.

Startled by the bright sunlight coming through the motel room window, he snapped into a sitting position like a sprung mousetrap. "Jesus! What time is it?"

Natalie stopped him from leaping off the bed. "Relax. It's only nine."

She still wore the feathery shoulder-length wig, but had removed the contacts that turned her pupils a matching shade of brown. Threads of red capillaries laced the whites of her eyes, and her eyelids looked bruised from fatigue. Dan glanced at the bed next to his, whose sheets lay undisturbed. "Don't tell me you—"

"I couldn't sleep anyway." She traced the lines of his cheekbones. "How do you feel?"

He should've had a ready answer to that question, but he didn't. Wrung out? Relieved? Exhilarated? All those things, and more. Remembering last night was like watching his own open-heart surgery on videotape: It hardly seemed real.

"Better," he said at last. "I feel better." He lifted his hand to her cheek, chickened out, touched her arm instead. "Thanks."

Without taking those violet eyes from his face, she grasped his hand in both of hers and raised it to her lips. The kiss alighted on his knuckle with the delicacy of a butterfly.

His pulse quickened with both desire and apprehension. "We—we'd better go...."

Despite his words, he offered only token resistance when Natalie leaned forward to place a whisper-soft kiss on his lips.

Now he did stroke her cheek. "Natalie? Is that really you?"

"Yes. It's me." She drew back a bit. "Does that bother you?"

"No." He let out a nervous chuckle. "It probably should, but no."

Forgetting for a moment that her hair wasn't real, he brushed his fingers through the wavy brown strands and, for the first time, permitted himself to savor the beauty of that bone-china skin and the black-light glow of those dark, dark eyes. A gravitational pull drew him toward her, his mouth opening as it met hers. In the hunger of their loneliness, they jawed the kiss as if devouring each other.

Dan jerked back, abashed. "I'm sorry, I'm such a mess." He massaged his sandpaper cheek and looked down at the clothes he'd slept in, which now smelled like a locker room. "I haven't showered or shaved—"

"Neither have I." She lunged forward to embrace him, and he crushed her to his chest, gratefully nuzzling the tender flesh of her neck to taste the salt of her sweat. His stubble left pink rashes on her paleness, but she didn't complain, even as he moved farther down her body with his kisses. Nor did he complain about the coarseness of her bare legs when she wrapped them around his naked thighs as they made love. Afterward, Natalie removed her wig and showered with him, Dan caressing the water-slicked smoothness of her scalp in silent adoration.

A continuing sense of unreality plagued him as the two of them dressed and groomed. Natalie put on her brown wig and contacts, Dan his fake glasses and false mustache. Neither of them spoke about what had happened; either they were reluctant to admit what they'd done, or they didn't want to jinx whatever magic had brought them together. Everything reverted to the way it had been, yet everything had changed.

They took the elevator down to ground level, and Natalie insisted that they stop for coffee in the dining room next to the motel lobby. The "complimentary continental breakfast" provided only Styrofoam cups of scorched Folgers with powdered nondairy creamer for taste, but Natalie gulped down two cups of the sludge with barely a wince.

"You *must* be desperate to stay awake." Dan chucked his own half-full cup in the trash.

"Yep." She upended her remaining coffee as if knocking back a shot of whiskey.

"Lucy scare you that much?"

Natalie's expression turned grim. "Lucy was one of the most experienced Violets I know. Any normal soul she could've booted out of her brain in two seconds. If she couldn't beat it, I don't know how I can."

"You can't stay awake forever."

"I know. That's why you can't trust me." She slipped her hand into his, glancing around the lobby as if committing a felony. "Don't let me out of your sight. If I start acting weird, knock me out. Punch me if you have to. Whatever it takes to—"

Her eyes fixed on something across the room.

"What is it?" He looked in that direction and saw a cadaverously thin black man in a gray suit seated opposite them, absorbed in the morning *Chronicle*.

"Maybe I'm just paranoid." She scrutinized the man's patrician face, which was fringed with a scrub of black wool beard. "I could swear he was on my flight last night."

The man folded his paper and nestled it under his arm as he rose and sauntered out of the lobby. He seemed perfectly at ease…but was there, perhaps, something a bit too studied in his nonchalance, a bit too deliberate in the way he avoided looking in their direction?

Dan tightened his grip on Natalie's hand. "Let's go."

By the time they reached the sidewalk outside the motel, the man was nowhere to be seen.

As he and Natalie got in their car and headed for the Hall of Justice to meet with Clark, Dan eyed each pedestrian they passed and the driver of every vehicle around them, wary of any stranger whose gaze lingered on them too long. The city became like the Gangster's Alley target range back at the police academy—a facade of hidden menace where jack-in-the-box malefactors might pop out of a window or door at any moment.

It wasn't long before he noticed the black Honda Accord that followed them around three different turns as they wound their way through the narrow midtown streets.

Natalie slumped against the passenger-side window and threw her head back as if about to sneeze, grunting as if in pain. Dan's eyes darted between the street ahead and the car reflected in the rearview mirror. Steering with one hand, he grabbed her arm and jerked her upright. "Hey! You okay?"

She blinked and shook off her fatigue. "Yeah...I'm fine. What's up?"

"I'm about to find out." He merged from the left lane into the right. The Honda did the same. As they approached the next intersection, Dan slowed his speed until the light turned yellow, then stepped on the accelerator. The Honda ran the red to keep up with him. With the car right on his back bumper, he could now see the driver in his mirror: Behind the wheel sat what looked like a big pink bubble wearing a baseball cap.

Dan grinned.

"What are you doing?" Natalie asked as he turned off Van Ness and started searching the crowded curbs of a side street for a parking space.

"Going to visit an old friend." Finding the perfect spot took a while; he needed a space fairly close to a traffic light that had another open space behind it. Fortunately, Preston was a persistent and artless tail. Dan clucked his tongue at himself for not having spotted the reporter long before that afternoon at Kamei's house.

He finally found a likely-looking spot and parked, and was gratified to see the Honda backing into the spot half a block behind him. "I'll only be a few minutes," he told Natalie. "Will you be okay?"

She gave a tentative nod. In the bright light of day, the dark discoloration around her eyes made her look frail and sickly. "Could you leave the keys?" she asked, her voice hoarse. "I'd like to run the AC."

"Uh...sure." He reinserted the key in the ignition and waited for the traffic light to turn red, his hand on the door handle. When the light changed, the cars backed up at the intersection, and Dan jumped out and ran down the street to the Honda.

Sid Preston saw him coming and threw his Honda into gear, but it was too late. The line of cars idled bumper-to-bumper, and no one would let him nose his way in. Through the windshield, Dan saw Preston pound the steering wheel and curse in soundproofed pantomime.

Striding up alongside the Honda, Dan tapped on the driver's-side window with a cheery smile. The reporter glared at him, but rolled down the window anyway.

"Mr. Preston! What a pleasant surprise."

The newsman pulled the bill of his Yankees cap down over his brow. "What do you want, Atwater?"

"Well, how about stepping out of the car for starters?"

"Why? I don't have to talk to you."

"On the contrary, you've been at the site of every single Violet murder, so that makes you a prime suspect."

"Give me a break! That's a load of BS and you know it."

"All right, then. How about I arrest you for obstruction of justice?"

Preston snorted with derision. "You'll never make that stick."

"Maybe not, but it'll keep your byline off the front page until your lawyer can bail you out."

Grinding his gum between his teeth, Preston spat an obscenity and put the car in park. He got out and leaned back against the Honda with folded arms. "Didn't they ever tell you not to screw with the Fourth Estate?"

Dan shrugged. "What can I say? You know how much I like making headlines. How did you find me, anyway?"

"Wasn't hard. I figured you'd have to come out of hiding to report to your boss, so I hung around Earl Clark for a few days. Saw you with him at the Kamei place and the morgue, subtracted the Groucho Marx disguise and—bingo!"

"Not bad. And the Violet murders? How did you put them together?"

The reporter bared his teeth in a smirk. "Now that *was* a beautiful thing, wasn't it? There I am, covering this gang-related shooting in New York, and Russell Travers is the Violet on the case. He suddenly disappears, and people start wondering if he's been whacked.

"I think there might be an angle, so I pester the N-double-A-C-C for more info. But they act all cagey, want to know why I'm so interested in Travers. I do some poking around and find that Travers is the fifth Violet to vanish in, like, three months. Not only that, but they've shut down the school where they teach the creepy kids. That's when I knew I was onto something big."

"Congratulations. Anything you've discovered that we should know?"

Preston's grin widened. "Maybe. What's it worth to you?"

Dan regarded him with the game face of a Persian rug dealer. "Depends what it is … and what you want for it."

"What it is is a license plate number. As for what I want … well, you can probably guess that."

He hath a lean and hungry look, Dan thought, frowning at the knifepoint glint in the reporter's eyes. "You want the scoop."

"Naturally. An exclusive: I want to be there when you bag him and credit for helping you catch him."

Dan nodded his appreciation. "That oughtta be good for a book deal, all right."

"So we have a deal?"

"Yes … assuming your lead pans out. If it's a dud, the deal's off."

"Fair enough. I'm a reasonable man."

Preston ducked his head through the open car window, stretched his arm across to the passenger seat, and yanked a yellow legal pad out from under a scattering of empty Mountain Dew cans. He offered Dan the pad, but snatched it away again.

"Don't cross me, Atwater." The smile had become a sneer. "I can make you either a hero or a stooge in this story."

"I think you already proved that." Dan took hold of the pad, and Preston let go of it with a triumphant grin.

The top pages were dog-eared, discolored with grime, and crowded with sloppy shorthand. Crude doodles of naked women cluttered the margins.

Preston peeled back the yellow sheets until he came to

one with a column of alphanumeric combinations. "I wrote down the plate numbers of every car I saw near the Gannon place and the séance shop. Only two showed up more than once: yours, and this one."

He tapped a line highlighted in pink marker that read "WA—3APM—821—gray Camaro." "I woulda traced it myself, but I don't have the police connections in Washington that I do in New York and L.A."

"Mmm." Dan's pulse quickened, but he acted unimpressed, even a little bored, by the information as he transcribed the license number into his own notebook.

"You better write my cell phone number there, too," Preston murmured, and dictated the digits. "Call me for the arrest."

"*If* there's an arrest. And only if you stay out of my way."

Tucking his notebook and pen back in his jacket pocket, he returned the legal pad to Preston, who was staring past his shoulder, snickering.

Dan scowled. "What're *you* laughing at?"

The reporter nodded toward the stoplight up the street. "Isn't that your car?"

With Preston's laughter rising in his ears, Dan whipped around in time to see the rented Buick driving through the intersection.

Shoving the reporter away from the Honda's door, Dan held out his hand. "Give me your keys!"

"What? You can't—"

He grabbed Preston's shirt. "NOW!"

"All right! Sheesh..."

Dan snatched the key ring from him and slung himself into the Honda's driver's seat. "You wreck that car and you're paying for it!" he heard Preston shout as the Accord peeled out from the curb.

The light at the intersection changed from yellow to red just as he got there, and cross-traffic began to roll. Dan leaned on the Honda's horn and stepped on the gas. Brakes squealed and horns snarled as he swerved between the cars to his left and right, nearly causing the Accord to fishtail and spin out.

With three cars now between him and Natalie, Dan saw a man on a motorcycle swing in behind the Buick and follow it into the left-turn lane. Although a black helmet hid the rider's face, he wore the same gray suit Dan had seen on the man in the motel lobby that morning.

"Oh, God." Dan veered into the adjacent lane of on-coming traffic in hopes of doing an end run around the intervening vehicles, but a Ford Explorer barreled toward him and barely missed smashing head-on into his front end. Trapped between currents of traffic with drivers on all sides yelling at him, he watched in despair as the Buick and the motorcycle disappeared over the hill ahead.

27

Auto-Abduction

NATALIE AWOKE IN DARKNESS.

The fact that she couldn't remember falling asleep shocked her into alertness, her eyes straining to shape the shadows. Drifting dust swirled in a conical beam of light before her, and she heard the soft whir of a projector fan.

"As you can see, the eighth victim established the pattern we have since come to recognize as the Violet Killer's signature." Dan's voice, emanating from somewhere on the other side of the light beam. "Note the staging of the body, the placement of the extracted intestines...."

Natalie looked to her left, where the cone of light spread a lurid crime scene photo of Arthur McCord across a rectangular screen.

"We see the pattern repeated in the mutilation and debasement of the ninth victim."

The screen went black, and the projector exchanged slides with a mechanical shifting sound. The light beam turned ruby red, splashing the screen with a shot of Lucy lying naked in a lake of blood. Although Dan had described the scene to her on the way back from the airport, Natalie still gasped at the carnage.

She searched the room around her for others' reactions,

but couldn't make out any faces. Was this the San Francisco police headquarters? Dan had been driving her there, last thing she remembered. Did the gentle motion of the car lull her to sleep? Had she somehow somnabulated her way into a meeting without realizing it?

Something was dripping off to her right. Probably condensation from an air conditioner vent.

Dan continued his lecture with the same passionless pedantry. "We can trace the growing rage of the UNSUB through the increasing boldness in his desecration of the corpses, beginning with the first victim...."

The slide changed again, and a morgue close-up of Jem's eyeless face flashed into view.

"His habit of taking the eyes as trophies tells us that we're dealing with a highly organized, obsessive killer."

Jem's wizened skin had blanched from a rich mahogany to a ghastly greenish gray. Natalie shivered. Had they just discovered his body? Was that why they'd scheduled the meeting?

The tempo of the dripping accelerated. The air conditioner must indeed have been working overtime, for the room grew quite cold and was permeated with the stale scent of mildew.

"With each successive victim, the killer embellished his atrocities...."

Autopsy photos of Gig, Sondra, Russell, and Sylvia replaced each other with clockwork regularity.

"Wait! I don't understand," Natalie blurted. "When did you find—"

"At first incidental, the slash marks on the torso evolved into part of the killer's ritual: the message of his murders."

Dan proceeded with his dry commentary as if he hadn't heard her.

"It's okay, Boo," a voice of indeterminate gender whispered to her. "They didn't suffer."

The breath nipped her ear like the exhalation from an open freezer. She started and looked around, but the whisperer was lost in darkness. The dripping was now accompanied by an irregular squishing sound, like the oozing of water-soaked shoes.

Evan's face loomed before her on the screen. Even the empty eye sockets and the red gash across the neck couldn't destroy the sweet soulfulness of his high forehead and full lips. Pressing her fists to her mouth, Natalie now recognized the unique inflections of the whispering voice.

Dan droned through a detailed analysis of Laurie Gannon's disembowelment, and the projector coughed up another slide. "Of course, we can see the culmination of the killer's psychopathology in his treatment of the tenth victim...."

Another livid cadaver, another pair of raw red eye sockets. But this time the face was Natalie's.

She tried to scream, but couldn't summon enough breath. The killer had wrapped the rope of her intestine around her neck in a crude noose, like the umbilical cord in a breech birth.

"...And so we can see that the UNSUB is likely to grow even more savage and depraved in his crimes until we apprehend him. A greater understanding of his methods and madness should help us do that." The slide show ended with a blank white screen. "Lights, please."

The room remained black as tar, although Natalie

imagined she could see darker shapes seething around her in the opaque shadows. Thorns of cold bit into her skin, and the odor of iron and mold saturated the air.

"Could someone get the lights, please?" Dan asked in peevish annoyance.

All around, the sound of dripping and squishing and dragging.

"I'm afraid you're mistaken." Arthur's voice, unmistakable yet strangely guttural and clotted with phlegm. "There are no lights here."

The rectangle of white on the projector screen vanished like the outline of a slamming door, and the shambling shadows pressed in upon Natalie, sightless fingers groping to welcome her....

Terror propelled Natalie out of one darkness and into another, the transition from nightmare to consciousness as seamless as the awakening of the blind.

Her eyes felt open, yet she could see nothing. Was this another dream? Or was she already dead?

She sought some sensation from her body, but none came through. Yet, her soul still ricocheted off the walls of her flesh, a lightning bug trapped in a jar. Someone had evidently knocked while she was asleep, boxing her in the nether regions of her own mind.

Natalie instinctively invoked the Twenty-third Psalm. Through years of meditation, she'd conditioned her brain and body to restore control to her whenever she recited the protective mantra. But now her will encountered some unforeseen surface tension, her thoughts sealed in an impenetrable bubble.

They got me while I was asleep.

Fear jangled through her. If what Lucy had told her was true, the killer might be slitting her stomach right now.

I never even saw the end. . . .

Natalie frantically sifted her memories for a means of escape. What else had Lucy said? *They knew my mantra and used it against me.* By mimicking the host Violet's mantra, the invading soul must fool the body into ceding control to it. If that was the case, how could she reconnect with her flesh?

Every house has a back door, she thought. *There must be another way in.*

She left off the Twenty-third Psalm in mid-verse and switched to the protective mantra Jem had taught her when she was only seven. It was a snatch of blues that his mother had once sung to him as a lullaby:

> *O Jesus, sweet Jesus, come hold me when I die*
> *'N' lay me in the bed of the big night sky.*

The blackness brightened into two blurred spots of light like those in a pair of unfocused binoculars. As Natalie repeated the refrain in her mind, the spots grew and defined themselves until they overlapped into a single image, which nevertheless wavered in and out of double vision.

She saw that she still rode in Dan's rental car, only now she sat in the driver's seat. The old mantra also restored some sense of her flesh, although her limbs felt like they were made of sponge; only the dull pressure of the steering wheel on her hands and the accelerator under her foot confirmed the solidity of her form.

With queasy helplessness, Natalie watched her hands, of their own volition, steer the car onto a street lined with grimy gray tenements and cheap motels. Though she quickened the pace of the mantra, she couldn't stop her body from parking the car and entering what had once been an office building whose front door bore a name that had long ago been spray-painted into illegibility. The outhouse odor of urine seeped into Natalie's awareness as she saw herself march through a garbage-strewn foyer and up a flight of concrete steps to a door that was missing its handle. Her hand knocked on it.

"I have her." The words sounded as distant and hollow as the mumble of a gramophone, and it took Natalie a moment to recognize her own voice. "Get ready," it said.

Footsteps scuffed toward the door, followed by the slingshot snap of rubber pulled tight. Three latex-covered fingers poked through the hole where the knob should have been and pulled the door inward.

No no no no! Natalie shrieked, but her body stepped into the room anyway. She caught a glimpse of floral wallpaper stained with mildew before her gaze swung around to confront the featureless black veil of the Faceless Man, who shut the door behind her.

"Did you—?"

"Don't speak," Natalie's voice snapped. "She's breaking through, and I'm not sure how long I can hold her. Let's get on with it."

Natalie's body stripped off her T-shirt and bra, then unzipped her jeans and pushed them to her ankles. Bare breasts dangling, it sat on the floor and shoved the pants, panties, and shoes off her feet into a jumbled heap.

"Well, what are you waiting for?" Her voice was sharp with impatience, her eyes glaring up at the Faceless Man.

The double image of the man split and merged and split again, resembling an amoeba that was struggling to divide. Crouching beside her naked body, he drew a carbon-steel knife from his belt—the kind used to clean deer carcasses—and poised the blade over her midriff, its tip grazing the inside of her navel.

O Jesus, sweet Jesus, come hold me when I die, Natalie repeated with fervent desperation, *'N' lay me in the bed of the big night sky!*

The mantra was now a prayer.

The knife quivered in the killer's grip. The fabric over his mouth palpitated like a beating heart.

"Come on!" Natalie's hands wrapped themselves around the Faceless Man's fist and drew the knife down. *"Do it!"*

Her skin began to yield to the blade's point, a single tear of blood leaking from the nick in her belly. With the petulance of a toddler determined to prove he can tie his own shoes, the Faceless Man wrested his hand free from her grasp and pulled the knife back, his arm tensing to drive the blade home.

O Jesus, sweet Jesus…!

As though struck by a thunderbolt, the killer stiffened and pitched forward on top of her, his limbs spastic and shaking.

Two small metal darts had lodged in his back, each trailing a wavy white wire. The wires led up to a device that resembled a man's electric razor, except that it sported a trigger instead of a switch.

The hand holding the taser belonged to the black man she'd seen on the plane.

Natalie pleaded to the man with her mind, but could not make herself heard. Instead, her body growled at him and pushed its way out from under the convulsing killer to lunge for the hunting knife. As her fingers closed on the handle, the stranger's brown leather dress shoe stomped on the blade, pinning it to the floor. He disengaged the top of the taser, uncovering the U-shaped spark gap of a stun gun. A thread of blue fire jumped across the gap with an electric crack.

No longer immobilized by the taser's current, the killer groaned and got to his knees.

Natalie wanted to shriek a warning to her rescuer, but her body obeyed its other master. It thrust its naked weight against the black man's leg and yanked the knife free. Rather than lashing out at the stranger, though, her hand turned the blade's point inward, aiming it at her own heart.

The stranger seized her wrist, straining to hold the knife at bay, and thrust the stun gun toward her arm. Another crack split the air, and Natalie's nervous system overloaded with the shock.

Just before her vision whited out, she saw the Faceless Man rise behind the stranger, his rubber-skinned hands reaching for the black man's throat.

After a blankness of unknown duration, Natalie's thoughts coalesced again. Her entire body stung as if wrapped in nettles, the way it did whenever someone hit the Panic Button on a SoulScan unit.

She opened her eyes to a sideways view of the floor, the hunting knife lying inches from her face. Natalie focused her will on the weapon, and her hand scuttled toward it like a palsied spider.

As her hearing returned, she became aware of the sound of scuffling feet, punctuated by grunts and sharp cries. Grabbing hold of the knife, Natalie rolled onto her back and saw that the Faceless Man had locked one arm around the stranger's neck while he slammed the man's right hand against the wall.

His fingers bruised, the black man dropped the stun gun and, in a lightning-quick motion, jerked his head back against the killer's masked face, smacking it just above the bridge of the nose.

Stunned, the killer let his choke hold slip, and the stranger thrust his elbow into the Faceless Man's solar plexus. Anticipating the move, the killer staggered back a step and grabbed the stranger's arm, twisting it behind his back. The black man's groan shrank to a rasp as the choke hold tightened on his windpipe again.

With coltish clumsiness, Natalie pushed herself into a crouch and charged at the Faceless Man, brandishing the knife. At the sight of her, he froze with indecision for an instant, then shoved the stranger at her. The two of them collided and toppled to the floor, while the killer's staccato footsteps pattered out the door and down the stairwell.

The stranger sat up, still coughing for breath. "You all right?" he rasped.

For the first time, Natalie looked down at her nude body and noticed the glistening red smear between her navel and her genitals. "Yeah. I think it's just a scratch. But—"

Without waiting for her to finish, the stranger scooped the stun gun off the floor and bounded after the killer.

Left alone, Natalie glanced from her heaped clothes to her bleeding belly, unsure what to do with herself.

A minute later, the black man returned, his posture more relaxed. "He's gone. Let's have a look at you."

He knelt beside Natalie and studied her wound. "This should be wrapped," he decided, and unbuttoned his dress shirt. Natalie gaped in astonishment when she saw the yards of Ace bandage wrapped around the man's chest.

"I think you need this more than I do." He removed the diaper pin that fastened the cloth strip in place and unwound the bandage. Natalie's eyes widened further as the "man's" unbound breasts swelled into fullness.

"Who *are* you?" she asked.

The stranger grinned and tore off "his" beard. Smooth and hairless, the face suddenly became familiar: Natalie had last seen it in a Seattle cemetery.

"Serena Mfume, at your service," the woman said. "Simon sends his regards."

28

Reunions

SERENA DIDN'T BOTHER TO COVER HER BREASTS before leaning toward Natalie with the Ace bandage. "Lift your arms."

Still in a shock-induced stupor, Natalie did as she was told. Serena wound the cloth strip around Natalie's midriff and safety-pinned it. The beige weave of the elastic strip darkened to purple as it absorbed the blood beneath.

"There. That oughtta hold you 'til a doctor can stitch it up." She sat back on her heels and buttoned up her shirt.

Her own clothes forgotten for the moment, Natalie gawked at her rescuer, too astonished even to express her gratitude. "Why are you here?"

"Simon was worried about you. He figured the killer might have an accomplice on the Other Side, and he didn't think the cops were prepared for that possibility." Serena shoved the fake beard in her pocket and picked up the stun gun. "Simon can be a bit of a tyrant sometimes, but he's really an old softie at heart."

"Yeah. I guess so." Natalie grimaced, remembering how she'd made him her prime suspect.

"Um…aren't you cold?" Serena indicated Natalie's clothes.

"Oh…yeah." Flustered, Natalie snatched up her shirt, pulled it right side out, and put it on without the bra. Balancing on one foot to insert a leg in her jeans, she heard Serena whistle from somewhere behind her.

"Looks like our friend left us a present."

Natalie dropped the pants and walked bare-legged over to where Serena knelt beside an Adidas gym bag. The black woman shrugged off her businessman's jacket and wrapped it around her hand, which she used to part the bag's open zipper. Light fell on a mass of crumpled clothes.

Tucked in one end of the bag, a shaggy toupee snaked a few blond curls into view.

For a moment, Natalie thought Laurie Gannon was knocking. Again she saw the little girl's view of the blond man in the jumpsuit, squatting beside the oil tank, his face pinched in an agony of indecision.

"That's it. That's the one he wore at the School."

Serena glanced up at her. "What?"

"The wig."

"I see." She folded her jacket around the bag as if swaddling a baby. "Maybe the folks in forensics can tell us something about our mystery man. We need to get this to your Fed friend."

"Dan—oh, God!" Natalie scrambled to finish dressing.

As soon as she was ready, she let Serena lead her down the stairs and around behind the concrete steps, where a burly black Harley leaned on its kickstand.

Natalie looked at the motorcycle as if it were a rhinoceros. "You brought it inside?"

"This is the Tenderloin. I couldn't leave it out *there*." Serena hooked the stun gun on her belt and nestled the wrapped gym bag in one of the bike's rear compartments. "We're lucky our masked man didn't notice it on his way out. You feel up to riding on back?"

"I guess...."

"Good. Get the door for me, will you?"

She nodded and propped the door open while Serena wheeled the Harley out onto the sidewalk. Straddling the front of the bike, she handed Natalie her helmet. "You better take this."

Natalie donned the headgear and climbed on the back of the leather seat, wrapping her arms around her rescuer's steel-hard waist.

The black woman flipped up the kickstand with her foot. "Hang on."

"Serena?"

"Yeah?"

"Thanks."

"Don't thank me yet. My work's just begun." She stomped on the starter, revved the throttle, and they roared off down Turk Street.

Piloting Sid Preston's Accord along Geary Boulevard, Dan hardly blinked as he squinted at each blue Buick and black motorcycle he passed. More than dedication to duty motivated his vigilance. If he kept his eyes on the street, he couldn't look at the dashboard clock, wouldn't dwell on how much time had elapsed since he'd last seen Natalie.

After calling in the APB, he'd driven through the downtown avenues in an ever-widening spiral, beginning his search at the point where the car and bike had disappeared from view. Every few minutes, he would pass one of the SFPD patrol cars engaged in the hunt, and he prayed that one of them would suddenly spin its lights, its siren proclaiming that Natalie was safe and on her way back to him. But each car prowled past him quiet and dark, and Dan's heart twisted with dying hope.

When his cell phone chirped, he almost didn't answer it. Preston had already called three times to demand his car back. The phone wouldn't shut up, though, so Dan snatched it off the seat beside him in annoyance. "Yeah?"

"Dan?"

Red taillights flashed on in front of him, but he nearly forgot to brake. "*Natalie?* Are you all right?"

"Yes, yes, I'm fine—"

"My God! I've got half the cops in the city looking for you. Where are you?"

"At a McDonald's pay phone."

"Tell me where—I'll have the police there in two minutes."

"No need. I already called them. Listen, can you meet me in the emergency room at St. Francis Memorial?"

"Emergency room?" Concern, like cold water, splashed over his joy of relief. "Lord, you *are* hurt, aren't you?"

"No, I'm fine—it's nothing, really. Can you come?"

"On my way. Look, Natalie, I—"

The car behind him honked, bullying him to move forward.

"—I'll see you there." He hung up and hit the gas.

* * *

Like many metropolitan hospital emergency rooms, the St. Francis ER was a chaos of conflicting crises. Overworked interns and nurses scurried in and out of the swinging doors to the surgery, attending to the most serious cases, while all the patients who could afford to wait sat on padded benches in the outer reception area. Dan was glad to see Natalie seated among them when he arrived.

Her face mirrored his relief, and she leapt off the bench and into his arms for a hug. Dan pressed his nose and lips into the peach-soft skin of her cheek, confirming her reality with touch and smell and taste. "Thank God...."

"It's okay." Her arms constricted around his back. "I'm okay."

He trembled, and his eyes filled with water. "I'm so sorry."

"It's okay. It wasn't your fault."

Dan would have held her like that for an hour or more, but she backed away and turned to her right. "Serena!"

With his tunnel vision trained on Natalie, he hadn't noticed until then that Detective Yee stood nearby, conversing with a tall, slender black woman who wore a man's business suit. At the sound of her name, the woman excused herself to the detective and stepped over to meet Dan.

Her outfit matched the one worn by the man on the motorcycle.

"Dan, this is Serena Mfume, one of Simon's students." Natalie gripped the woman's shoulder in camaraderie. "She saved my life."

Dan extended a stiff arm to Mfume. Gratitude collided with guilt and an ugly streak of jealousy inside him. *It should have been me....*

"Thank you," he said, shaking her hand.

She brushed off the thanks with a dismissive wave. "Anything I can do to help."

"Speaking of which, she brought us a bag of the killer's goodies." Yee came forward to join their group. "Could be the break we've been looking for."

"Great." *She saved Natalie's life,* Dan reminded himself. But Mfume's twin successes rankled him. Not only was she a better bodyguard than he was, she was also a better detective.

In a feeble effort to redeem himself, he reached into his jacket pocket for the license plate number Preston had given him. "By the way, Stuart, I was wondering if your guys could run this for me—"

Before he could pass his notebook to Yee, a woman wearing surgical scrubs and oval wire-framed glasses pushed open one of the swinging doors to the surgery and called out, "Ms. Lindstrom? I can treat you now."

Mfume grinned and gave Natalie a nudge. "That's your cue, girl."

Dan put his hand in the small of Natalie's back and shepherded her toward the door, but the doctor motioned for them to stop. "I'm sorry, sir. Only patients and personnel are allowed in here."

He fumbled his Bureau badge out of his pocket. "This woman is a material witness in a murder investigation. I have to remain with her at all...Natalie?"

All at once, she seemed oblivious to both him and the physician. Her head swiveled to the right, like a radar dish honing in on an enemy plane.

Dan tensed. "What is it?"

Natalie didn't answer, but instead took a tentative step toward one of the nearby benches of waiting patients. A bookish man with reddish-brown hair and sideburns hunched there, massaging his forehead. He muttered something to himself, his eyes closed behind thick horn-rimmed glasses. The words diffused into the general murmur of the waiting room, but from what Dan could discern, they sounded like a series of numbers.

Apparently sensing that someone was watching him, the man shut his mouth and glanced up at Natalie, the lenses of his glasses flashing reflected light. While she was still a few feet away, he stood and headed toward the ER exit with the unhurried gait of a smoker going out for a cigarette.

"STOP!" She hastened to cut him off.

The man broke into a run, elbowing aside an indignant matron as he fled out the door. Natalie sprinted after him.

The perplexed doctor pointed in the direction her patient had gone. "Wait—I thought she was—"

Dan didn't stay long enough to hear what she said. Racing to keep Natalie in sight, he charged out of the hospital and down to the corner of Hyde and Bush Streets. Mfume paced him, stride for stride. The two of them caught up to Natalie when she stopped short at the next intersection.

"What is it?" Dan panted. "*Who* is it?"

Natalie scanned the streets in every direction, clutching her stomach. Her hand couldn't quite hide the blood that had seeped into her shirt.

"It was Evan," she said. "He's alive."

29

The Poser

"I'M TELLING YOU, IT WAS HIM—AH!" LYING ON THE examination table, Natalie flinched as the doctor pulled the thread of another stitch tight. The topical anesthetic apparently couldn't kill the strangeness of the sensation.

The physician, an intern named Grimes, poked her surgical needle back into the skin of Natalie's stomach. "Almost done," she promised.

Dan rubbed his chin. "You're sure what you heard was his…"

"Mantra. Yes."

"Couldn't someone else—another Violet—have the same mantra?"

Natalie's eyes blazed. "No! You see—"

Grimes paused in her sewing. "Lie still, please."

The patient growled with frustration, then relaxed her abdominal muscles again. "I mean, it's possible for two Violets to have the same mantra, but usually different ones work for different people. The mantra is any bit of repeated language that helps you concentrate, helps you keep your personality intact and connected with your body. For Arthur, it was Zen koans; for Jem, African American hymns. And for Evan, it was the multiplication tables. That's what I heard both the homeless guy at the airport and the man here in the waiting room repeating to themselves."

"But we talked to Evan after he disappeared. Russell Travers summoned him. Evan described how the killer got him, and a SoulScan confirmed the whole thing."

"The SoulScan could only confirm that Russell had summoned *someone*—not that it was Evan."

"You're saying a dead soul *impersonated* Evan?"

"Why not? A dead soul impersonated me."

Dan felt his face flush, remembering how he'd been fooled. "But haven't you talked to Evan? After what you've told me, I would've thought—"

"No." Natalie looked away, her mouth small. "I was afraid to. I thought he would knock, but he didn't. Now I know why."

He chose his next words with caution; he didn't want her to hear how much the prospect of Evan's survival depressed him. "Natalie, don't you think this might be wishful thinking?"

The cords of muscle in her neck tightened. "You have Evan's testimony on tape, don't you?"

"Yeah...."

Dr. Grimes snipped the thread of the last stitch with her scissors. "That should do it." She pointed to the line of parallel dashes that ran along Natalie's stomach like tiny train tracks. "You might have a light scar there, but not too bad. And you probably shouldn't get your navel pierced anytime soon."

Natalie chuckled. "Don't need to worry about that."

Grimes daubed Neosporin on the sutured wound and taped a square pad of gauze over it. "Keep it clean and dressed, and you ought to be able to get the stitches out in-side of three weeks. For now, you're good to go."

"Thanks." Natalie hopped off the table and pulled on the T-shirt Dan handed her. "Let's go watch that video."

"Whatever you say." He waved his thanks to Dr. Grimes and followed Natalie out to rejoin Yee and Mfume in the reception area.

Dan was not surprised to find Earl Clark waiting for them when they arrived at the Hall of Justice. He was also not surprised to find Sid Preston there as well, looking very ticked off.

Clark sighed. "Agent Atwater, would you kindly return this gentleman's car?"

Digging the Honda's keys out of his pocket, Dan dan-gled them in front of Preston with his index finger and thumb. With a crab-claw snap, the reporter plucked the key ring from his hand.

"That's another one you owe me, G-man," he spat, and stamped out of the building.

"You want to tell me how you ended up with him?" Clark asked when Preston was gone.

"I think God's punishing me," Dan replied, only half joking. "But he gave me a license number we might be able to use."

"Well, I hope you got something out of him." Clark tipped his head toward Yee and Natalie. "Stu. Ms. Lind-strom—glad to see you're still in one piece. And you must be Ms. Mfume." He shook the newcomer's hand. "Good work. We already have that gym bag under a microscope."

Dan drew a deep breath to preserve his bland expression.

"Did you find the video of Evan's deposition?" Natalie asked.

"Yep." Clark motioned for them all to follow him down the adjacent hallway. "We dug it out, but I don't know what you think it'll tell you. Seems like Evan Markham to me."

"Maybe. But I want to be sure."

When Clark veered toward an office door, Yee broke off from their group. "Earl, I'm going to see if forensics found anything. Catch you guys later."

"Wait! Before you go…" Dan tore the license plate number out of his notebook and handed it to the detective. "See if you can trace this for me."

"Sure." Yee pocketed the slip of paper and proceeded down the hall as Clark ushered the rest of them into a meeting room, where a television and VCR waited on a two-tiered cart.

While Dan and the others seated themselves on a semicircle of folding chairs in front of the TV, Clark switched on the set and grabbed the recorder's remote control. He cautioned Natalie with a look. "You ready for this?"

She rubbed her arms as if to ward off a chill and gave him the go-ahead.

Clark pressed the remote's Play button, and the placid blue of the TV screen dissolved into a burst of black-and-white snow as the VCR adjusted the tape's tracking. When the picture cleared, they saw a three-quarter-profile close-up of Russell Travers, his bald scalp scabbed with electrodes and sprouting wires. Dan shifted in his seat when he saw the drooping face with its fishbowl glasses; he'd seen the tape before, of course, but not since this dead man had tried to seduce him with Natalie's body.

Captions at the bottom of the screen gave Travers's name and the name of Evan Markham, the witness he was summoning. A bracket on the right side of the screen showed the real-time readout from the SoulScan unit, green brainwaves spiking to verify the presence of the occupying soul. Clark had evidently cued the tape up to the moment of inhabitation, for Travers hunched into a fetal curl, raising his arms as if to shield himself from a beating. In his blue-veined fists, he held a silver chain from which hung a circular metal pendant. The pendant rotated toward the camera, revealing two snakes entwined to form the figure-eight symbol for infinity, each with its tail in the other's mouth.

Natalie stiffened. It was the twin of the one in her apartment. Dan recalled the grief in her eyes as she'd held it.

But she can't be pining for him now, he silently insisted. *Not after last night....*

In the video, Travers's posture relaxed as he ceded control to the summoned witness. He squinted at his surroundings through the thick lenses of the glasses, discarded the pendant on the table in front of him, and slouched back in his chair with a James Dean defiance.

"Who are you?" asked a female voice from off-screen. Dan knew the interviewer was Karen Spence, one of his colleagues at Quantico.

The man wearing Travers's face gave a rictus grin. "Evan Markham. Isn't that who you were expecting?"

"Can you tell us how you died, Evan?"

The man seemed amused by the interrogation. No doubt Evan had served as conduit for many such interviews, and now he had to answer all the same questions he'd heard dozens of times in the past.

"Someone wrapped a piece of wire around my neck and pulled." He mimed the action with ghoulish flair. "The pressure built in my head until it felt like every artery in my brain burst, and I died. That clear enough for you?"

Dan glanced at Natalie to gauge her reaction, but she kept watching the screen with a determined stare.

On the videotape, Spence's detached tone did not waver. "Did you see the individual who did this to you?"

"Are you kidding? After what he did to Sondra? If I'd *seen* him, you'd be talking to him right now instead of me."

"He attacked you from behind, then?"

"What do *you* think?"

"I'll take that as a yes. Now, after Ms. Avebury's disappearance, you went into hiding on your own, against the Corps' advice—"

"They wanted to lock me in one of their goddamn safe houses!" He took off his glasses to wipe the tears of rage from his eyes. "The woman I loved had just been butchered. Was I supposed to grieve in a prison?"

Natalie winced.

"It must have been terrible for you." Spence's tone became more sympathetic. "We want to punish the killer as much as you do. That's why we need your help. Where were you when he found you?"

Casting aside the spectacles, he sagged back in the

chair. "Virginia Beach. It was one of Sondra's favorite vacation spots."

"Do you know how the killer found you there?"

"No."

"Do you have any idea where he took your body?"

"How the hell should I know? I was *dead* at the time, if you recall…."

Natalie tensed. "Stop! Roll it back a little."

Raising an eyebrow in surprise, Clark hit the remote's Rewind button. Travers unsaid his last few remarks in reverse-scan mode, and Clark let the tape roll forward again.

"—one of Sondra's favorite vacation spots."

"Do you know how the killer found you there?"

"No."

"Do you have any idea where he took your body?"

"How the hell should I know? I was *dead*—"

Natalie jumped from her chair. *"There!* Pause it!"

Clark froze the frame, capturing Travers with his mouth open in mid-sentence.

Standing to one side of the television screen, Natalie pointed to Travers's left arm. "You see how he brushes this hand past his ear and down the back of his head as he talks? That's the habit of someone who's used to having long hair. I know, because I do it myself even when I'm not wearing a wig. Evan almost never wore a wig, and when he did, it was always a very short toupee. Evan is also righthanded; this person took off the glasses with his *left* hand."

Dan and Clark gave each other a quizzical look.

"That's not all," Mfume added. "Rewind it to the beginning."

Clark backed the tape up to the point of inhabitation: Travers relaxed in his chair, squinted at his surroundings.

"Notice how he glances down at the necklace he's holding before throwing it on the table," Mfume observed. "That's because he needs to *see* what the touchstone is. He needs to see who he's supposed to be."

Dan shivered; the room's temperature seemed to have plunged about ten degrees. "But the dead person would still have had to touch the necklace at some point during his lifetime. That's the way a touchstone works, right? How many people could've come in contact with it besides Evan?"

"Not many." Natalie brushed the video image of the pendant with her fingertips. "It was our secret."

The wistfulness in her voice made Dan grit his teeth. "Do you know of anyone else he might have shown it to?"

Her face tightened. "Sondra, I suppose."

"She had undercover training," Serena casually mentioned. "Was a whiz at impersonations."

Everyone gaped at her.

"We worked together in the Corps' Intelligence Division awhile." She smiled. "That's classified, by the way. Tell anyone, and I'll have to kill you."

Dan looked to Natalie. "You think that's her?" He indicated Travers, who repeated his answers to the interrogation as the tape replayed.

"I don't know. But I want to find out."

Clark stopped the VCR and switched off the TV. "We

obviously need to confront this impostor again. Only problem is, how do we get 'im to tell the truth? What do you use to threaten someone who's already dead?"

Natalie's expression turned hard and cold. "Same threat you use on someone who's still alive: imprisonment."

30

Violets within Violets

WITH A RIPPING SOUND, MFUME DUCT-TAPED THE last sheet of aluminum foil over the layers of chicken wire and rubber insulation, cutting the tape off with an X-Acto knife. "Well, that's it." Only the ridges of her brows, cheeks, and chin showed in the darkness, lit from underneath by the beam of Natalie's flashlight. "You really think this can trap a ghost?"

"It worked for Arthur." Natalie swept the beam around the narrow interior of the transformed utility closet. The foil-lined walls returned the light in dull reflections, a cell made of blurred mirrors. They'd covered everything, including the electrical outlets and the socket for the overhead lightbulb.

Dan tossed a half-used roll of Reynolds Wrap beside a pair of bare cardboard tubes. "Whether it really works or not, we need to convince our impostor 'Evan' that it does. Still...not bad for a three-hour job."

He pushed open the closet door and led the two women out through the rickety booth they'd fashioned from plywood and two-by-fours they'd bought at Home

Depot. It, too, was lined with layers of metal and insulation, and they each had to duck through the low makeshift door as they reemerged into the hallway of the police head-quarters.

The former contents of the closet—bottles of disinfec-tant, jugs of bleach and hand soap, and an array of mops, brooms, and vacuum cleaners—cluttered the corridor in haphazard clusters, which the SFPD officers had to step over and around as they passed. Several of them paused to gawk at the odd structure, Stuart Yee among them. He greeted Dan with a grin.

"Love what you've done with the place. Mind telling me what it's for?"

"It's a holding pen for a prisoner," Dan explained, "only this one happens to be dead."

"Okay, but what's with the garden shed?" Yee kicked the corner of the booth.

"Hey, take it easy! Don't break it before we've even used it." He shooed the detective back a step. "It's sort of an air-lock—a buffer zone, so the soul won't escape when we open the door to come out."

"You saying our janitor's closet's going to be haunted from now on?"

"Only if we screw up."

"I'll have an exorcist standing by."

"Thanks for the vote of confidence."

"Don't mention it. Anyway, I wanted to let you know I looked up that plate number you gave me." Yee unfolded a computer printout of the Washington state DMV informa-tion and handed it to him. "Camaro's registered to Clement

Maddox, a Seattle TV repairman, thirty-seven years old, widowed. No priors that we can find, but we're still looking."

"Great." Dan peered at the name on the form and felt the niggling itch of recognition.

MADDOX, CLEMENT EVERETT.

Where had he seen it before?

Yee turned to Mfume. "We've also gone through the gym bag and its contents. Found some lock picks as well as the rest of the disguise he used at the School. Couldn't get any decent prints, sad to say, but forensics did get some skin cell samples off the inside of that toupee, which we've sent out for DNA analysis."

"Will that tell you anything about the guy?" she asked.

"Not unless the FBI already has his DNA on file. But if we ever find a suspect that matches, we'll nail him in court."

"Hmm. Let's see if our mystery ghost has any ideas." Dan touched Natalie's shoulder. "You sure you want to do this? Serena could—"

"No." Natalie had removed her wig and contacts, and her eyes gleamed like amethysts. "I *have* to do this."

Dan squeezed her hand. "Okay."

"We put a battery in this." Mfume hefted a SoulScan unit off a cart parked in the corridor. "Should last at least an hour. You want me in there with you?"

"Nah. The fewer Violets we have inside, the better."

With a flashlight in one hand, Dan grabbed the wooden chair he'd chosen for Natalie and carried it into the utility closet, where he placed it near the back wall. Mfume set the SoulScan on an overturned milk crate by the door and unwrapped the coiled electrode wires, while Dan set his flashlight on top of the unit and stepped out to get a metal folding chair for himself. He reentered the closet with Natalie, who carried an extra flashlight and a hank of nylon rope.

Mfume slapped the back of the wooden chair. "Make yourself comfortable."

Natalie sat down, and Mfume took the rope and wound it around the other woman's ankles and wrists, binding them to the chair's legs and arms as though preparing her for a Houdini escape.

"Make sure those knots are tight," Natalie said.

When the rope was secure, Dan raised his flashlight beam so Mfume could attach the SoulScan electrodes to Natalie's head. He wasn't going to record an official deposition, so he didn't really need the machine's readout, but he wanted that Panic Button within easy reach if the interrogation got ugly.

Mfume finished her work and squeezed past him on her way out. "Give a holler when you want me to slam the doors."

"Check."

Dan set one of the two flashlights on the SoulScan unit, shining it on Natalie's midsection, and held the other in his hand, directing it at her mouth so as not to blind her. In the darkness above the beam, her eyes became pinpoints of reflected light, her head a Medusa of wires snaking into shadow.

Kneeling beside her chair, Dan took hold of her right hand. "Good luck."

Her fingers tightened on his. "Thanks. You, too."

She opened her palm. Reaching into his jacket pocket, Dan took out the snake pendant and placed it in her hand. The serpents glinted under the flashlight's beam for an instant before her fingers curled over them.

Dan sat on the folding chair and watched for the first signs of inhabitation. If their soul cage worked, the electromagnetic entity that Natalie summoned could only enter the closet through the open door behind him. He tried not to dwell on the fact that the soul might actually pass *through* him to get to her.

Natalie settled into a rhythmic breathing pattern, and the waves on the top three lines of the SoulScan screen rolled with conditioned regularity.

Time crawled by in the stifling confines of the converted alcove. With nothing to look at but wavy green lines and Natalie's blank stare, Dan suppressed a yawn more than once.

After about half an hour of silence, Mfume stuck her head back through the door. "Anything yet?"

"Nope." Dan sighed and stretched. "Hope we didn't make this thing *too* ghostproof...."

A loud creaking interrupted him. The joints of Natalie's chair groaned as she rocked from side to side, her arms and legs straining against the knotted rope. The three flat lines at the bottom of the SoulScan screen spiked into jagged peaks.

Dan waved Mfume back. "We got something. Shut the doors."

She withdrew, and the padded door closed with the muffled suction of a coffin lid. Dan kept his flashlight trained on Natalie, who almost tipped the chair over with her thrashing.

After more than a minute, the chair stopped creaking, and Natalie slumped forward. Dan angled the flashlight upward to note her facial expression as she sat up.

With the subtlety of a magician palming an ace, she uncurled her fingers for a glimpse of the snake pendant.

He needs to know who he's supposed to be.

"Who are you?" Dan asked.

"Evan—Evan Markham." Her voice was deeper, her brows lower. She squinted at him through the beam. "Aren't you the guy I worked with on the Ripper case? Dan, isn't it?"

He's good, whoever he is, Dan thought. "I'd love to chat about old times, *Evan,* but I need your help with something."

"Do what I can for you." Concern flickered through Natalie's jaded expression when she surveyed the foil-covered walls of the janitor's closet. "Where are we?"

"Glad you asked, *Evan.* You remember the late, great Arthur McCord, don't you?"

"He was like a father to me. What about him?"

"You ever visit his little shop there in Hollywood, *Evan?* It was like this." Dan jiggled the flashlight beam over the surrounding sheets of aluminum. "It's a modified Faraday cage. Keeps souls from getting in. It can also keep them from getting out."

Natalie's nostrils flared. "What are you trying to say?"

"Nothing, *Evan.* I was only wondering if you'd like to reconsider your answer to my first question: Who *are* you?"

Her lip curled in a feral snarl. "You know damn well who I am!"

"Oh, really, *Evan*? You sure you don't want to think about that?" Dan tapped a fingernail on the plastic disk of the SoulScan's Panic Button. *Tic-tic-tic-tic.*

Raw fear and seething resentment swirled in her eyes, but she said nothing.

"Cat got your tongue, *Evan*? Maybe bouncing off these walls for a few days will make you more sociable." He put his palm flat against the Panic Button and spotlighted it with the flashlight.

She glared at him a moment, her face in shadow, then laughed and eased back in her chair. "And if I'm *not* Evan... who would I be?"

Taking his hand off the SoulScan, Dan directed the light back toward her. "Only one person knew Evan well enough to play him so convincingly. Isn't that right, Sondra?"

She chuckled. "Bravo, Dan! You're smarter than you look."

"Not smart enough to figure out why you put on this charade. Care to enlighten me?"

"Sure... *if* you open that door."

"Not until we finish our conversation."

"Tsk-tsk-tsk! Such mistrust from an old colleague."

"Your time in this room is only as long as you make it, Sondra."

She sighed. "When the killer got me, we knew it was only a matter of time before he went after Evan, too, so we staged his disappearance. I had touched most of Evan's personal stuff during our time together, so any Violets who tried to summon him would get me instead. By pretending to *be* him, I made everyone think Evan was dead, too."

"But the killer would know that he hadn't murdered Evan. What was the point?"

"We weren't trying to fool the killer. We only wanted to fool the Corps."

"Why?"

"Because they would've put Evan under Security protection, and he wouldn't have been able to complete his quest."

"Which is?"

"To find the killer and torture him to death." She said it with a twinkle in her eyes, like a kid thinking about Christmas.

It took Dan a moment to believe what he'd heard. "You mean...?"

"Actually, Evan promised that I could do it. When he finds the guy, he'll summon me, and I can punish the bastard with Evan's hands. Isn't that romantic?"

Her face hovered before him in the dark, smiling and mad and utterly lost to humanity. He had no idea what to say to her. "Sondra...I know what you've been through...."

"Do you, Dan?" Half-moons of sardonic merriment lit up the undersides of her brows, her eyes, her grinning lips. "Do you know what it's like to *die young*?"

He grimaced, remembering Alan Pelletier's accusing stare. "I think so."

"Ah! Then you know that the dying itself isn't the bad part. It's painful, yes, and inconvenient certainly, but it doesn't last long.

"What *does* last is the regret: You float around in the tar of the afterlife with nothing to do but think about all the fun you'll never have, the friends you'll never see, the love you'll never know. And every once in a while, you'll cross souls with some old fart who lived to be ninety-something, and he'll be cooing about all his great-grandchildren or whatever, and you'll get a glimpse of all the things you *could* have had if only some cretin with a knife hadn't picked you out of a crowd and torn apart your body to vent his frustration about his own worthless existence. And that's when the hell *really* starts, because you realize you now have all Eternity to dream about what might have been and never will be."

She giggled. "But I don't need to tell *you* that, do I, Dan? You know all about it, don't you? I guess that means we're *both* dead."

Dan's mouth felt stuffed with sand. "You know, I can't let you do this."

"Oh, come on, Dan! Like you wouldn't do the same if anyone hurt your precious Natalie."

His hand drifted toward the Panic Button again. "I can keep you here."

"It doesn't matter. Evan will kill the son of a bitch, with or without me."

"Where *is* Evan?"

"I don't know. And neither do you." Her face threatened to vanish in the darkness, leaving only the ivory crescent of her grin.

"I can't guarantee Evan's safety if he gets in our way."

"I can't guarantee your safety if you get in *his* way. May I go now?"

Dan sighed and thumped on the door behind him. "Serena!"

Mfume yanked open the exit, which Dan indicated with his hand. "Good-bye, Sondra."

"I'm sure we'll be crossing souls again soon, Dan." She winked at him. "Catch you on the flip side!"

Natalie's eyes dimmed, and her head dropped on her chest, the slack face dipping into the flashlight beam. The fingers of her hand relaxed, and the pendant fell to the floor with a slither of chain.

Kneeling before her chair, Dan gently patted her cheek.

"What did you find out?" Mfume called from behind him.

"That we're in deeper doo-doo than I thought."

When Natalie lifted her chin, Dan glanced at the SoulScan monitor to make sure that Sondra was really gone. "You okay?" he asked.

Natalie nodded, but her gaze was watery and shaken. She shrugged and stretched her cramped muscles. "What are you going to do about Evan?"

"The only thing I can do: get to the killer before he does." Dan picked at a stubborn knot with his fingernails. "Christ, Serena! Where did you learn to tie rope like this— the Girl Scouts?"

"Try CIA Special Ops," she replied in an arch tone.

"Oh."

She brushed him aside and finished untying Natalie herself.

The three of them emerged from the utility closet to find Earl Clark waiting for them in the hallway. "I hear we have one less victim to deal with," he commented dryly.

Dan rotated his head to work a crick out of his neck.

"That's the *good* news. The bad news is, the would-be victim wants to take vigilante vengeance on our killer."

"What odds do you give him?"

"About as good as ours. Evan Markham's worked at Quantico longer than I have and has more firsthand knowledge of serial killers than most of the Bureau's best."

"You think he might lead us to the killer?"

"Sure—if we can find him."

"That won't be easy." Natalie rubbed the rash red rope burns on her wrists. "Evan knows all the usual law-enforcement methods for locating suspects."

"That may be," Dan conceded, "but he still needs money and transportation to get around. I say we start by looking over his financial records: bank statements, credit card transactions, ATM activity, and so forth."

"I'll get some people on it." Clark glanced with concern at Natalie. "You've had a long day, Ms. Lindstrom. I'll have some police escort you back to your motel."

Her mouth hung open in confusion. "I thought I was going with Dan...."

"Agent Atwater needs to focus on the case." Clark glared in his direction. "Another agent will relieve him as your bodyguard."

Should've seen this coming, Dan thought. Given the blunders he'd made, he couldn't really blame Earl for sacking him.

"No," Natalie answered. "I'm staying with Dan."

The SAC drew a long breath. "Ms. Lindstrom, whatever your personal feelings in the matter, the fact is that Agent Atwater recklessly endangered your life—"

"It wasn't his fault."

Dan exchanged a perplexed look with Mfume. He was about to say something, but checked himself.

"It was *my* fault," Natalie continued. "I tricked him into leaving me alone so I could escape Bureau surveillance."

Clark crossed his arms. "That ain't the way I heard it."

"Obviously, Dan felt responsible for the incident, but it was entirely my doing. I now see how stupid I was, and I promise it won't happen again."

The SAC puckered his lips in displeasure. "You realize you're a material witness in this investigation, don't you? Our success—and other people's lives—may depend on your safety."

Her bravado faltered. "I know," she said softly.

He harrumphed and turned to Mfume. "Would you give them some backup, at least?"

She grinned. "Oh, I'll be around."

Dan bit his lip, but did not object.

"Here, you'll need this." Clark tossed him the key to his own Bureau Taurus. "I can catch a ride with Stuart Yee."

"Thanks." Dan accepted the offer with both gratitude and chagrin, for his rented Buick had been abandoned in the depths of the Tenderloin, where the cops found it and impounded it for evidence.

As a further reminder of his failure, he saw the black Harley and its helmeted rider gliding along behind him as he drove Natalie back to his motel. Mfume was discreet enough not to follow them into their room, but the thought that she lurked nearby, watching them like some ninja chaperone, set Dan on edge.

To keep his mind off her, he spread a bunch of the manila folders Clark had given him over his bed and sifted through pages of School employee records. He felt sure he'd seen MADDOX, CLEMENT EVERETT before, but he'd pored over so much evidence that remembering where he'd come across the name was akin to recalling what he'd eaten for lunch on Tuesday a year ago.

Natalie removed her wig and contacts and lay down on the bed beside his, gazing at the ceiling. Since leaving the station, she'd spiraled back into a near-catatonic daze, hardly speaking a word in the past two hours.

Probably just shock and exhaustion catching up with her, Dan told himself. But he couldn't help looking at her distant, worried expression and wondering: Was she thinking about *him*?

The idea bothered him more than he wanted to admit.

He set aside the sheaf of papers he'd been thumbing through and cleared his throat. "Thanks for taking the rap for me this afternoon."

He said it at half-volume. If she didn't respond, he'd let the matter drop.

She lolled her head toward him. "What?"

"You know, with Earl. You didn't have to do that." Dan threaded and unthreaded his fingers. "I don't really deserve it."

She frowned at him with an expression both tender and severe, like a mother chiding her child for crying too much. "It wasn't your fault."

"Still, I let you down. If Serena hadn't been there..." He left the consequences unsaid. "I couldn't live with myself if anything happened to you."

Natalie slid herself off the bed and crossed over to sit beside him, enfolding him in a hug. "I know."

Dan layered his arms over hers. "I want you to know... whatever happens, I only want the best for you."

She drew back, and he imagined her drifting away from him like an asteroid in deep space, vanishing into memory.

Instead, she cupped his face in her hands and made him look into her eyes. "I'm glad Evan's alive," she said, "but I'm not in love with him."

She kissed him, and he held her there. They fell back onto the sheets, their bare feet kicking manila folders and stapled faxes off the bed in a paper avalanche. Dan took great care, though, not to press too hard on the tender area swathed by the gauze on her stomach.

Later, when they drowsed together, naked but for her bandage, he gently pried himself loose from her arms. "Back in a sec," he whispered.

A lioness at rest, she eyed him with a lazy wariness as he padded over to his suitcase and dug though the rumpled clothes inside. "What are you doing?"

"Making sure you don't get away from me again." Climbing back into bed, he handcuffed her left wrist to his right. "Sorry."

She lifted her arm, yanking his with it, and rattled the cuff, giggling. "Why, Dan, how kinky!" And she snuggled up against him, her bare head pillowed on his chest, their chained hands clasped between them.

In a rent-by-the-week motel called The Excelsior down in San Francisco's Western Addition district, a young man blustered into one of the establishment's small, Spartan rooms and dropped himself onto the bed's flaccid box spring. He ripped the rusty-brown hairpiece from his shaved scalp and lay there in the dark, massaging his head and muttering to himself.

"... six times six is thirty-six, six times seven is forty-two, six times eight is forty-eight, six times nine is—"

He snapped his jaw shut, nearly biting his tongue. She'd be livid if she caught him doing it again after the mess he'd made that afternoon, and he feared her wrath more than death itself.

The muttering had become so habitual of late that he often babbled on without realizing it. He'd told her that it was to keep the others away. In truth, he wanted to keep *her* out, to carve himself a tiny respite of peace in his head. But she knew him too well, and she always got in.

Even now, her rage surged into him with the relentless ferocity of a Fury. He clawed the sheets beneath him, moaning with either the ecstasy of orgasm or the agony of rape, and his skull thrummed with the force of her knocking, like a crystal goblet on the verge of shattering.

"I'm *trying*, Sondra," he whimpered. "I'm trying *so hard*." Hugging his legs to his chest, he pounded his head into the pillow and wept.

31

Eureka

WAKING FIRST IN THE MORNING, DAN LOUNGED IN bed for nearly an hour, unwilling to disturb Natalie by jostling the handcuffs that linked their wrists. He lay on his side, enjoying the warmth of her body on his, the blank peacefulness of her face.

Then she stirred, and they spoke soundless words to each other with their eyes and hands and lips.

Propping herself on one elbow, Natalie waved her manacled wrist at him. "You can unlock us now."

"I wish I could." Dan scratched his head with his free hand and grinned sheepishly. "Unfortunately, I left the key in my suitcase."

Natalie fell back on her pillow, laughing. "Call us the Two-Headed Monster!"

"Ha, ha...very funny. Scoot over—we'll get out on your side."

Thigh to thigh, they clambered from the bed in tandem and crossed the room with synchronous strides, as if practicing for a nude three-legged race.

The stiff dryness of paper crumpled under Dan's bare feet, and he glanced down at the pages of evidence strewn across the floor, some now indented with footprints. "Oops."

"Can't wait to hear you explain *that* to Earl," Natalie quipped. "Keys?"

"Right." He scrounged the handcuff key out of his bag and freed them both.

Natalie shook the circulation back into her fingers and gave him a seductive look. "Now...where were we?"

Snaking his arms around her waist, he pulled her close for a deep kiss, then drew back with a sigh. "We were about to get dressed and head down to the station. I expect Earl's already looking at his watch."

She pouted with exaggerated displeasure, rising up on her tiptoes to stare him in the eye. "Well, we'll just have to make up for it later." She underscored her determination with another kiss before stepping away to get dressed.

After putting on his T-shirt and slacks, Dan stooped to gather the documents at the foot of the bed, the papers scattered like molted feathers from some mythical Bird of Bureaucracy.

"What a mess." He scooped a fan of pages back into its folder, but paused when one of the sheets caught his attention. Paper-clipped on top of a stack of stapled job applications in the School employee files, it bore the boldface title IRIS SEMPLE CONDUIT ACADEMY—PROSPECTIVE EMPLOYEE PSYCHOLOGICAL EVALUATIONS. Below that, a list of about a dozen names in alphabetical order. One of the names had a ruler-straight line drawn through it, along with the remark *See report* written in blue ballpoint ink beside it.

MADDOX, Clement Everett.

Natalie came up beside him, her arms bent behind her to hook her bra. "What is it?"

Dan displayed the list. "Eureka," he said.

Since the School had rejected Maddox as an employee, his psychological evaluation form was not among the files Dan had with him. He phoned Clark to see if they could locate the records, and the SAC had the report in hand by the time Dan and Natalie entered his temporary office at SFPD headquarters.

"The Corps faxed it over." Clark gave Dan the three-page evaluation. "Ordinarily, they keep these things confidential, but Delbert Sinclair bent the rules for us." He tapped the report's top page. "Maddox sounds like a real straitjacket case, you ask me."

Dan strained to decipher the interviewing psychiatrist's handwritten notes. "He claimed he could contact the dead electronically?"

"Yeah—on TVs and radios, no less. He was apparently obsessed with speaking to his dead wife. Even demanded a coroner's inquest into her death, hoping a Violet might be called to summon her. The courts denied his request because it was obvious she'd died of breast cancer.

"That's when he tried to get a job at the School—anything to get close to Violets. Said he wanted to share his discoveries with the Corps, wanted them to sponsor his 'research.' They showed him the door in short order."

Natalie looked at Dan. "You think he's trying to teach the Corps a lesson?"

He finished skimming the report. "Being snubbed by

the Corps might have inflamed his hatred of Violets in general—that matches the profile. The belief that he possesses Violet-like powers would also fit with the delusions implied by the 'Master of the Doors' letter...."

"*And* we have him placed at two of the crime scenes," Clark added. "Three, if you count his connection to the School."

Dan shook his head. "It's still pretty circumstantial. We can prove he's crazy—but being crazy isn't a crime." He passed the psychological evaluation back to Clark. "You think we have enough here to get a search warrant?"

"Coupled with your profile of the killer, yes. And if the judge doesn't buy it, well...I still have Mr. Sinclair's phone number. That man pulls more strings than Geppetto."

Sinclair's name struck a spark in Dan's mind. "Could he send me an official Corps ID?"

"Probably. Why?"

"If we find Maddox and he's as arrogant as we think he is, he'd relish bragging about his 'research' to a Corps official. Might let some important facts slip out."

Clark frowned, but nodded. "I'll see what I can do. But I want local police there to back you up. We can't let Maddox slip away from us if he gets spooked. I'll call Seattle and let 'em know you're coming."

Natalie folded her arms. "Where does that leave me?"

Dan winced at her accusatory tone. "I think it'd be best for you to stay here...."

"We'll have a couple of officers take you back to the motel and post a watch outside your room," Clark said. "With any luck, this is the last time we'll need to inconvenience you like this."

"Oh, I'm sure you'll find some other way to inconvenience me."

She kept a straight face, but with a sassy gleam in her eyes. Dan nearly burst out laughing. As they left Clark's office, he slipped his arm around her waist and felt her hand slide under the tail of his coat to rest against the small of his back.

Leaning against the wall in the hallway, Mfume smirked like a kid who's caught her older brother necking on the living room sofa.

Dan dropped his hand to his side. "You're in a good mood today."

"So are you." Mfume's grin widened.

Even the cool ivory of Natalie's face reddened a bit right then. Dan hastened to steer the conversation to business.

"I have to fly to Seattle to investigate a suspect. We've got police protection for Natalie, but I'd feel better if you were with her, too."

"Don't worry. I'll strap her to the bed if I have to." Mfume winked at Natalie, who rolled her eyes.

"Fine," Dan retorted, "but don't forget to strap yourself down, too. Whatever soul inhabited Lucy and Natalie could get into you as well. I suggest you sleep in shifts."

"Wise plan." Mfume's expression sobered. "Good luck."

"You, too." He grasped the hand she offered and leaned forward to whisper in her ear. "Could you give us a minute?"

"No problem." With a conspiratorial smile, she waved at Natalie. "See ya soon, girlfriend."

Natalie sighed as Mfume sauntered off down the hallway. "Another babysitter." She put her arm around Dan's waist. "I sometimes wonder if we'll ever have time alone."

"I know." He pulled her close. "You gonna be okay?"

"That depends." Her cheek pressed against his. "Come back alive, okay?"

"Only if you promise to be here when I get back."

They kissed, and swayed in each other's arms as if slow-dancing to a private waltz. Over Natalie's shoulder, Dan saw that Mfume had returned and was now feigning interest in the black-and-white photos of former police chiefs mounted on the wall.

He cupped his hands around Natalie's temples and peered into her eyes, wishing that he could see their true color, that he could feel the smoothness of her scalp instead of the starchy nylon locks of the wig.

Tell her! an internal voice urged. But he didn't. Not then.

Dan gave her shoulders a final squeeze. "I'd better get going."

"Yeah." Natalie edged back, her fingertips lingering on his jacket as she let go of him.

"Save me a seat on the carousel?"

His goofy smile teased a laugh out of her. "You bet!"

With no further excuses to stay, he waved good-bye and walked on down the hallway alone. Glancing back, he saw Mfume rejoin Natalie, who stood perfectly still as they watched him leave.

Dan almost reached the station's parking lot before he remembered that he didn't have a car. He'd returned the keys to the Bureau's Taurus to Earl Clark earlier that morning.

With a sigh, Dan took out his cell phone to call for a cab

to the airport. Too bad he couldn't take Sid Preston's Honda again....

Seeing the reporter's sour frown in his mind reminded Dan of the deal they'd made. *That's another one you owe me, G-man.*

Teeth grinding, Dan dug out his notebook and looked up Preston's cell phone number. His finger slowed, though, as he punched the number into his own phone.

Don't cross me, Atwater. I can make you either a hero or a stooge in this story.

"Screw him." Dan hit the phone's flash button, then ripped out the notebook page with Preston's number and threw it in the nearest trash can.

32

Bad Reception

SEATTLE RAIN SPATTERED THE REAR WINDOW OF the surveillance van with melting blotches of refraction, obscuring Dan's view of the dingy TV repair shop across the street. He could see the old Camaro easily enough, however. Sulking at the curb in front of the shop, the fog-colored car looked like it had dropped from the overcast sky above.

"Our guys saw it pull up around midnight," Harv Rollins said. The heavyset Seattle detective crouched beside him and adjusted the wire taped to Dan's bare back. "Hasn't moved since."

"Hmm. He must've driven nonstop." Dan flexed his shoulders, getting used to the wire; it felt like a vine had taken root in his back. "We ready to go?"

"Ready when you are. We've got four plainclothes people out front and three covering the back. That won't necessarily help you if Maddox goes ballistic, though."

"I know." Dan shrugged on his dress shirt and buttoned it up to hide the eavesdropping gear. "If I find sufficient evidence, I'll try and coax him outside for the arrest. If you hear me say 'I've seen enough,' get ready to move. Otherwise, sit tight."

"Got it." Rollins signaled the driver, who piloted the van around the corner and parked it out of sight of the electronics shop. While Dan put on his suit jacket and raincoat, Rollins sat on a low stool in front of the short-range communications gear he'd use to confer with his plainclothes officers and to record Dan's conversation with Maddox.

"Sure you don't want a gun with you?" the detective asked as Dan got out of the van armed only with an umbrella.

"Yeah. I don't want to scare him," Dan replied, though that wasn't really the reason.

Stepping out onto the sidewalk, he mushroomed up the black hood of the umbrella and walked back around the corner. Scanning the street, he noted that a well-dressed thirty-something couple, both blond, monitored his movements through the front window of a Bohemian café. A blue Camry had parked in the spot behind the Camaro, and as Dan approached, the Toyota's driver hunched over toward the passenger side and pawed through the contents of the glove compartment. Outside the guitar store adjacent to Maddox's place, a man in a gray slicker stood in the rain and window-shopped, the slicker's hood pulled up over his head. The hump on his shoulders indicated the presence of a backpack under the slicker, and the cowllike hood angled toward Dan as he neared the electronics shop.

The sign over the store dubbed it Clem's Gadget Garage, and amateurish lettering painted on the front window read "TVs VCRs Stereos Bought Sold Repaired." Behind the glass, tall towers of televisions, amplifiers, and cassette players listed against one another, a metropolis of screens, buttons, and knobs.

A sun-yellowed sheet of notebook paper taped to the glass of the front door claimed the shop was "Temporarily Closed." Dan pressed the plastic button on the wall to his right, but heard only the popcorn percussion of raindrops on his umbrella. He tried the button again, then rapped on the door in case the buzzer was broken.

Nothing.

Shading his eyes to reduce the glare, Dan peered through the door, but lurched back when his reflection abruptly became a different face. An unshaven man in military fatigues shouted at Dan through the glass.

"We're *closed*!" He stabbed a finger at the paper sign for emphasis.

Despite the collar-length hair and stubble-covered jaw, Dan recognized the face from the DMV records. "Mr. Maddox? Clement Maddox?"

Another muted shout. "Who wants to know?"

"The name's Tate—Julius Tate. North American Afterlife Communications Corps." He pulled out the bogus ID Delbert Sinclair had procured for him and held it up. "Can I have a few words with you?"

Maddox examined the badge with surly suspicion and unlocked the door. "What do you want?" he asked, blocking the entrance.

"It's about your work. Our recent research confirms the possibility of electronic soul reception, and the Corps wants your input."

"They do, huh?" A smug I-told-you-so grin. "That figures."

"Uh...mind if I come in?" Dan glanced skyward to remind Maddox of the rain.

"Oh—sure." He pushed the door open and stood to one side, keeping his right hand in the pocket of his Army jacket.

Dan collapsed the umbrella and shook it off before entering. The store's interior consisted of little more than a counter, a cash register, and shelf units crammed with dismantled electronic devices that leaked entrails of insulated wire. The air stung Dan's mucous membranes with an acrid mélange of hot solder, burnt circuit board, and dust, and a sibilant hiss from somewhere deep within the building made it sound as if the place were breathing.

"I'm afraid the Corps owes you an apology, Mr. Maddox," Dan said. "We had no idea of the far-reaching implications of your research."

"Tell me about it." Maddox now stood between him and the exit. When he pulled his hand from his coat pocket, the cloth sagged with an unseen, angular weight.

Dan pretended not to notice, but avoided turning his back to the other man. "Of course, we now see what a valuable asset you could be."

"That so?" Maddox folded his arms, a chess player confident of checkmate. "What's your offer?"

Surveying the room, Dan saw nothing out of the ordinary. He eyed the dark open doorway behind the counter. "You'll be handsomely compensated for your contribution—*if* you can prove your claims."

Maddox's smile vanished. "It's not about the money." He closed the distance between them until their noses nearly touched. "It's *never* been about the money."

Dan met his glare without blinking. "And what *is* it about, Mr. Maddox?"

"Control." The word hung in the air like pesticide. "I want complete control of the project."

Ice-water tremors trickled down Dan's spine. "Of course," he said, keeping his tone calm, businesslike. "*If* you can prove what you've told us."

Maddox gave a gloating chuckle. "Oh, I can prove it, all right."

He flipped up the drawbridge leaf of the wooden counter and motioned for Dan to pass through the doorway beyond.

Trying to keep Maddox in his peripheral vision, Dan advanced into the shop's back room. The hissing he'd heard before grew louder and seemed to leak from several mouths, like a chorus of asps. As his eyes adjusted to the gloom, he saw a mattress with dirty, rumpled sheets lying on the floor next to a weary Frigidaire icebox. On his right, an open door exposed a grungy bathroom. A dim, grayish glow emanated from the left, pulsing in the darkness without relieving it. Dan turned toward the light source and discovered more than thirty television sets stacked on shelves that surrounded one end of the room. The oblong screens all shimmered with the snow of dead channels, their speakers exhaling white noise.

"Well?" Maddox pointed to the TVs like a proud father. "Do you see them?"

Dan saw nothing on the screens but a blizzard of black and white spots. "I'm afraid I don't understand...."

"Sometimes you have to wait awhile." Squatting until he was eye level with one of the televisions, Maddox stared at the snow, his face bathed in phosphor-dot moonlight. "They come and go. Depends on the receptivity of the touchstone."

He slapped the top of the TV near the set's rabbit ears. For the first time, Dan noticed that a man's wristwatch had been lashed to one of the telescoping metal rods with a bit of wire. In fact, he now saw that each of the TVs had some incongruous object tied to its antenna: a locket containing a faded baby picture, a comb with blond hair still caught in its teeth, a woman's glove flattened like a shed snakeskin.

"*Listen.*"

Maddox twisted the volume knob of another set and inclined his ear to the speaker as its static rasp rose to a waterfall roar. "There! You hear her?"

Dan held his breath and listened. There did seem to be a voice caught behind that curtain of static—a distant, plaintive cry, like that of a child trapped deep in a well. *Interference from another station,* Dan told himself, yet the skin of his arms pimpled with gooseflesh.

Maddox beamed at him. "Ah! You *do* hear her, don't you?"

Without waiting for a reply, he hurried over to a long wooden workbench along the opposite wall. Strewn with soldering irons, needle-nose pliers, and plastic cups filled with assorted resistors, transistors, and integrated circuits, the bench held nine more snow-speckled TVs.

"Right now, the reception isn't good enough to permit dependable communication. I'm convinced that resonant frequencies are the key." Quivering with enthusiasm, Maddox patted the top of a device that resembled an oscilloscope, which he'd hooked to the center TV with telephone cords. "Imagine being able to tune in your dead grandfather as easily as *60 Minutes* or *Friends*!"

Dan watched the glowing green line that spiked across the oscilloscope's round screen. It looked exactly like a SoulScan readout. He licked his dry lips. "And how do you go about…*finding* these resonant frequencies?"

Maddox glanced around, motioned for Dan to lean closer. His voice dropped to a whisper, as though he feared the TVs themselves might hear what he said. *"I'm studying the souls of dead Violets."*

He indicated a bulletin board mounted on the wall behind the workbench. Dozens of newspaper clippings, dry and brittle as autumn leaves, had been thumbtacked to the board's cork expanse, boasting headlines such as CONDUIT CONVICTS KILLER WITH VICTIM'S TEARS, VIOLET VERIFIES AUTHENTICITY OF NEWLY DISCOVERED VERMEER, and CLASSICAL MUSIC CONDUIT KAMEI MURDERED IN HER HOME. Dan recognized photos of Jem Whitman, Gig Marshall, Russell Travers, Sylvia Perez…and Natalie.

"Their souls are more resonant than ours." Maddox surveyed the clippings with an envious awe. "That's why they can open themselves to the dead. If I can replicate that resonance electronically, we can *all* share their power."

Dan touched the television set hooked to the oscilloscope. Perhaps it was only the power of suggestion, but the longer he stared at the screen, the more the shifting pattern of dots resolved itself into defined patches of light and dark. Two elliptical smudges for eyes, a gaping O of a mouth.

"Is this one of them?" But he already knew the answer to the question.

A stuffed Tigger with matted polyester fur dangled from one pole of the TV's antenna like bait.

Laurie...

"Yep." Maddox stroked the picture tube. "With proper equipment, I'm sure I can perfect the technology."

Dan glanced from the Tigger to the artifacts tied to the other television antennas. "Where do you get your touchstones?"

Maddox stiffened, suddenly wary. "You know...thrift stores, estate sales, things like that."

"Must be hard to find touchstones for dead Violets at the local Goodwill."

A glare like the gleam of an unsheathed sword. "You have to know where to look."

Dan brightened his tone. "No doubt the Corps can help you with that. What about this one over here?"

He moved toward a television that sat apart from the others, but Maddox blocked his way. "That one's special."

"Hmm." Dan noted the diamond engagement ring looped around the antenna. "Well...unless there was something else you wanted to show me—"

A small, shiny object on the workbench stopped him: a pendant with two snakes twined into an infinity sign. He'd only seen two like it. One lay secure in the evidence files at the Hall of Justice in San Francisco. And the other...

Dan drew a breath to steady his voice. "I think I've seen enough, Mr. Maddox."

"Then you'll sponsor my research?" The other man probed him with a sidelong look.

"Yes. In fact, if you'd like to accompany me to our downtown office right now, you can give us your terms."

Maddox massaged the stubble on his cheek, chewing on the proposition.

"I'll even introduce you to Simon McCord," Dan added in an offhand manner. "He's in Seattle right now. Might be able to assist you."

Excitement glimmered on Maddox's face—the thrill of a fan about to meet a superstar. "Yeah...maybe."

"Of course, if you're busy, I understand. We can meet another time—"

"No." Maddox's gaze lingered on the television with the engagement ring. "No, the sooner, the better. Let's go."

He headed for the door without bothering to shut off the TVs. Dan lagged behind. The white noise had differentiated itself into a fugue of conflicting whispers, as if a roomful of deaf-mutes were desperately trying to speak to one another. The suggestion of a face coalesced out of the fog of specks on each screen like wraiths struggling to materialize, the phosphor-dot pits of their eyes pleading for release, their mouths frantic with unintelligible cries....

Dan hastened to rejoin Maddox. When they stepped out the front door into the rain, he gulped the fresh outside air in relief.

While Maddox locked up, Dan opened his umbrella and glanced across the street. The couple seated in the coffeehouse window abruptly left their table. The Camry was still parked at the curb, but its driver had disappeared from view, as had the man in the hooded slicker.

"My car's over this way." Dan pointed to a maroon Cadillac along the opposite curb, a short distance from where the blond couple had just emerged from the café.

Maddox pulled his baggy Army jacket tight around his shoulders, blinking rain out of his eyes. "Well, let's get to it."

Tilting his umbrella to shield Maddox from the downpour, Dan steered him toward the curb, waiting for a break in the traffic. The couple loitered outside the café, the woman shaking her folded umbrella as if unable to open it.

Without warning, the passenger door of the Camry swung open, and the man who hunkered inside stumbled out onto the sidewalk. Maddox and Dan turned in surprise as the man stood and raised a camera to his eye.

"Mr. Maddox, how do you feel about being the FBI's number-one suspect in the Violet murders?" Sid Preston shouted. *Whirr*-click-*whirr*-click-*whirr*-click went the camera.

Maddox backpedaled in panic. The woman across the street dropped her umbrella and pulled out a gun, while her partner waved a badge in the air to stop the flow of cars in the street. Both muttered angry words, their mouths tilted toward their shirt collars.

Dan would've yelled at Preston, but he didn't have time. He threw down his own umbrella and made a grab for Maddox's arm. "We only want to ask you a few questions—"

The air bellowed out of his lungs as Maddox threw his weight against him. Dan staggered sideways, tripped on the brim of the upturned umbrella, and fell on the pavement. Maddox sprinted away up the sidewalk.

Whirr-click-*whirr*-click-*whirr*-click went Preston's camera before the stocky blond Seattle cop blocked the reporter, barking at him to get back.

His female partner charged across the street at a diagonal to intercept Maddox. *"Stop! Police!"*

Dan pushed himself to his feet, his bruised side still stinging, and saw that two other plainclothes officers had jumped out of parked cars to join the pursuit. He limped toward them as they converged on the fleeing suspect.

Surrounded on three sides, Maddox skidded to a stop, eyes wild. His back against the wall of a vintage clothing store, he whimpered with an almost pitiable anguish and yanked an old Army revolver out of his right-hand coat pocket.

The blond woman leveled her gun at him. "Drop it!"

He nearly got the barrel in his mouth before she pulled the trigger.

Her aim was good. The first bullet slammed into Maddox's shoulder, throwing him off balance, and his flailing arm dropped the pistol. The second shot hit his upper thigh, and he collapsed. Gouts of blood tainted the rainwater that washed the sidewalk.

The three plainclothes officers closed in. "Call an ambulance," the blond woman said into the microphone on her shirt collar. As Dan stepped up behind her, she kneeled to put pressure on Maddox's leg wound.

The suspect rolled onto his side, the matted strands of his hair dripping water in his eyes. His pale face turned bluish, and its features became smooth and untroubled. "Amy…"

He closed his eyes, a slight smile on his lips.

The cop leaned more heavily on his leaking wound. "Don't go to sleep on me, Clem! Tell me about Amy. Who's Amy?"

"His wife," Dan said when Maddox failed to answer. "I guess he was determined to see her again, no matter what."

The other officers collected Maddox's revolver and stood guard against the growing crowd of spectators until the ambulance arrived.

With all the excitement half a block up the street, no one noticed the dark-haired young man who slipped out the front door of Clem's Gadget Garage, mumbling to himself.

"—nine times three is twenty-seven, nine times four is thirty-six, nine times five is forty—"

He cut off the phrase and glanced around with a look of alarm. Satisfied that no one had heard him, he pulled up the plastic hood of his slicker and walked away from the shooting with his head bowed toward the pavement.

33

Doubts

THE EKG MONITOR GAVE A REGULAR, IF UNENTHU-
siastic, beep to show that the man in ICU 6 was still alive.
With bandages on his shoulder and leg and an IV attached
to his arm, he had not opened his eyes or moved under his
own power since arriving at Swedish Medical Center. Nevertheless, an armed Seattle police officer stood watch in the
room, for the man in the bed was Clement Everett Maddox,
the Violet Killer.

Dan slouched in a chair opposite the bed, his fingers
steepled in front of his mouth, and contemplated Maddox's
corpse-pallid face. He'd been sitting there for almost two
hours, ever since the suspected murderer had come out of
surgery.

Harv Rollins waddled through the door, his raincoat
still damp from the downpour outside, and nodded toward
the bed. "What's the prognosis?"

"Still critical. Shock from the blood loss. Doctor figures
it'll be a week before he regains consciousness, if at all."

Rollins snorted. "Save us all a lot of trouble if he didn't."

Wrinkling his nose at the detective's remark, Dan rose
from his chair. "What did you find?"

"What *didn't* we find? A roll of piano wire, a knife, a box of surgical gloves, a bunch of bomb-making materials, trophies from several of the victims—our guys are still bagging up the stuff. Including *this*."

He fished a Polaroid out of his pocket and held it up. The glossy square showed an open cabinet in Maddox's shop. On its shelf lay a flattened mask of black crepe—part mourning veil, part executioner's hood.

"Good work, Harv," Dan said tonelessly.

Rollins tucked the photo back in his coat and patted the pocket. "If he ever does wake up, we'll put him away for life. Death penalty, if they try him in California."

"Yeah." He took another long look at Maddox and let out a dry chuckle.

"What's so funny?" Rollins asked.

"Not funny, just ironic." Dan indicated the comatose patient. "If he were either alive *or* dead, he'd be able to speak in his own defense."

He ignored Rollins's frown and walked out the door.

Dan put off calling Natalie that night, afraid she might hear the gloom in his voice as he told her the "good" news. He tried phoning her the following morning, but one of the SFPD officers who'd been guarding her motel room answered instead. He said that she and Serena had gone out to brunch to celebrate the arrest.

Dejected, Dan hung up the phone and donned his fake mustache and glasses before leaving his motel. He didn't want to answer any questions about the Violet murders and, most of all, didn't want anyone to congratulate him on the killer's capture. Arriving at Seattle's Public Safety Building, he passed unnoticed through the flock of reporters outside and skulked to his temporary office without even stopping to grab a Danish.

Earl Clark was waiting for him inside.

"Is that a disguise," the SAC asked, "or a fashion statement?"

"Neither." Dan plucked off the mustache. "It's a way of life."

Clark clapped him on the back. "Cheer up! You're the man of the hour. By the way...I saved you a copy."

He unfolded that morning's *New York Post* and held it up. VIOLET KILLER GUNNED DOWN, the headline shouted. MURDERER CAUGHT DESPITE FBI INCOMPETENCE. The lead photo showed paramedics loading Maddox into the back of an ambulance; below that was a smaller picture of Dan falling on the sidewalk beside his overturned umbrella, with Maddox running away in the background.

"Not my best angle," Dan admitted.

Clark laughed and dropped the tabloid in the wastebasket by the desk. "Relax. I've told the Bureau that you were the one who led us to Maddox."

"Yes...I was."

The director's smile curdled. "You don't seem happy about that. Detective Rollins tells me you have some doubts about the arrest."

"Yes, sir."

"Uh-oh. You're addressing me with respect. Now I *know* something's wrong." He propped himself against the desk. "Out with it, boy. What's on your mind?"

Dan drew a deep breath and shook his head. "It doesn't fit, Earl."

"How can you say that? For God's sake, you *saw* the man's shop: It's a stalker's shrine to Violets. Seattle PD found the murder weapons and mask on the premises, not to mention all his souvenirs from the victims."

"I know all that—"

"Did you know this?" He picked up a set of stapled forms off the desk. "They found a pair of Nike sneakers that fit the imprints in the Gannon carpet. A fiber sample taken from the sole of one of the shoes matched the carpet fiber."

"Look, I grant you that Maddox is a nut. At the very least, he's guilty of multiple counts of breaking and entering and petty theft. But if he's the killer, why would he risk going *back* to the crime scene to collect his trophies? Why not take one with him after each murder?"

"Maybe it's his way of reliving the murders—getting his jollies all over again. He wouldn't be the first psycho to do that, you know."

Dan reluctantly conceded the point. Some sociopaths derived a perverse thrill from revisiting the sites of their murders.

"Fair enough," he said, "but what about Maddox's DNA? Our initial results say it doesn't match the samples taken from the blond toupee Natalie and Serena found in the gym bag."

Clark shrugged. "The toupee was probably another trophy from one of the victims. What better way to gloat over someone's death than to carry a piece of them on your head all day? Maddox might've seen it as a way to steal the murdered Violet's mental powers. Fits your profile, doesn't it?"

"Yeah. My profile." The fact that he was arguing against his own logic made Dan feel even dumber.

"And you still haven't answered the most obvious question: If Maddox isn't the killer, where did the mask and weapons come from?"

Touché.

"I don't know," Dan confessed. "Someone must've planted them there."

"Of course. I suppose this is all connected to the Kennedy assassination, too."

Dan's face warmed with chagrin. "Don't patronize me, Earl. And what about the dead soul that helped kill Lucinda Kamei? It knew her mantra. How do you explain that?"

"Easy—it didn't happen. Kamei probably dreamed or hallucinated the whole thing. We figure Maddox must've drugged her to carry her up to the tower room. Used some stuff we didn't catch in the autopsy's toxicology screen."

"Oh, really? And what about Natalie driving off into the Tenderloin? Was that drugs?"

Clark had to chew on that one for a moment. "Maybe. Maybe hypnosis." He hesitated. "Or maybe Maddox has a closer relationship with his dead wife than we'd like to think."

"You might be right about that." Dan thought of the TV set with the engagement ring on its antenna—the set Maddox wouldn't let him near.

"Whatever the case, Maddox is the man with the motive, method, and opportunity. Agreed?"

Dan raised his hands in surrender. "Okay, okay! All I'm saying is that I think it's premature to let our guard down 'til we've reviewed all the evidence."

"Review all you want. Me, I'm going *home*. Thanks to you, Charisse won't kill me for missing our anniversary." Clark put a hand on Dan's shoulder. "I know you're worried about the shooting, but you got the right guy this time."

Dan grimaced. "Whatever you say."

The SAC sighed and moved toward the office door. "Oh! Almost forgot." He pointed to a thick manila envelope on the desk. "Evan Markham's financials, if you still want 'em. If you find where he's hiding, tell him it's safe to come out now."

Clark slapped Dan's back again and left him to confront his doubts alone.

Still unopened, the manila envelope lay on the corner of Dan's motel bed that night while he rummaged through the loose pages of notes, photocopied documents, crime scene photos, and autopsy reports, searching for something concrete upon which to hang his hazy misgivings. For what seemed to be the thousandth time, he reread the "Master of the Doors" letter, scoured the interior of Arthur McCord's soul-cage shop, scrutinized Lucinda Kamei's ravaged body, all in the hope that he might see a telltale detail he'd missed before.

Finally, with his back stiff and his eyes sore, he cast aside the latest file he'd riffled through and glanced at his watch.

It was 6:23 P.M. Maybe Natalie would be back at her motel now.

Unfolding his cramped legs, he reached over to grab the telephone off the shelf by the bed. By now, he didn't even need to look up the number before dialing; he'd already called four times in the past two hours.

"Walkright Inn," the desk clerk answered. "How may I help you?"

"Room one twenty-two, please."

"Hold while I put you through." She must've recognized his voice from the previous calls, for her tone betrayed weary annoyance.

Two chirrups in the earpiece, then a click. "Hello?"

Natalie's voice soothed Dan's headache like ointment on a burn. Had it really been only two days since he'd seen her?

He smiled. "Hey!"

"Dan! I was beginning to wonder if I'd ever hear from you. What's going on?"

"Yeah...sorry I've been out of touch. Things have been crazy around here."

"I bet! You weren't hurt, were you?"

"Only a couple bruises. My own clumsiness. You hear about the arrest?"

"Only the basics. Everyone around here seems to think they have a strong case against Maddox, though."

Dan drew a long breath. "Yeah. Here, too."

"Is he going to live?"

"It's touchy, but yeah, they think he'll pull through."

There was a long pause at the other end. "Do you think he'll be able to lead them to the bodies of Jem and the others?"

"I suppose so." He wanted to sound more reassuring than that. "Um...I tried calling earlier, but you were gone. Cops said you and Serena went out to eat. How was it?"

"Great. We went to a nice seafood place along Fisherman's Wharf, then did a little window-shopping before she had to go to the airport."

Dan sat up. "Airport?"

"Yeah. I saw her off at the security checkpoint, then took a cab back here." She chuckled. "I might have to learn how to drive—those cabbies are nuts."

"You mean Serena's not there?"

"That's what I just said, isn't it? Actually, she should be back in Seattle in an hour or so."

"What about the police? Do you still have a guard outside the room?"

"No...there didn't seem much point. Dan, you're starting to scare me. What is it?"

"Hopefully nothing. Look, do me a favor. Stay in your room with the door locked tonight. I'll try to get a flight out first thing in the morning and pick you up at the motel."

"Okay." The brightness drained from her voice. "You don't think it's over, do you?"

This time, the long pause was his. "I don't know," he said. "But don't sleep too deeply tonight."

A sigh. "You don't need to worry about *that* now."

Her grim tone saddened him. "I still want to pick up where we left off the other morning," he murmured.

Very softly: "Me, too."

"See you tomorrow."

"Yeah. See you."

" 'Night."

Reluctant to hang up, Dan waited for her to disconnect first. She seemed to be doing the same thing.

" 'Night," she replied at last.

A click and a dial tone gave Dan permission to set the receiver back in its cradle.

Groaning, he turned back to the disheveled evidence with dread. He picked a case file almost at random and skimmed it, then another, and another. After half an hour, though, he gave up. He'd seen this stuff so many times already that his overloaded brain turned the text on the page to gibberish.

Tossing the most recent file on top of its siblings, he happened to glance toward the manila envelope with Evan Markham's financial records. At least it would be something new to look at.

He tore open the envelope as though it were a piece of junk mail and skimmed the contents. Visa charges stopped after Markham's disappearance. Disappointing, but no surprise. Evan was too smart to tip the Corps to his whereabouts by using a credit card. Ditto ATM transactions. That meant he needed to withdraw a substantial amount of cash before his supposed "murder."

Dan scanned the printout of Evan's bank withdrawals and deposits, starting with the date of Sondra Avebury's disappearance. Frowning at the figures, he worked his way backward through the bank statements, the furrows on his brow deepening as he turned the pages faster and faster.

Struck by an idea, he set aside the financial records and pawed through the morass of paper in front of him until he unearthed Lucinda Kamei's autopsy report. Several postmortem photographs had been paper-clipped inside the folder. The one on top showed a close-up of Kamei's eyeless face and bare, bleached-white shoulders.

There, just below her clavicle, a crusted red gash curled to form the number 9.

Dan stared at the numeral as if it had suddenly burned itself into Kamei's skin like stigmata. Hands shaking, he dropped the autopsy folder and seized the phone.

The desk clerk put him through to Natalie's room again, but the phone rang without answer.

As soon as she got off the phone with Dan, Natalie returned to rereading *Sense and Sensibility*, but found it impossible to keep her mind on the story. Dan's cryptic warning circled around in her head, crystallizing the fears that had been casting shadow-pictures on the back wall of her mind.

Don't sleep too deeply tonight....

The book flopped closed in her lap. Natalie started upright in her chair, catching herself as she was about to nod off. A week of subsisting on less than two hours of sleep a night had finally taken its toll.

Vaulting out of her seat, she paced the hotel room floor, rubbing her arms to rouse herself and debating what to do. She considered switching on the TV, but feared it would put her to sleep faster than Jane Austen.

"I'd kill for a cup of coffee right now."

She couldn't believe she'd heard herself say that. Once planted, though, the concept of coffee spread tickling tendrils in her head. Walkright Inn boasted that it offered free coffee twenty-four hours a day. Given how wretched its morning java was, Natalie could only imagine how stale and scorched the night coffee might be, but at least it would have caffeine, and the bitterness might actually help her stay awake. The dining room was only a few feet from the front desk, so she'd never be alone; she could run there, grab a cup of sludge, and be back behind the locked door of her room in five minutes. And it was certainly safer than falling asleep.

Unlocking her door, she crept out into the hallway with the pointless stealth of a dieter sneaking to her own refrigerator. The motel was sparsely occupied even for a weeknight during the off-season, and Natalie encountered no one until she reached the lobby, where a bleached-blond woman with heavy makeup sat behind the front desk reading a V.C. Andrews novel.

So far, so good, Natalie thought as she passed through the open archway into the adjacent dining room. No food was there at this hour except for the chips and candy bars in the glass-fronted vending machine, but a two-burner coffeemaker on the counter supported a half-full pot of oil-black liquid. Its nutty odor beckoned her.

She warily eyed the room's other occupants. To her right, a potbellied man in shorts and bare feet stood with arms folded across his chest, watching CNN Headline News on a TV mounted in the corner. To her left, a wheelchair-bound man with frizzy shoulder-length hair played a Game Boy, his thumbs furiously flicking as the unit buzzed and beeped. Neither of them showed the slightest interest in her.

Crossing to the coffeemaker, Natalie snatched up a Styrofoam cup and shoveled scoops of sugar and clumped Cremora into it before pouring in the dubious brew.

Lightened to a hazel color, the liquid tasted sour but bracing. Good enough.

She took another sip and turned to leave, but was startled to discover that the handicapped man had rolled his wheelchair up behind her. He regarded her with slate-gray eyes.

"Hey, Boo," Evan said.

34

Significant Others

SHE ALMOST DROPPED HER COFFEE ON HIM.

"My God, Evan, what are you doing here? Did something happen...?" She indicated the wheelchair.

"Oh." He chuckled. "Nah, just traveling incognito."

"You can say that again." If he hadn't spoken, she wouldn't have recognized him. It wasn't merely the frizzy wig and baggy thrift-store clothing; his face had grown gaunt, and lines of weariness scarred his brow. The gray darkness around his eyes might have been makeup but probably wasn't. "Where have you *been*?"

"Around." He avoided her stare.

"So I heard. Sondra told us about your little revenge plan."

"That was Sondra's plan, not mine. I only wanted to protect you. I still do."

The quiet earnestness of his voice, the soulful melancholy of his expression—for a moment, he resurrected the Evan she'd known back at the School. "Why show yourself now?" she asked, softening her tone.

"Because you're in danger."

A shiver skittered over Natalie's skin. "What makes you say that?"

He glanced over his shoulder. The potbellied man shook his head at whatever the CNN anchorwoman told him. "Could we talk somewhere else?" Evan whispered.

"Not until you tell me what you know." Setting her coffee on the counter, she pulled a chair out from one of the dining tables and sat facing Evan's wheelchair. "They caught Clement Maddox. Why am I still in danger?"

He slowly rotated his chair to give himself a better view of the dining room entrance and the lobby beyond. "Maddox didn't do the murders. Not all of them, anyway."

"You sound awfully sure of that. How would you know?"

"I read about the bomb in the papers." He panned the room like a security camera. "Maddox is a decent electrician, but whoever made that bomb had specialized training. *Government* training. And who better to frame Maddox than the people collecting the evidence?"

"But why would the government want to kill us? We're worth more to them alive."

"Maybe. Maybe not. The Feds have buried a lot of bodies that the voters don't know about. We're the only ones who can bring those people back and ask 'em what they know."

"They've bent over backward to protect me—"

"Protect you? Or hold you hostage until they can finish you off, the way they did with Lucy?"

"If they wanted me dead, why am I still alive? They could have done it anytime."

"They need to make it look good. As long as they can blame some lone psycho, the killings won't arouse the suspicions of the press or the public."

Natalie shook her head. "Dan would never be part of something like that."

Evan arched his eyebrows in mild surprise. "Dan Atwater? The FBI agent who miraculously beat a murder rap after shooting an innocent man? The man who first suggested Clem Maddox was the killer, then conveniently had him shot before he could be questioned?"

"No!"

Evan tapped an index finger on his lips. "You know, it's curious—the Feds didn't know where Arthur was until you took Agent Atwater to meet him."

"No!" She said it loud enough that even the man watching TV turned his head. Her eyes teared up, and she couldn't keep herself from trembling.

"Look . . . I might be wrong," Evan said to soothe her. "All I'm saying is that we should lie low for a while until I find out who we can trust."

Natalie blotted her eyes with the sleeve of her pullover sweater. When she didn't reply, Evan took hold of her hand.

"Since Sondra died, I've been thinking a lot about our times back at the School." He wove his fingers in between hers. "I've been thinking they were the only good days of my life."

She tried to read his contact-covered eyes. How many times during the past eight years had she fantasized about him suddenly reappearing to confess his mistakes and proclaim his undying love? Now all she could think about was Dan.

Evan gave a weak smile, perhaps sensing that his words didn't have the impact he'd hoped for. "Remember when Mrs. Osgood took our Life Sciences class out into the maple orchard to hunt for bugs? We ended up spending the whole hour kissing behind a tree. I think we came back to class with one lousy beetle between us!"

"Yeah." Natalie chuckled, but the memory felt as dead to her as those that passed through her mind when someone knocked. "If those days were so good, why didn't you even call me? And I must've written you ten million times, and you never wrote back."

"Because I thought it was better that you forget me." Evan squeezed her hand to the point of painfulness, and the color drained from his face. "For your sake, I'm glad they never sent you to Quantico. It was even worse than I'd heard."

"I can take it, Evan," she replied a bit harshly. "It's what I do for a living."

"Not like this." He stared into an unseen abyss, his shoulders sagging with the soulless exhaustion of the damned. "Reliving atrocities day after day. Torture murders, rape killings—I wouldn't put my worst enemy through that."

"But you didn't mind having Sondra there with you."

He laughed, a sound like someone hacking up a piece of unchewed meat. "Yeah, Sondra. We loved each other like two convicts sharing the same cell."

"You mean you didn't choose her over me?"

"Choose? I've never *had* a choice." He pressed her hand between his palms. "Until now."

She looked at him as though he'd mistaken her for another woman. "What do you expect me to do, Evan?"

"Come with me." His glance strayed toward the pot-bellied man, who lost interest in the news and ambled out of the room. "I know a place that's safe."

The steam had stopped rising from the murky coffee in Natalie's cup. She wished she could drink more of it to clear her head. What if Evan was right about the danger? If only she could talk to Dan...

"Look, let me make a quick phone call—"

"To *him*?" Evan's words sharpened to a stiletto point. "Why not simply call Corps Security and cut out the middleman?"

"All right, that's it. Good-bye, Evan."

Natalie rose to leave, but he clung to her hand. "Please. Don't go."

His lonely, frightened face softened her anger but not her resolve, and she pried herself loose from him. "I'm sorry."

"So am I," he rasped as she turned away.

Natalie heard the wheelchair squeak, and she spun around in time to see Evan spring to his feet. The sparking stun gun flashed toward her before she could cry out, shutting down her consciousness like a blown fuse.

Evan caught her leaden body and swung it into the seat of the empty wheelchair. Dropping the stun gun back in his pocket, he pulled the shoulder-length black wig off his scalp and draped it over Natalie's drooping head to cover her own auburn hairpiece. He ran his hand over the short brunet toupee he still wore to make sure it hadn't slipped, then stooped to place Natalie's feet on the wheelchair's footplates.

"Is everything okay?"

Looking up, he saw that the desk clerk had stepped into

view of the dining room archway. She scowled at him with an I-hope-this-isn't-something-I-have-to-deal-with frown.

Evan gave her a reassuring smile as he got to his feet. "Yeah, we're fine." He patted Natalie's shoulder. "She's a little tired, that's all."

Natalie's corneas stirred beneath her eyelids, and a soft moan escaped her lips.

Forcing his smile even wider, Evan pushed the wheelchair out into the lobby. "I'd better get the poor thing to bed. 'Night!"

He waved a cheery good-bye to the desk clerk, who smiled with relief and wished them pleasant dreams.

Natalie groaned and swayed her head while he pushed her down the hallway and around a corner to one of the motel's side exits. As soon as they were safely out of view of the lobby, Evan zapped her with the stun gun again. She jerked once and lay still.

Muttering multiplication tables under his breath, he rolled her out the exit door and toward the van he'd parked outside.

35

Answers
and Questions

DAN STOOD SENTINEL BESIDE SEA-TAC'S GATE N14, waiting for the passengers of United Flight 1238 from San Francisco to disembark. The setting recalled the time he greeted Natalie at the airport in his nerdy disguise, and a small, desperate part of him hoped to see her now, queasy from the plane ride but alive and smiling. He knew he wouldn't see her, though.

The door of Gate N14 opened, and travelers carrying tote bags and computer cases poured out into the waiting area. Dan scanned the procession of strangers, praying that the airline had given him the correct flight information. Despite his vigilance, he almost let the woman in the fashionable knit sweater and skirt and knee-high leather boots pass right by him. She now wore long, glossy black hair, and he had to stare at her face for several seconds before he recognized her.

"I appreciate the welcome," Serena murmured as he approached, "but you don't seem real happy to see me."

Dan took two plane tickets from his jacket pocket. "Our

flight boards in thirty minutes. Buy you a cup of coffee before we go?"

As soon as the Fasten Seatbelt signs went off, Dan lowered Serena's tray table and covered it with scraps of evidence he yanked out of his carry-on book bag.

"I must've been blind." He tapped the autopsy close-up of Lucinda Kamei. "That 9 should have told the whole story."

Serena frowned at the photo. "I'm *still* blind. What about it?"

"Initially, I thought it indicated the number of victims—the killer's way of bragging about his body count, which he did again in the 'Master of the Doors' letter," Dan said. "I was *meant* to think the body count was nine. *But Evan Markham wasn't a victim.* The killer planted these clues to reinforce our belief that Evan was murdered, and there are only two people who'd do that: Sondra Avebury and Evan himself."

"Seems like you're basing your whole theory on this 9 being the number of victims. What if it means something else entirely?"

"Fair question. That's one reason why it didn't strike me until I saw this." He drew Markham's financial records out of their manila envelope and folded back the first few pages. "Evan needed cash in order to operate without attracting the Corps' attention. I figured he saved up in advance, so I checked the size of his bank deposits to see if they took a sudden dip before he 'died.' It turns out they did ... but not when I expected."

He traced a line between two consecutive dollar amounts on the list. "From this week to that one, the portion of Evan's paycheck that made it into his bank account dropped by almost two thirds. Look at the dates."

Serena's mouth fell open. "This was more than six months ago!"

"Yeah. Or about five months before Jem Whitman, the first victim, disappeared. I haven't checked yet, but I'll bet that Sondra started shoving money under her mattress at the same time."

"You mean she was an accomplice to her own murder?" Judging from Serena's expression, he might as well have said that Sondra was abducted by aliens.

"It sounds crazy to me, too, but if Evan's our killer, then Sondra's been helping him. She's most likely the one who inhabited Lucy and Natalie. Probably Russell Travers and Sylvia Perez, too, since they were both taken in their sleep. Sondra knew them all well and must've figured out a way to get around their protective mantras, particularly when they're asleep and their guard was down."

That was the first moment he'd ever seen Serena look truly worried. "What about the others? Jem Whitman and Gig Marshall were killed before Sondra disappeared. And then there's Laurie Gannon and Arthur McCord...."

"I think Evan and Sondra needed to kill a couple of Violets before their own 'murders.' Being the first to disappear would have drawn too much attention to them. Jem and Gig were both older, less physically intimidating—easier for Evan to take on his own. Allowing himself to be seen as the 'Faceless Man' by the first few victims also gave the Corps and the Feds a phantom suspect to chase. To keep us guessing, they picked victims from different parts of the country, so their own 'murders' would be viewed as part of the fictional Violet Killer's nationwide rampage.

"I doubt killing Laurie Gannon was part of their original plan. They probably figured she'd go up in smoke with the rest of the students at the School. But she interrupted Evan while he was planting the bomb, and he lost his nerve and never started the bomb's timer. Even though he was in disguise at the time, she'd seen him without his mask, and she could lead people to the bomb he'd left behind, so he followed her to the West Coast to kill her before she could tell anyone."

"Why didn't Sondra inhabit her?"

"Sondra had never come into physical contact with Laurie, and so she couldn't use her as a touchstone the way she did with the Violets she knew personally, like Natalie, Lucy, and the others. Jem Whitman was able to reach Laurie because he'd been one of her teachers."

"And Arthur?"

"McCord's soul cage must have kept Sondra out. She and Evan probably underestimated its effectiveness. I suspect Evan had been counting on Sondra to take over McCord's body. She couldn't, and Evan had to battle Arthur alone, which was why McCord's murder was so messy."

"What about Sondra's story that she and Evan wanted revenge on the Violet Killer?"

"A lie. Once we discovered that she'd been masquerading as Evan, Sondra had to divert suspicion away from him by inventing a plausible explanation for why they'd staged his death."

Scowling, Serena slid the autopsy photo aside to uncover a *New York Post* picture of Clement Maddox, his eyes bulging like a rabid bulldog's. "And how does *he* fit in with all this?"

"Maddox was seeking an artificial way to contact the dead, and he thought the souls of Violets might hold the secrets he needed. When Violets started turning up dead, he saw it as an opportunity to procure some souls for his research. After each murder, he followed in the real killer's footsteps, breaking into the victim's house to steal a touchstone. Unfortunately for Clem, Evan found out what he was up to, probably by spying on our investigation. Once Evan tracked him to Seattle, Maddox became the perfect patsy."

"Because Maddox fits the profile."

Dan winced. "Ah, yes—the profile. A textbook case, wouldn't you say? In fact, our UNSUB's MO is a hodgepodge of traits from other serial killers." He ticked them off on his fingers. "You've got the ritual disembowelment from Jack the Ripper, an arrogant letter to the press like the Zodiac, the taking of body parts like Dahmer. And who would know more about profiling than Evan and Sondra, who summoned serial murder victims every day at Quantico?"

"You're saying they *made up* the Violet Killer? Why?"

"They needed a scapegoat for their murders, someone with obvious motives that would disguise their own. All along, I was perplexed by the inconsistencies in the UNSUB's MO. Why, for example, did he suddenly go from hiding the bodies to posing the corpses for our benefit? Although you sometimes see that kind of escalation in violence with serial killers, I think that, in this case, Evan and

Sondra were *inventing* the Violet Killer character as they went along."

Dan shuffled through the scattered photos, placing an autopsy close-up of Arthur McCord next to the one of Lucinda Kamei. He indicated the eye sockets of both victims. "See how McCord's eyes have been crudely punctured, while Kamei's have been neatly plucked out? I'll bet Arthur nearly got a look at Evan's face, which is why Evan had to blind him.

"If we'd known that the killer was someone Arthur would recognize, it might have led us to Evan sooner, so he and Sondra made the Violet Killer a 'collector' of eyes. They carefully stole Lucy's, and sent this note to the *Chronicle* bragging how the killer was supposedly saving the eyes in a jar." He tapped on a photocopy of the "Master of the Doors" letter.

Serena slowly nodded. "So the whole ritualistic murder routine was just a put-on."

"Yep." Dan shook his head. "That's what bothered me about this case from Day One: The killer never seemed to be *enjoying* his work. Laurie Gannon sensed reluctance in the murderer, both when he planted the bomb at the School and when he killed her. A true sociopath wouldn't hesitate—he'd revel in the kill. Even the mutilation of the bodies had a kind of... *staged* quality to it, as if the murderer were merely playing the part of a sadist."

"If that's the case, what *is* their real motive?"

"I don't know," Dan sighed. "That's one question only the killers themselves can answer."

Fingering the autopsy photos again, Serena stared at

the 9 on Lucinda Kamei's chest. "Does Natalie know about this?"

"No. I haven't been able to reach her since I put the pieces together." A tremor crept into his voice, and he cleared his throat to get rid of it. "I called Stuart Yee and asked him to check on her. He thinks I'm overreacting, but he promised to send some cops to her motel."

"I don't think you're overreacting. I only hope you're in time." She looked at him with grim readiness. "What do you want me to do?"

"Get the truth out of Sondra." Dan scraped the evidence back into his book bag as the plane began its long, slow descent into the Bay Area.

36

Road Trip

WHEN NATALIE CAME TO, SHE FOUND HER ARMS
and feet bound together behind her back and her mouth
sealed with duct tape. A coarse blanket had been draped
over her, mummifying her with its mustiness. Only the
thinnest of carpeting cushioned her from the metal on
which she lay, and she could feel the floor beneath her vi-
brate with the hum of a motor. Whenever the engine's
grinding acceleration subsided, she heard Evan's ceaseless
mumbling, his mantra reduced to the chittering of a frightened mole.

Natalie twisted her wrists and slid her ankles against
each other to worm free of the ropes, but Evan had apparently taken the same knot-tying classes as Serena. With her
legs and arms bent behind her, her body became an awkward triangle that made it nearly impossible for her to
move at all.

For a while, the vehicle sped and slowed and turned.
Then the speed leveled off and the route straightened.
Evan had evidently moved from surface streets onto the
freeway.

He's taking me out of the city, Natalie realized. Again, she
wriggled in vain to loosen the ropes, her wrists stinging

with abrasion, the blanket smothering her with her own hot breath.

Evan drove on, muttering to himself all the way.

They traveled for what seemed like hours, and the monotony of the trip eventually overcame Natalie's terror. With nothing to see but blackness, she slipped in and out of a fitful doze as the miles slid past below her.

She'd been asleep for an indeterminate amount of time when the sudden cessation of sound and movement awakened her. She heard scuffling around her, and the blanket lifted from her face. Evan smiled down, as eager and secretive as a boy cutting class.

"We're here."

He ripped the tape from her mouth, making her gasp in pain and relief. Before she could scream for help, Natalie felt the familiar edge of a hunting knife graze her throat. "There's no one for miles around," Evan informed her. "We can talk here."

She steadied her breath before speaking. "*Where* are we?"

"A little ways north of Big Sur." He yanked open the van's side door to reveal a panorama of darkness and spun-sugar fog. "Isn't it beautiful?"

"Mmm." Still roped like a rodeo calf, Natalie got only a sideways view of the landscape outside. Though she could see almost nothing, she smelled salt water and heard the rush of rolling waves.

Evan sat in the open doorway and gazed out into the night, his face barely visible in the ambient light. "It's like that time we all went to Cape Cod. Remember? The fog feels so close and makes the world around you seem so small, yet you know that it's hiding this huge ocean and, beyond that, all kinds of foreign countries. We couldn't see more than ten yards out that day, but all the time I kept thinking about what it'd be like to fly straight into that fog and end up in England or France or somewhere."

"Yeah." Natalie squirmed in place to massage some circulation back into her limbs. "Why did you bring me here?"

"Like I said, I just want to talk." Setting the knife at his side, he hid his face in his hands. "I'm so tired."

Natalie swallowed, keeping her voice soft and sympathetic. "Why is that, Evan?"

"It's hard. You don't know how hard." He rested his forehead on his knees, and seemed to be talking to an unseen third person. "We both agreed I should be the one, but I don't think I can take much more. Not by myself."

"It's all right. You did your best." Natalie picked her words as though they were steps in a minefield. "You can rest now—"

"*No.*" Evan snapped upright, the oval of his shadowed face black and implacable as polished jet. "I've got to keep going. I've got to save them."

"Save them? From what?"

"From the fear. You should know that better than anyone, Boo." He peered out into the fog. "It's not fair. Most people live their whole lives without even thinking about the Black Room that's waiting for them. But we don't get that chance. For us, any little happiness we have is tainted by the constant reminder that it's all going to end."

His voice broke, and he spat out a bitter breath. "Sondra was right. Better to quit life like a bad habit, before you develop a taste for it."

The cold mist penetrated Natalie's pullover, and her teeth began to chatter. "Is that why you wanted to kill the children?"

Evan slowly nodded. "To deliver them from a life of grief, a life of Corps slavery? Yes. Sondra was right—I should have blown the School to bits. But...the way the little girl looked at me..."

He wrung his hands, and Natalie recognized the reluctance of Laurie Gannon's Faceless Man. "You killed her anyway, though, didn't you? The little girl."

"I had to. She saw me."

"What about Jem?" Natalie asked. "And Arthur, and Lucy, and the rest? Why them?"

Evan shrugged, as if the answer were obvious. "They were my friends. I had to save them."

Natalie's heart shivered. "Am I your friend, Evan?"

"Yes." A tremolo of anguish in his voice, he picked up the knife and bent over her. He brushed the knuckles of his free hand across her cheek. "I'd do it for you, but..."

Trembling, he tore the wig from her head and stroked the marble slickness of her scalp. "You are all the things that make life so unbearable. So precious and beautiful that I never want to say good-bye."

She felt the knife press in on her trachea as she swallowed. "I know what it's like," she whispered, afraid that any movement of her throat might cause the blade to cut. "All my life, I've been terrified of death—too afraid to leave my room sometimes. And yet, even when I did everything I could to stay alive, there didn't seem any point in living.

"When you left was the worst: I thought if I was going to be alone in a room forever anyway, I might as well be dead.

The only thing that made me want to go on was the hope that, someday, I might see you again."

The knife quivered. Natalie heard him sniff dripping mucus back up his nose.

She forced her teeth to stop chattering long enough to smile. "I don't want to say good-bye either, Evan. Not again. Not ever."

Another sniffle. "Oh, Boo…you don't know how much I've wanted to hear you say that."

"As much as I've wanted to say it. I know you've done what you have out of love. I can see that now. And I want to help."

At that, Evan lowered the knife and hugged her, sobbing.

"It's okay," Natalie cooed. "We're together now."

"Yeah. We are." Wiping his face on his sleeve, he positioned the knife blade under the knot that bound her arms to her feet. Natalie's pulse quickened.

When he started to saw the rope, however, his whole body tensed with a sudden cramp.

"*No,*" he breathed. "*Not now.*"

The hunting knife thudded onto the floor, and Evan rolled back against the wall of the van, hands spread over his temples.

"*One times one is one! One times two is two! One times three is three!*" He sneered the words through clenched teeth like a bad ventriloquist.

Natalie writhed in the ropes to see if the knot had weakened. It hadn't. "Come on, Evan. Fight her!"

"*One times twelve is twelve! Two times one is two! Two times three…two times THREE…!*"

Evan paused, his face scrunched up as if racking his brain for the answer. Then his jaw fell open, air leaking out of his larynx, and his hands dropped to his lap. Natalie whimpered.

"Never leave a man to do a woman's job," he murmured with Sondra's cold confidence.

Pushing himself forward, he reached over Natalie to retrieve the knife.

37

Conversation in the Cage

IT WAS PAST MIDNIGHT WHEN DAN HEFTED THE
SoulScan unit into place beside his folding chair and ducked
back out of the foil-lined utility closet to get Serena. She
waited for him in the corridor, her head stripped bare, conferring in grave whispers with Stuart Yee.

"You find her?" Dan asked the detective, though he already knew the answer.

Yee shook his head. "All her stuff's still in the room, but
she isn't."

"What did they say at the motel?"

"Desk clerk doesn't recall seeing her leave. Of course, it's
hard to ask a witness for a positive ID when you don't know
the hair or eye color of the person you're looking for."

"Did the clerk see anything unusual?"

Yee pushed back the open flaps of his suit jacket. "A
dark-haired woman in a wheelchair apparently fell asleep
or passed out while sitting in the motel dining room. A
young man with short brown hair, heavy brows, and an unshaven face told the clerk that he was going to put the

woman to bed, and he wheeled her out of the lobby. We've questioned other employees, however, and no one remembers a handicapped woman checking in."

Dan's heart contracted. "How long ago?"

"About three hours." The words bore an unspoken apology, like that of a surgeon whose operation has failed.

Dan looked at Serena, who mirrored his frown.

"Then we'd better get started," he said.

While Yee remained at the booth's entrance, ready to shut the doors, Dan led Serena into the closet and tied her to the wooden chair. Fumbling to attach the SoulScan wires to her scalp in the flashlight's paltry glow, he dropped one of the electrodes in her lap.

"Keep it together," Serena chided him. "You won't help her by panicking."

Taking a deep breath, Dan finished hooking her up to the machine and pulled Evan Markham's snake pendant out of his pocket.

"I won't need that," Serena said. "Sondra's an old CIA buddy, you recall. I can use myself as the touchstone."

Dan nodded and put away the necklace. He took his seat and switched on the SoulScan monitor as Serena shut her eyes, murmuring a silent invocation.

The lower lines on the monitor rippled with a seismic tremor, but flattened into stillness again.

Serena crimped her mouth in frustration. "Uh-oh."

"What?" Dan hunched forward. "What is it?"

"I'm getting a busy signal."

"A *what*?"

"You got her?" Yee called through the door behind him.

"No! Hold on." He leaned toward Serena again. "What do you mean, a busy signal?"

"I've grabbed snatches of Sondra, but she has another mind to hang on to and keeps slipping away from me. That means she's inhabiting another Violet."

Dan's pulse jumped a groove. "Natalie?"

"I don't know." Serena knit her brows. "Whoever's on the other end is pushing hard to get rid of Sondra. Give me a minute and I might be able to reel her in."

Fidgeting in powerless impatience, Dan glanced from the plaster calm of Serena's face to the stubborn flatness of the lines on the SoulScan screen. Against his better judgment, he checked his watch. The glowing blue display read 12:38, and his panic edged into despair.

Then he heard Serena gasp, and the lines on the SoulScan monitor erupted with jagged scratches of green.

"Doors!" he shouted to Yee.

The entrance to the utility closet thudded shut as Serena bared her teeth and snarled. Dan recognized her expression when she glowered at him.

"Welcome back, Sondra."

She smiled without a trace of humor. "Dan. Figures you'd be the one to interrupt me."

Interrupt? Then there was a chance...

"Where's Natalie, Sondra?"

She chuckled. "On her way to Paradise."

"Cut the crap." He pointed to the Panic Button. "Tell me where she is, or you'll spend the rest of Eternity in this box."

Her grin shriveled like rotting fruit. "You think I care? You think I'd mind being alone for the first time in my mis-

erable existence? No dead people buzzing in my ears…
that would be a relief."

Dan raised his voice. "We already know Evan's the Violet Killer. It's only a matter of time before we catch him. If
you help us, we can spare him the death penalty."

Sondra went on as if he hadn't spoken. "You don't know
how lucky you are. You only have to die *once*."

"We're wasting time." His volume surged to a shout.
"Where's Natalie?"

"You remember the Randolph Exeter case, don't you? I
summoned his last victim: a twelve-year-old girl. He pulled
all her teeth with pliers before forcing his penis in her
mouth."

"That's enough! *Where's Natalie?*"

"Then he carefully slit off her eyelids so she'd have to
watch him while he raped her—"

"I said that's *ENOUGH!*"

"But that's all in a day's work for a Violet. Corps duty,
and all that."

Dan lunged out of his chair and seized her neck.
"WHERE IS SHE, YOU SICK BITCH?"

Sondra smirked, eyes flaring with mad fanaticism.
"That's it," she croaked. "Put this one out of her misery!"

He took his shaking hands from her throat and
straightened himself, his words dropping to a whisper. "I'll
ask you once more: *Where is Natalie?*"

"In a place where she'll never die again." She smiled
with the unshakable certainty of the insane. "If you *really*
loved her, you'd have sent her there yourself."

Without another word, Dan whipped around and
slapped the Panic Button.

Serena bucked in the chair like a condemned convict as electric current purged her neurons of consciousness. Her eyes bugged wide, white moons in the dark, and she flopped into stillness.

Dan glanced at the SoulScan screen. Its lines lay flat. He untied her wrists before she came to.

She sat up and rubbed her forehead, wetness collecting in her eyelashes, her facial muscles quivering with the tics of an electroshock therapy patient. "You didn't need to do that."

"Sorry." He knelt to loosen the knots at her ankles. "You better start saying your protective mantra. We're not letting her out of here."

Serena gave a tired nod and mumbled to herself.

"You get anything from Sondra's memories?" Dan asked as he freed her left leg. "Anything that might help us find Natalie?"

She groaned, and her whispering sputtered to a stop.

"Serena?" Looking up, he saw that she had slumped sideways, eyelids fluttering, lips quivering. With a queasy dread, he turned back toward the SoulScan.

A chaos of green squiggles danced across the monitor.

The machine jumped off the milk crate to land on the floor with a crack, and Dan felt the bundle of insulated electrode wires constrict around his neck.

"You wanna trap me here?" Serena's voice hissed in his ear. "Then I want *you* to keep me company."

She knew Serena's mantra, Dan realized, an instant too late. Unable to cry out, he thrashed from side to side, batting his arms at the woman behind him. But Sondra held on, and used Serena's CIA-trained muscles to draw the cord tighter.

Dan's blood-starved brain squirmed, and the darkness in the foil-lined closet grew dimmer still. In reflex, he yanked the .38 out of his shoulder holster and angled it back over his shoulder, cocking the hammer.

"Go ahead," said the voice behind him.

Dan's finger quivered on the trigger. *It's Serena! You'd be killing Serena!*

Pointing the gun barrel at the ceiling, he quick-fired four shots. The fifth bullet went into the wall as Sondra grabbed his arm and wrenched it behind his back, dislocating his shoulder.

The cord slipped off his neck when she let go of it, and oxygen washed into his lungs. Dan would've screamed, but his lacerated throat could only manage a rattling gasp. With the searing pain in his shoulder, he barely felt Sondra twist the gun out of his hand.

Remembering that her right ankle was still tied to the chair, Dan grabbed one of the chair legs and tipped her over. Sondra yelped in surprise, smacking her head against the wall as she clattered to the floor. Pieces of surgical tape still stuck to her scalp where she'd ripped away the electrodes. She kicked wildly to free her leg from the anchor of the overturned chair while Dan spun around to get on top of her.

Just then, the door to their left swung open, and Stuart Yee thrust his own pistol into the utility closet, drawing a bead on Serena. "Hold it!"

"Don't shoot!" Dan rasped, still gasping for breath.

When she saw the open door, Sondra gave him a perverse parody of Serena's trademark grin. "I guess this is my cue to go. See you 'round, Dan."

She raised the .38 until it pointed directly at Dan's head.

Natalie, he thought.

And Sondra pulled the trigger.

38

Crossing Souls

DAN DID NOT FEEL THE BULLET THAT TORPEDOED through his skull. Before his brain cells could process the pain, the explosion from the gun barrel had churned his gray matter to mush. By the time his blood speckled the closet's foiled wall and his body fell to the floor, he was long gone.

You've got to make peace with your life while you can, so you can wave it good-bye when the time comes.

Jem's words came back to Dan as he struggled to orient himself in the directionless world of the dead. There was so much he hadn't done: He wanted to help his niece hunt for Easter eggs again, wanted to hug his mom, wanted to fish off the end of a dock with his dad and catch nothing. He wished he could apologize to Susan once more, and wished he could beg forgiveness of Alan Pelletier's wife and children. Most of all, he longed to hold Natalie in his arms and gaze into those gorgeous eyes of hers. And now—too late, too late for it all.

Except, perhaps, for one thing.

Unable to see, hear, smell, touch, or taste, Dan possessed only the sense of his own mind, which suddenly seemed vast in extent. Infinitesimal dendrites of his soul stretched to every atom he'd ever touched, from the grains of sand on Maui where he'd walked with Susan on their honeymoon to the skin on Sid Preston's palm. Trillions upon trillions of touchstones, each exerting a tiny quantum pull upon the energy of his being.

Natalie is a touchstone, he thought. *If I can find her... if there's a chance...* Propelled by hope, he set out in search of her.

He didn't count on crossing souls with Alan Pelletier.

Like matter and antimatter, the disembodied spirits of victim and killer attracted one another as if bent on mutual annihilation. There was a mind-warping dislocation of personality, and Pelletier boiled into Dan like molten magma.

A puppet of the other man's mind, Dan saw himself standing before a dark wooden door—although he didn't *see* the scene so much as he *remembered* it. His callused brown hands fumbled to select the right key on his key ring in the dim light cast by the caged bulb above him.

"Freeze!" shouted a voice from down the alley to his right.

He did not think the voice was speaking to him. He was, after all, the night janitor at this Laundromat, just here to do his job.

"Drop it, and put your hands on your head *now!*" another voice barked.

The voices seemed to be directed at him, yet he had no idea why. He turned to see what they wanted, the keys still in his hand.

No, please, no! Dan pleaded in helpless horror as the scene unfolded with the inevitability of a television rerun. He barely glimpsed the three uniformed men at the end of the alley before the bullets cratered his flesh with red wells of agony.

The next thing he knew, he was on his back. He tried to breathe, and his lungs filled with fluid, the holes in his chest wheezing and bubbling. The thought that he might be dying seemed too incredible to be believed: He *couldn't* die. Who'd take care of Andrea and the kids? Bobby was only eight and Olivia barely out of diapers....

The three uniformed men looked down at him, white faces frightened beneath the hoods of their crash helmets. Who were they? Why had they done this to him? One of them took off his jacket and bent down to press it on the leaking wounds. Dan gazed up into his own face and felt an unquenchable rage flare within him. No forgiveness, no absolution, only endless hatred for this man who'd robbed him of his family and future.

Was this to be his punishment—a doom of everlasting self-loathing?

Oh, God, Natalie, why did you lie to me?

He nearly surrendered to damnation then, when a strange thing happened. Just as Pelletier's wrath and grief engulfed Dan, his own guilt and anguish permeated the other man's being. Alan Pelletier saw two of his close friends gunned down right in front of him, learned the fear of pursuing a killer through night-blackened city streets. His guts knotted with regret as he discovered that an innocent man had died by his hand, and his face burned with shame as he filed out of the courtroom past the murdered man's wife, brothers, and mother. He withered in front of a television set, watching the Cartoon Network while his marriage, once happy, collapsed under the weight of his remorse. For an instant, the two men became one, and, with perfect empathy, finally understood one another.

I guess I can't really blame you, Pelletier admitted, his words an echo in Dan's thoughts. *In your place, I mighta done the same thing.*

The red tide of their mingled anger and sorrow receded, leaving them cleansed and free.

I can't tell you how sorry I am, Dan said.

You just did, Pelletier replied. *And now I believe it.*

With that, his soul released Dan back into the void.

Natalie . . .

The urgency of Dan's search returned a hundredfold. How long had he been with Pelletier? Time seemed to have no meaning here, yet every second that passed might mean Natalie's murder.

Racing like an electron in a power grid, Dan hurtled from one touchstone of his life to another, yet every path led to a dead end. And there were more souls to cross: One moment, he became an old Anasazi blessing the birth of his grandson in the shadow of a Mesa Verde adobe wall. The next, a Fortune 500 CEO teeing off on the back nine at Coral Gables. After that, a baby girl dying a crib death, her parents' doting touch the only joy she ever knew. Homesick souls, adrift in limbo, shuffling through their memories as if poring over a stack of old postcards. They corroded Dan's determination with hopeless longing, dissolving him in the caustic dreamland of their solipsistic afterlives.

As if telegraphing a distress signal, he concentrated on the image of Natalie astride her carousel steed until his entire being vibrated with the memory, broadcasting it to the universe. *Please hear me, Natalie,* he prayed. *Summon me—call me to you!*

An inescapable maelstrom of force caught him in its vortex, and Dan spiraled into its maw like water funneling down a drain. The pull was so strong that he instinctively resisted it at first, terrified that it might drag him into another self-obsessed soul, into Hell, into oblivion.

The next moment, he became aware of the prickling of toes and fingers—a *real* sensation, not merely the memory of one. Wrists chafed under coils of rope, a thigh ached from the pressure of a hard floor, braless breasts listed to one side beneath the lint-speckled weave of a pullover sweater.

I'm inside her, he thought with awe. *I'm part of Natalie.*

Other senses phased into his awareness: the salt smell of sweat and cold sea air. A distant churn of waves and the nearby mumbling of a man. The dark blur in his vision resolved itself into the cockeyed silhouette of a huddled figure. It hugged its knees and rocked back and forth.

Lying helpless on the van floor, Natalie shuddered with recognition as he settled into her skin. "Dan?" she breathed. "No! Not you...."

Yes, it's me, he answered in her mind.

He felt her lips quiver. "How?"

Never mind—I'm okay. I want to get you out of here.

"Dan, I can't—"

Hush! Don't speak!

Too late, Dan noticed that the muttering had stopped. The hunched figure lifted its head.

"You said his name, didn't you?" The voice quavered with the wounded disbelief of the betrayed.

Natalie hurried to placate him. "Evan, I didn't—"

"You're still thinking of *him*." He reared up like a horse set to trample her. "All those things you said about wanting *us* to be together, and you're still thinking of *him*."

Natalie! How can I inhabit Evan? Dan asked.

Have you ever touched him? she asked in return.

No, I never touched Violets… before.…

Let me make contact with him, she answered. *Then you can jump between us.*

Evan pressed his hands to the sides of his head, seething. "I *saved* you, you ungrateful bitch! She was going to kill you, and I pushed her out! I *saved* you!"

"I know! And I *do* love you. Cut me loose and I'll prove it to you."

"Oh, really?" Evan bent down until his lips brushed her cheek and his breath steamed into her ear. "Do you really want us to be together, always?"

"Yes. Forever."

Get ready, she told Dan.

Evan ran his left hand over her bare temple and down to the nape of her neck. "In that case, I should just slit your throat. That way, I can summon you whenever I want."

His fingers closed around her neck, and he reached for the hunting knife with his right arm. Gagging, Natalie jerked her head up, mouth open, and clamped her teeth on Evan's wrist.

NOW! she shouted at Dan.

Dan heard Evan's surprised cry and tasted his blood on Natalie's tongue. Then his consciousness imploded as Natalie thrust him from her mind with a bolt of focused thought.

An instant later, a tearing pain flared in his left arm. His vision faded in from black, and he had the jarring impression of being turned upside-down, for his perspective abruptly changed 180 degrees: He now looked down on Natalie, who still bit into his throbbing wrist. The bleeding wound forgotten, he gazed, transfixed, at the beauty of her smooth brow and angular cheeks, a face he'd feared he would never see again.

Natalie gave him an uncertain look and released his arm. "Dan?"

He managed to work Evan's sluggish lips and tongue. "Yeah...."

He longed to tell her all the things he'd bottled up inside, to kiss her and clutch her to his chest. But already he could feel Evan pounding on his psyche, eroding Dan's tenuous control over this body.

His right hand tightened its grip on the hunting knife.

Natalie squirmed as he lowered the quivering blade toward her. "You okay?"

The mental levee that held back Evan's personality crumbled, and fury flooded Dan's thoughts. *Ungrateful bitch! Sondra was right—I'd be doing her a favor.*

"Dan! Don't let him in!" Natalie sounded far away, calling to him across a great chasm. "Start saying the times tables—it's how he reconnects with his body!"

Bitterness swelled in him. In his mind, he saw her as a teenager, running a few paces ahead of him through a maple orchard on a crisp autumn day. Red pimples dotted her pale skin but couldn't spoil the bright loveliness of her face when she glanced back to laugh at him. *One cut, and she'd be mine forever....*

Dan shoved the thought aside. *One times one is one, one times two is two, one times three is three....*

He forced the multiplication tables through his mind, and Evan's anger subsided. Wresting command of his hand again, Dan maneuvered the knife blade in among the ropes that bound Natalie's hands and feet and cut her loose.

NO! Evan shrieked from the back of the brain they shared. *NO, YOU CAN'T HAVE HER! SHE'S MINE!*

The arm that held the knife twitched with the conflicting orders of two masters. Groaning with effort, Dan aimed the blade at Evan's heart.

"Don't!"

Natalie's cry perplexed him, and he strained to hold the knife at bay.

She sat up and shook free of the nylon cord. "If you kill him, I'll never be free of him."

Dan whimpered with frustration and drew a sharp breath. *Four times four is sixteen, four times five is twenty, four times six....*

With a grunt, he pried open his hand and let the knife fall to the floor.

"I—I d-don't know—how l-long I can—stay." His tongue seemed swollen, anesthetized. "You'd b-better—tie me up."

Snatching up the knife, Natalie held the blade between her teeth while she took the remnants of rope and looped them around the hands that Dan forced behind his back.

Eight times three is twenty-four, eight times four is thirty-two, eight times five is ... is ... is ...

"Hurry," Dan gasped, falling forward onto the floor.

Natalie lassoed his ankles together with the remaining

rope just before the legs began to twist and kick. A quadri-
plegic numbness crept up Dan's torso as Evan reclaimed
what was his.

Not yet! Not yet! Dan pleaded. *I have to tell her....*

"Nnaaalee!" Her name came out as a Down's syndrome
slur. He strained to martial command of Evan's mouth one
more time. "I...I love..."

Evan's body thrashed like a hooked marlin, and Natalie
needed all her strength to lash his legs and arms together.
She'd barely secured the knots when she heard Dan's words
trail off. Scrambling over the wriggling body, she peered
into his face in time to see the last light of his soul seep
from Evan's eyes.

She took the knife from her mouth and stroked his
cheek. "I love you, too."

The face spasmed to life at her touch.

"Thank God, Boo! I knew you wouldn't let him kill me."

She recoiled, brandishing the knife, while Evan tried to
slither closer to her. "You don't need to be frightened—I'm
sorry I scared you before."

Tight-lipped, Natalie backed out the open door of the
van, planting her feet on the gravel of the embankment
without taking her eyes off him.

Evan floundered more frantically, but Natalie was every
bit as good at rope-tying as he was.

"Look—those things I said before—I was upset. You
know I'd never hurt you! Boo? *BOO!*"

Natalie slid the van door shut. Walking around the vehicle, she stabbed the hunting knife into the sidewalls of all
four tires, then stuck the weapon's blade under the waistband of her jeans.

The mist had cleared a bit, and a hazy blotch of moon illuminated the seaside clearing where Evan had parked the van. Tall evergreens encircled the scenic viewpoint on one side, while a steep, rocky embankment sloped down to the surf on the other. A curve of asphalt on the edge of the gravel oval led off into darkness among the trees.

Natalie took a cold, cleansing draft of night air into her lungs and allowed herself one tear—only one—before heading down that road in search of a police call box.

39

D.C. in December

DELBERT SINCLAIR DID NOT LOOK PLEASED. AFTER thundering threats and condemnation for nearly half an hour, the Director of Corps Security had lapsed into the ominous silence of a hurricane's eye.

"Is that your final decision, then?" he asked at last, his face still blotched with scarlet patches.

Standing in front of his desk, Natalie restrained the impulse to hang her head like a shamed schoolgirl. "Yes, sir."

"You realize what this means, don't you? For you ... and your *family*." He lingered on the last word.

"Yes, sir."

"We'll be watching you, day and night. If you so much as jaywalk or miss a credit card payment, we'll know about it. And you can forget about getting another job."

"Yes, sir."

"Then you won't reconsider?"

"No, sir."

"Well, have it your way." Sinclair picked up the vellum Certificate of Commendation he'd intended to bestow upon her for capturing the Violet Killer and ripped it into scraps. "Escort Ms. Lindstrom from the building," he commanded Agent Brace, who waited at his right hand like an attentive Doberman.

"That won't be necessary." Natalie took her heavy overcoat from the rack by the door. "I know my way out."

With the coat over her arm, she stalked out of Sinclair's office and along the maroon-carpeted hallway to the elevator. She hit the call button, but then changed her mind and took the polished marble stairs down to the ground floor instead. Not that the elevator bothered her; she merely wanted to stroll through the self-important grandeur of the Depression-era building, with its Greco-Roman pilasters and arched windows, one last time. She hadn't seen the inside of the Corps' headquarters since her induction ceremony at age eighteen. With any luck, she might never see it again.

When she descended to the rotunda of the lobby, Natalie spotted Serena there, leaning against the circular wall among the pretentious statues of Iris Semple, Gideon Wicke, and other Violets that lined the circumference.

"Hey! How's my girl?" Serena stepped forward to hug her.

"Didn't expect to find *you* here," Natalie said warmly. "D.C.'s a long way from Seattle."

Serena shrugged. "Simon gave me some time off. Like I said, he's really a big softie at heart." Her smile lacked its usual cockiness, and she looked a bit peaked despite the makeup and wig she wore. She glanced toward the stairs, where Agent Brace now stood, eyeing the women from behind mirrored sunglasses. "How'd things go up there?"

Natalie chuckled. "About what you'd expect."

"You really quit?"

"Call it maternity leave."

Serena raised her eyebrows, and Natalie answered her with a grin.

"Well. Our little Natalie's gonna be a mama!" Her mouth flattened a bit. "Does *he* know?"

Even after three months, Serena still couldn't seem to say Dan's name.

"Yeah. He knows."

Serena nodded, but her gaze wandered. "Heard they gave Evan life. That gonna be enough?"

Natalie sighed. "They've got him in solitary on round-the-clock suicide watch. We should be okay for the next forty years or so. What about Maddox?"

"Seattle cops let him go. They agreed not to try him for burglary, and he agreed not to sue them for shooting him. They'll keep an eye on him, but he seems pretty harmless."

Natalie hesitated. "And Sondra?"

"Yee and I sealed her up in that damn closet—but *good*, this time. I swear I've still got bruises from that night." Serena drew a long breath, working up her nerve. "I wanted to tell you again how sorry I am. I should've stopped it, somehow." Her stare turned glassy, and she stood at attention, like a Marine awaiting court-martial.

Natalie shook her head. "There was nothing you could've done. And if things hadn't happened the way they did—"

"I know. He told me." Serena's eyes regained some of their former twinkle. "You let me know if you need a kick-ass godmother for that kid of yours!"

"You've got the job." From the corner of her eye, Natalie saw Brace descending the stairs. "I'd better go."

Serena nodded and followed her toward the exit. "I'm starved. You want to grab dinner somewhere? Girls' night out, on me."

"Sure. I'd like that." Natalie paused, as if recalling a forgotten engagement. "I need to take care of some things back at the hotel first. Can you pick me up at five?"

"You got it! Where you staying?"

"The Harrington. Room one-seventeen."

"Check. Need a ride there?"

"No, I'll be all right. See you at five."

As they reached the front entrance, Natalie donned her coat and took a stocking cap out of her pocket.

"He's right, you know." Serena grinned—a big, old Serena-style grin. "You *do* look good as a blonde."

Natalie laughed and brushed a hand over the sandy-colored bristles on the crown of her head. Allowed to grow for several weeks, the hair nearly obscured the tattooed node points on her scalp. "Thanks. After all this time, it itches."

Pulling on her cap, she waved good-bye and pushed her way through the revolving glass doors and out into Judiciary Square. Dirty snow dusted the nation's capital like ash, and the cold air bit her cheeks, but she enjoyed the ten-block tramp back to the Harrington. Festive Christmas decorations adorned the street lamps, promising a season of good cheer to usher in the winter that had just begun.

Warmth thawed Natalie's numb nose as she reentered her hotel room and locked the door behind her. With unhurried thoroughness, she drew the drapes, switched off all the lights, and stripped off her cap, gloves, and coat. Settling into the darkness as though it were a hot bath, she lay on the bed and folded her arms across her chest.

"Talk to me, Dan," she whispered, and smiled in anticipation as she shut her eyes.

About the Author

A graduate of the prestigious Clarion West Writers Workshop and a First Place winner in the Writers of the Future Contest, Stephen Woodworth has written and published speculative fiction for more than a decade. His work has appeared in such venues as *The Magazine of Fantasy & Science Fiction*, *Weird Tales*, *Aboriginal Science Fiction*, *Gothic.Net*, and *Strange Horizons*. *Through Violet Eyes* is his first novel.

Look for

WITH RED HANDS

the next thrilling novel from

Stephen
Woodworth

on sale December 28, 2004

Here's a special preview. . . .

THE SHOCKING NEW THRILLER FROM THE AUTHOR OF
THROUGH VIOLET EYES

WITH RED HANDS

STEPHEN
WOODWORTH

With Red Hands

on sale December 28, 2004

Prescott Hyland Jr. fidgeted in his chair, discomfited by the oxford shirt and Dockers he wore. Left to choose his own wardrobe, he'd be in a wife-beater T-shirt and board shorts, but Lathrop insisted he go for the preppie look.

"And lose the rings," the attorney had commanded, referring to the silver bands that pierced Scott's ears and eyebrows. "The press will be on your tail twenty-four/seven until this thing is over."

Scott smoothed his left eyebrow. The holes were already starting to close. Lathrop had accomplished in five minutes what his parents had failed to do for three years.

If only Dad could see me now . . .

The thought unnerved Scott, and he pushed himself straight up in the chair, focusing on what the lawyer was saying as if his life depended on it, which it did. Although Scott was still technically a minor at seventeen, the State had pushed to try him as an adult in order to seek the death penalty.

"I don't need to tell you, we've got a lot of points against us." Malcolm Lathrop leaned forward in his Corinthian-leather-upholstered throne and consulted some papers on his desk as if reviewing a grocery list. "Although your parents' bedroom appeared to have been ransacked, almost nothing of value was taken, and every other room in the house was left untouched—including yours."

Scott shifted in his chair and said nothing.

Not a single ruffled hair disturbed the perfect rayon wave of Lathrop's pompadour. "Then there's the broken window, where the 'burglar' supposedly entered the house. Unfortunately, the police found glass fragments *outside* the window, not inside. And as for those little accounting 'mistakes' you made at your father's business—well, the less said, the better."

Scott picked at a hangnail but still said nothing. Lathrop had forbidden him to say anything more about the case, even in private.

The attorney rose and strolled around the enormous walnut altar of the desk. "The good news is, we now have your parents on our side."

"My parents?" Scott's scalp prickled. In his mind, he saw his dad blown back against the headboard of the bed, a crimson impact crater in his chest. His mom screamed and sat up as his father's body slumped against her, still convulsing in its death throes, and the shotgun barrel swung around to aim at the widening oval of her left eye. . . .

Lathrop regarded the boy as if he'd just slouched out of a cave. "You *are* familiar with the North American Afterlife Communications Corps, aren't you?"

"Yeah." Last year, his dad had dropped a bundle on a brand-new painting by Picasso or some other dead guy. It looked like something you'd stick on your refrigerator with Snoopy magnets.

He'd seen dead-talkers in cop shows and movies, too, of course. Purple-eyed freaks known as "Violets," they'd allow murder victims to take over their bodies and speak with their voices. But they wouldn't matter as long as you wore a mask to keep the people you killed from seeing your face . . . would they?

"The Corps' conduit for the L.A. Crime Division recently

contacted me," Lathrop informed him. "He's kindly offered to summon Elizabeth Hyland and Prescott Hyland Sr. to testify at the trial."

Scott's face went numb as the blood drained from it. "But . . ."

Lathrop held up his hand. "Not to worry. They'll tell us the truth about what happened that night."

He propped himself on the edge of the desk and folded his arms, putting on a more sympathetic face. His eyes remained keen and cold, however. "We know you were framed, Scott. Can you think of anyone who'd want to kill your parents and set you up to take the blame?"

Scott suddenly felt like an actor who'd forgotten his lines. "Sir?"

"How about your dad's business partner?" Lathrop glanced at a sheet of paper on the desk. "Avery Park. Our private investigators found that he has no credible alibi for the night of the killings. And he does stand to gain by your father's death, doesn't he?"

"Yeah, I guess." The lawyer's insinuations gave Scott the queasy sensation of being hypnotized: Lathrop was telling him what to believe.

"Never fear, Scott. We won't let him get away with it." Lathrop tapped a button on the intercom beside him. "Jan, would you show in Mr. Pearsall?"

A moment later, the office door opened. With the poise of a game-show model, Lathrop's receptionist ushered a pudgy, troll-like man resembling an alcoholic undertaker into the room and shut the door behind him. Scott stood to greet him, but the man crossed the ocean of carpet with an unhurried air, hands in his pockets. His pear-shaped body made the jacket of his cheap suit limp on the chest and tight at the waist, and his toupee looked like a dead poodle, its permed hair three shades lighter than the coarse brown brush of his mustache. A pair of Oakley sunglasses sunk his eyes in shadow.

"Scott, I'd like you to meet Lyman Pearsall, the conduit I told you about."

At Lathrop's prompt, Scott shook the newcomer's hand. He noticed how Pearsall grimaced at the touch, the man's lips moving as if he were silently repeating a phrase he didn't want to forget. Scott shivered, remembering how the Violets in the movies would always mumble some sort of mystical gobbledygook whenever dead people were around.

"Mr. Pearsall has requested a two-million-dollar retainer for his services," Lathrop said. "With your permission, I'll pay him now, and you can reimburse me when you inherit your parents' trust later this year."

"Sure." Scott stared at Pearsall's flabby face, the submerged menace of his unseen eyes. "Thanks."

Lathrop indicated the twin chairs in front of him. "Let's all sit down and get to know each other, shall we?"

He moved back around behind the desk while the other two seated themselves, still staring at one another. Pearsall casually removed his sunglasses.

His violet irises burned Scott's face with invisible fire.

"Now, then, Mr. Hyland," he said, his voice a cobra's rasp, "tell me everything you remember about your mom and dad...."

Natalie knew the session was going to be bad, even before Corinne Harris opened the black leather-bound case containing her dead father's pipe. She could tell from the moment she set foot in Corinne's immaculate living room, each object placed with fanatical precision, the white carpet brushed so that every shag bristle bent north, like compass needles. She could see it in her host's eyes as they avoided looking into Natalie's own violet irises, could sense it in the way Corinne stalled for time with small talk and offers of excessive hospitality.

"I've made some lemonade." She set a tray of finger sandwiches on the glass-topped coffee table. "Or I could brew some coffee? Or tea?"

"No, thanks. Water'll be fine." Natalie smiled at the tumbler sweating on the coaster in front of her.

"Oh . . . fine." Like a parakeet alighting on its perch, the woman settled herself at the far end of the sofa, knees together, and interlaced her thin fingers. "So . . . you said you have a daughter?"

"Yes. Callie. She'll be six next June."

"That's such a sweet age!" Corinne gushed.

"And your kids?" Natalie inquired, more from politeness than curiosity.

"Both teenage boys, I'm afraid. Tom's seventeen, Josh fifteen. They were adorable before the skateboards and rap music. Now they give Darryl fits." She smiled as if apologizing for her own sense of humor. "You and your husband must be thrilled to have a little girl."

Natalie's smile flattened. "Callie's father passed away before she was born."

Corinne put her hands to her mouth in horror. "I'm sorry! I had no idea."

Natalie waved off the faux pas. "It's all right. Really." She took a sip of water and swirled the ice cubes in the glass like tea leaves in a cup. "When did your dad die?"

Corinne's mouth crinkled. She'd managed to avoid any mention of Conrad Eagleton since Natalie had arrived, and now she could no longer pretend that she was simply enjoying afternoon tea. "Sixteen years ago."

A knot tightened in Natalie's stomach. When Corinne had phoned to schedule the appointment, she'd sobbed into the receiver as though prostrate before her father's corpse. "How old was he?"

"Fifty-six." Corinne smoothed her skirt. "He had a bad heart."

"And why have you waited so long to contact him?" Natalie asked, although she could guess the answer.

Corinne shrugged and gave an airy giggle. "I don't know. There was Darryl and the kids to think about. Darryl . . . he'd think this's all a big waste of money."

"Your husband doesn't know?"

"He doesn't need to." She crossed her arms in adolescent defiance. "It's my money. I saved it up from my allowance."

Allowance? Natalie thought. *Darryl sounds like a real peach.* "You sure you're ready for this? Reconciliation with a dead loved one is never easy."

"I just want to show him that I've changed. That everything turned out okay."

Natalie nodded. "Did you find a touchstone?"

"I think so." With the care of a museum curator, she lifted the small, oblong black case from the coffee table and pried open the lid. "Will this work?"

The pipe lay cushioned in dingy green velvet, its darkly grained wooden bowl pointed downward like the butt of a dueling pistol. Deep bite marks scarred the tip of its black plastic stem, and Natalie could smell the sweet yet stale cherry scent of tobacco that seeped from the case. Despite the countless times she'd summoned souls, she still felt the familiar twinge of dread.

"Yeah. That'll do."

Actually, she could have used Corinne herself as the touchstone, for every individual or object a dead person touched during his or her lifetime retained a quantum connection with the electromagnetic energy of that person's soul. Natalie, however, preferred to use a personal item from the deceased because physical contact with a Violet made most clients uncomfortable.

With a deep breath, Natalie twisted her long sandy-blond hair into a hasty bun, which she fastened in place with a plastic hairclip. Having real hair was one of the perks of working in the private sector. When she was a member of the NAACC's Crime Division, she'd been required to keep her head shaved so the electrodes of a SoulScan electroencephalograph could be attached to the twenty node points on her scalp. The device would then confirm when a dead person's soul inhabited her brain. Fortunately, she didn't have to bother with that now; seeing Natalie with a bunch of wires sticking out of her head would probably make a client like Corinne Harris run screaming.

Natalie took the pipe from its case, silently mouthing the words of her "spectator" mantra. The repeated verse would hold her consciousness in a state of suspension, yet allow her to eavesdrop on the thoughts of the inhabiting soul while it occupied her mind:

Row, row, row your boat,
Gently down the stream.
Merrily! Merrily! Merrily! Merrily!
Life is but a dream. . . .

An encroaching numbness prickled in her extremities, as if her fingers and toes had gone to sleep. Memories that weren't hers sifted into her skull. Natalie pressed the pipe between her palms and shuddered.

Conrad Eagleton was knocking.

An old Cadillac Fleetwood brougham sat before her with its hood up, billowing steam from its blown water hose. The summer sun baked her balding crown, and the armpits of her dress shirt sagged with sweat.

She was late. She'd miss the meeting, and Clarkson would get the contract. Twenty years with the same company, and this is what I end up with! Crappy car, lousy job, miserable life! She kicked the Caddy with her patent-leather dress shoe, kicked it until her toes crumpled with pain and her heart spluttered like the burst water hose. . . .

Natalie's pulse stammered in sympathy. Conrad Eagleton's bitterness throbbed in her temples as he relived his fatal heart attack, and she hastened to calm her autonomic functions before her own heart gave out.

Row, row, row your boat. . . .

With long, yogic breaths, Natalie slowed her rabbit-quick heartbeat back to its normal rhythm. Through fluttering eyelids, she saw Corinne wave her hands excitedly and leap to her feet.

"Wait! Wait! I forgot something."

She fluttered out of the living room, leaving Natalie to squirm on the sofa in semiconsciousness.

Corinne returned with a framed family photo of her, Darryl, and their two sons. She brandished the portrait as if it were a report card lined with A's. "He'll want to see this."

Natalie didn't answer. Her tongue felt like a dead slug in her mouth, and her hands tightened on the pipe until its stem snapped. She dropped the pieces in her lap.

Life is but a dream. . . .

With the clinical detachment of a psychiatrist analyzing someone else's nightmare, Natalie watched as Conrad Eagleton opened her eyes and gaped at the spotless white interior of the living room and the aging woman he didn't recognize as his daughter. "What the hell . . . *where am I?*"

The martinet bark quavered with fear. *Easy, Conrad,* Natalie cooed to him in the mind they now shared. *There's nothing to be afraid of.*

Eagleton clapped Natalie's hands over her ears, trying to shut out the internal voice. In doing so, he touched the soft skin of her cheeks, noticed the fine-boned grace of her smooth, ivory arms. Her delicate hands trembled as he looked down at them. "What's happened to me?"

Corinne leaned forward, her eyes and mouth round O's of awe. "Daddy?"

Conrad shrank from her. "Who are you?"

Her lips curled into the crescent of an uncertain smile. "It's me, Daddy. Cory!"

He squinted at her puffy, pleading face. Dye kept her hair brown and Botox erased her crow's-feet, but she couldn't hide the subtle drooping of her cheeks and chin and the perpetually tired look in her eyes.

"Cory? You were only twenty-four when . . ." His words fell to a whisper. "Has it been that long?"

Fidgeting in the ensuing silence, Corinne snatched up her family portrait as if grabbing a fire extinguisher. "Tommy's almost grown up now," she said, pointing to the older boy. "Darryl's been a wonderful father to him. And this's Josh. I think he looks like you."

Conrad snorted. "You found some schmuck to take care of you, eh?"

Corinne's smile guttered like a wind-struck taper. "But you'd like Darryl, Daddy. He's a city councilman, and . . . well . . ." She spread her hands, inviting him to admire the impeccable decor.

Conrad stood, hands on hips, and gave the room a cursory inspection. "I'm surprised he was willing to take you. Especially when you already had a kid with that loser . . . what was his name?"

"Ronnie." Corinne hugged the framed photo to her chest. "That was a long time ago."

"Some things never change. How long you think it'll take you to drive this one away?"

"Daddy!"

Cut her some slack, Conrad, Natalie chided him.

"Shut up!" He pounded Natalie's fists against the sides of her head. "You have no idea what she did to me!"

Right then, Natalie considered faking the rest of the session. She could push Conrad out of her head with her protective mantra, then play his role for Corinne, giving her the reconciliation she longed for. *Tell them what they want to hear,* Arthur McCord, her cynical Violet mentor, once said. *They like it better than the truth anyway.* But long ago, Natalie vowed never to lie to her clients the way Arthur had to his, so she let Conrad Eagleton's wrath erupt from her mouth.

Corinne seemed to shrink into her corner of the couch. "Daddy, what's wrong? What're you talking about?"

"You know damn well what I'm talking about!" Natalie's wiry frame vibrated with his anger. "You're a worthless leech, Cory, and you always have been."

"That's not true!"

"The hell it isn't! Why d'you think your mother stuck me with you? She knew. Probably why Ronnie dumped you, too. And this idiot"—he flailed a hand toward the photo she held—"what's-his-name. Darren? I *pity* him."

"But I've *changed.*"

"Yeah, just like you'd 'changed' when you came crawling home from Seattle with Tommy in your tummy."

"I know, I made a mistake, but I've settled down now. . . ."

"Settled down, or found someone else to sponge off?" He pointed to the hard gray world outside the living room window. "You think I would've been out on the I-5 in hundred-degree heat if I hadn't had to support you and your stupid kid? I worked myself to *death* for you."

"I'm sorry! I'm sorry!" she blubbered. "I never meant to hurt you."

His laugh was the inextinguishable crackle of a fire in a coal mine. "'Hurt' me? Cory, you *killed* me." He loomed toward her. "You hear me? You killed me, and if you think you can make it all better with your pathetic apology, you're even more hopeless than I thought!"

You're not being fair, Natalie interjected.

"*Fair?* What do you know about *fair?*" Conrad shouted at the ceiling—a rebuttal to God. "Is it fair that I had to come home after working thirteen-hour days to cook and clean up after her? Is it fair that women wouldn't give me the time of day because I had a brat hung around my neck?"

Corinne wheezed sobs like a leaky accordion.

That's enough, Natalie warned Eagleton. *If you don't apologize right now, I'll send you back.*

For a moment, fear short-circuited his anger. Like most souls, he dreaded the black void of the afterlife.

He surveyed the sterile whiteness of the living room, the gray day outside the window. The rosebushes that lined the front flower bed had been pruned to a skeleton of thorns, the lawn mowed to crew-cut shortness. His gaze returned to his daughter, and he ground Natalie's teeth.

"Send me back if you want. There's nothing here for me anyway."

Corinne flinched as if slapped, bawling like a colicky infant.

The Lord is my shepherd, Natalie recited, *I shall not want....*

With the words of the Twenty-third Psalm, her protective mantra, circling in her head, she mopped Conrad Eagleton's consciousness from her mind. He didn't fight her, but his hatred left the acid sting of bile in her brain. As sensation returned to her limbs, Natalie dropped heavily onto the couch, still shaking with feverish rage.

Corinne didn't even lift her head from her hands. Dampness seeped between her fingers. "I didn't even tell him I love him."

Natalie massaged her temples. "He didn't give you the opportunity."

"No wonder he hates me." The daughter tightened herself into an armadillo ball.

Whining little brat, Natalie thought, then shook the words out of her head. Conrad's contempt still hissed through her neurons like quicklime, but she ignored it and moved to put an arm around Corinne's shoulders. "It's not your fault."

"It *is*!" Corinne's fingers knotted around clumps of her hair. "I never listened to him, never appreciated him." She spoke with such venom that she, too, seemed possessed by her father.

"You may have made some mistakes," Natalie said quietly, "but that doesn't mean you didn't love him. And it doesn't mean he shouldn't love you."

Corinne blotted her eyes with her wrists. "I thought if I could talk to him again, tell him I was sorry, we could make it all right."

"Sometimes you can never make it all right." In her mind, Natalie saw her own father smile and wave over his shoulder to her as he left her crying on the front steps of the School, condemning her to a quarter-century of Corps servitude. "You just have to go on and make your own life right."

The words didn't console Corinne Harris, née Eagleton. Perhaps nothing could. She wept herself dry, muttering self-recriminations. "It's okay," Natalie murmured over and over as she cradled the woman in her arms. "It's not your fault."

Eventually, Corinne dwindled into silence, her open eyes as blank as a desert sky. When several minutes passed without a word, Natalie gingerly pried herself from her client's embrace and rose from the couch.

"I'd better go now. You know where to reach me if you need to."

Corinne didn't respond. Natalie let herself out of the house.

The session had lasted so long that she ran late to pick up Callie at day care. Hunched forward with her perpetual death grip on the steering wheel, Natalie ran a yellow light for the first time in her life. The tan Chrysler LeBaron that had been tailing her all day accelerated through the red light to keep within a car length of her. In her rearview mirror, Natalie saw the driver, a black man with wraparound eye-shades, shake his head.

"Sorry," she apologized, as though George could actually hear her from inside the LeBaron.

She slowed her Volvo to a few miles an hour below the speed limit and crawled through the surface streets from Tustin up to Fullerton. Taking the 55 north might have been quicker, but freeway traffic still made her skittish. Natalie had been too afraid of auto accidents even to get behind the wheel of a car until she turned twenty-seven, but the duties of parenthood ultimately forced her to learn to drive. Flexing one cramped hand, then the other, she wondered if she'd ever get used to piloting one of these death machines.

She glared at the traffic ahead, but it couldn't take all the blame for her anxiety. The session with Corinne had been a disaster, and for the thousandth time Natalie questioned whether she did any good as a family counselor, particularly when she was barely on speaking terms with her own dad. . . .

Brake lights flashed in front of her, and she panic-stopped. Rubber squealed behind her as the LeBaron screeched to a halt inches from her rear bumper.

She glanced again in the rearview mirror at George's frowning reflection and exhaled her bottled tension. *God, I'm starting to act like a real L.A. driver. I better relax before I get both of us killed.*

Maybe she should go back to work for the Corps, she thought. No doubt they'd welcome her with open arms and a steady paycheck. But they'd also want Callie, and Natalie wouldn't allow that. Not yet, at least.

It was nearly four-thirty when she pulled into the parking lot of the Tiny Tykes TLC Center, a former preschool that had been converted to a private day-care facility. George, she saw, parked the LeBaron on the street outside.

Out of habit, Natalie switched off the engine and dug her contact lenses out of her purse. Once she put in the first one, though, she paused and cast an ashamed glance at her eyes in the rearview mirror—one blue, one violet.

What a wonderful role model you are, she silently sneered at her reflection. *Bet Callie can hardly wait to get her first pair of lenses.* Nevertheless, she went ahead and put in the second lens before getting out of the car.

A fresco of three gigantic alphabet blocks with the letters TLC masked the entire front wall of the day-care center, the dark windows camouflaged in the design of bright primary colors. By this time, the indoor activities would be done for the day, so Natalie headed straight for the small playground to the right of the school building. The overcast sky and waning daylight dyed the grass gray, and the few toddlers who remained rode the merry-go-round and teeter-totter with winter lethargy.

Seated on an orange plastic chair far too small for her, a plump woman rested her folded arms on her belly and darted her eyes from the children to her wristwatch and back again. Catching sight of Natalie, she heaved herself forward to get to her feet and hurried to meet her. "Ms. Lindstrom! Ms. Lindstrom!"

"Hi, Ms. Bushnell. Sorry I'm late."

"No, no problem-o." Panting between words, Ms. Bushnell pulled a folded glossy brochure out of the back pocket of her plus-size jeans and thrust it in Natalie's hands. "I got some info on that school I told you about."

"Oh. Thanks." Natalie grimaced at the photo of the forbidding Victorian mansion on the front cover. Cursive script below it read, *The Iris Semple Conduit Academy: An Introduction.*

"They've got good people there." Ms. Bushnell tapped the picture. "Experts. I'm sure they could help Callie. You know . . . with her education."

"Uh-huh."

"And it's all free! They'd pay for everything."

"I'm sure they would."

"I really think it'd be the best thing for her." Ms. Bushnell's genial face adopted a look of matronly concern. "The fits, the way she talks to herself or zones out completely—ordinary schools simply aren't equipped to deal with those things. And it can be upsetting for the other children."

Natalie nodded, her jaw tightening.

"At the Academy, she'll have a chance to meet kids . . . like her. I'm sure she'll find it easier to make friends there."

"Mmm. You're probably right." Natalie folded the brochure in quarters and crammed it in her purse. "I'll give it some thought."

Ms. Bushnell beamed. "Want to help however I can. She's a darling little girl."

"Thanks." Natalie gave her a plastic smile and moved off toward the square wooden cell of a sandbox in the far corner of the playground.

A small girl with her brown hair tied up in pigtails crouched there on the miniature dunes. Her denim overalls powdered with white dust, she pushed a blue plastic bucket with both hands to bulldoze sand onto a growing mound in front of her. Patting the sand into an igloo-shaped hill, she used a stick to stir shallow holes in the dome, her singsongy voice drifting on the air like the notes of a distant calliope.

". . . make a room for you, and one for Mommy, and one for me . . ."

Natalie frowned as she drew close enough to catch the words. Callie apparently sensed her displeasure, for she stopped talking and scrunched up her face as if making a birthday wish. Her violet eyes wide, she looked up at her mother with the exaggerated innocence of a child who's been caught playing with matches.

"Hey, kiddo." Natalie squatted beside the sandbox. "Whatcha making?"

Callie prodded the mound of sand with her stick. "A house."

"Uh-huh. And are we going to live there?"

"Yeah."

"Just you and me?"

Her daughter's lips puckered. "Yeah. . . ."

Natalie drew a deep breath. "Who were you talking to?"

Callie continued to jab the stick in the sand. "Nobody."

"Was it Daddy?"

Her daughter's eyes remained downcast.

Natalie sighed. She'd asked Dan to leave their daughter alone. *She has to live her own life*, she told him, and he agreed . . . or so he'd said.

"Honey, I told you not to talk to Daddy at school. If he knocks, just tell him to go away."

"He doesn't knock. I call him."

Natalie stared at her, amazement mingling with apprehension. She knew that Dan had occasionally inhabited Callie ever since she was a baby. In fact, Callie's first word had been *Da-Da*. But now she'd evidently figured out how to use herself as a touchstone to summon Dan whenever she wanted.

She needs to be trained, Natalie thought. Summoning the dead without knowing how to get rid of them was dangerous. Callie could lose control of her body for hours or even days if the inhabiting soul refused to leave on its own. In the meantime, it could make her do whatever it wanted. Natalie had found that out the hard way.

"We'll talk about this later," she told her daughter. With a grunt, Natalie hefted Callie out of the sandbox and carried her toward the parking lot. "Right now I'm starving. How about a pizza?"

The cloud of guilt lifted from the girl's face. "With olives and pepperoni?"

"You bet."

"Yay!" Callie raised her little fists in a touchdown Y.

Natalie chuckled. *She has his smile.*

"I was hoping I might catch you here." An older woman in a business suit stepped into their path. "Motherhood agrees with you."

Natalie squinted at the woman's stern, bronze-colored face, at the graying hair tied back in a French braid. "Inez? Why on earth . . ."

"I need your help." Inez took a thick padded envelope from under her arm and held it aloft. "Scott Hyland's trying to get away with murder."